PRAISE FOR TAHOE HEAT

"IN TAHOE HEAT, BORG MASTERFULLY WRITES A SEQUENCE OF EVENTS SO INTENSE THAT IT BELONGS IN AN EARLY TOM CLANCY NOVEL"

- Caleb Cage, Nevada Review

"TAHOE HEAT IS A RIVETING THRILLER"

- John Burroughs, Midwest Book Review

"WILL KEEP READERS TURNING THE PAGES AS OWEN RACES TO CATCH A VICIOUS KILLER"

- Barbara Bibel, Booklist

"THE READER CAN'T HELP BUT ROOT FOR McKENNA AS THE BIG, GENEROUS, IRISH-BLOODED, STREET-WISE-YET-BOOK-SMART FORMER COP"

- Taylor Flynn, Tahoe Mountain News

"TODD BORG'S SERIES OF TAHOE BOOKS HAVE WON OVER READERS FROM ALL OVER THE COUNTRY"

- Sam Bauman, Nevada Appeal

PRAISE FOR TAHOE NIGHT

"BORG HAS WRITTEN ANOTHER WHITE-KNUCKLE THRILLER... A sure bet for mystery buffs waiting for the next Robert B. Parker and Lee Child novels."

- Jo Ann Vicarel, Library Journal

"AN ACTION-PACKED THRILLER WITH A NICE-GUY HERO, AN EVEN NICER DOG..."

- Kirkus Reviews

"A KILLER PLOT... EVERY ONE OF ITS 350 PAGES WANTS TO GET TURNED... FAST"
- *Taylor Flynn, Tahoe Mountain News*

"PLENTY OF ACTION TO KEEP YOU ON THE EDGE OF YOUR SEAT... An excellent addition to this series."
- *Gayle Wedgwood, Mystery News*

"ANOTHER PAGE-TURNER OF A MYSTERY, with more twists and turns than a roller coaster ride."
- *Midwest Book Review*

"A FASCINATING STORY OF FORGERY, MURDER..."
- *Nancy Hayden, Tahoe Daily Tribune*

PRAISE FOR TAHOE AVALANCHE

ONE OF THE TOP 5 MYSTERIES OF THE YEAR!
- *Gayle Wedgwood, Mystery News*

"BORG IS A SUPERB STORYTELLER...A MASTER OF THE GENRE"
- *Midwest Book Review*

"TAHOE AVALANCHE WAS SOOOO GOOD... A FASCINATING MYSTERY with some really devious characters"
- *Merry Cutler, Annie's Book Stop, Sharon, Massachusetts*

"EXPLODES INTO A COMPLEX PLOT THAT LEADS TO MURDER AND INTRIGUE"
- *Nancy Hayden, Tahoe Daily Tribune*

"READERS WILL BE KEPT ON THE EDGE OF THEIR SEATS"
- *Sheryl McLaughlin, Douglas Times*

"WORTHY OF RECOGNITION"
- *Jo Ann Vicarel, Library Journal*

TAHOE HIJACK

by

Todd Borg

THRILLER PRESS

Thriller Press First Edition, August 2011

TAHOE HIJACK
Copyright © 2011 by Todd Borg

Library of Congress Control Number: 2011924675

ISBN: 978-1-931296-19-9

Cover design and map by Keith Carlson

Manufactured in the United States of America

For Kit

ACKNOWLEDGMENTS

When I write mysteries, I inevitably stray into legal and law-enforcement territory about which I know little. Three people provided enormous help in this area.

With much patience, Chris Campion answered countless questions about many of the law enforcement issues in this story. He was a huge help.

Jenny Ross went through the manuscript and sorted out my unreasonable legal constructions, then figured out how to make them work. In the process, she fixed a good deal of other problems as well. Can't thank her enough.

Some time back, Truckee PD Sergeant Marty Schoenberg gave me a night tour of the cop side of Truckee, one part of which was the Truckee jail. That jail finally makes an appearance in this book. I keep using other things I learned from Marty as well.

The three of them deserve the credit for any law-related things that I got right. I claim credit for all of the mistakes.

I set another world record for copy problems, which Liz Johnston corrected in her edit. She also gave me many helpful suggestions on the story.

I invented new ways to mangle sentences and paragraphs and chapters, which Eric Berglund unmangled. More importantly, Eric seems to understand exactly what I'm trying to say, and he finds much better ways to say it.

Christel Hall uncovered significant continuity problems, dozens of glitches in my wording, and fixed many typos. The book is much better as a result of her efforts.

Extraordinary artist Keith Carlson produced another fantastic cover, with strong images, brilliant colors, and bold graphics. Over the years, I have watched countless people pick up the books, stare at the covers and decide that if the covers were that enticing, the stories were probably worth checking out. I hope the stories have lived up to the cover promise.

As always, Kit is my first and last defense against bad writing. Only she and I know what she has to wade through when I hand her that first draft. I'm hoping she can continue to keep the secret...

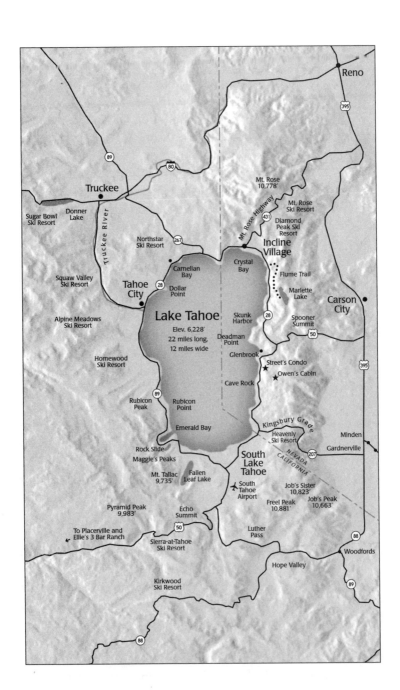

PROLOGUE

When the yacht rounded Rubicon Point, the man lifted his flask of Irish whiskey, took a last sip of Celtic fire, and exhaled hard. Liquid courage, my ass, he thought. Anesthesia, nothing more. The Celts who sacked Rome didn't imbibe before the charge for any reason other than emotional prophylaxis. Egregious tasks require serious mitigation. Numb the nervous system, full speed ahead.

Time to begin.

The man threw the flask overboard, then thrust his arms through the straps of his backpack. He reached down to the leather sheath that protruded from a thigh pocket on his jeans and pulled out his custom full-tang knife with the polished tanto point, rip teeth, and a handle engraved with the Celtic Cross. He palmed the knife, made a single nod to his partner, a smaller man at the bow of the Tahoe Dreamscape, then walked toward the closest passengers, two people who stood on the port side of the foredeck.

The boat was coming down Lake Tahoe's West Shore on a course that would bring it adjacent to the Rubicon cliffs. The Tahoe Dreamscape was one of Tahoe's largest boats and was used as a private charter for large groups. An event planner in Reno had booked the Dreamscape for their Afternoon Appetizer Cruise to Emerald Bay. A bunch of consultants had come up the mountain to sample the lake views and the cool mountain weather of fall while Reno still baked in the desert heat.

The man and his partner had gotten onboard with the rest of the passengers. They'd worked up a business story in case anybody asked. They ran back-country corporate retreats complete with power conditioning and attitude coaching, and they were on the cruise at the request of one of the consultants. But no one asked. They didn't even have to show tickets.

Some of the passengers were along the other side of the boat, crowded against the starboard rail, waiting to glimpse the entrance to Emerald Bay, a shallow, narrow opening to a deep fjord-like body that was tucked in among the mountains that lined the West Shore. As the Dreamscape cruised south, the passengers had their cameras out, eager to see the famous bay with its island and the Vikingsholm, the Norwegian-style castle at the head of the bay.

But the man had no intention of letting the boat get past the rocks of Rubicon.

The Rubicon shore was the top edge of a great underwater cliff, 1200 vertical feet of rock that descended three-quarters of the way toward the floor of the big lake. Because of the great water depth, sunlight entering the water traveled down until it was exhausted. With no bottom close enough to bounce the light back, the water off Rubicon Point was a deep indigo. It was the depth of this part of the lake that made it perfect for his needs.

The crowd was nothing like the big groups of August, but it was a good-sized group for a September weekday: 47 consultants served by a crew of 4 and the 3-person catering firm.

Earlier on the Dreamscape's windy trip across Tahoe, many of the travelers stayed inside the salon or out on the wind-sheltered rear deck. For much of the journey, the two men had the foredeck to themselves. No one had noticed as they put their things in place. Their movements were casual enough that even the crew on the bridge above them was unaware of anything other than two men moving around, curious about the boat.

The man approached the two passengers. He grabbed the elbow of one, a person dressed in a hooded sweatshirt with the hood up against the wind. He held out his knife.

"Come with me." The man spoke with a ragged voice as if to disguise it. "Don't say a word, or you die."

The passenger gasped, but stayed silent. The other person started to speak, a rising shout.

"Quiet!" the man said in a harsh whisper, "or I start cutting!" He flicked his hand like a trick shooter spinning his 6-gun, and the shiny knife twirled in the air. The man caught it and made a thrusting motion with his knife. "If you make another sound, if you say anything, talk to anybody, blood will flow."

The man walked his hostage across the deck toward the bow of the boat. He kept his knife low and out of sight. Even if the captain on the bridge above saw him, it would look like he was escorting someone to a better view.

When they got to the bow, he spoke to his hostage.

"Lean on the rail. Now swing your leg up and over to the outside of the rail. Do it! Now your other leg."

The hostage did as he demanded, feet on the very edge of the bow. The hostage gripped the rail to keep from falling into the lake. The man positioned himself between his hostage and the Dreamscape's crew on the bridge so that they could not see that the hostage was standing outside the railing.

The man pulled three short cords from his pocket. He used one to tie the hostage's wrists together as the hostage gripped the railing. Near the hostage's feet were two lengths of heavy rusted anchor chain that the man's partner had pulled out of his backpack and piled at the edge of the bow. The chain lay just in front of a gear locker, out of sight of the crew. The chains attached to nothing and merely served as twenty-five-pound weights in the form of heavy metal links.

The man bent down, and used the second cord to tie one of the chains to the hostage's ankle. He straightened and, threatening to cut the hostage's fingers with his knife, pried the hostage's hands from the rail.

"Turn away from the boat," he said. "I'll hold the back of your belt to keep you from falling overboard. Do it!"

He forced the struggling hostage to turn away from the rail and face the water. Because the rail projected out six inches beyond the edge of the deck, it forced the hostage to lean out at an angle from the boat as the hostage taker held onto the belt. The man squeezed the hostage's belt against the boat railing and tied the third cord around them.

The man pulled a fourth and longer cord out of his pocket. With a few simple and well-practiced knots, he attached a line between himself and the hostage and created an arrangement that allowed him to dump the hostage into the lake with a single jerk on the cord.

"You're being held to the rail by the cord," the hostage taker said. "If you stay still, you will be safe. But the knot is a slipknot, and I can pull my cord to release it. If you try to turn around to grab the railing, I will send you into the water with the anchor chain. That chain will pull you to the bottom like an elevator on high-speed descent."

Facing out toward the lake, with the sweatshirt hood up, the terror on the hostage's face was not visible to anyone.

The hostage taker pulled out a cellphone that he'd lifted in the salon from the purse of a woman who briefly looked away during the excitement at the beginning of the cruise. The man looked up at the boat's bridge above him and dialed the number of the Tahoe Dreamscape's captain.

"Ken Richards, Tahoe Dreamscape," the captain answered.

"Look down at your foredeck. I have a hostage who is outside of the bow rail, kept from falling into the water by a cord. My hostage is tied to a heavy chain. I have a release cord. If I pull on the cord, the hostage and the heavy chain will fall into the water." He paused to let his statements soak in. "Cut your engine power, or I will send the hostage to the bottom of the lake."

There was no immediate response from the captain. The boat didn't slow. The captain was probably in shock, the hostage taker thought. Time to elaborate.

"The hostage has no chance and will be dead twenty-five or thirty stories down, about the depth where the last of the sun gives way to blackness! Do you understand? THIS IS A HIJACKING! CUT YOUR POWER IMMEDIATELY, OR I PULL THE CORD!"

The boat immediately slowed as the engines wound down. Within seconds, the boat coasted to a crawl, on its way to a stop. Without power, it began to rotate as it drifted, its bow turning clockwise toward the shore cliffs.

Captain Ken Richards covered the phone, and yelled at his chief mate. "Call nine-one-one! We've got a hijacker!"

He put the phone back to his mouth. "Stay calm," Richards

said to the hijacker. "We'll do whatever you say."

Richards watched the hijacker from above. He was large, or maybe it was just the man's bulky jacket. He had big hair, a bushy beard and moustache, and his eyes were covered by large sunglasses. On the man's back was a large blue backpack. The man looked frantic, turning from the tourists on the starboard side, to the bridge, to the cliff shoreline fifty yards away.

As with all of the tour boats, Richards and his crew had been previously briefed by the FBI as a routine caution. He remembered the basics of the drill should someone take hostages on the boat. Stay calm. Buy time. Make the hostage taker believe that they were trying to do what he wanted.

Richards was about to speak into his phone when he saw a tourist point to the hostage taker. The tourist yelled something. A group of other tourists turned to look. One of them shouted, his voice tense. More tourists focused on the hostage taker. A cacophony of raised voices came through the windows of the bridge. Four words carried above the din.

"HE'S GOT A BOMB!"

People screamed and ran toward the stern of the Tahoe Dreamscape. Two people fell. Others tripped over them.

The chief mate got through on his 9-1-1 call. He began explaining in earnest.

Richards turned back to his phone.

"What do you want?" he said, his voice raised and tense. He realized that he'd already broken the first rule of staying calm. Richards stared down at the man and saw for the first time what looked like a thin black wire arcing from the man's pocket to the backpack. Christ, the guy really was wired. The pack could easily hold enough explosives to sink the Dreamscape.

"I'm very disappointed in you, Captain Richards!" the hijacker shouted into the phone. "I asked you to cut your engine, but you hesitated! You don't seem to realize that I am now in charge of this boat. Do you understand me?!"

"Yes, of course," Richards said.

The hijacker was outraged "I don't think you do," he said into his stolen phone. He pocketed the phone, took three steps over to his partner. The cord to the hostage was now stretched tight. The man spoke to his partner.

"The captain of the boat said there is something in the water," he said to his partner. He gestured toward the water directly below the bow. "Do you see anything?"

The man's partner turned, bent down and stared out at the water. "I don't see any..."

The partner's words were cut off as the man with the backpack grabbed his partner by the hair and slammed him forward, crushing his throat against the railing.

The smaller man reached for his neck. His mouth opened wide, but no air flowed. The hijacker picked up the second pile of chain. He looped the chain around the neck of his suffocating partner, made a crude knot with the chain, then, leaning the man against the railing, lifted up the man's feet and dumped him and the chain over the rail and into the lake.

The man and the chain created a small splash.

The hostage saw it and made a guttural, choking howl.

The hijacker pulled the phone from his pocket. "NOW DO YOU BELIEVE THAT I'M IN CHARGE?!" he screamed into the phone.

"Yes," came the captain's weak voice. Almost a whimper.

"We could have made this simple, Captain Richards," the hijacker said. "But you complicated things with your delay. Are you ready to do as I ask?"

"Yes." The captain's voice in the phone sounded fragile and desperate. "Please... please don't hurt anyone else. We'll do whatever you want."

"I want a meeting with a man. Your crew is probably talking to law enforcement as we speak. Tell the law to find him and get him out to this boat as fast as you can. If you drag your feet, I drop the hostage into the lake to join the other man twelve hundred feet below!"

"Yes, sir," the captain said. "Who is the man you want to meet?"

"He used to be a homicide inspector in San Francisco. Now he's a private investigator in Tahoe. His name is Owen McKenna."

ONE

A loud ring. Something wet and cold on my cheek. In my eye. Ouch. Another ring. A bad way to wake up from a rocking-chair nap.

Spot's nose. Insistent. A Great Dane's nose in your eye is like a cold stick of butter. I pushed him away, wiped my eye with my sleeve. Another ring. I squinted. Something sparkled through the blur. Spot's earring catching the light coming in the window. I looked at the clock. 2:47 p.m. Another ring. I stood up, blinking my eye. My eyelashes were glued by doggie nose juice. A fifth ring. I walked over to my kitchen nook and grabbed the phone. The caller had hung up. I only heard dial tone.

"Why can't you let me sleep when I'm finally out?" I said, knowing that it was the phone that made Spot prod me in the eye.

Spot wagged.

I wasn't a nap taker, but I'd been awake a good part of the last three nights, trying to puzzle out a phone caller's claim that he knew who killed Grace Sun, a murder that went unsolved during the last month of my career as Homicide Inspector with the San Francisco PD. I'd gotten a call at midnight each of the previous three nights.

The readout on my phone had said the caller's number was private. Probably not a telemarketer at midnight, so I had answered.

"I know who killed Grace Sun," the caller said.

"Who is this?" I said.

The caller ignored me. "I read how you got some DNA evidence but no suspect to match. Check out Thomas Watson.

Just bought a condo on the West Shore. The Blue Sky, Blue Water development." The caller hung up.

The next night he called again and was even more agitated. Did I go arrest Watson? Why not? The guy was a killer! Did I want murderers to go free?

I told him that a tip from an anonymous caller did not constitute probable cause. Told him that I was now a private investigator, that I had no authority to do police work. He swore and hung up.

The next day I passed the information on to cops I know in several of the various law enforcement jurisdictions that cover Lake Tahoe.

The third night, the man called again. I told him that I'd passed on his info to the authorities involved, that there was nothing else I could do. He strung a bunch of insults together, told me I'd be sorry, and hung up again.

This morning, I'd called Street Casey. She came up the mountain to have breakfast with me. We chatted about the phone calls while I cobbled together some scrambled eggs. They tasted a bit rubbery, but you work with the skills you have, limited as they are. We ate out on my deck, a modest expanse of weathered cedar with an immodest view of Lake Tahoe, one thousand feet below. Across the lake, the Sierra crest still had accents of snow even though the last serious accumulations were four months earlier in May.

"It sounds like Grace Sun's murder was a frustrating case," Street said.

"Yeah. You work cases in Homicide, you expect that a majority will remain unsolved. But when the victims are kids or old people or women in the prime of their lives, it stays with you."

"You didn't know Grace Sun," Street said.

"No. But during the investigation I met her cousin, Melody Sun, who was her roommate. Melody discovered the body. I came to understand that Melody and Grace were close. In talking to Melody, I learned about Grace a little bit. It bothered me that we got nowhere on the case."

"Why was Grace killed?" Street asked.

"We never knew. Melody and Grace lived in an apartment in North Beach, under Coit Tower. The place was torn apart, but we never found a clear indication of why she was killed."

"You think Grace interrupted a burglar, and that got her killed?"

"Possibly," I said. "But there was a pot of fresh tea and two teacups on the table. Tea had been poured and drunk. Earlier that morning, Melody and Grace had left the apartment together. Neither of them had made tea in the morning. And Grace was at work the entire day before she went home. So we narrowed the tea time down to sometime after Grace went home and before Melody went home. We determined that Grace had been dead about an hour when Melody arrived."

"So Grace came home," Street said. "Then someone she knew came over and they had tea. Then that person left and someone else came in and killed Grace?"

"Could be. But one cup had Grace's prints on it, and the other was clean. Which suggested that the other tea drinker killed her, then wiped his prints off the cup. Before she died, Grace fought with the killer, scraped his skin with her fingernails, and got herself hit over the head with a cast iron frying pan, which caved in her skull and killed her. Then the killer ransacked the apartment. Drawers emptied, clothes pulled out of closets, cushions ripped off of couches and chairs. Filing cabinets opened and dumped on the floor. Books swept out of bookcases."

Street made a slow nod and shut her eyes for a moment.

"The surprise came after we brought the body in. The medical examiner found a journal inside Grace's shirt. She had a sweater over her shirt, and its bulk obscured the shape of the journal underneath."

"You think the killer was after the journal?"

"We couldn't tell. The fact that she'd hidden it there suggested as much. Maybe she had the journal with her when she came home. She may have come inside, heard the burglar, and quickly slipped it inside her shirt before he saw her. Or perhaps when someone knocked – the person she had tea with – maybe Grace realized that it was a person who was interested in the journal. So she hid it under her shirt."

"It must have been very valuable," Street said.

"Right. Except there was nothing valuable that we could find."

"What was in the journal?"

"It was written in Chinese. Unfortunately, at some point in the past, the journal had been dropped in water, dirty water. Most of the writing had gotten blurred. We had an expert look at it, but he could tell very little other than a few details about the daily minutia of life during the gold rush. It was boring enough that nothing stood out."

Street thought about it. "You got the burglar's DNA from the skin under Grace's nails?"

"Yeah. She'd gouged a surprising amount of bloody skin off of him. It was easy for the lab to get DNA from it."

"She obviously fought hard, but it didn't do her any good," Street said. "She still died, and you never found the perpetrator."

I nodded.

"It would have been incredibly difficult for Melody to come home and discover the body."

"Yeah. She called nine-one-one. In the tape of that call, she was sort of composed. But by the time we got there, she'd pretty much come unglued. She was sitting in the apartment hallway, knees to chest, head banging on her knees, hysterical."

Street took the last bite of her rubber eggs, drank the last of her coffee. "It sounds like the burglar was looking for something specific instead of cash in a safe, or necklaces and earrings in a jewelry box. Something that could be inside of books or hidden in the furniture. Something like the journal Grace was hiding. Did Melody notice anything missing?"

"No. That was another strange thing about the burglary. Two days later – time she'd mostly spent sedated and staying at a friend's – I went with her back to the apartment. The cleanup crew had done a pretty good job, and Melody kept her emotions under relative control. She went through the apartment and could find nothing missing. Even a couple of weeks later, she still never noticed anything missing."

"And now an anonymous caller is saying that the killer is a

guy who lives here at the lake," Street said.

I nodded.

"Have you ever heard of this Thomas Watson?"

I shook my head.

"What will you do about that?" Street asked.

"I called Bains at the El Dorado Sheriff's Office, Santiago at Placer County, and Mallory at South Lake Tahoe PD."

"And Diamond?"

"Of course," I said.

"He have an idea?" Street said.

"No. In fact, he said, 'why tell me?' and I said, 'a Mex intellectual who happens to be a cop for Douglas County might have an idea that the rest of us would miss.'"

"He probably scoffed at you for saying that," Street said.

"Yes, that's exactly what he did."

Spot was out on the deck with us, snoozing in the sun, when a distant whistle of a bird caused him to lift his head and stare at the sky. Street and I followed his gaze to see a large raptor circling. It had huge wings with primary flight feathers separated at the wingtips. Its wings were held straight out like a seven-foot 1 X 10 board. Which meant Bald Eagle. It came around in a big soaring circle, and the sun flashed on its white head and tail feathers.

It was a welcome change of subject, and we three focused for a time on the eagle. Eventually, Street had to leave to meet an entomologist colleague.

After Street left, I took Spot out for a long mountain hike to clear my brain, then came back and ate lunch. Spot watched me.

"You stare as if a peanut butter sandwich and a glass of milk is God's answer to a dog's prayers," I said.

Spot licked his chops. His nose flexed. He looked from the sandwich to me then back to the sandwich. His stare was so intense, it might toast the bread if I held it still.

I stood up, tore off a chunk of peanut butter sandwich, and stirred it down to the bottom of his bowl, thinking it might encourage him to eat some of the dried sawdust chunks that are supposed to pass for dog food.

Spot stuck his nose in the bowl, rooted around in circles and pulled out the sandwich morsel without touching the dog food. Then he lay down on his new cedar-chip mattress, a custom affair that was five feet long so he could stretch out. Even so, his feet and tail flopped over the edges and onto the floorboards.

After lunch, my sleep deficit caught up with me. The rocking chair beckoned.

Now I was awake and had answered the phone to a dial tone. I set the phone down only to have it ring again.

"Hello?" I tried a second time.

"Thought you were asleep or something," Diamond Martinez said.

"Sergeant," I said.

"Thought you would want to know that we've got a hostage situation on the lake. Guy out on the Tahoe Dreamscape dropped another guy overboard with a chain tied to him."

I was still groggy. "Intentional? Or accidental?"

"Intentional. He's currently got a hostage tied to the front of the boat. Threatening to drop him overboard, too."

"And you called me because…"

"I'm in my patrol unit. I was just having a side-by-side with Ramos and another FBI agent on Lower Kingsbury when he got a call from dispatch. Turns out the hostage taker wants to talk to you. Ramos is currently on his phone to the Captain of the boat, Ken Richards. Hold on, Ramos just folded his phone. He's saying something to me."

A pause. Muffled voices.

Diamond said, "I'm going to hand my phone through his window."

There was some wind noise, then a voice.

"Owen McKenna, Special Agent Ramos here. Diamond filled you in." A statement, not a question.

"You have a hostage taker on the Dreamscape," I said.

"Yeah. Wants you out on the boat."

"Any idea why me?" I said.

"No. Captain Richards says that the hostage taker's got a heavy chain on the hostage. The hostage taker says he's going to drop the hostage in the lake unless you come out to the boat to talk. Apparently, the hostage taker is very agitated. We don't know more than that."

I tipped my head left and right, forward and back, trying to loosen a sore neck that was fast seizing up. I reached up and rubbed the muscles.

"Can you get me out there?" I asked.

"Yes. We have a boat available to us."

"Any idea who this hostage taker is?"

"No. Agent Bukowski is with me. He's trained in hostage negotiation. He'll be able to give you an idea of how to proceed. We'll be at your house in five or ten minutes."

We hung up.

I put fresh water and Spot's untouched food out on the deck and put Spot on the long chain, the lightweight variety that couldn't be used to sink people in 1635 feet of ice-cold water. I grabbed my windbreaker and was waiting outside as a black Chevy Suburban pulled up. I got in the back seat, driver's side.

"McKenna, meet Bukowski," Ramos said from the driver's seat. He glanced at me in the rearview mirror, shifted into reverse, backed out of my little parking pad and drove down the long private road that I share with my upscale neighbors. "Bukowski is up from the Sacramento office. He's helping us on a different matter."

Bukowski turned around in the front seat. He reached across the back of the seat to shake my hand. He was maybe 35, younger than Ramos and me. Unlike Ramos, who always dressed just two notches shy of tux and tails and whose shiny black hair and tiny black moustache looked like they were barbered every morning, Bukowski wore a crisp white shirt with no jacket. His hair was greased and brushed up into messy tufts that angled backward. Despite the casual dress, his face looked earnest and focused and worried.

"Do you have any experience with hostage situations?" he asked me.

"Not enough to matter," I said. "Give it to me from the beginning."

"You set up a dialogue with several principles as your guiding focus," Bukowski said. "Slow it down, calm it down, reduce the tension. Make the hostage taker think that you're doing everything you can to work with him."

"What about his demands?"

"You tell him, 'Let me see what I can do. It'll take some time. But I'll make some calls. I think you and I can work this out. I want a peaceful resolution to this. And I'll keep working on it as long as the hostage stays safe.' Like that," Bukowski said. "You make your calls. You check back with him. You stay in his sight so that he can see you working on his demands. Your presence and your talk with him becomes his reassurance that someone cares. It's all about empathy. Most hostage takers, if they think someone is listening to them, they chill a little. It's when they think someone is blowing them off or planning a SWAT assault that they detonate their bombs."

"This guy has a bomb?" I said.

"It looks like it. A large backpack with a wire going into it."

Ramos got to the bottom of my neighbors' winding private drive and made a hard left onto the highway, accelerating fast enough to make the wheels squeal.

"What if he demands something I can't reasonably try to get for him?" I asked. "Ten million in cash and a helicopter."

Bukowski nodded. "Right. The forty-virgins-and-a-tropical-island demand. Sometimes they do that. If so, you say, 'I don't think I can get that for you. But what I can do is tell the authorities that we need time to work this out. I can guarantee your safety as long as the hostage stays safe.' When he asks for something you can give him, say, cigarettes, you ask him to give you something in return."

"Like getting the hostage into a safer position," I said.

"Right. If he agrees, you give him just one cigarette."

"Got it."

"If the hostage taker wants food, you give him a single small item, and get another concession in return."

I nodded. "Any idea what the hostage taker wants?"

Bukowski looked at Ramos.

"None," Ramos said over his shoulder. "Captain Richards only said that he is intense bordering on frantic and demanding to speak to you."

"Weapon?"

"Other than the bomb, none that the captain can see," Ramos said, looking at me in the mirror. He used his front teeth to bite some micro roughness off his lower lip, hit the button to roll down his window, spit it out. "Is this out of the blue?" he asked me in the mirror. "Or is anything going down that you know of?"

"Don't know if it's related, but I got a call each of the last three nights," I said. "A guy claimed that he knew who killed a woman in a case I was involved in before I quit the SFPD. A woman named Grace Sun."

We entered the Cave Rock tunnel, Ramos accelerating through the dark. I tensed involuntarily as we popped out of the southbound tunnel opening where the young man had fallen to his death a few weeks before.

"Caller ID himself?" Ramos asked. "Or you get it off your phone?

"No to both. The readout said 'private.'"

"He say who it was he claims killed the woman?" Ramos asked.

"Yeah. Somebody named Thomas Watson."

Ramos swerved a little as he looked at me in the rearview mirror.

"You know Watson?" I asked.

Ramos looked at Bukowski. "Legal name of Tommy Watts, right?"

Bukowski nodded.

"Christ," Ramos said. He glanced at me in the mirror, then looked back at the road as he came around a curve, heading toward Skyland. He accelerated. "That's why Bukowski is up at the lake. We've been working with ATF on a case involving a company we think is running guns. One of the agents they had on it disappeared a few months ago. There's an import corporation called TransPacificTronics that purchases Chinese stuff through a Malaysian intermediary. We don't know yet how it works. It appears that the Malaysian purchase orders detail electronic goods, but in actuality represent automatic weapons. Somehow those weapons are brought across the Pacific, then transferred onto fishing boats and brought onshore into Mexican fishing villages. The guns are in small containers buried in the holds with the fish. These guys are bold and aren't just targeting Mexico. We intercepted two shipments coming into California coastal towns as well. Morro Bay and Mendocino. We believe they've also used Tomales Bay and Crescent City. The fishermen plead ignorance."

"Like they have no idea how the weapons got in the holds of their boats," I said.

"Right. We don't know the volume of weapons, and we don't know where they are all going. They probably end up in drug cartels or at gun shows. We do know that a bunch of them have gone to a militia group called the Red Blood Patriots. We confiscated some of their weapons in a motel raid and matched the serial numbers to the Chinese factory that made the weapons – an outfit that Tommy Watts has worked with – but we haven't been able to accurately trace the supply chain to this continent. Even so, we're sure that Tommy Watts is involved with the guns that end up going to militia groups."

"Multiple militias?" I said.

"We're assuming several. Watson is a businessman. He's perfected a money-making enterprise. Can't imagine he would stop with just one customer."

I was surprised. Ramos had never before been forthcoming with me. We had worked with each other in the past, but there'd always been a divide for us to bridge.

"You think this import company is owned by Thomas Watson?" I asked.

"No, no. This is a big outfit. Watson is a relative small-timer. TransPacificTronics' ownership is a consortium in Singapore. The consortium is a partner in a private equity group. None of that information is publicly available. This stuff is like an onion. Companies that own other companies. The international aspect makes it harder to peel."

He paused as he steered through a curve. "Tommy Watts grew up as a poor cowboy in West Texas, went to the U.S. Naval Academy, served in the Navy for ten years, most of that time in the Far East. Then he quit and suddenly started living a better life.

He has condos in San Diego and Mexico City in addition to his new place here in Tahoe. He's associated with known smugglers and has dinner with guys who work for TransPacificTronics. He travels extensively in the Far East, especially mainland China. His cover is as a weapons consultant hiring out to the independent contractors who provide security and protection to international corporations. We think his consulting is bogus and that he is actually a critical part of TransPacificTronics' supply chain, procuring the weapons where they are made. We have hearsay evidence linking him to a bid request for Chinese AK Forty-Sevens, but we can't attach anything incriminating to him."

"You bring him in for questioning?"

"We've knocked on his door several times, both when he was alone and when he had company, but he doesn't answer. We followed him in his car. When he got out, we asked him if we could speak to him. He ignored us. We stopped by the Chips-n-Brew in Tahoe City when he was enjoying his afternoon libation. He and his two pals calmly stood up and left, never uttering a word."

"Knows the rules," I said. "You think my phone caller could be right?" I asked. "Can you see Watson for the murder of Grace Sun?"

Ramos shook his head. "From what we've learned watching him? Not his style. His guns have probably been used in killings. But personally murdering a woman? I doubt it."

"Any idea why Watson bought a place here?" I asked.

"Probably wanted a Tahoe vacation getaway, same as everyone else. But he also uses it to wine and dine his vendors in an effort to get a lower bid. China may be a closed society compared to most countries, but they're like any other place when it comes to business. You get the best deal from the people whose palms you grease and whose stomachs you feed. Last month, Watson rented a three-cabin cruiser from one of the marinas. He had a caterer come onboard to put on a gourmet spread for three Chinese businessmen. Dessert was three showgirls who moonlight for a high-priced escort business."

"My caller said that Watson's place is in something called the Blue Sky, Blue Water condos," I said. "I'm not familiar with it."

"It's that new development on the West Shore where the old Masterson place used to be."

"I don't know Masterson, either."

"Masterson was a movie producer who was a friend of the ballplayer Ty Cobb. Used to live on the East Shore next to Cobb in Glenbrook, then built a big estate on the West Shore. A couple of years ago, some big money from LA tore it down and put up a gated community. Four buildings, a dozen units each. Nice beach, pool, tennis courts, boat buoys for each unit, underground garages, all the trimmings. Watson moved in a couple of months ago."

Ramos turned his head to get a glimpse of the water as he drove. He sighed. "This lake is a bucolic place. Happy tourists enjoying their vacations in the mountains. Kids playing at the beach. Most calls to the sheriffs' departments are about bear problems. Now you get some unusual phone calls about an old murder, and a guy hijacks a charter boat, and it's the same month that Thomas Watson moves into the basin. The hostage taker wants to talk to you. If it's the same guy who's been calling you, he must be real motivated to convince you that our Naval Academy cowboy is your San Francisco murderer. Makes you wonder why. But it could be nothing more than a wacko who knew of the woman's murder in The City and wants to get his fifteen minutes by taking a hostage and making an outrageous claim."

"We'll know shortly," I said.

TWO

Ramos turned onto Elks Point Road at Round Hill, and drove toward Nevada Beach. He went through a private gate, then turned down a driveway. Ramos pulled up to a three-car garage that projected out from a large house on the lake. He parked and we got out.

"Where are we?" I said.

"Mark and Mabel Cardman. They run an IT service business. Their clients are big Bay Area companies. We saved them from an identity theft problem a few years ago, and they've been trying to do us favors ever since."

"The Cardmans have a boat," I said.

"And we don't," Ramos said. "It's come in handy a few times."

We hustled around to the dock, Ramos carrying a small battery-powered megaphone. Ramos knew the combination for the electronic lock on the boathouse. We were in a Four Winns sport boat a few minutes later.

Ramos drove the small craft the way he did everything else, carefully and with precision. He eased out from the East Shore at no-wake speed. When we were a good distance from shore, he ran the speed up a bit but still kept it slow as we headed southwest, quartering the swell out of the south. The boat rocked up the front of each wave, then made a dramatic tip over the top and down the back side. Ramos picked it right, as the prop stayed in the water at each wave top.

It was obvious he'd had boating experience as he turned south toward the big hotels, drove into the calm waters in the lee of the south wind, and punched the throttle up.

"Tell me what the caller said," Ramos shouted over the engine roar.

"He called at midnight. I answered the phone. A man's voice said, 'I know who killed Grace Sun.' I asked who the caller was. The caller ignored me and said, 'I read how you got some DNA evidence but no suspect to match. Check out Thomas Watson. He's got a condo on the lake, Blue Sky, Blue Water on the West Shore.' Then the caller hung up. The second and third nights he wanted to know if I'd arrested Thomas Watson. He was very frustrated when I told him that I was a private citizen and could only pass on his information to local law enforcement."

"Did you pass it on?" Ramos asked.

"Yeah. I didn't know where Blue Sky is, but if it is on the West Shore, it has to be Placer County or El Dorado county. So I called Santiago at Placer and Bains at El Dorado. I also mentioned it to Diamond and Mallory."

"For good measure," Ramos said.

"For good measure," I said.

"But you didn't call us," he said.

Bukowski shot Ramos a look.

"Figured you guys got more important things to focus on than wacko callers," I said. "I also called Joe Breeze at SFPD. He worked with me on the Sun murder."

"Any of your cop pals heard of Thomas Watson?" Ramos asked.

"No."

Near Edgewood Golf Course, Ramos turned the boat west across the southern part of the lake and pushed the throttle forward even more. When we came to Baldwin Beach, he put the boat into a sweeping turn to the starboard, and we headed north up the West Shore toward Emerald Bay and Rubicon Point beyond. It was a longer path, but Ramos had avoided a punishing and possibly dangerous ride across the windy open water of the big lake. Despite Ramos's fast speed, his route around the giant lake still took 45 minutes to approach Rubicon Point.

Ramos had compact binoculars hanging on a cord around his neck. Every couple of minutes, he raised them to his eyes, then made a small course adjustment. Bukowski never said a word. He stared toward the Dreamscape with an intense frown creasing his forehead.

Ramos spoke on his phone as he drove. He eventually folded his phone and turned to me. "Sergeant Bains has gotten to the Dreamscape. He's established incident command. I told him we were bringing you out. We've offered him our full support."

"He's a good guy. Worked with him on the avalanche case."

When we were about a quarter mile away from the Dreamscape, Ramos throttled back, and the boat dropped off plane and settled down, stern low and bow high, trailing a large wake. I now understood his plan, as we were perfectly lined up with the Dreamscape's stern.

"The Dreamscape is drifting," Ramos said. "No anchor, because it's about eleven hundred and fifty feet too deep. She's currently pointing north. If the hostage taker remains at the bow, we can approach the stern without being seen."

At 50 yards out, Ramos cut the throttle to idle, and we approached without wake or engine roar, either of which might alert the hostage taker.

"You got a plan to save the hostage if the hostage taker drops him overboard?" I said in a low voice.

"We talked about it," Ramos said. "El Dorado Sheriff's Department has a dive team. They've got a boat on the way. The thinking is that while you distract the hostage taker and buy time, they drop two divers in at the Dreamscape's stern, out of sight from the hostage taker. If the divers stay directly under the boat, their bubbles will rise up along the hull, and won't be visible to the hostage taker. If the hostage gets dropped, the hope is that they might be able to grab him before he plunges on past. After they grab the hostage, the divers will inflate their BCDs."

I'd been diving years before in Maui, but it took me a moment to remember the term. "Bouyancy Compensation Devices," I said.

"Yeah. Two BCDs make for a lot of buoyancy."

Ramos eased the boat up to the boarding platform at the stern of the Dreamscape, throttling into neutral and then reverse to slow our approach. He turned to port at the last moment, bringing the starboard side of the speedboat alongside. The Dreamscape looked close to 100 feet long and had maybe 20 or more feet of beam, so we were effectively hidden from the hijacker at the bow. One of the Dreamscape deckhands squatted down and grasped the gunwale of the sport boat.

Ramos turned to me. "Agent Bukowski will get out here. Bains wants you and me to re-approach the Dreamscape near the bow so that I can announce to the hostage taker that I'm bringing you as he requested."

Bukowski jumped out onto the boarding platform of the Dreamscape.

Ramos jockeyed the boat as if it were a car in a tight parking place. I understood that instead of white lines, the constraints on his movement were the sightlines from the hostage taker. Ramos wanted to stay out of his sight.

Ramos got us turned around, and he throttled up, driving away from the Dreamscape's stern, keeping in line with the big boat so that we stayed hidden from its bow. After a minute, he sped up. A half-mile out, he turned, and we traced a big curve until we were again approaching the Dreamscape, this time from its starboard side.

When we got close, Ramos slowed, then lifted his megaphone to his mouth.

"I have Owen McKenna onboard," his amplified voice announced. As we drew closer, he slowed and repeated his announcement.

The hijacker turned to face us and took a single step away from his hostage.

Even from a distance, I could see that the hostage taker was a thick man whose head seemed swaddled in a spherical bush of hair that wrapped from the sides of his head down under his chin to a big beard. With his sunglasses, almost no part of his face was visible.

The man wore blue jeans with multiple pockets. The hijacker carried a large blue backpack that appeared to sag under a heavy load. His dark blue jacket was open at the front and revealed an unusual belt made up of multiple black rectangles. It reminded me of a picture I'd once seen of a suicide bomber wearing a similar belt. Just in case the backpack bomb wasn't powerful enough, the C-4 plastic in the belt would add some extra punch.

The hostage was slim like a teenaged boy, wearing jeans and a baggy hooded sweatshirt with the hood up obscuring his face. The hostage was outside the bow rail, perched on the boat's edge, facing the water.

Despite the ice-cold water of Tahoe, I didn't dwell on the danger to the hostage until I saw the pile of heavy chain at the boy's feet.

Ramos turned toward me and whispered, his voice barely audible over the speedboat's engine. "Remember the principles…"

I nodded and whispered back. "Get him talking, keep it calm, try to buy time, show empathy and respect, expect a concession for each of any demands we can comfortably meet."

Ramos gave me a look of surprise, as if competence in others was hard for him to comprehend. He pulled the throttle to neutral, and the speedboat once again eased next to the big boat. We touched the hull about twenty feet back from the bow curve and under a railing gate that was up above us at pier level.

A deckhand lowered a boarding ladder down to us. Ramos held onto it while I climbed up.

"Owen McKenna!" yelled the hostage taker as soon as I was on deck. He held a cord that stretched to the hostage. I nodded, made a small wave of acknowledgment, and walked toward him. As I got closer, the hostage's position looked even more precarious, perched on the very edge of the bow, facing a certain death should the hostage taker drop him overboard.

The hostage taker was so tense that he seemed about to explode.

When I was in easy hearing range, I spoke. "I'm Owen," I said.

At that came a gasping, whimpering cry from the hostage. "Owen! Help me!" A terrified voice that I recognized. A gut punch that knocked out my wind and made my vision go black.

The hostage was my girlfriend.

Street Casey.

THREE

"Street!" I shouted.

"Finally got your attention, McKenna?" The hijacker wagged the cord that drooped from him to the rail and then stretched tight to Street.

"Stay calm, sweetheart," I said, my voice shaking. "We'll get you to safety." I couldn't think. My heart hurt. A sudden headache seared. I tried to remember the negotiation principles, but I was in a black rage.

"I told you what I wanted on the phone," the hijacker said. "But you ignored me."

"No, I didn't." I struggled to say the words. My brain felt like it was being squeezed in a vice. "I told you the truth. I passed your information on to the county sheriff's offices."

"DON'T TELL ME WHAT YOU DID! I'M TALKING ABOUT WHAT YOU DIDN'T DO!" He reached down to a thigh pocket on his pants, his sleeve riding up and exposing a tattoo on his wrist. The blue marks were indistinct but looked like two infinity symbols. He pulled out a knife, a custom piece with an ornate design engraved on the handle. The man flipped the blade into the air, grabbed it in a flash of movement, then twirled it over and around the fingers of one hand like a magician with a coin. The spinning knife flashed in the sunlight. With a snap of his wrist, it disappeared into the sheath.

"I'm sorry," I said. "I'll do whatever you want. Just please let me get Street back inside the boat railing."

"She will be safe if you do EXACTLY AS I WANT!"

I was blowing it. The hijacker was in control. I was his puppet. I wasn't buying time, I wasn't calming him. Worst of all, Street was in greater danger since I set foot on the boat.

I took a deep breath, trying to calm myself.

"How can I help?" I said. "I want to help."

"Sure, McKenna. That's why you didn't do a damn thing when I called! Three phone calls. I gave you every chance! Now you will do as I want!"

"Yes, of course. Whatever you want." The words grated. But Street was hanging by a thread, her feet tied to an anchor chain. What else could I say? How could I calm him down? "You can call me Owen," I said. "What's your name?" It sounded ridiculous. It would never work.

"You don't need my name, McKenna! I know the whole psychological routine you guys use with hostage takers. It won't work on me. What you need to do is listen to me! You understand?" He paced two steps. His cord that controlled Street's tether went tight. He turned, paced two steps back. One of his athletic shoes was untied, laces dragging. I worried that he would trip on the laces, jerk the cord. It would release the line that held Street.

"That's what I'm here for," I said, desperately trying to speak in a calm voice. "I'm listening. Tell me what you want."

"I want you to shut up!" He kept his left hand in his pocket. A black wire came out of the pocket, ran up and inside the backpack.

I nodded understanding. I waited. My temper was on a tripwire. Blood pressure at stroke level.

The man paced, radiating pressure and anger as great as mine. "I gave you the murderer of Grace Sun! I told you where he lives. I'm serving you justice on a plate, but you cops just sit on your asses!"

"Thomas Watson," I said, nodding. "I'll go after him myself. Look, maybe we can sit and talk. If you untie Street, we can go inside the boat. Find a quiet place. I'll guarantee your safety."

"I told you to SHUT UP! You do anything but listen, I'll drop her! You open your mouth one more time, I swear!" He pointed at the big chain by Street's feet. "That anchor is heavy. She'll be twelve hundred feet deep in a couple of minutes. You know what the pressure is down there? She won't even be half way down before the air in her lungs is squeezed to nothing. You know what that means, McKenna? Before her ribs snap under the crushing pressure, her lungs will flood with ice cold water. She couldn't stop it even if she wanted to. It's not a pleasant death, McKenna!"

I held my hands out, palms forward, fingers up. I took a step back, a gesture of compliance.

The man marched his two-step pacing pattern, his big backpack swinging, the rip cord stretching taut at each turn, his loose laces nearly catching. He panted as if he were running up a mountain.

"Thomas Watson. You bring him in and check his DNA. You understand? Don't give me any shit about not being able to get a search warrant. You cops know how to make stuff up, plant some contraband. You promise me that you'll bring him in. Promise me right now, or your girlfriend goes into the lake!" He pulled his cord tight. On the other side of the rail Street was wracked with violent shivers.

I made a solemn nod. He had told me not to say another word, then told me to promise. So I spoke as softly as I could and still be heard. "I promise."

"Louder!" he said again.

Bukowski had said that I shouldn't promise what I couldn't provide. The hostage taker would know it was a false promise. It could backfire.

"I promise I'll do my best to bring Thomas Watson in."

"No!" he said. "Promise you'll bring him in! I didn't say promise to do your best. You're condescending to me! You cops are all the same!" His pacing was frantic. A caged tiger. "I make it simple for you. But you play your little game, never doing what I want. You insult my intelligence! Too late, McKenna!"

He pulled his left hand out of his pocket, held it high so that his switch device at the end of the wire was easy to see.

I tensed, wondering at what point I should sprint forward to try to intercept him or catch Street. But if he pressed the switch, nothing I did would prevent us from being vaporized.

I gestured again with my hands. "I'm sorry. Please, let's talk."

He seemed not to hear me. His eyes were aflame. With his other hand, he unhitched the trip line from his belt, twisted his body, readying himself to jerk Street's line. He took a step back, tripped on his loose shoelaces.

He tried to catch himself, tried to step back again, lifting on the stuck shoe.

The hostage taker fell back hard, dropping the line to Street. I leaped toward Street.

The man's butt hit the bow rail. The heavy backpack flipped him over the rail backward, and he fell out of my sight. Then came a splash as I grabbed Street from behind. The hostage taker's voice was suddenly small, wafting up from over the edge of the bow. "Can't swi..." he got out before his words were choked with water.

I pulled Street toward me, and leaned just enough forward to see over the edge of the bow.

The hostage taker was in the water, thrashing in panic. He gasped, sucked in water, made a horrible gargled choke as his head went below the water. Then silence.

I gripped Street and turned away as Bukowski rushed past me and dove over the rail after the hostage taker.

I held Street with one arm around her body, got out my pocketknife with the other hand, and cut the cords that tied her.

She trembled as I lifted her over the rail and set her down, and we hugged as if we were grabbing onto life itself.

FOUR

Sergeant Bains appeared next to me. I put my windbreaker over Street's shoulders and walked her into the Dreamscape's salon, accompanied by Bains. We found a corner table with a wrap-around bench seat. When Bains saw that we'd be okay, he left us and went back out on deck. I kept my arm around Street. She exuded terror and shock. She hadn't uttered a word since her first exclamation when she heard my voice. I held her in silence, rubbed her back, pressed my lips to her temple.

A few minutes later, Bains came back into the lounge. With him was Agent Bukowski, dripping wet and shivering. A deckhand rushed up with two towels, draped one around his shoulders and handed him the other one.

"He went down like a rock," Bukowski said. "His backpack must have been really heavy. I watched him struggle. He ripped at the straps, trying to get the pack off, but it was stuck."

Bukowski rubbed his head with the towel, then used it on his clothes. He shook, it seemed, not just from the cold, but like he was shaken from the emotion of the situation.

"At first," Bukowski said, "just after I dived in, I thought I might catch him. He was sinking with his back down, the heavy pack pulling him. I tried to reach for him, and he reached up toward me. His sunglasses had come off and the horror on his face was something I'll never forget. I'm a good swimmer, and I pulled hard after him, but he was sinking even faster. Then he made a burst of bubbles and his face changed from horror to slack. His mouth and eyes went wide open in death." Bukowski made a single, involuntary shiver.

He continued, "I was maybe thirty feet below the surface, and he was probably another thirty feet below me when I gave up. Then he disappeared from my sight. Blue pack and clothes fading into the dark blue deep. The way he was sinking, he's probably already at the bottom, dead as dead gets."

He sat down near Street, leaned toward her, and spoke in a low, earnest voice. "I'm very sorry for your trouble. That was a terrible thing out there. Are you okay? Can we get you anything?"

Street shook her head. "No thanks," she said in a tiny voice.

Bukowski turned away from Street as if to block her vision as he took his Glock 23 out of his concealed-carry holster, released the magazine and racked the slide to eject the cartridge in the chamber. He took the bullets out of the magazine and wrapped all the pieces in the towel. He bent down, pulled an S & W Airweight out of his ankle holster. He took out the five bullets, and wrapped them in the towel as well.

The lounge door pushed inward and Ramos walked in. He glanced at me, nodded at Bains.

"I saw it from out on the water," Ramos said, "but I couldn't hear all the words. You find out who this hostage taker was?"

"No. But he was my midnight phone caller," I said. "He repeated the same demand as on the phone. He wants Thomas Watson brought in for the murder of Grace Sun. He took this dramatic action to get my attention."

"Anything notable about him?"

"Other than what you could see from a distance, he had a tattoo on his wrist. It looked like two infinity symbols."

Ramos shook his head. "We'd have to have a full time researcher on militia tats and gang tats just to keep up with current trends." Ramos reached for a chair and pulled it up to the table. He picked a scrap of plastic packaging off the chair seat, flipped it onto the table. It was one of those little containers that disposable contacts come in.

"Any other clue to his identity?" Ramos asked.

"No. My guess is the same as yours. Someone who's come up against Thomas Watson in the past and got burned bad. Someone who maybe knows the truth of Grace Sun's death."

Ramos turned to Bains, gave him a questioning look.

"No idea," Bains said.

"Ma'am?" Ramos said, finally acknowledging Street.

She didn't look up. She just stared ahead, her face largely obscured by the large hood. She shook her head.

"What about the other guy he dumped overboard?" Ramos asked. "He say anything that would hint about who he was?"

I shook my head. "Nothing."

Ramos looked out at the bright sun on the water, his eyes narrowed. "That guy had some kind of monster motivation to take Street hostage all just to get you on Tommy Watts's case. And how did he expect it to end? If you gave him the exact response he wanted, was he going to let Street go?"

I hugged Street harder, chin to the top of her head. I didn't have an answer, so I didn't speak.

"You're the only one who's really spoken to this guy, Owen," Ramos said. "On the phone and in person. What do you make of his beef with Watson? He give you any idea what it was about?"

"No. He just wanted me to pursue Watson for Grace Sun's murder. But he didn't say why he believed that Watson did it or why he cared about it. When I tried to talk to him, he nearly lost it. He made me promise that I'd bring Watson in."

"You think he knew Grace Sun? Like maybe he had a thing for her, and that was what motivated him?"

"I doubt it. When he mentioned her on the phone, it was impersonal. His emotion was directed toward Watson."

"What about you? Why did this guy pick you?"

"Again, no specific indication. Just the obvious assumption that he learned that I had worked the Grace Sun murder, and he figured that I would have a vested interest. I think he also thought that, as an ex-cop, I would have some authority that I could use in pursuit of Watson."

Ramos sighed and said, "Unbelievable. A very elaborate scheme just to get you to go after Watson. Then he trips and his gig collapses."

"Best laid plans," I said.

Bains came over, tugged up on the seams of his pants and squatted down next to Street. In a low voice he said, "Okay if I get a statement from you tomorrow?"

She nodded.

"Thank you very much," he said, his politeness touching.

FIVE

Ramos and Bukowski took Street and me back across the lake in the speedboat. We loaded into their vehicle, and they dropped us off at my cabin. Ramos didn't ask questions of Street. He knew that Bains would get her statement tomorrow. Any further questions could be answered later, when she was more comfortable.

Street was still in a kind of shock. Talking didn't seem appropriate. Instead, I steered her out onto the deck and put her on the chaise that faced the mountains across the lake and the lowering western sun. Spot ignored me and went immediately to Street, sensing, as most dogs do, the wounded person in any group. He was attentive to her, if subdued, and after a hello-sniff he lay on the deck boards to her side, lifted his head and rested his chin on her thighs. She pet him absently.

Despite the sun's heat, Street shivered. I got my Navajo lap blanket and wrapped it around her shoulders, then brought her a small glass of foothill zin.

I pulled the other chaise near, and we sat and watched the sunset. Spot's eyelids wavered, then closed.

We were silent. Street drank her entire glass of wine in fifteen minutes, possibly a new record. It appeared that she stared toward the summit of Rubicon Peak above the West Shore, one of the high mountains that looked down on Rubicon Point where she'd been strapped to an anchor chain a short time ago.

Eventually, she spoke.

"I don't think he was crazy like he seemed," she said.

"No?"

"He acted crazy. He stomped around and shouted. He was extremely agitated. But I don't think that was really him."

"Why do you think that?"

"Something he whispered," she said.

"What do you mean?"

"After he had me tied to the rail. After he called the boat captain. Probably when you were on your way out to the boat. He came over next to me, leaned out and looked at me. He raised his sunglasses so I could see his eyes. His eyes were piercing blue, and they radiated intelligence. He seemed rational. Then he whispered, 'I don't want to kill you, I'll try not to kill you, but I will if I have to. I'm sorry if it comes to that.' He said it in a calm, collected way. Not like the frantic way he'd been shouting."

"What do you make of that?" I asked.

Street thought about it. "It suggests to me that he wasn't a natural thug. I don't think he was unhinged the way he appeared."

"I thought the man was ready for an institution," I said. "But you think that his crazed demeanor was an act."

"Maybe. Probably."

"The implication being…" I said.

"I think he wanted everyone to think he was wacko, that he was acting out this crazy idea. But in reality, I think he had a careful plan. The plan included acting crazy because it was more likely to be effective."

"You mean, effective at summoning me out to the boat and getting me to promise that I'd try to get the law after Thomas Watson."

"Right," she said.

"Did it seem to you that that was the whole point of taking you hostage? Demanding that I pursue Watson? Or was there going to be something else that he demanded?"

"Of course, I can't know the answer, but I'm guessing that it was all about Thomas Watson. He knew that if he took me hostage, you would do whatever he asked."

"Have you ever seen him before?"

Street shook her head. "Not that I know of. But cut off his hair and beard, he would look like an entirely different person."

"Did you get any sense of how he knew about us?" I asked.

"No. Certainly he could have watched us over time, or talked to any number of people in the area. I'm not well known, but you have a public profile of sorts."

"What about the boat cruise? Was that information in the paper or something?"

"Not that I know of," Street said. "But he could have found out about it any of several ways. The organizer had printed a list of all of our names and contact info and emailed it to everyone who went on the cruise. If the man who grabbed me had access to any of those people, he could have found out. And at our lunch meeting in Reno they handed out printed copies of instructions on how to get to the Tahoe Dreamscape's pier, where the parking lot was and so forth."

"If he had tailed you to the lunch meeting, would there be any opportunity for him to get a copy of that list?"

"There was a table just outside of the meeting room where the buffet was held. The table had a clipboard with the lunch sign-in sheet. Next to it was a stack of the printed sheets with the charter boat information. Anybody could have helped themselves while we were having lunch."

"Seems innocent enough, leaving such info out at a lunch. No one would think that it could contribute to a hostage taking. But careful plan or not, it backfired in a big way," I said.

"Yeah. But other than falling in the lake, everything else was orchestrated. The chains. The way he tied me to the boat rail. How he set it all up without being noticed. His call to the boat captain. And then…" she stopped.

"Dropping his partner overboard," I said.

Street nodded, staring toward the mountains but seeing darker images. As Spot fell into a sleep fog, his head started to slide off of Street's legs. Then, like a school boy snoozing in class, he caught himself with a jerk. His eyes opened, drooping, and he shifted his weight on his elbows so that his head could remain on Street's lap and under her delicious touch. Then he gradually began to drop off again, renewing the cycle.

"You think that murdering his partner was premeditated just like taking you hostage was?"

She thought about it. "Yeah. You can't suddenly decide to murder someone without being extremely impulsive, and in spite of the crazy act, he didn't seem impulsive to me. So I think that the murder was part of the plan as well." Street turned and frowned at me. "I remember when the fire starter kidnapped me. Like this hostage taker, the arsonist radiated intelligence. The difference is that when the arsonist was cranked up, he looked demented. His plan was simple revenge. Whereas this guy was different."

"Rational?"

"Yeah, I think so," Street said. "But feral, too. Why would a person go to such lengths to get you to pursue Thomas Watson? I would think a smart guy could figure out lots of ways to get what he wanted without resorting to such an extreme act."

"So either he was not as smart and rational as you think, or there was something else going on that we're not aware of."

"Like what?" Street asked.

"I don't know. Did you get a look at his partner?"

"Yes, but nothing much about him stood out. He was smallish, maybe five and a half feet, and thin. But rugged looking. Like he'd worked construction all of his life. His skin was tan and wrinkled even though I don't think he was more than forty or so."

"Hair?" I asked.

"Coarse, short hair. Brownish gray like a schnauzer dog."

"Eyes?"

Street shook her head. "I didn't see them."

"If the hostage taker's hair was fake, maybe his partner's hair was fake, too."

"I doubt it. It was cut too short to hide any of his features. And he wasn't carefully choreographed, either. I think he was just as he appeared, a helper who was probably paid to do a job."

"Did the hijacker appear to focus on his helper?" I asked. "When he looked at him, was the look intense or casual?"

"I don't know. I didn't see any look of hate. But I don't think the hijacker would have revealed his feelings in a look. He was under more control than that. Anyway, I was mostly facing away from them, toward the water."

I nodded. "Maybe the plan was something completely different. A diversion of some kind. A way to draw all area law enforcement while something else went down in the Tahoe Basin with no police around to stop it."

"It's outrageous to think that he may have taken me hostage for that purpose."

"Yeah. The crime is the same, but it trivializes what you went through and makes it even more infuriating."

"But if diversion was the purpose, it certainly appeared to work. While I was tied up, I saw boats from a couple of sheriff's departments. They were probably all out there."

"We'll hear in the next day or so if some other crime was committed," I said.

"Because the hijacker demonstrated his willingness to murder," Street said, "if he really wanted Thomas Watson taken off the streets, it would figure that he could have just killed Watson. But he didn't. Instead, he enlisted you to get him out of circulation another way. I wonder why?"

"Maybe Watson would be very difficult to murder. Maybe he has a bodyguard at all times. Maybe he never comes out of his condo. Or maybe he is hyper-vigilant, and he would recognize the hostage taker if he came anywhere near."

Street said, "So he supposedly found out that Watson killed Grace Sun, and he learned that you were on the case, yet were unsuccessful at finding the killer. Even though you've been off the force for a few years, you still have a vested interest in finding the killer. That's correct, isn't it?"

"Right," I said.

"The hostage taker could have developed his whole plan knowing that you would be motivated to get Watson before the judicial system. You would have the additional motivation of being afraid that he'd take me hostage again if you didn't."

I nodded. "True. At least, I don't have to worry about that."

Street stared down at the huge lake below us. She took a deep breath and shut her eyes. She picked up her wine glass, realized it was empty, put it back down. I went inside, came back out with the wine and refilled both of our glasses.

Street took a sip, then spoke. "I've never been more afraid than I was out on that boat. I thought I was going to be sacrificed to his plan, just like the guy he came with. I stood there shivering, imagining what it would feel like to have that chain anchor pulling me down into the freezing blackness, the pressure bursting my eardrums, ice water pushing into my brain, my lungs being crushed. No human can survive more than a fraction of the depth of that lake. The thought was terrifying."

"You went through it because you're connected to me," I said. "I'm so sorry that my world puts you at risk." I put my arm around her shoulders. The rough wool of the blanket felt warm.

Street held her wine up so that the lowering sun shined through it and fractured into burgundy rays that danced over her face. "We don't fall in love with someone because it is practical or safe," she said.

"You don't," I said. "But I've heard some women say they married for money. I'm sure men do, too. Physical and psychic safety can't be far removed from that."

"As a scientist, I'm all about pragmatism and efficacy, but I could never see myself getting involved with a guy because he had a good job or a low-risk lifestyle. Maybe I'm not the romantic that you are, but I still fell in love with a guy who doesn't make much money, who'd rather study art than pursue a practical hobby, who doesn't even have a TV, who is unreasonably tall. You fell in love with a skinny woman who spends her life studying bugs. What kind of strange creatures are we?" Street turned to look at me.

"You?" I said. "Passionate, brilliant, gorgeous. Me? Lucky."

The sun had finally warmed Street enough that her nervous shivering subsided. She pushed the blanket off of her shoulders.

"What are you going to do about what happened?" she asked.

"Track down Thomas Watson. See if he might be Grace Sun's killer. In the process, I might get an idea of who the hostage taker and his partner were."

"Don't you think that's giving in to the hijacker's manipulation?"

"Absolutely."

"I know your code requires you to honor all promises, but your promise was to a guy who is now dead. A guy who murdered and terrorized people."

"Yeah. But the main reason I'll look up Watson is that if he is in fact Grace's killer, I want to track him down for her sake. A killer has gone unpunished. I want to rectify that."

"How are you going to get to him?"

"Don't know," I said.

We finished our wine.

Street said she wanted to sleep at her condo. I took it as her testing her strength and independence. You can get taken as a hostage and threatened with death and still sleep alone.

I knew not to protest.

We got in the Jeep and I drove her down the mountain.

Once inside Street's condo, she pulled a Night Harvest cab out of her wine rack and went to work with the opener. This was a serious break in pattern for her. A glass and a half at my cabin, then coming home and getting serious about the grapes. I said nothing.

She poured us each a glass and then proceeded to cook some kind of veggie dinner with spinach and sun-dried tomato in an unleavened dough, one of those meals that sounded drab but tasted wonderful. I always assumed an inverse relationship between taste and healthfulness, but Street was gradually convincing me that it might not be a universal law of food.

Later, we sat in front of her gas fireplace.

"Maybe you should give up this pursuit," she said. "If this Watson turns out to be Grace Sun's murderer, the case will be closed. Why the hijacker sent you on this chase is something we'll never know. Isn't that something you can walk away from?"

"That's what I've been telling myself. But I can't stop thinking about it."

"Why?"

"I don't know," I said. "It's too messy. Too many unanswered questions."

"But most of life is like that, right? Everywhere I turn I see messiness. I try to make some sense of my own little world by selectively shutting off the inputs and putting on some soft music. But outside of these walls, there is so much random chaos. So much danger."

"That's just it," I said. "Weren't you the one who told me about finding order in chaos? That chaotic environments are subject to natural order? You said that rushing rivers produce regular eddies.

Turbulent, mixing air masses create repeating cloud forms. Eons of shifting tectonic plates produce ordered geologic layers. I still remember that picture you once showed me of a gravel pit where the stones were magically ordered. At the bottom were the smallest pebbles, and as it went higher, the pebbles got larger until the highest layer was made up of cobbles."

"And this connects to the killer who took me hostage," Street said, doubt in her voice.

"Sort of. I think that what I'm looking for in the hijacker experience is order in chaos. This hijacking seems so random. The man's apparent purpose, the man's action, the surprising result. I don't understand any of it. So I'm hoping I can make some sense out of it. If I keep poking around, asking questions, maybe somebody will say something that will make me see the repeating pattern, see the order."

"And if that doesn't happen?"

I shrugged. "Always in the past, if I turned over enough rocks, eventually a snake crawled out. As long as it isn't a rattlesnake striking before I'm ready, it's a good result."

"I don't want to think that," Street said.

"But even then I'd have something to follow."

"Or you would die from the bite. Talk about a messy ending."

"Good point," I said.

"Then you'll think about resuming your previous life?"

"Yes."

We sat in silence in front of the fire, and sipped our wine. Then Street said she wanted to try going to bed. I went with her into her bedroom, tucked her in. Spot put his paw up on Street's bed, then pushed his head in next to us.

I rubbed Street's back, kissed her goodnight, and let myself out.

Spot and I got in the Jeep and were up the mountain at my cabin ten minutes later.

SIX

Before I got to my cabin door, Spot was there sniffing it in the dark, the knob, the lock, the door jamb. He paid particular attention to the knob.

"You find something, boy?" I whispered. I put the key in and turned the lock. Then I grabbed his chest and shook him a little. "Find the suspect, Spot!" I said in a loud whisper. "Find the suspect!"

I turned the doorknob with two fingertips, hoping to preserve any existing prints and smacked his rear. But instead of racing into the cabin, he just stood there and continued to sniff the knob.

No one had burgled my cabin. No crime had been committed. I had little interest and even less justification in calling Diamond or pulling out my fingerprint equipment.

I went out on the deck and looked at the night sky. Spot pushed at my hand with his nose. I rubbed his head.

The twinkling stars seemed so calm and peaceful from a distance. Yet I knew from Street that appearances deceive, that the universe was an unimaginably violent place. The stars were seething cauldrons that gave birth to new elements. Some exploded, their end-stage theatrics so dramatic that they annihilated entire solar systems.

I got the portable and dialed Agent Ramos.

"Question about Thomas Watson," I said when he answered. "You said he's a people person, eats dinner with a group and such. What about when he's at his new place here in Tahoe? Could a guy get to him? Does he have a bodyguard insulating him from the world?"

"Yes, he has a bodyguard, and he won't respond to your knock or call, either. You want to talk to him, you'll have to catch him when he's out in public."

"Recommendation on where to get to him?"

"Try the Chips-n-Brew in Tahoe City. He's a regular around three in the afternoon. Sits at the bar with his bodyguard."

"Descriptors?" I asked.

"Watson's in his middle thirties, five-eleven, one ninety-five, reddish hair slicked back like a fifties greaser, the kind of skin you get when you take a red-headed Scotsman with no melanin and stick him under the sun for a couple of decades too long."

"Clothing?"

"He's got two approaches," Ramos said. "His work style is loose khakis and polo shirts. His party style is tight-crotch jeans and silver cowboy boots."

"Thanks," I said.

SEVEN

Two hours later the phone rang.
I fumbled it off the little table I'd made out of stacked art books. "Hello?"

"This is turning out to be difficult." It was Street. Typical understatement.

"Sleeping?" I said.

"After what happened," she said.

"You want to come back up to my cabin?"

"Please."

"I'll be there in a few minutes."

When Spot and I pulled in, Street came out before I could shut off the Jeep. She locked the door, ran out through the wash of my headlights, and got in.

We drove back up the mountain. As I walked her into my cabin, I could feel the shakes in her body.

We didn't talk, just sat together in front of the small fire I'd made in the woodstove. After an hour we went to bed, and I wrapped her in my arms and held her through the night.

Sleepovers were uncommon for us. My ideal world would have us together every night. Perhaps Street's model world might include me in the same way, but that would require rewriting a childhood so bleak that she ran away at 15 and vowed never to get very close to anyone again.

After being with her for a few years, I was beginning to sense that her fear of loss and betrayal was lessening. But I had no illusions that the trauma her abusive parents had created would ever go away. So I was content to take Street on her terms and be glad for any time that I got with her.

We slept late, and I made a breakfast of oatmeal with cantaloupe and blueberries on the side. The sun had risen enough that we sat out on the deck, the solar radiation canceling the cold air of a late-September morning at 7200 feet.

"What's this?" Street said, sampling her oatmeal. "The bacon-and-eggs carnivore is going healthy?"

"Don't sound so skeptical. It was only a couple of weeks ago I ate that veggie tufa thing that Ryan Lear served us for dinner."

"Tufa is the name of those limestone formations that have formed over the centuries at Mono Lake. I think you mean tofu," Street said.

"Ah."

"And now a zero-fat breakfast," Street said. "Like Alexander the Great becoming a pacifist."

"Just what I was thinking," I said.

After breakfast, Bains called and asked about meeting with Street. I handed Street the phone and she made a plan to meet Bains at the county offices in South Lake Tahoe where she would give him a statement and then sit down with a local artist the county uses and work up sketches of the hostage taker and his partner.

Street wanted to shower and change clothes before her appointment with Sergeant Bains, so Spot and I took her back down the mountain to her condo and said goodbye.

I drove north around the lake to Tahoe City. I found a place to park at one of the shopping areas near the Chips-n-Brew, the place where, according to Agent Ramos, Thomas Watson was an afternoon regular. I told Spot to be good, walked over and looked in through the large front window.

The restaurant was comprised of a single large room in a Starbucks-meets-brewpub layout, with many small tables made of dark, varnished wood. At the back of the room were three huge stainless-steel tanks that contained the house microbrews. To one side was a long bar made of the same wood as the tables. At the center of the bar were six barstools for people who didn't want a table.

Above the bar was a black chalkboard on which an artist had

used colored chalk to list the menu items and decorate around the menu with cute pictures of rainbow trout and Kokanee salmon. Across the room was another chalkboard with pictures of beer steins filled with beer. The drawings were organized according to the color of the brew, darkest on the left and palest on the right. Under each beer was the name of the brew.

At one end of the bar was the order area, and at the other end, the pick-up area from which patrons could carry their food to one of the small tables or over to the bar.

I continued down the sidewalk, visualizing the restaurant layout, wondering how I might accomplish my task. A UPS driver stepped in front of me. She hauled a two-wheeler loaded with boxes into the Bookshelf bookstore. I stood looking in the window at the books displayed, thinking through an idea.

Two blocks down, I turned into an alley and found a dumpster behind a store. There were several empty cardboard boxes in the dumpster. I pulled out a smallish one, about ten inches long on each side. Another three blocks down was a shop that sold various sundries including some office supplies. They had a small dispenser of clear packing tape. I carried it and the empty box back to my Jeep.

Spot wasn't so interested in the tape as he was in the box, which had no doubt absorbed lots of dumpster smells. While Spot sniffed, I called Jack Santiago, the Placer County sergeant I had met sometime back. The secretary transferred me to someone else who told me that Santiago wouldn't mind if he gave me Santiago's cell number. I dialed the number, and Santiago answered.

"Heard about you on the charter boat, McKenna," he said when he found out it was me. "Hell of a way to enjoy an outing on the lake. Lemme guess. You're calling about Watson comma Thomas, AKA Tommy Watts, our new, part-time resident of Placer County, subject of the hostage taker's ill will."

"Good guess."

"Lieutenant Davison got the story from Agent Bukowski this morning. We don't want a murderer in our happy little mountain paradise any more than you do. What can I do for you?"

"Wondered if you might have time for a quick chat this afternoon," I said. "I'll be in the Tahoe City area around three."

"I can probably swing that. Where do you want to meet?"

"How about the Chips-n-Brew?" I said.

"Three o'clock?" Santiago said. "See you there."

"Any chance you could change into your civvies?"

"You watching a drop or something?"

"No. We can just talk more freely when we're incognito."

"I'll see what I can do."

I hung up and spent a little time with my packing tape, carefully sealing the empty box where it had been opened, leaving the old address label in place. I tore off one long piece of tape and two short pieces. I used the short pieces to attach the long piece on the side of the box with the adhesive facing out. Unless you touched it or looked closely, the box looked normal, and the reversed tape was not visible.

When I was done, I had an extra hour to kill, so I took Spot down to the water at The Commons park where he spent some time playing with a yellow lab. Whenever the lab ran into the water and swam around, Spot ran up and down the water's edge, making big frustrated woofing sounds. Realizing he was alone in the water, the lab came out, raced around with Spot for a bit, then went back into the water. The lab was unable to resist the water, a foreign concept for most Danes.

The lab's owner sat next to me on a bench.

"We're breaking the leash law," he said.

"Yeah," I said.

"Hope the cops don't come around."

"Yeah," I said.

Out on the lake, five Jet Skis put down high-speed S-curves, their wakes intersecting in formation. It looked like a water version of the Blue Angels, frothy waves in place of smoke trails.

"The thing about cops," the yellow lab's owner said, "all they do is try to catch people doing something wrong."

"Ah," I said.

"'Course, I suppose it's good somebody is after the bad guys," he said. "Not like we're bad guys 'cause we let our dogs play."

"Yeah," I said.

"Not very talkative, are you," he said. "Or maybe you're a cop, ha, ha."

"Ex-cop," I said.

"Oh. Sorry." He stood up and whistled. "Ochre!" he yelled.

The yellow lab came running. The man clipped a leash onto his dog and hurried away.

I put Spot back into the Jeep, picked up my box and walked to the Chips-n-Brew. Santiago was just pulling up in an unmarked. He drove past the restaurant, found an opening half a block down, and parked. I was glad to see that he was wearing jeans and a sweatshirt.

We shook hands and went inside.

"What's in the box?"

"Delivery for the manager."

"Oh."

There were four men at the bar, each with a beer. Two of the beers were brown with heavy foam heads, two yellow with a few wimpy bubbles. The right-most guy had bad skin and red hair slicked back. Thomas Watson getting his afternoon bump just as Ramos had said. He wore a green short-sleeved Polo shirt that contrasted with his red pigmentation. The bodyguard to his left was large the way a walrus is large. Thick and roundish, with no muscle definition. His sides bulged out like they were filled with gel, making a continuous two-foot contact with the men on either side of him. Still, he radiated professional-with-experience. If he got hold of you, you'd be in trouble whether he sat on your chest or snapped your neck. Santiago didn't react. Probably when Bukowski told him about Watson, he didn't show him a picture of Watson. Or maybe he did, and Santiago played it very cool.

There were several vacant tables. I steered Santiago to one near the front. He pulled out a chair that would have him facing the window.

"Tell you what," I said. "I'm waiting on someone else who might walk by. Mind if I take that chair?"

"No problem." Santiago stepped behind the table, took the chair that backed up to the window, and sat down. He was now facing the bar.

"Drinks and food on me," I said. "What'll you have? I'll go order."

"The special." He pointed to the chalkboard.

I stood up. "I'll give this box to the manager, then be right back with our beer."

I carried the box over to the counter near Thomas Watson. He leaned his elbows on the counter. Although tiny compared to the beef pot pie next door, Watson was a thick guy, with meaty forearms below the short sleeves of his shirt. The bare arms were going to make my task easier. I set the box on the counter with the reversed tape facing Watson's arm.

I caught the eye of a beer jockey. "I've got a delivery for the manager."

The kid said, "Stanley is out for the next…" he looked at a clock on the wall, "'bout fifteen minutes."

"Oh. Maybe I should come back." I reached for the box, turned, pretended to bang my knee under the bar, exclaimed and jerked and pushed the box over against Watson's arm.

"Oh, I'm sorry," I said. I made like I was losing my balance and grabbed his shoulder with one hand. I used my other hand to push the box and tape firmly against his skin.

Watson pulled his arm to the side, surprised to see that the box was stuck to him.

"Your box is stuck to me." He reached to pull it off. The box separated from the tape, which was plastered to his skin.

"I'm sorry," I said again. I grabbed the tape and jerked it off his arm. The sound of hair ripping out of skin was audible.

"DAMN!" he shouted. He rubbed his arm.

"I'm really sorry. I sure didn't mean to hurt you."

I took the box and tape and hurried back to the table. Santiago was frowning at me.

"We better get out of here," I said in a low voice. I turned and walked out. Santiago joined me on the sidewalk a few seconds later.

"Did you get a good look at the guy I just bumped into?"

"Yeah. What the hell kind of stunt was that?"

I walked down the sidewalk at a fast pace.

"That was Watson," I said as Santiago caught up with me.

"The guy you fell against was Thomas Watson? But I don't understand what the box… Christ, now I get it. That was a setup. This whole gig was about using that tape to get a forest of arm hair from the guy who may have killed the woman in San Francisco."

"Yup." I held up the tape.

He looked at the tape up close. "And you got a bunch of roots, too. Perfect for DNA sampling."

"Yup."

"So this wasn't about talking to me at all."

"Nope," I said.

Santiago walked in silence for a moment. "Maybe I'm figuring this out," he said. "You wanted an officer of the law to witness that the hair on the tape did, in fact, come from Thomas Watson. That makes it more likely that the evidence would be admissible in court."

"Yup."

"But you didn't tell me about your plan in advance because then a jury could interpret it as my plan, which, as an officer of the law, would be construed as an illegal search and seizure without a search warrant."

I nodded.

"However, you, as a private citizen, can acquire the DNA of a suspect without repercussions unless the suspect files assault charges against you, which is unlikely considering the method you devised."

"That's my hope," I said.

He shook his head back and forth. "Wait 'til I tell the boys."

"You'll take charge of the tape evidence?" I said. I handed it to him.

He nodded. "I can send it to the lab. I'll see if they can give us the rush treatment. If the DNA is a match, we'll need an arrest warrant. But how can we get one? The crime was in San Francisco?"

"True, but we – they – already have a John Doe DNA warrant," I said.

"Great," Santiago said. "A John Doe DNA warrant doesn't identify a suspect by name but by DNA profile. And it gives any law enforcement officer the authority to arrest the suspect if his DNA matches." He held up the tape with Watson's arm hair. "So if this does the job, I can bring him in myself." He grinned. "I'm thinking I'll talk to the lieutenant and see what we've got on the schedule. Maybe we can spare a couple of deputies, have them watch Watson in case he realizes what happened and decides to run. We don't have the budget to follow him far, but we could at least get a sense of where he's going and alert our colleagues down the highway."

"Good idea," I said.

"Maybe next time we really can get a bite, huh? They have good fish."

"Count on it," I said.

EIGHT

When I got back to my office on the far side of the lake, I fired up the coffee maker while I sorted mail. Spot focused on his office olfactory inspection. I poured coffee. At first, Spot was interested in the walls. Then he moved to the side of my desk.

"You just sniffed all of that two days ago," I said. "No one's been in here since then. There can't be that many new smells."

Spot looked at me and wagged. In typical Great Dane style, his tail wipered so far to the side that it came over the edge of my desk, endangering my tenuous organization of office detritus. I moved my stapler, my tape dispenser, and my pen mug that Diamond had given me in a misplaced effort to get me to share his new enthusiasm for French philosophers. The mug had a picture of a golfer who's just sliced his ball into a pond. The golfer's shirt said, 'Sartre,' and next to the pond it said, 'An Existential Lie.' Diamond explained that it was a triple entendre, but I didn't really get it, and his disappointment in my ignorance was obvious. But it held a lot of pens.

I dialed Agent Ramos. I was pulling an old croissant out of my mini-fridge when he answered. I set the croissant on the desk.

"McKenna calling," I said. Spot stared at the croissant.

"Ah," Ramos said. "I talked to an informant who's gotten close to TransPacificTronics. He's helped us in the past. He said that Watson currently stays at the Marriot when he's in San Francisco, but that a few years ago – when Grace Sun was murdered – he used to stay in one of the suites at the Club Pacific Crest Hotel. So I called the Club Pacific and squeezed the reception desk manager."

"Squeezed?" I said.

"My term," Ramos said. "Some people find that dealing with FBI agents is intimidating. Like dealing with cops, only more so. And sometimes that reaction encourages people to reveal information they need not. Anyway, I found out that Watson was in San Francisco and stayed at the Club Pacific the day the Sun woman was murdered. It's not much, but it's something."

Spot took a half-step forward, his head over the edge of the desk, in striking distance of the croissant. His nostrils flexed. I pulled the croissant to safety.

"Be interesting if we could get a warrant to pull his credit card records," I said. "Maybe Sun and Watson ate at the same cafés in North Beach or hung out at the same bars on the wharf."

"I revisited our file on Watson," Ramos said. "But I didn't see anything suggestive in light of these recent events."

I took a bite of the croissant. It was enough past stale that petrified rock was only a week off. Spot studied me. He ran his giant tongue down one jowl and back up the other.

Ramos said, "Watson has made some enemies. But none seem like good matches for the guy who fell into the lake. Wrong area, wrong MO, wrong physical type. I'm looking for any guys who might have been burned badly enough by Watson to want to do something as crazy as taking Street hostage."

Spot's eyes were laser beams. I looked at the hard croissant, but I couldn't see any little red dots of light on it. I tossed it in a behind-the-back-and-over-the-head pop-up. Spot was ready, having played my brand of ball before. He did the little bounce off his front paws, stood on his hind legs, his head arcing toward the ceiling, and caught the pastry like Willie Mays leaping up at the outfield fence. He didn't chew that I could see, just snapped two or three times and swallowed. Then he gave me an expectant look.

"One croissant is the maximum recommended serving," I said.

"Pardon me," Ramos said in my ear.

"Sorry," I said. "Spot and I were discussing doggie nutrition."

Ramos paused. "I've been upstaged by dog food," he said, no

humor in his voice.

"So," I said, "you've got Watson's proximity to Grace Sun the day she was murdered. That's good."

"It's still not probable cause."

"That's the reason I called," I said. "We may not need it." I told him about getting Watson's arm hair on the packing tape.

Ramos was silent for a moment. Eventually he said, "Sounds like you engineered a good maneuver. It might just hold up in court." It was a compliment of sorts, another unusual experience for me, coming from Ramos.

"Do you have the tape with the hair?" Ramos asked.

"Santiago has it. Placer County will have it analyzed."

"If Watson's DNA matches what your San Francisco boys pulled out from under Grace Sun's fingernails, and we get a murder conviction, that'll take Watson out of the smuggling business without us having to nail him on it."

"We'll know in a day or three," I said.

Shortly after we hung up, Street walked in. She was wearing heavy jeans and a long-sleeved, navy flannel shirt buttoned all the way to the collar. Over the shirt was a red fleece vest. I could see thick wool socks above the rims of her running shoes. Her hair flowed out from under a red, wool baseball cap, the kind designed to keep hunters warm in a Minnesota November. She was dressed as if the weather were 30 degrees colder than the sunny, Tahoe fall, a lingering reaction to her imagined plunge to the depths of the freezing lake.

Spot lifted his head toward Street's face, his nose just two inches shy of her chin. He wagged as if it had been a few weeks rather than a few hours since we'd seen her.

"Go okay?" I said as Street rubbed his head and ears.

"Yes. The statement was easy. I just told Sergeant Bains what happened, all of which everyone involved already knew. The artist was trickier to work with. I'm sure that she's really very good, but every time I'd say something and she'd try something, it just didn't come out looking like anything. At one point she'd drawn a very good portrait of a gorilla with a bushy beard, and I started laughing. I know she thought it was rude of me, but I just couldn't help it. In the end, we pretty much realized that the only part of this guy's face that I really saw was when he pulled off his sunglasses for that one moment. I feel like I might recognize his blue eyes if I saw them again. But he was so close to me when he took off his glasses that I couldn't really describe his face. Add to that my stress and I'm afraid I was really no help to the artist."

"Never know," I said.

Street told me she wanted to hear about my day, but had to get over to her lab to make a phone call. She gave me a kiss, pet Spot, and left.

I told her I'd stop by later.

I dialed my old work number I still had memorized from years before. I asked to be put through to Joe Breeze, the cop who was working homicide with me when Grace Sun was killed. Three transfers later, he said hello.

"Owen McKenna calling," I said.

"Like a ghost in my ear," he said. "Tall guy, right?"

"Memory like a bear trap," I said.

"Sure, now it's coming back to me. We did everything but sleep together for what, five years? I can even picture your face if I try hard. But I still don't forgive you that the ladies always spoke to you instead of me when we did our song and dance. I tell myself it's just the tall boy thing. Women are always impressed by size. If we were the same height, I'da probably had it all over you."

"No doubt."

"What's up?" Breeze asked.

"You remember the Grace Sun case? Had a boat hijacker up here at the lake. Claimed that Grace's murderer was a guy named Thomas Watson."

"Heard about the hijacking. But y'all obviously did a good job keeping the lid on the connection to Grace's murder, because I didn't know about that. Who's Watson?"

I gave Joe the gist of what had happened and how I'd sampled Watson's DNA.

"We'll know in a couple of days if the DNA matches what was under Grace's fingernails," I said.

"Good work, McKenna. Be sweet if we could close Grace's

case. But I wonder what motivated the hostage taker. Kinda out there, him going to all that trouble."

"Why I called. Remember the journal that Grace had inside her shirt when we found the body?"

"Yeah," Breeze said. "Written in Chinese. And it was water stained. Blurred the writing all to hell."

"Most of it, anyway. I'd like to take another look at it."

"You think something in it would point to Watson?"

"Maybe. Maybe not," I said.

"If this Watson's DNA matches what Grace had under her nails, what difference would it make? We could close the case."

"True," I said. "But it still wouldn't explain why the hostage taker went to all the trouble."

"You think the journal will point to the hijacker?"

"Who knows?" I said. "I remember during Grace's case, we had that professor try to translate the journal. He couldn't get much out of the blurry characters. But he did figure out that the journal was probably a hundred years old or more. So it's unlikely that anything in it is going to connect to this situation. Nevertheless, I'd like to take another look at it. Can't hurt, right? It's still with the other evidence, right?"

"No doubt. You want to come down to The City and take a look?"

"I thought you could FedEx it to me," I said.

"You know I can't do that."

"Why not? I was the detective on the case. I have a valid reason for looking at the journal."

"Technically, you're not even a law enforcement officer anymore," Breeze said.

"This is a compelling exception. I'm a consulting expert. I may find something that leads to the killer."

"It would break the chain of custody," Breeze said.

"No it wouldn't. The Evidence Custodian has you sign for it. You document when and where you put it in FedEx's hands. I sign for it on my end. I document that I never let it out of my sight. Then I send it back to you."

Breeze blew air into the phone. "No matter what you say, sending the journal to you would be irregular. If you compromise our case and we lose a conviction, my career would be on the line."

"I thought you were nearing retirement, anyway."

"Funny guy. Chrissakes, McKenna. It's like you never left. Next thing, you're gonna be telling me all over again about the time you helped catch the Propane Killer."

Breeze was referring to the case where he and I and two other cops went into an apartment building where a suspected arsonist-murderer hung out with his drug-shooting buddies. When we heard a child screaming, we made a no-knock entry into an apartment and came upon a man sexually assaulting a seven-year-old girl. We arrested the man, and the crime scene technicians collected irrefutable evidence. Later, when we confirmed to our own satisfaction that the molester and the arsonist-murderer were the same person, we didn't have a strong enough case to prosecute the man for murder. I had an idea that compromised the sex evidence and destroyed the state's sexual assault case. But it helped us find sufficient evidence to convict the same man of murder and put him on Death Row. Afterward, the DA gave me a wink-and-a-nod reprimand for my transgressions.

"This could be a parallel situation," I said. "Information in that journal could lead me to different, better evidence."

Breeze was silent for a bit. "Give me your shipping address," he said.

I recited the number.

"How you gonna read the journal, anyway?" Breeze said. His voice radiated doubt. "That Berkeley professor couldn't even help us."

"Met an ER doctor when I moved up to Tahoe. He's fluent in Mandarin. I'll see if he can help."

Breeze grunted, then hung up.

NINE

I'd just gotten to my office the next morning when Sergeant Santiago called me on my cell.

"Got the lab report. They matched Thomas Watson's DNA with the DNA you collected from under Grace Sun's fingernails three years ago," he said.

"You pick Watson up?"

"Byron was on the Watson rotation. He had tailed Watson to the supermarket. Forsythe met Byron in the parking lot. They arrested Watson in the produce aisle while his bodyguard was at the ice cream cooler. Watson was cool. Went without a fuss. Which we appreciated when we found his concealed carry."

"Heavy equipment?"

"Forty cal Browning in a concealment T-shirt."

"Is he in the Truckee jail?" I asked.

"Until we transfer him to San Francisco," Santiago said.

"I'd like to talk to him when it's convenient," I said.

"Sure you would. But the guy hasn't said one word. Not even to Byron and Forsythe."

"Never seen that before," I said.

"No kidding. It's like he went to law school himself."

"He ask to call his lawyer, yet?"

"Nope. That surprised me. Most dirtballs aren't lawyered up, but a guy like this seems like he'd be pretty tight with a lawyer somewhere. But maybe he doesn't have one. "

"You're cops. And he's in your jail. That would make some people reticent. But maybe he'll talk to me. I'm a civilian. Practically harmless."

"How did I forget that," Santiago said. "All you did was rip out his hair, and now he's a candidate for the big injection at

San Quentin. You're like his best bud. Anyway, you know the routine. The lead inspector at SFPD will be the first to talk to Watson. Anyone else would need explicit permission from the lead inspector to talk to Watson."

"Right," I said. "But who says we have to follow routine? Besides, I would just be a guy who stops by the jail, maybe to inspect the plumbing or something. I could say a few words to Watson while the rest of you are having coffee."

Santiago was silent for a long moment.

"We do have a faucet that keeps dripping," he finally said.

"Be there in an hour," I said.

The Truckee jail was a low-profile building with little signage. Most locals probably didn't know where it was or even that it existed. I parked on the street and left Spot in the Jeep. He had his head out the back window and made a bark that morphed into a groan as I walked away. I turned around, held my finger up to my lips, then shook it at him. He barked again. Like a windshield wiper, his tail wag was set on intermittent, waiting to see if the conditions would get more exciting before it shifted to normal speed.

I called out, "That's a zero on the sign language obedience scale."

He barked again. No respect.

"Any change in the patient?" I asked Santiago when he met me just outside of the front door.

"Nope. Like a monk, he's so quiet. And he sits in the lotus position. What's that called when they do the moaning thing?"

"I don't know. Tibetan absolutions? Gregorian chants?"

"Yeah, that. I keep expecting him to start chanting."

"When's the transfer?"

"The San Francisco boys are coming for him tomorrow."

Santiago took me into the jail. A uniformed Nevada County Sheriff's deputy who looked about twenty-one was on duty at the door. Another was at the desk.

"Two cops on guard," I said to Santiago.

"High-value prisoner demands plural guards," Santiago said. "Owen McKenna, meet Barry Downywood and John Farnum."

We said our how-do-you-dos.

"Sidearm?" Santiago said to me.

"I don't carry," I said.

He gave me a quick, puzzled look, then took out his own gun and put it in the safety locker.

We walked with Deputy Farnum through to the cells. Thomas Watson sat cross-legged on the bench, his eyes shut, his arms down, palms facing out. His legs were thick like his arms. It didn't look like he'd be able to get them into the lotus position, but cross-legged was close.

"Owen McKenna to see you, Watson," Santiago said.

Farnum unlocked the cell gate, let me in, locked it behind me.

"You want me to stay nearby?" Santiago glanced at Watson. "He's in a tough business, might be a tough guy."

"I'll be fine," I said, knowing that he'd said it just to rile Watson.

"Let Barry and John know when you want out." Santiago and Farnum walked away.

I leaned against the wall opposite the prisoner. Watson ignored me and stared off to my side.

Watson had probably learned my name after I arranged to sample his arm hair. If not, I imagined that someone, one of the arresting cops maybe, would have said something about the DNA warrant, which would have tipped Watson off to the real reason I stuck the tape on his arm. He didn't need to look at me to know that I was the person who started the sequence that landed him in jail. But Watson exhibited no recognition of me.

"I'd like permission to ask you a few questions," I said.

"You can ask," Watson said. "Doesn't mean I've got any answers for you."

"You no doubt know about the hijacking incident on the lake a few days ago," I continued. "I'm here to ask you if you have an idea of who the hostage taker was."

Watson didn't respond, so I recapped how the hostage taker had put on his grand performance ostensibly just to convince me to go after Watson. "He claimed, with great confidence I might add, that you were Sun's killer. The hostage taker killed one man, nearly killed a woman, and put an entire boatload of passengers at risk, all because he was determined to have me bring you in for Sun's murder."

I paused. Watson stared at the wall.

"Why would a hijacker do all that just to get me to go after you? The only answer I could think of was that either you killed Grace Sun, and the hijacker was trying to serve the cause of justice, or the hostage taker had a real negative thing for you, separate from his desire for justice in the killing of Grace Sun."

Watson didn't speak.

Maybe I could just keep talking. Wear him down.

"The hijacker was obviously out to get you. You would be the most likely person to know his identity. When you think of it, a lot of people would know if someone really hated them, right? Can you tell me who the hijacker was?"

Watson shut his eyes. Took a deep breath, held it while he rotated his shoulders, then relaxed them and let his breath out slowly. He appeared to go into a trance. Or a coma.

"I forgot to explain that the hostage taker tripped and fell into the lake wearing a heavy backpack," I said. "He drowned. So you don't need to worry that there could be any repercussions from telling me who he was. And besides, it's not like anyone could get to you inside of San Quentin or wherever you're going on permanent vacation."

Watson was so still, it was as if he had stopped breathing. His eyes had drifted open until they showed slits of white. His lips had gone slack. He looked like he'd had a stroke. Maybe I could insult him into speaking.

"Maybe you're just silent because you're scared. You were the big man in your previous world, your wallet full of the proceeds from smuggling weapons into the country. Now you're a little man in jail, and this jail is the Taj Mahal compared to the snake pit where you're going. You know that newbies at the state's country clubs are required to provide special entertainment for the long-term residents, right? Some don't survive. And of the ones that do, the physical and emotional trauma is so severe that some of them end up unable to care for themselves."

Watson took a long, slow, deep breath, his ribs rising, belly pushing out. He held it for a ten-count, then exhaled, slow as a tire puncture that lets you drive a dozen miles before the rim hits the pavement. At the end, his body relaxed another notch, flesh sagging, all tension leaving his face as if he had died.

I waited for a minute, but I saw no sign of inhalation. It was as if Watson had so thoroughly transcended the limitations of earthly life that he no longer needed the earthly requirement of air. He was gone to me.

"Deputy Downywood? Farnum?" I called out. "I'm ready."

I heard a distant buzzer. Santiago appeared a minute later. He opened the gate and let me out. We were back to Downywood's desk when a voice came from behind.

"My guess is that the hostage taker was Nick O'Connell."

I turned and walked back to the cell. Watson hadn't changed position. He still sat cross-legged, arms in his lap, palms up, eyes closed.

"Who was Nick O'Connell?" I said through the bars.

Watson kept his eyes shut as he spoke. "Meanest psychopath you could meet. Be glad he's at the bottom of the lake."

"You knew him?"

"Met him once or twice. Mostly just heard things."

"Like what?" I asked.

"He used to work for Carlos, leader of the Nogales Cartel. He was Carlos's knife man. But O'Connell stole a shipment and disappeared. Then O'Connell started working with Davy Halstead, leader of the Red Blood Patriots."

"You're kidding."

"It was a big mistake. Davy didn't know how wicked O'Connell was. It was a lucky break for Davy that O'Connell died. Otherwise, O'Connell might have fomented rebellion and tried to take over the militia."

"Fomented?" It was the kind of word Diamond would use.

"Yeah. Incite. Provoke."

"Does the militia want to get into the drug business?" I asked.

"Already is. Davy Halstead is a pro. But in this case, I think Davy wanted O'Connell's expertise in other ways. O'Connell didn't steal a shipment of drugs. He stole a shipment of money.

Carlos was so upset that he put out the word to the other cartel bosses. He let them know that O'Connell was an unacceptable risk because he knew too much and because he wasn't afraid of anyone. So they made an agreement to take him out on sight."

"The cartels got together on a common purpose?"

"Yeah. Three of them. All deadly enemies. All trying to kill the same man." Watson still had his eyes closed. He hadn't moved position. "Now they won't have to trouble themselves."

"You sound pretty convinced the hijacker was O'Connell."

"Makes sense, that's all."

"What kind of drugs do the Red Blood Patriots sell?"

"These guys in the drug business, they're scum," Watson said, ignoring my question. "I hope they all kill each other." There was venom in his voice.

"You don't approve of illegal drugs," I said.

"Drugs rot people's minds."

"Yet you peddle illegal guns."

Watson made a dismissive snorting noise. I was so tedious. "If O'Connell were still alive," he said, "I'd skin him alive myself if I could tie him down before he killed me."

"What's a knife man do?" I asked.

"Bodyguard. O'Connell was Carlos's personal bodyguard. It's a new trend for the drug bosses. Guns are loud, bring unwanted attention. A knife man operates on stealth. A guy who's good with a blade can get the job done and move on to the next and the next and maybe no one has discovered the first job, yet. Plus, the soldiers are used to guns. They don't fear them. But everyone is afraid of getting stuck with a blade. O'Connell studied Samurai techniques. I watched him use his knife, once. Did a twirling thing that was impressive. Word was that he was so fast, he could go in below your sternum, reach up and cut out your heart and show it to you before you lost consciousness and died."

"Why would O'Connell go from a drug cartel to a militia?"

"Who knows? Maybe he wanted to be the big cheese in a smaller store. Maybe he planned on kicking out Davy Halstead and taking over the Patriots. He could've pulled it off."

I watched Watson sit motionless. He had emotion in his voice but no emotion on his face.

"This hijacker O'Connell, or whoever he was," I said, "had a partner. He was a small guy who didn't say anything, just helped the hijacker carry their stuff onboard. The hijacker killed him. Knocked him out, strapped an anchor chain around his neck, and dumped him overboard. Any idea who he was?"

Watson shook his head. "Could be anybody. A lot of these guys, they just want to hang out with someone tough. Makes them feel tough by association."

"How do you know that? You one of them?"

"I'm a businessman. In my trade, some of my customers have associates and employees who are not quite Harvard Law material. The rest of society doesn't know the extent of this population. But there are a lot of them. Country guys who live in tents or under pieces of old plywood. Guys who are easily organized using the basic principle of distrust of government. You don't have to spout much about the oppressor class before people want to sign up to oppose them."

"You went to the Naval Academy," I said. "Doesn't that make you part of the oppressor class?"

"I help these people. I empower them." Watson made it sound like he was a missionary bringing enlightenment to the pagans.

"Hijacking a boat and taking a hostage is a dramatic way to get the world's attention," I said. "Was Nick O'Connell that kind of guy? Would he go to such lengths?"

"That's the reason why I think it was Nick. His MO was melodrama. Impulsiveness carried to a neurological extreme. He had no governor. That's what made him so dangerous, so effective at bending others to his desires."

I thought about it. "Did you kill Grace Sun?" I asked.

"No." His tone made it sound like I was an idiot for asking.

"Yet your DNA matches what was under Grace Sun's fingernails."

Watson's eyes were shut. He made a single, dismissive head shake.

"If O'Connell was the hijacker," I said, "why would he try to implicate you in Grace Sun's death?"

"I don't know."

"What did O'Connell have against you?"

Watson still hadn't opened his eyes. I waited, but he didn't answer.

"Did O'Connell know Grace Sun?"

Silence.

"If O'Connell wanted you out of his way for something, and if he was as ruthless as you say, why didn't he take you out himself? Why put me onto you?"

No answer.

"Okay, let's say that Nick O'Connell was like you say, quick with a knife. And let's assume that you are right, and he was the one who hijacked the boat. The obvious question is why. Why would he involve me when he could have made no end of trouble for you without me?"

More silence.

I prodded, "You don't know? Or you won't say?"

Nothing. Watson was done talking. I called to be let out.

"Santiago around?" I asked Downywood when he came to let me out.

"Outside, on his cell. Been talking a long time."

I raised a hand toward Santiago as I went by. He nodded at me as he kept talking.

Spot had his head out the rear window as I approached. He wagged with vigor, no doubt the pure joy of seeing his master. Then he gradually turned, still wagging, until he faced well off to my side. Turns out he wasn't looking at me at all.

I looked behind me. A pit bull was out in front of her owner. The pit bull had a bright pink Frisbee in her mouth and carried it high and proud as she trotted. I got to the Jeep, grabbed Spot's head and rubbed it hard. Spot paid me no attention. He watched the pit bull and wagged harder.

I knew when I wasn't wanted. I was getting into the Jeep when Santiago walked up.

"Any luck?"

"The patient rallied for a bit, then became non-responsive," I said. "You know about the Red Blood Patriots?"

Santiago flared his nostrils. "Bunch of psychos who march around in the woods like soldier wannabes. I've got a buddy in the department who works the West Slope of the Sierra.

He's seen these guys. Thinks they're more dangerous than the motorcycle meth gangs. Some people dismiss them as harmless boys playing pretend with guns. 'Cept, these guys carry modern assault rifles and rant about the Second Amendment and the coming government takeover." Santiago frowned. "Why do you ask? Something about our inmate?"

"Watson thinks that a guy named Nick O'Connell was the hostage taker and that he was involved with the Patriots."

Santiago shook his head in disgust. "You want me to call Agent Ramos, spread the word?"

"Please. Okay if I come back tomorrow? Maybe I can wear him down, get him to talk some more."

"We'll give you a VIP pass if you like. But his big transfer is set for two in the afternoon."

"Got it."

TEN

The next day I was back at the Truckee jail first thing in the morning. They let me into Watson's cell. As before, he was sitting on his bench, his legs crossed. But this time his eyes were open, and there was tension in his face.

"More questions for you, Watson," I said.

Watson looked at me and slowly unfolded his legs. He stood up, wincing as he put weight on his left leg.

"Too long sitting like that will freeze you up," I said.

He shook his head. "It's not that. It's an old injury." Watson bent down, pulled up his pant leg and rubbed his skin where there was a nasty purple-brown divot in his shin. "A few years ago, I tripped on a street grate in San Francisco and landed shin first on the curb of the sidewalk. It still throbs."

"Two o'clock today, you're on your way to check in to San Francisco's finest hotel. Yesterday, you refused to answer some questions. I'm thinking you were just tired, right? Can we try again?"

Watson said, "I'll answer your questions. At least you're looking into this case. Maybe you'll get me off."

"I'm not trying to get you off. That's a lawyer's job."

"You are investigating the case. You're the only one asking questions. You may learn something that will exonerate me."

"No information can exonerate a guilty man," I said.

"I'm not guilty."

"You still say that you didn't kill Grace Sun."

"Correct."

"Then how did she claw your skin hard enough to fill her fingernails?"

"She didn't claw me. She never touched me except for when

we met and shook hands. I have no idea how my skin got under her fingernails. It must be a mistake. I've read about how some labs are sloppy in their record-keeping. They mislabeled their samples or something. Either way, I didn't kill her."

"You're admitting that you met her."

"Of course. At least I think it was her. I have nothing to hide." Watson walked to the front corner of the cell, grasped two of the cell bars, slumped his head and spoke toward the corner. "I talked to a woman who may have been Grace Sun one afternoon a day or two before she was killed. Maybe it was the same day. My memory of those days is fuzzy because I didn't find out about her murder until weeks later. Anyway, if it was Grace I met, we never touched beyond a single handshake."

"Why and where did you speak to her?"

"I was at the San Francisco Library doing some research on nineteenth century Chinese gold miners. A librarian told me that a woman had been looking up similar information. She said that the woman had been in at lunchtime for the last three days. I waited to see if she might come in again that day, and she did. We spoke at some length. Our interests intersected some, but not a great deal."

"And those interests are…?"

"The woman was apparently interested in the history of the Chinese miners because her great, great grandfather was a miner who came from China. She wanted to know more about what his experience was like. I was more interested in the differences between the Chinese miners and the other miners. I wanted to know why Californians of the time demonized the Chinese and not the Irish and other immigrant groups who came for the Gold Rush. Presumably it was racism, but it may have had other cultural components."

"Are you an anthropologist?"

Watson shook his head. "Not in any academic way. But, yeah, I suppose that's what my interest was."

He sounded sincere, but it didn't seem very believable. The idea of researching Gold Rush racism seemed the kind of subject that only academics would pursue.

"Are you writing a book or something?" I asked.

"No. Well, maybe. I'm just fascinated by the Gold Rush. I'm like those people who are fixated on the Civil War. I read everything I can find. I visit the places. I tour mining sites. I go to museums. The Gold Rush created the state of California as we know it. The Gold Rush created the city of San Francisco. The Gold Rush was a huge part of the reason the railroads were built, and it financed the railroads. The second, later gold and silver rush in Virginia City financed the Union Army in the Civil War. It's been argued that the Confederates might have won if the north hadn't had that giant flow of gold and silver from the tunnels under Virginia City. Anyway, it's my hobby. And when the librarian told me that a woman was looking up some of the same things I was, I was intrigued. So we met. We spoke. We shared some stories. Then we parted, and I never saw her again."

"What kind of stories did you share?"

"Small stuff. Nothing significant," he said.

"Like?"

"Like her great, great grandfather was the opposing side in Mulligan's War."

"What's that?"

"Seamus Mulligan was an Irish miner and one of the first Irish property owners in the foothills. Apparently, he had a small parcel, but in good gold territory. His neighbor landowner was Gan Sun, one of the first Chinese property owners. For several years they had an intense dispute over the property line. Mulligan and his son tried to lynch Gan Sun. Sun fled up a hill, and Mulligan and his son chased him. It was a steep hill, covered with loose rock. Mulligan lost his footing, fell, and slid a long way down. Mulligan hit his head and died. For the rest of his life, Mulligan's son continued to threaten Gan Sun with death.

"The other miners in the area hated Sun the way they hated all the Chinese. But they hated old man Mulligan even more. So they let Gan Sun be. Over the years, they always referred to the incident as Mulligan's War. A war that Gan Sun won by default."

"You learned this from Grace."

"Yeah."

"Why didn't you come forward when she was murdered? You

might have been able to provide useful information."

"Because I didn't know she was murdered. I had left the country on what I later learned was the day after she was killed. I caught the early flight and hadn't seen any newspaper. Not that I pay much attention to crime news, anyway. I didn't come back home for three weeks. By then the media had dropped the story. It wasn't until a few weeks after I returned to the country that I saw my first reference to the murder. I was flipping through some old Chronicles at Club Pacific, the hotel where I used to stay in The City. I was looking at the news from when I was gone, and I saw a reference to the murder victim Grace Sun. The article mentioned that she was an amateur historian who specialized in Chinese miners during the Gold Rush. They printed a picture of her. It was fuzzy, but it looked like the woman I'd met at the library. That was the first time I wondered if the woman I'd met might have been the woman who was murdered. I never did find out for certain. The woman hadn't told me her last name."

"Tell me more about your conversation at the library."

Watson breathed deep and sighed. "What difference does it make?"

"I'm investigating," I said. "I ask questions. You answer."

"I asked the woman about her research. She explained that her Chinese grandfather, two greats removed, came to this country in the early eighteen fifties, two or three years after the start of the gold rush. He worked for several companies in the foothills near what is now Placerville. The woman wanted to learn more about him."

"And did she?"

"I think she mostly learned about the Chinese miners in general and their contribution to the placer mines. Like their fellow countrymen who were later hired to build the railroads, the Chinese miners were mostly limited to doing menial work for daily pay. The mining companies used them to build the flumes, the wooden troughs. They also dug up river sediment and ran it with water through custom sluices. You probably know how it worked. If you adjust the water speed and the angles and such, you can make it so that most of the mud flows out with the water, while the heavier gold dust drops to the bottom." Watson turned and looked at me. "I suppose you don't want to know these details. Like the woman at the library, it was my area of interest as well, so I kind of get lost in the subject."

"I'm interested," I said, noticing how expert Watson was about the era. "Go on. Anything that drew Grace's interest might be useful to me in trying to figure out what happened."

"Well," Watson continued, "people think that the Chinese came to try to get rich mining gold, and quite a few did, but the reality was that China was mostly a source of manual labor for the mining companies. See, before eighteen sixty-nine when they completed the transcontinental railroad, which Chinese laborers built, it was easier to bring workers all the way across the Pacific than to get them across the U.S. from the East Coast. So the mining companies and the railroad companies put the word out that they would hire Chinese. It was a mutually beneficial relationship. Even the ship captains who engaged in human transport from China helped by allowing the Chinese to sign a contract to pay for their passage over time once they began working in California. Soon, the Chinese were the largest single ethnic group in the fast-exploding population of California. In fact, the reason why San Francisco ultimately had the largest concentrated population of Chinese outside of China was because of the immigrant labor during the nineteenth century.

"The Chinese worked hard, didn't complain, and they kept out of trouble. Of course, the Chinese could rarely work their own claims. Even if they tried, white claim-jumpers would run them off and steal their claims. But some of the Chinese worked abandoned claims on their off-hours. They sifted through the waste tailings for a bit of gold dust here and there. And the Chinese invented some filtering techniques where they used cloth to catch the gold dust, then burned the cloth to process the gold. A kind of smelting. They also developed the rocker, a type of see-saw device that sifted tailings through screens.

"I think the woman thought that her great, great grandfather had been quite successful at these techniques, because he was eventually able to buy some land from one of the railroad companies."

"I thought you could get land for free back then under the

Homestead Act," I said.

"Yes, that was passed in eighteen sixty-two. And it even allowed foreigners who intended to become U.S. citizens to get land. But around the same time, much of the best land in the area – millions of acres – was given to the Union Pacific and the Central Pacific railroads. The purpose was for the companies to sell the land off to finance building the railroads. So this woman's grandfather bought a little piece from the Union Pacific. She said he wanted to farm it even though it was bad farmland because it was steep foothill land. She learned that he cleared trees and terraced the steep hillsides and was quite successful at growing several crops. But the land also had a stream flowing through it, and she thought that her ancestor may have found gold in the stream."

"Grace told you this?"

"The woman I believe was Grace, yes. I remember because she showed a bit of anger in the library."

"Why wouldn't she be happy about her ancestor creating a farm?"

"Because the governor of California, a guy named Bigler who was both a racist and a demagogue, saw that political gain could be had by stirring up anti-Chinese hatred. He pushed the idea that Chinese were inferior people and that only whites should be allowed to benefit from California's riches. He made speeches and so inflamed anti-Chinese hatred that Chinese were lynched several times. Their tents and houses were burned. Many of the atrocities were well documented."

"Like with the Native Americans," I said.

"Yes and no," Watson said, shaking his head. "What we did to them was much worse. That was mass extermination. Genocide. But the Chinese were treated very badly, too. White men could murder Chinese and not even be prosecuted."

I had a hard time reconciling this man's intelligent speech with that of a gunrunner. But he was a U.S. Naval Academy graduate.

"Anyway," Watson continued, "the woman – Grace – said that this swell of hatred caused her ancestor to lose half his land. Two white brothers – no relation to Mulligan – had a claim that stopped producing. They were angry that the Chinaman had done well. So they took his land. First, they beat him, then killed his best friend. Then they forced him to sell his farm for pennies, threatening him with death if he didn't sign the bill of sale. The bill of sale gave them legal title to the land. What they didn't know was that Gan Sun had two parcels. He only signed one of them over to the brothers.

"A hundred fifty years later, this woman – Grace Sun – was mad as hell at Governor Bigler. She said that Bigler was scum and that his legacy still harmed many people today. She said that her daughter was denied half of whatever rightful inheritance would have passed down to her all because of Bigler's legalized racism."

"It was probably her cousin that she mentioned," I said.

"No, she said her daughter."

"Did she say what her daughter's name was?"

Watson shook his head. "Not that I recall. It was years ago. My memory is like everyone else's. You can't trust details years later."

"But you're sure she referred to a daughter."

"Yeah. I remember because I had a nasty thought about it, and it stuck in my mind. The woman – Grace – had these enormous hands, like a big blacksmith or something. For some reason, I just couldn't picture a woman holding a baby with those hands. I know it's rude of me to think so. But when she mentioned a daughter, that imagery stuck in my mind."

I thanked Watson and left the jail.

ELEVEN

When I got home, I made several calls, reporting what I'd learned to Ramos, Santiago, Bains, and, for good measure even though it was out of his jurisdiction, Diamond.

Then I called Joe Breeze back at San Francisco PD.

The receptionist said he was out and would be back in five or ten minutes and could he call me back. I remembered what it was like. Breeze would have a hundred other things to do that were more important than talking to me. So I asked to be put on hold.

I put the phone on speaker, set it down, got out my cell, and called Street.

"Want to come up the mountain for a celebration dinner?" I asked when she answered.

"What are we celebrating?"

"I've told you that I always wanted to try baking bread, right?"

"I remember."

"I found a recipe online that I thought sounded good, so I bought the ingredients."

"You're kidding," Street asked.

"You sound doubtful."

"Why would I doubt the cooking skills of a guy who thinks pumpkin pie equals a serving of vegetables, and the whipped cream on top equals a glass of non-fat milk?"

"Am I wrong about that?" I said.

"And I remember that attempt at cookies a year ago." She made a small short sound like the beginning of a laugh. Nothing robust, but it was beautiful music after the black pain of being taken hostage.

"Hey, I got the flames put out all by myself," I said. "Never even thought of calling the fire department. Anyway, imagine the delicious smell of baking bread filling my little cabin," I said.

"That's just it," Street said. "Probably the only way I'll ever smell that in your cabin is by using my imagination. The alchemy of leavened bread is not simple, Owen," she said.

"How hard can it be? You mix up flour, water, yeast, and a few other ingredients, right?"

There was a pause before she spoke. "What time should I be there?"

"Seven?"

"Okay."

We hung up. The speaker phone was still silent. So I found the recipe I'd stuck to the fridge and started pulling out my bread ingredients. Whole wheat flour, oats, yeast, molasses, brown sugar, salt. I put all the dry stuff in a big bowl, stirred it around with a spoon. People say bread is tricky, but it seemed pretty easy to me. I stirred too fast at one point and got flour all over the counter and floor, but otherwise I felt like a professional baker. I measured out some room-temperature water, stirred in the molasses and was pouring the result into the bowl when Joe came on the line.

"Breeze," he said.

I picked up the phone. "McKenna calling. I've been waiting so long I thought maybe you retired."

"You keep calling, I will," Breeze said. "I heard that the DNA of the guy you told me about matches what we got from under Grace's nails, and they picked him up."

"Yeah. Thomas Watson is currently residing in the Truckee jail, awaiting transfer today to your backyard."

"Can't wait," Breeze said.

I kept stirring my bread dough. It was getting very thick.

"I've been thinking about Grace," Breeze said. "The more we learned about that woman, the more we all wished we'd known her before she was killed. I remember how her neighbors and her colleagues at work all said that she was the sweetest person any of them had ever met."

"The picture of Grace," I said.

"Right. Like her name was made for her. By the way, Grace's journal went out this morning, in case you're wondering."

"Appreciate that. I have a lead on who the hijacker might have been. I'm trying to learn what his connection was to Watson. So I need your help again."

"I break all the rules for you, put my ass on the line, and you got more favors to ask?"

"Right. Can you look in the file and see what kind of contact info you have on Melody Sun, the next of kin? I'd like to call her and let her know."

I heard Joe sigh on the phone. "Take me a few minutes to go downstairs and dig through the files. Call you back?"

"Please. Also look and see if there are any other relations mentioned, specifically, a daughter."

I hung up. My bread mixture was now unstirrable. I had expected that it would set up, but I didn't expect cement. Maybe I'd put in too much flour. But I thought I should try kneading it before I added more water. I put the dough on my wooden cutting board.

The kneading was work the way squeezing rocks was work. And the little bit of dough that hadn't turned solid stuck to my hands like glue. Maybe I was supposed to grease my hands. I scraped as much gunk off my hands as I could, scrubbed them under water to get them clean, and dried them off. I found olive oil spray and sprayed it on my hands. Tried kneading again. Now the dough didn't stick to me, but it was still progressing its transformation from sandstone to granite. So I dipped it under the faucet to work some moisture into it.

The water didn't soak in. It just made a slick coating on the surface of the ball of dough. The dough slipped out of my hands, rolled across the counter, fell onto the floor and slid to the far wall.

Spot jumped up, and the phone rang.

"Spot, no!" I said as I grabbed the phone.

It was Joe Breeze. "Got a pen?" he said.

Spot was already at the dough. Spot will eat pretty much anything other than dirt and pine cones. But instead of grabbing the dough off the floor, he sniffed it suspiciously.

"Ready," I said to Breeze. "Spot, move away!" I said to Spot.

Spot didn't back away, but he shook his head as if he'd gotten pepper in his nose.

"This is the phone number and address where Melody and Grace lived," Joe said. He read off a number with a 415 area code. San Francisco. The address was in North Beach. "I also have the number of the neighbor woman who Melody stayed with after the murder. Woman named Veronica Place."

"I remember," I said. "The older lady who still used her stage name from her acting career."

Breeze read off a second number with the same area code and an address in North Beach.

"I hope she's still around," I said.

"I hope she's still alive, wherever she is," Breeze said. "She was quite old when the murder happened."

"Any other contact info? Email? Work address?"

"Here's Grace's work number. The insurance company." He read it off. "But there was no mention of a daughter. What's that about?"

"Watson said he met Grace, talked to her at the San Francisco Library," I said. "He said that Grace mentioned her daughter. To my recollection, we never heard any mention of a daughter."

"Doesn't ring a bell for me, either. Not like my memory is fresh on this. Hold on, let me look through these papers again."

I heard the phone being set down. Folder slapping the desk. Pages flipping. Spot had backed away from the ball of bread dough. He sat down and stared at the dough like it was an alien creature that might move of its own accord.

"Nope," Breeze said. "In the summary it says that Grace Sun was single, fifty-one, and her only known relative was cousin Melody Sun, forty-eight.

"Got it. Thanks."

"Keep me in the corral on this?"

"Will do," I said.

We hung up.

Spot was still staring at the bread dough from the safe distance of a couple of feet. I picked the dough up. It was coated with dust and grit. I ran it under water again and rubbed it. Some of the dirt came off, some got rubbed into the dough. More fiber. Hopefully, the heat of baking would kill any germs.

I put the dough back on the cutting board and tried kneading it again, working the slippery moisture into it when there was a knock at the door. Spot didn't bark, which meant it was Street or Diamond or maybe Mallory from the SLTPD.

"Come in," I called out.

Diamond walked in carrying a manila folder. Spot wagged and sniffed him as he passed by. Diamond gave Spot a single head pat like he was ringing the little signal bell at the post office counter. Spot wagged harder. Diamond came over to my kitchen nook and frowned. "You are cooking," he said with the same tone he would use to remark on me chain-sawing out my front wall for a new window or dragging a hose inside to clean the bathroom.

"A treat for my sweet," I said.

Diamond looked into the bowl where I was kneading. "Lemme guess. Giant roadkill dumpling. What was the original organism? Porcupine?"

"Bread," I said. "I'm baking bread."

"Awfully dark."

"I thought Mexicans were more sophisticated than your basic puffed-air, white, sponge bread. This is whole wheat. Healthy. I even added oatmeal for fiber. And one adds molasses to whole wheat. So yes, it is supposed to be dark."

"You added an entire bottle?" he said.

"You should probably stick with beans and rice and leave the artier foods to me," I said. "Bread is high-art. It requires the touch of a neurosurgeon, the nose of a sommelier, the ear of a concert pianist."

"Baking bread needs a pianist's ear?"

"Trust me," I said.

Diamond shook his head in disbelief and set a manila folder with some papers in it on the counter. "Heard from Agent Ramos that the Red Blood Patriots might be involved with Thomas Watson, the man the hijacker pointed you toward. Brought you an article about them. Nasty group."

"Thanks," I said, as I held the dough under running water

again. "Good to know whatever I can about those boys."

The dough was starting to flex and bend once again.

Diamond nodded, rang Spot's head again, and left.

I put the ball of dough in the center of a glass pie pan and set it in the oven to rise. I'd found a hint online about turning on the oven light to give it a little warmth to aid rising. What a pro.

I dialed the number that Joe said used to be Melody's and Grace's apartment. A recording said the number was no longer in service.

I dialed their older neighbor Veronica Place. She answered on the third ring.

"Hello?"

I knew it was her because she had a stage voice, husky and strong enough that she could still probably project out over a full house.

"Ms. Place, my name is Owen McKenna. We met three years ago under stressful circumstances." I went on to explain that I was with SFPD and worked the Grace Sun murder. "I tried to do a follow-up call to Melody because it appears that we have caught the killer. But the number is not in service."

"Oh, my word," Veronica Place said with dramatic flair. With her deep voice, she sounded like a drag queen who didn't bother to talk in falsetto. "I haven't seen Melody for a very long time. I suppose it's over two years. That girl was so scared to go back into that apartment that she lived with me for two or three months. Then she finally got up her courage and moved back in. But it gave her the terrors. She would come running back down the block and pound on my door at midnight, begging to sleep with me. I still remember her standing on my doorstep, that long black hair all stringy and wet with tears and sweat and fear. Poor Melody lost something important the day her cousin died. Eventually, she sold the apartment and bought a townhouse in Woodside, down the peninsula near Palo Alto or Mountain View, or one of those techie places. She said she's at the base of the mountains where the redwoods grow. It sounds lovely. She wanted to start over. New house, new job, new life. Can't say that I blame her."

"What was her new job? Or her old one, for that matter?"

"Oh, I have no idea. At my age, I remember the nature of people, but I can't keep track of the pedestrian details of their lives."

"Would you happen to have her new number and address?"

"Certainly. One thing I learned in stage work is that you have to be organized. You can't risk missing your line or your entrance just because you forgot to make notes on your script. Hold on. Here it is in my little book. Melody Sun." She gave me the phone and address.

"Another question that came up," I said. "Do you remember Grace's daughter?"

"I never knew Grace had a daughter."

"Did you ever see another woman with Grace? Someone…" I paused as I did some quick subtraction to account for Grace having a child when she was very young. "Someone in her late twenties or early thirties?"

"Well, of course there were other women around. Grace and Melody had friends. Co-workers. I saw lots of other women over the years. But I never thought one of them might be a daughter, and I don't think something like that would have escaped me. And certainly Grace never mentioned a daughter."

"Thank you so much, Ms. Place. I really appreciate it."

"Say hi to Melody from Veronica," she said.

"Will do."

"Mr. McKenna, may I call you Owen?"

"Yes, of course."

"Owen," she said, "you sound like a real man, a solid man. If you're ever in the area and you want to visit, I'm nearly always home. I build a martini that will make your hair stand up and wave like you're Vincent Price."

"I bet you do, Veronica. Thanks for the invitation."

We hung up and I dialed the number for Melody's address in Woodside.

A man answered. When I asked for Melody, he said I had a wrong number.

I Googled the address Veronica gave me and got yet another phone number. I dialed that, and a young woman answered.

"Redwood Bank and Holding Company."

I tried to think fast. Why would a bank be in the data bases for Melody's residential address?

"I'm hoping you can help me," I said. "I'm inquiring about ownership on a townhouse I'd like to buy. Your bank came up. Perhaps this property is in foreclosure? Could you please direct me to the appropriate department?"

"Yes, of course. I'll transfer you to our real estate division."

The phone rang, and another woman answered. I explained that I was interested in the property and asked if she could give me information.

"We've listed that property through Bonnard Realty. I'll give you their number." I wrote it down as she spoke. I thanked her, hung up, and dialed that number.

I gave the property address to the receptionist, then asked for the listing realtor.

"That would be Sheila Stone. Please hold."

"Sheila Stone," said a woman.

"I'm an investor looking to shift some of my portfolio into bank-owned properties. I'm interested in a townhouse you have listed in Woodside." I gave her the address. "I understand that it is owned by Redwood Bank and Holding Company. Is it still available?"

"Yes, it is, and it's a lovely property, a great setting near the redwoods and horse country. These townhouses are in demand. This one will sell fast. Can we set up an appointment?"

"Perhaps, but tell me, please. If it's a good property that will sell fast, why didn't the owner sell it? How did it end up in foreclosure?"

"It's another one of those sub-prime mortgage casualties. The owner realized there'd been a run-up in value in the short time since she bought it, so she got into one of those shady refinance deals where she borrowed one hundred and ten percent of the appraisal on the assumption that the property would keep going up in value. Of course the opposite happened, and she ended up owing much more than the house was worth. So, like a lot of upside-down borrowers, she walked." The woman sounded disgusted.

"Along with her refi money."

"Right. You don't want to know how realtors feel..." She stopped talking.

I didn't want to get into that conversation, so I kept quiet.

"Anyway," she continued, "I'd love to set up an appointment. The lender's loss is your gain."

"Let me go take a look at it. I'll call if I want to get inside."

I next called the insurance office where Grace worked at the time of her death. I got handed around to three different women. Two of the women said they knew Grace well. Neither of them had heard of a daughter.

One of Grace's colleagues, a woman named Frances Mirra, was especially effusive about Grace. I asked about Grace's work.

"She was an adjuster. You know, someone whose job it is to reduce the payouts on claims. It's the worst job in the business. You get these people who have endured something terrible – a flood or something – and you're supposed to go in there and say that their home was rundown and not worth very much before the flood, and their family heirlooms were just old furniture that had no value. It can get pretty bleak. But after a few years with the company, Grace wouldn't do it. She said that fair is fair, and she'd file these reports that supported the claims. So the insurance company put in a new manager. Danielle Rimbottom. A scruffy blonde who only cared about cats and chocolate and whose only trump card on Grace was that Danielle had these perfect hands, long, slender fingers, perfect nails. She flaunted those hands constantly, just to make Grace feel extra unwanted. Danielle was determined to get rid of Grace from the beginning.

"So Grace – who was like a Girl Scout or something, always prepared beyond any reasonable point – Grace went into preparation-for-combat mode. 'Document, document, document,' she always said. She collected all of the materials that could impact her different cases. She organized and collated and wrote up transcripts of conversations – every phone call – highlighting every important point. She collected all the cost estimates on claims and correlated them with actual expenses. She even edited a video collage of customer claims and the resulting insurance abuses.

"When the day came that Danielle Rimbottom asked her

into the conference room where the bosses were waiting for the inquisition, what happened was that Grace pulled out her documentation, notes, case files, and the video that she played on her laptop, and the whole premise that Grace was the Achilles heel of the team collapsed. Instead of Grace being fired, Danielle was pretty much destroyed. She raised up those pretty little hands to her horrified mouth and ran out in shame.

"Afterward, Grace came back to our little group in the office and said that it came down to being prepared. You could be a superhero, but if you were caught off guard, you'd go down. However, if you were prepared, you could be the class nerd and you would still triumph."

I thanked the woman for her time and hung up.

An hour later there was a knock at the door. Spot jumped up, tail on high speed, which meant it was Street.

TWELVE

I opened the door.

Street stood there wearing tight black jeans over thin black boots with enough heel to add two inches to her height. She had on a black turtle neck and over it a sweater with an elaborate, ornate design of red and orange and black. Persian, maybe. It seemed a sign of healing that she was wearing attractive clothes instead of being swaddled in multiple thick layers.

Spot pushed past me and leaned up against her as she bent over to hug him.

I gave her a little kiss.

"Will an Oakstone cab suffice?"

She nodded.

I got out the large glasses, poured a short inch for her and three inches for me. We chatted a bit, and I told her about my endeavors.

Street said, "The only thing I can think of that would explain a daughter that no one knew about would be if Grace had a daughter years ago that she gave up for adoption. She may have kept quiet about it. No one would know, possibly not even her cousin Melody."

"Could be," I said as I pondered the idea.

"Then what if that daughter searched out her biological mother?" Street said. "Grace would suddenly have a new, very important person in her life. She might not tell her cousin or others she was close to. But she might tell a stranger."

"Ah," I said. It made good sense.

"She'd be bursting with this news, but hesitant to tell people she knew lest they judge her harshly. So she might test-drive the idea by telling a stranger like Thomas Watson at the library, just to see how it felt."

"You might be onto something," I said. "I'll have to look into it. Although in all of my different traces over the years, I don't remember ever tracking down any kids given up for adoption. This will be new territory."

"I know a woman who teaches at UC Davis," Street said. "The daughter she'd given up for adoption found her online and sent her an email. She was scared to death and overjoyed at the same time. They ended up meeting. Now they see each other quite often. Let me call her and see if there is a standard way to track these things."

Street went out on the deck to use her cell.

I opened the oven door to see how much my bread dough had risen in the couple hours since I made it.

I wasn't sure, but it looked to have expanded at least a quarter inch. Too late to wait any longer, so I consulted the recipe, turned the oven on to 350 and set the timer for 35 minutes.

Street was still on the deck, talking on her phone.

I went to work on my stir-fry. I put on a pot of brown rice to simmer, then cut up an onion, chopped several cloves of garlic, cut chicken into strips, and sautéed it with the garlic and onion. I chopped celery, green pepper, red pepper, and carrots, and put them in the pan. I saved the sugar-snap peas and the stir-fry sauce. I'd add them shortly before I served it up.

Street came back inside.

"There is an entire online world that has sprung up around biological parents and children reconnecting years after adoption," Street said. "I gave Grace's name to the woman at Davis and told her what you told me. She went through the various websites she knew and came up with a woman who had posted on a bulletin board for biological parents and children looking to reconnect. It was three years and six months ago. The woman posting gave her name as Arianna, thirty-two years old. She wrote that she lives on the West Coast and that she was adopted as a newborn. The only information she'd learned from her adoptive parents was that her birth mother's first name was Grace, and that her mother was nineteen years old when she gave birth at Saint Anne's Hospital in San Francisco."

"Was there any information that suggested that Grace got in touch with her or that they ever met?"

"No. Any direct communication between them would have been private unless they put information about meeting on Facebook or some other public site."

"Was there contact information for Arianna?"

"Just an email. I wrote it down." Street handed me a folded scrap of paper she'd torn off of an envelope.

"Thanks. You're amazing," I said.

"I'm practically like a private investigator or something," Street said.

"Yeah. We could switch businesses, except I wouldn't like studying bugs. I'll send this woman a message."

Street suddenly wrinkled her nose. "The stir-fry smells great, but what's that strange smell?"

"I don't know what you mean. The only thing I smell is the wonderful aroma of baking bread."

Street looked at me, squinting just a little. "Aroma? Euphemisms we know and love." She walked into the kitchen nook and peeked into the oven. "Oh, a mini-loaf! Fun. You made a partial recipe so it would be like a personal dinner serving."

"Well, not quite. But I'm sure you'll love it."

I could see a question forming on Street's face, but she thought better of it and didn't speak.

When the timer went off, I pulled out the bread. It was heavy and very brown.

"I don't think I can wait until this cools down," I said. "The excitement of fresh, warm, baked bread is too much to resist." I got out my knife to slice off the end of the ball. After sawing a bit, the knife hadn't broken the crust. "I forgot to sharpen the knife," I said.

"Fresh bread always requires an extra-sharp knife," Street said.

I stropped the knife multiple times, and tested the edge on my fingernail. The knife was now a razor. I went at the bread again. It was like trying to cut a cobblestone. I finally stabbed the tip of the knife into the bread and by levering and tearing and pulling, I was able to break a chunk off.

Another hacking, ripping maneuver split the chunk into two small pieces. I had been a little worried about the hardness of the shell. But when the inside of the bread also appeared to be hard, I thought it best to test it myself before giving it to Street. So I gave it a bite.

Street watched me as I masticated.

"Well?" she said.

I tried to talk as I chewed. "The, uh, bread isn't really, well, chewable in the normal sense."

"Normal sense being like you chew it up and swallow it?"

"Yeah," I mumbled, still trying to work enough moisture into the bread to be able to give my jaws a proper workout without breaking teeth. I felt a little grit and then a string of hair. I pulled at it, but it broke off. No doubt remnants of the roll across the floor.

While I was still chewing, I made the decision to spare Street the same frustration. So I took the other little chunk and tossed it to Spot, knowing that he probably wouldn't even bite down on it more than once before swallowing it.

In fact, he did bite down several times, then spit it out.

Eventually, I gave up, spit my piece into a paper towel, walked over and picked up Spot's reject.

"Not quite up to restaurant standards?" Street said.

"I guess I was too focused on the stir-fry," I said.

"Right," Street said.

I added the peas to the stir-fry mixture, stirred in some sauce and served it up a couple of minutes later. It was tasty.

"I don't know what I did wrong on the bread," I said as we ate. "Maybe I got a faulty recipe."

Street nodded. "I'm sure that's it. Happens all the time. Artisans develop great chemistry recipes for faux stone and then accidentally post them under the Bread heading. But the stir-fry is great."

After dinner, Street finished the last of her single small portion of wine, kissed me goodnight, and left. I understood her need to go home and be independent, but it left a physical ache in my chest as real as if I'd pulled a rib muscle.

I put on a Miles and Trane CD, poured another inch of wine and got out my monograph on Thomas Hill. Partly, I wanted to look at the magnificent nineteenth century landscapes. Partly, I wanted to see if he painted any pictures of Chinese miners.

I sat in the rocker in front of the woodstove and turned the pages the way a little kid looks at a picture book. No great mental inquiry. No scholarly questions. No academic analysis necessary. Something much better. The childlike gaze at a new world as only a picture book can present. Youthful imagination of a different life. Questions that begin with 'What if...,' and 'Why is the...'

Thomas Hill was born in England in 1829, emigrated to the U.S. and came of age in New England. He moved to San Francisco after the Gold Rush. Along with masters like Albert Bierstadt, Hill became one of California's major painters of Romantic Realism. And his most famous paintings were of Yosemite and the Sierra and Mt. Shasta.

I turned the pages one by one. Moving slowly. Pausing on each image. They took me back over a century to a time when people in the Eastern U.S. were still trying to understand the magnitude of the western landscape. I stared at each image, imagining what it would be like to see these astonishing places before highways and cars and hotels and fast food restaurants arrived.

I'd seen some of the paintings in person, like the giant canvas hanging in the Oakland Museum.

Grand as Hill's work was in real life, the book in my lap was still special. I missed Street, but Hill worked his magic on my eyes, Miles and Trane worked on my ears, the heat of the woodstove played on my skin, Spot's head was on my knee, and the Oakstone cab worked from the inside out.

Unfortunately, my book had no images of miners, Chinese or otherwise. I could only imagine the life of Gan Sun and the legacy that he left his great, great granddaughter Grace, a legacy that probably resulted in her murder.

THIRTEEN

In the morning, I sat down and composed an email to Grace's possible biological daughter.

Dear Arianna,

Please forgive this intrusion into your life. I got your name from someone who knows about adoption websites. She determined that you are the birth daughter of Grace Sun and that you were likely in contact with her prior to her death. If this is not the case, please accept my apologies and disregard this note.

If you are Grace's daughter, I'm writing to let you know that my name is Owen McKenna, and I was one of the homicide inspectors who worked on Grace's case. I'm sorry to bring up such an upsetting event, but I thought that you would want to know that we may have found her killer.

A man whose DNA matches the DNA found on Grace is currently in jail awaiting trial.

Please write back to me to confirm that you are the daughter of Grace and you have received this email.

Sincerely,
Owen McKenna

I sent the email and considered what its impact would be. Upset and discomfort and rage, mixed, I hoped, with some small relief. I had no assurance that the woman would write back. Nor did I even know if her email address was current. But if it was, I was one step closer to the closure Street talked about. After Grace's daughter Arianna, Grace's cousin Melody would be the last step.

My cellphone rang two cups of coffee later.

"Hello?"

"Just got an unusual email," a voice said. Male, slight Mexican accent.

"Diamond," I said. "Tell me."

"The email is from a Gmail account, and the subject says Adopted Daughter. I'll read it.

"Dear Sergeant Martinez,

"I'm hoping that you won't attempt to betray my trust and trace this email. I am responding to an email from a Mr. Owen McKenna. I looked online at some newspaper articles and found out that he's a friend of yours. I have reason to mistrust emails. His account could have been hacked. So instead of responding to a potentially fake email, I'm writing you as a security measure. A hacker can approach me under disguise, but a hacker wouldn't be able to guess who I might approach. I'm sorry if this seems paranoid, but believe me, I have reason to be paranoid.

"Therefore, may I please ask you to call Mr. McKenna and verify if in fact it was he who wrote me? Because he was involved in Grace Sun's murder case, and because he has apparently been asking questions about me, I worry that he may be being followed or monitored without knowing it. The man who is after me has sent me emails before, and he might try to gain access to Mr. McKenna's computer and his email, thinking I would then respond.

"If Mr. McKenna sent the email, please tell him that yes, I am Grace Sun's daughter. Meeting her was the best and the worst thing that ever happened to me. She was wonderful to me in a way that no one has ever been. But then she was murdered. Meeting her nearly destroyed my life.

"After Grace died, a man – I don't know who he is – called me about something he wanted that belonged to Grace. When I didn't respond, he found out where I lived and tried to kill me. I barely escaped and have been on the run ever since. I've been in hiding for three years. I rented an apartment under an assumed name and began paying my bills with cash. My life sort of went back to normal, and I began to think that maybe I wasn't marked anymore.

"But then Mr. McKenna wrote. Now I worry that something bad is going to start all over again.

"In his email, Mr. McKenna wrote that he has caught the killer of my birthmother Grace. I am pleased and relieved about that. I know that my attacker was somehow connected to Grace because he called me right after Grace was murdered. But I've no particular reason to think that the person McKenna caught – that Grace's killer – is the same man who tried to kill me.

"Sorry for sounding mistrustful, but I'm petrified all over again. You can email me, but please don't try to find me. Please. I beg you.

"The email is signed 'Anna,'" Diamond said.

"Can you write a quick email response? Obviously it is better to have it come from you."

"Sure. I'm at my desk. What do you want to say?"

"Dear Anna, This is Owen McKenna. I'm speaking to Sergeant Diamond Martinez over the phone, and he is writing down my words to you.

"I'm sorry you are living a nightmare, and I don't want to add to your stress. Please consider calling me. If you like..."

"Whoa, slow down," Diamond said. "I ain't a secretary used to dictation."

"Sorry." I continued at a slower pace. "If you like, you can set up your phone to have a blocked number so it can't be seen by anyone receiving your call. Maybe your phone line is already that way. Otherwise, communicating through Diamond is a good idea.

"In the meantime, can you tell me anything about the attacker? Can you give me a description of what he looked like? Do you have any ideas about his identity? There may be a chance we can catch him without you having to reveal your whereabouts. Signed Owen."

"That's it?" Diamond said.

"You think it's okay?" I asked.

"Ain't Samuel Richardson, but I guess it gets the job done."

"Who's Richardson?"

"You and this Anna writing letters back and forth remind

me of Richardson, an eighteenth century English dude who wrote epistolary novels. I should add your phone number and hit send?"

"Yeah," I said.

"Done," Diamond said. "What do you make of it?"

"I don't know. She certainly sounds terrified. Of course, it could be that she is a drama queen and is exaggerating the circumstances or imagining it altogether. But she sounds sincere. And what would be the motivation to make this up? If she really is on the run and in hiding, that is a huge reaction to her fear. So whoever has scared her was very effective. No one should have to live in a state of terror."

"I wonder why she didn't call the cops," Diamond said. "Makes you think it's because her story doesn't hold water. But there could be another reason."

"If she calls, I'll ask."

"Let's hope that Thomas Watson is Anna's attacker in addition to being Grace's killer," Diamond said. "Or maybe Nick the Knife or his partner was her attacker. If so, she'd possibly be in the clear."

"Yeah. Both Watson and Nick O'Connell are connected to Grace."

Diamond stopped talking because my phone beeped in our ears.

"Hold on, I've got incoming," I said. I looked at my phone readout. It said private. "Maybe this is our answer. I'll call you back."

"Later," Diamond said and hung up.

FOURTEEN

I pressed my answer button and said, "Owen McKenna."

"Okay, Mr. McKenna, we'll give this a try," a woman's shaky voice said. "This is Anna Quinn." The tremor in her voice was so strong, it sounded as if she'd start crying at any moment. She made a hiccup sound, and her breath caught. "I'm sorry. I don't mean to be upset. But what happened three years ago was so frightening, it turned my life upside down. I can't bear the thought that I'm going to be dragged back to that."

"I'm sorry about the circumstances, Anna," I said. "But it's good you called. I don't want to give you false hopes, but maybe I can help you with this stalker. Not long after Grace's murder, I left the police department. But I'm still in law enforcement, working as a private investigator in Tahoe."

"Oh, God, if I could know I was rid of him forever! If I could get my life back! Can you do this? Can you find him without talking to me in person?"

"Maybe. I would need you to tell me everything possible about the circumstances."

"Okay. Where should I start?"

"Do you have any idea who this man is?" I asked.

"No, I don't."

"You've never seen him before?"

"No," she said.

"He didn't say anything or do anything to suggest his identity?"

"No."

"Was there any indication of why he was after you?"

"Yes. I got a phone call before he attacked me. Right after Grace's murder."

"Tell me about it," I said.

"It was the day after she died. This man with a ragged voice called and left a message saying he wanted a journal that Grace gave me."

"What was in the journal?"

"That's just it. She never gave me a journal. Let me back up and say that several different times, Grace gave me gifts. It started the first day I met her. I'd contacted her by email, and she wrote back. We had quite an intense email relationship. Then we met at the de Young Museum. That day she gave me a photograph of herself and her grandfather, Ming Sun. My great grandfather. The photo had been taken years before when Grace was in her teens. She wanted me to get a sense of my heritage.

"A couple of days later, we met at a coffee shop. That time she gave me a ring that was made by Ming Sun. She said it meant a lot to her and she wanted me to have it. Another day, we went to the library where she showed me some books about the Gold Rush. There was a mention in there of a Gan Sun. Gan was Ming's grandfather. Which made him my grandfather three greats removed. Grace said that she had something he'd made, and that one day she would give it to me. So in the ten times or so that we met before she died, she gave me lots of gifts. Little things, mostly. Things with sentimental value.

"The last time I saw Grace was the same day she died. I visited her in the morning, and we made plans to have dinner the next night. She had decided to give me the thing that Gan Sun had made. She would only say that it was very valuable and that she would tell me about it at dinner.

"Then she was murdered, and shortly afterward I got the message on my voicemail from the man who wanted a journal. He said it belonged to him, and he would pay me a five hundred dollar reward for giving it back to him. He told me to meet him in front of the Transamerica Pyramid the next day at noon to give him the journal and collect my reward.

"But I didn't go, partly because I didn't know anything about a journal, and partly because I was frightened. Something about his voice scared me. The next time he called, I was home and answered the phone. He told me that I was very bad for not meeting him and that he was only giving me one more chance. I got the sense that if I disobeyed him, something bad would happen to me. It was terrifying!"

"It was smart not to go," I said. "Did you tell the police about him or about seeing Grace the morning she was killed? I don't remember talking to you."

"No, I didn't tell anyone. Grace's murder had me so off-balance. If I told the cops about the gifts and about visiting her the same day she was killed, I knew I'd be pulled into a huge entanglement of legal stuff, depositions and court appearances and related stuff. Maybe that was stupid. But I knew that none of it had anything to do with me. As far as Grace knew, I didn't even exist until a few weeks before. Same with the police. So I knew that if I went on not existing, it wouldn't make any difference."

She continued, "The more I thought about it, the more it seemed that the guy who wanted the journal was dangerous. So I gathered my few things in a bag and left the apartment. I didn't tell my roommate where I was going. I just apologized, paid her my share of the rent for an extra month, and said that I hoped she could find another roommate soon. I stayed in a couple of motels at first, then eventually got a room at an old-fashioned boarding house. I used a fake name and paid cash for rent. I run a website design business. As long as I have a computer, I can work from anywhere."

"How were you able to leave your apartment and all of your things so fast? Most of us would need weeks to prepare for a move, especially if we were moving to a life on the road and had to get rid of everything."

"It's a long story," Anna said. "For twelve years, my partner was a woman named Tara Sperri. We met at USC and moved in together. We had many good years. But you know how even the best relationships can run down. We were both so focused on our careers. Tara is an attorney working as a public defender for Alameda County. I started out as an elementary teacher in Fremont, and then quit to begin my website design business.

"When Tara and I finally decided to call it quits, we had a huge garage sale, then sold our house. I wanted to be rid of all of my material things and get down to nothing more than the few things I take on the road when I travel. A change of clothes. My notebook computer. It was a way to make a clean break and start over.

"I found a woman who was renting the extra bedroom in her apartment, so I had shelter. But I was devastated. I lay there every night, sleepless, thinking that my life had come to nothing. Tara was gone. I had no home. My adoptive parents had been gone for some time, so I had no family. That was when I decided to look up my biological mother. It was breaking up with Tara that led me to Grace.

"When I met Grace, it was like coming home again. A connection that was more than what I had with my friends. I never dreamed it was the beginning of a nightmare."

"In the intervening three years, you've still never spoken to the police about Grace's murder or about the attacker?" I said.

"No," she said.

I wanted to give Anna the lecture about how reluctant witnesses were one of the biggest problems that cops have fighting crime. But I didn't want to risk this tenuous connection with Grace Sun's biological daughter and the information she might have.

"Didn't it occur to you that the caller may have been Grace's killer?" I asked.

"Yes. But I was still afraid to tell the police." She was silent a long moment.

"When I was in college," Anna finally said, "Tara and I had a best friend named Mandy Melane. In our junior year, Mandy broke up with her boyfriend. He started stalking her. So she went to the police and got a restraining order. She was so afraid of him that she moved out of her dorm and back into her parents' house in Torrance. It didn't make any difference. Her ex-boyfriend murdered her a week later. Her ex-boyfriend was several years older than her, and he had two friends who were cops. At the time, we wondered if that's how he found out where she was living."

Anna was panting.

I didn't know what to say.

"I thought I'd lost my attacker," she said. "But somehow he

got the information about my new place."

"What happened?"

"He broke into my room in the middle of the night. I'd locked the door to my bedroom, but my housemates had left the front door of the house unlocked. He broke the lock on my bedroom door. He came in holding a fancy knife, and he did this rotating thing with it to terrify me. Then he threw it at me."

"You escaped?"

"Yes. I had worried about this psycho coming after me for over a month. In the short time I knew Grace, she probably told me three different times that you can best confront your fears by making a plan for any eventuality. It was like she was psychic, like she knew something might happen to me. I learned so much from her! Anyway, she made such a point about being prepared!

"So I made an escape plan in case my stalker ever found out where I was living and broke in. I always slept wearing shorts and T-shirt and moccasins, and I kept my little purse next to the bed. I had a bag of things in the trunk of my car. My spare car key was on my bracelet, which I never take off, even in the shower. And I put a heavy book inside a pillowcase and knotted the end. I kept it on my bed.

"When he came into the room and twirled his knife, I was so terrified, I wanted to scream. But I did what I had practiced and threw the pillowcase with the book at him. He threw the knife at me. But I was already rolling out of bed and grabbing my purse as the knife stuck in the headboard where my head had been. I don't even know if the book hit him. But it gave me an extra second or two. I lifted the window and dove out onto the fire escape. I shut it behind me and slid the bolt I'd installed on the outside of the window. I got away in my car.

"It was the scariest thing I've ever experienced. I only survived because I practiced my plan many times."

"Was the room light enough to see what this guy looked like?" I asked.

"No, but I couldn't have anyway, because he wore a ski mask. My only clue that might help you is that when he reached to pull his knife from its sheath, his sleeve rose up and I saw a tattoo on his wrist. It was made of squiggly blue lines, but I couldn't tell what it said. I was so traumatized. I get shaky-scared when I think of it now, three years later."

"Have you ever heard of someone named Nick O'Connell?" I asked.

"No. Why?" she said. Then, "Wait, I did hear that name. Not Nick. But O'Connell. Let me think. It was Grace who mentioned the name. Something she learned about grandpa Gan Sun. It was in the book on the Gold Rush. There was something called the Mulligan War. Some land dispute back in the nineteenth century. The name O'Connell was somehow connected, but I forget how."

"Do you remember any of the details?"

"No. Just that she mentioned the name."

"What book was it in? Can you remember the title or the author?"

"No. I never even looked at the front of the book."

"What about where it was shelved? Could you find the area in the library?"

"You have to understand that the San Francisco Library is very dramatic. I kept looking at the design of the building. Compared to the library where I grew up, I've never even… Well, never mind where I'm from. Anyway, Grace led me through the place and we went up and down, but I couldn't even tell you what floor we ended up on. There were lots of shelves and lots of books and, except when Grace was pointing in a book, all I saw was the building. Kind of like modern art."

I gave Anna a quick explanation of the hostage crisis that ended with the hostage taker's death. I explained how the hostage taker had a tattoo and did knife tricks, and how he also accused Thomas Watson of killing Grace. I told Anna that when I went to talk to Thomas Watson, he thought that the hostage taker was a man named Nick O'Connell, a man who did knife tricks and had a number tattooed on his wrist.

"So we believe it was Nick O'Connell who drowned," I said. "O'Connell's knife tricks sound like your attacker. And his connection to Grace through Thomas Watson adds more credibility to the idea that it was he who came after you."

"But we don't know for a fact that O'Connell was my stalker," she said. "Maybe lots of sickos spin knives. Maybe there is a gang someplace where their group identity is all about knife tricks."

"That could be," I said. "The knife twirling is an unusual marker, and it could just be a coincidence. But the fact that O'Connell both twirled knives and also knew about Grace's murder is very compelling. Two coincidences like that are rare. Add in the tattoo and it becomes more rare. Your stalker may well be dead."

"I want to think so," Anna said. "You don't know how much I want to think so. Tell me, why do you think this Nick O'Connell hijacked the boat? Why would he go to so much trouble to get you to catch the killer of my mother?"

"We don't know why. No doubt he had some kind of serious beef with Watson and wanted the pleasure of seeing the law come down on him. But that wouldn't justify his actions. So we really don't know."

Anna didn't say anything.

"Is there anything else about your stalker that you can think of?" I asked.

"Not really," she said. "He wore a mask. Twirled the knife. Had the tattoo. Wanted a journal I don't have. Wanted it enough to kill me for it."

"Anna, I think you should consider giving all of this information, your whole story, to the police. Depending on where you are living, you could maybe get some protection. If, for example, you are staying in San Francisco or are willing to go to San Francisco, I could help get you into a safe house. They have a couple of places that no one knows about, places that are provided by private citizens, places that cops don't even know about. Or, if you came to Tahoe, we have some options here, as well."

"You think my attacker may have been the dead hijacker, yet you still talk about a safe house?"

"Basic principle," I said. "Always be cautious, always err toward safety. Consider all the evidence with an open mind, but don't believe it until it's been proven. This is a strange case. You'll want to lie low until we figure it out."

She was quiet for a bit. "I thought about going to the police.

A hundred times over the last three years. But then I'd have to once again reveal who I am and where I live. Right now, most of my customers pay me online. I deposit the few checks I get into the ATM machine. No one knows who I am. I get my cash from a different ATM. But my bank is small, so if I changed where I live, I'd probably have to change banks. Which means I'd have to give a new bank info like my address. That info would go into the databases. If my stalker is someone other than the dead guy, someone who has some kind of connection, if he could call someone he knows at the bank…"

"They're pretty secure," I said, immediately regretting the statement.

"Right," she said with obvious derision. "That's why hackers routinely get a hundred thousand social security numbers at a time out of bank computers. That's why those geeks get into the Pentagon's computers and steal military secrets. Because computers are so secure."

"You're right. Sorry."

Anna didn't respond. I'd stepped over the line.

"Look, Anna, let me look into this and see what I can find out," I said, knowing there was little if anything I could discover based on what she'd said.

Again, no response.

"Is there a way I can reach you that's faster than email?"

"If I feel like it, I'll call you," she said and hung up.

FIFTEEN

There was a knock at the door. Spot growled, which meant it wasn't someone he knew.

A FedEx driver handed me a package, had me sign for it. The return address was Joe Breeze's SFPD office. Spot walked next to me, sniffing it as I carried it to my little kitchen table and pulled open the tear strip.

The journal was as I remembered it, a cloth-bound notebook about 5 inches wide by 8 inches tall. The cover cloth was a faded purple silk with a large purple-black stain that was shaped like a mottled eggplant and went from the edges of the pages up across the lower half of the cover.

I flipped through the pages, revisiting the mildew smell and the rows of Chinese characters that were mostly blurred beyond recognition. It was a poignant sight, countless hours and maybe years of careful work lost when the journal had gotten soaked.

I dialed my friend Doc Lee's cell number, got his voicemail and left a message. He called back a half hour later.

"I was in the ER when you called," he said, his small voice delicate and precise. "I'm on break."

"I'm working on a case that involves a notebook with Chinese writing in it. I'm wondering if you could look at it. Any chance you'd like leftover chicken stir-fry for lunch?" I asked.

"I grew up eating leftover chicken stir-fry," he said. There was no judgment in his voice, just observation.

"Then you could demonstrate your cross-race tolerance of culinary hubris. White guys, as you no doubt know, think they are the best chefs around."

"You're a funny guy. When I taste it, I'll probably think you meant culinary malfeasance. My shift is over soon. I'll be there in an hour and," he paused, "fifty minutes."

I hung up thinking that while Doc Lee's fetish for precision didn't make him everybody's favorite bud, I would want nothing else if I were on the operating table, and he was slicing through my insides.

Just before the appointed time, I put the previous evening's leftovers on the stovetop to warm.

Spot put his nose all over Doc Lee when I opened the front door an hour and fifty minutes later.

"He's smelling the ER," Doc Lee said as he held his arms out and above Spot like a pelican drying its wings. He moved into my cabin, heading for the rocker. "Antiseptic and blood. Intriguing for a dog."

"Spot, let the doctor alone," I said. Spot ignored me. As Doc Lee sat down, Spot started sniffing his neck and ear. I pulled him away and pointed to the braided rug in front of the woodstove.

Spot looked at me, then slowly turned two circles, lay down and sighed.

"What is this case?" Doc Lee asked.

I handed him the journal. "A woman named Grace Sun was found murdered in San Francisco three years ago. She had this tucked in her shirt. It could be that she was trying to hide it from her killer. The hijacker on the Dreamscape claimed that his purpose in taking Street hostage was to convince me that a man named Thomas Watson was Grace's killer. So the two are connected."

Doc Lee had opened the notebook and touched the pages as if they were written in Braille. "Sounds complicated," he said.

"Yeah. We never knew why Grace was murdered. Thomas Watson says he didn't murder her, even though his DNA matches that of skin tissue found under Grace's fingernails."

"Pretty bold claim for him to make when you've got his DNA."

"Right. So I'm trying to understand what the hijacker had to do with the case."

"And then the hijacker drowned," Doc Lee said. "Quite the enigma."

I nodded. "Maybe this notebook can provide some

information about why Grace was murdered."

"Of course, you had other people investigate this back when It happened."

"We had a couple of Berkeley profs look at it," I said. "One was an archivist. He thought the paper was over a hundred years old and probably made in China during the early or mid-nineteenth century. The other prof teaches Asian Studies and knows Mandarin. He said it looked like the journal was written by a man who was a miner by trade. He thought the journal was a diary that focused on the man's work. But so much of it was blurred that he couldn't tell much."

Doc Lee was flipping pages. "Looks like it was dropped into water. Dirty water."

"Yeah. What do you think? Can you read any of the blurred characters?"

"Not much. First, I should say that I'm not a hanzi expert."

"Is that what the Chinese characters are called?"

"Yes. As kanji is to Japanese, hanzi is to Chinese. In fact, kanji was originally derived from hanzi."

"You're fluent in Mandarin, right?"

"Yes. It's a long tradition in my family even though we've been in this country for six generations. Everyone always speaks both Mandarin and English at home."

"Did you learn to write in Mandarin?"

"Yes, but I didn't do it enough to get very good."

Coming from Doc Lee, I imagined that that still made him an expert.

I gestured at the journal. "Can you tell from the blurred characters if that is written in Mandarin, or is written Mandarin the same as other Chinese dialects?"

"The answer to your first question is, yes, it appears to be Mandarin. The answer to your second is that all the different kinds of Chinese languages share the same written hanzi. The characters are interchangeable. But the words vary. While the various Chinese languages are often referred to as dialects, they are dissimilar enough that they should probably be called separate languages."

Doc Lee paused, flipped some pages. "Chinese is really a huge family of languages. Nearly three hundred different tongues. The languages are all related, and over the centuries the Chinese government has used its influence to make the hanzi characters universal. It is similar to the way the Romance languages all use the same Latin alphabet. And they even share a bunch of words."

"Words that are the same in both English and, say, Spanish," I said.

"Right," Doc Lee said. "Take the word international. It is spelled the same in English, French, and German and nearly the same in Spanish and Italian. And it means the same thing in each language, too. That also happens with some different Chinese languages. And like Dutch and German, some Chinese languages can be understood by speakers of a few very similar languages. But most people can still only understand their own language. Also, Chinese is one of the language groups that are tonal. Many words can be said with different tones or pitches. A high tone, a medium tone, a low tone. Tones can also rise or fall. Of course, we use different pitches and rising or falling tones in English, too, but they give us different inflections or nuances in our meaning. Whereas, in Chinese, the different tones give entirely different meanings to the words. So pronunciation of words varies widely from one Chinese language to the next."

Doc Lee turned another page in the journal. "While this is Mandarin, it isn't contemporary. There are some unusual constructions that suggest its age. But as you said, the journal was made one hundred or two hundred years ago."

"What can you tell me from it?"

Doc Lee stared at a page, flipped forward a few pages, squinted at it hard, then turned toward the end of the journal and spent quite a long time.

"The first part is in one pen, and the second part was written with multiple pens. The style of the characters and the style of the writing in each part are both a bit different as well. I think this journal was written by two different people."

"You're kidding," I said. "The Berkeley prof didn't say anything about that."

"Berkeley professors are busy. How much did you pay him

or her?"

"Him. And I don't think we paid anything."

"Well, there's your answer," Doc Lee said.

"I'm not paying you," I said.

"I thought I was getting a stir-fry lunch."

"Leftovers don't usually constitute remuneration," I said.

"Chicken stir-fry leftovers do. Unless you kill it."

I thought about my bread from the night before, sitting like a heavy field rock in my kitchen garbage can. "I would never kill food," I said.

"That's what I thought," Doc Lee said.

"What else can you glean from the journal?" I asked.

"Glean," Doc Lee said. "Is that a cop word?"

"Sure."

"Well, there are comments in here about mining, as the professor said. About digging in the riverbeds. Directing the water to wash away the sediment. And there is a reference to some kind of a land dispute, but whatever he wanted to say about it got blurred. The name mentioned is Mulligan."

"Like the Chinese writer was involved in a dispute with an Irish miner?"

"Ninety percent of it is blurred, but yes, that's what I'd guess." He paused. After a minute, he spoke.

"This presentation is somewhat formal. As if the writer had a fair amount of education. But if he was a miner, it would be very unusual for him to be educated. Most of the miners who came from China during the Gold Rush were uneducated farmers. Just like most of the white settlers who came west from the East Coast. Same with all of the people who emigrated to the U.S. from Europe during the same era. They were mostly motivated by a search for a better life. Of course, there were some educated people who struck out for the New World. But most of the educated had good positions in society, and they tended to stay where they were."

"Yet you think that notebook was written by someone with a formal education."

"Not formal in the sense of having gone to school. But perhaps this person's parents tried very hard to educate him at home. For example, see these few clear characters in the middle of this blurred page?" He held the book up for me to see.

"What does it say?" I asked.

"There isn't a literal English translation for it. But the writer is sort of saying that the food that Caucasians eat is abhorrent."

"As opposed to saying that white man's food sucks," I said.

"Yes, exactly. The way it is written doesn't seem like something from the journal of an uneducated miner."

"Can you tell anything about the content? What the man is saying regardless of the style?"

"What the journal is about…" Doc Lee's voice trailed off. He flipped pages. "The blurred characters make it seem very disjointed. Let me study it for a bit."

I took that to mean that he wanted quiet.

I went into the kitchen nook, served the rice and stir-fry into bowls and brought them out to the living room along with two Sierra Nevada Pale Ales.

We ate in our laps. Spot lifted his head and sniffed the air long and hard, nostrils flexing, brain circuits calculating the chances of the possible reward that might come from lying still to curry my favor versus getting up and generating my admonishment.

I don't think of myself as a glutton like Spot, but I was done with my food and beer by the time Doc Lee had taken his fifth careful bite. He drank his beer like Street does, in tiny sips. When he dabbed at the corner of his mouth with the tip of his little finger, I realized I'd forgotten napkins. I jumped up, went to the kitchen, tore off a paper towel, and brought it out to him.

"Sorry. Like eating with the Philistines," I said.

Doc Lee put his index finger inside of the paper towel and wiped his lips in the same precise arc that a woman uses to put on lipstick.

He continued to flip pages as he ate. Now and then he made a hmmm sound. Once, a slight intake of breath.

I brought my dishes back to the kitchen and fetched a second beer. I watched as Doc Lee looked at the book. He was to some degree the classic Asian-American cliché. Brilliance combined with studiousness. I didn't know his family and hence had no idea of what combination of nature/nurture produced him. But his first-in-every-class history was easy to see in the picture before me. Doc Lee could no more sit and tell jokes and guzzle beer with the boys during Monday Night Football than he could ride a bull in a Cheyenne rodeo.

In time, he spoke. "As I already said, I think that this is really two journals," he said. "The first two-thirds or so were written by one man, the last third by another."

"You say man. Do you mean to be gender-specific?"

"Yes. Partly, of course, because the first part appears to be the diary of a miner, and nearly all of the miners were men. And partly because the style of the way the characters were written is masculine. Although he doesn't state his gender that I can see."

"You can tell whether the writer was male or female just by looking at the Chinese characters?"

"Usually, yes. Not so much the character choices in terms of voice or content, but the style of the handwriting. It is the same as when you look at something written in English. Experts will tell you that handwriting does not reveal gender or age or income or anything else. But of course what they really mean is that handwriting cannot reveal these things conclusively. Yet, by some mysterious connection between genes and motor skills, writing style does in fact tend to reveal gender, whether in Roman cursive or Chinese characters. In all of the scientific journals I keep up with, I still haven't read a satisfactory explanation of how that comes to be. Nevertheless, in the same way that facial structure suggests boy or girl, handwriting does the same." He gestured with the journal. "For the same reason, I think the last third of the journal was also written by a man, although I think that this second man was not a miner but a construction laborer specializing in masonry."

"Really? The professor never mentioned any such thing."

"Bear in mind that this is only a guess based on some things the writer says, a different style of handwriting for the last part of the journal, and also a different style of voice. Chinese syntax. My sense of dating for the second part of the journal comes from a statement about motorized carriages. It could be a reference to some kind of mechanized device for construction. But it could also suggest motor vehicles. If the first writer was mining during the Gold Rush, and the second was around during the early stages of the horseless carriage, then that would indicate that the second writer was at least two generations removed from the first writer. Also, while the writing styles are different, they are not as different as that of two strangers. It makes me wonder if perhaps the second writer is the grandson of the first."

"That would explain why two people wrote in the same journal."

"Yes." Doc Lee nodded. "It could have been handed down."

"And the masonry idea?"

Doc Lee set his unfinished bowl on the little side table and sipped some more beer. "A reference to laying stones. Hard to tell, though. The blurred characters in the second portion of the journal are very hard to make out. It almost looks as if the journal is a fairy tale about sky people who lived in the Sky Palace."

"Sky people? You think it is fiction? Storytelling?" I asked.

"I can't tell. Maybe. Or it could be a metaphor. Although the second writer doesn't write in the formal educated style of the first, and the writing isn't sophisticated, his style makes him appear quite bright."

"Anything else you can decipher from the journal?"

Doc Lee frowned. "In general, nothing seems very remarkable. It seems like two diaries, like a grandson picked up where his grandfather left off. But one thing caught my eye. Here, in the first part of the journal," he pointed at a page, "is a reference to yellow metal beneath the tent." Doc Lee turned to the back of the journal where he had held his finger. "And back here near the end of the second part of the journal it says that the hiding place needs to last forever." Doc Lee looked up at me. "Makes you wonder if they refer to the same thing."

"Like the first writer had some gold and hid it under his tent? And the second writer was looking for a better hiding place? Two people, each with gold or something else that was valuable, hiding it? The Berkeley professor never mentioned anything like this."

Doc Lee's eyebrows went up and down a single time. "A common cultural characteristic of Chinese people is to be very frugal. If a Chinaman had some gold, he would not necessarily think to spend it. He might pass it on to his grandson. He might also pass on the tendency to hoard it."

Doc Lee pulled up his sleeve to look at his gold watch. His watchband was the same blue as his shirt.

"I better be going," he said.

"Any last observations?" I asked, looking at the journal in his lap.

Doc Lee flipped through the pages one more time. He stopped near the end, then turned back a few pages. "Something interesting where he talks about the people in the Sky Palace," he said. "I noticed this before. It is probably nothing, though."

"What?"

"The characters are all blurred. But it looks like this writer mentions an important person with a recording box. The choice of characters is awkward. But the closest meaning I can reconstruct would be as if this important observer recorded the place with the recording box. And the way the characters are made, there is emphasis on the words for the place."

"Like a physical place?" I said.

"Yes, I think so."

"Could be a photographer took a picture of a significant place," I said.

"That's what I thought."

"Does it say who the photographer is?"

"No. There is only the reference to the observer being important."

"Maybe the simple fact of having a camera made the observer seem important," I said.

"Sure." Doc Lee nodded. "The Sky Palace could make the observer seem more important as well." He looked at his watch again, then stood up.

Spot jumped to his feet and stared at Doc Lee's unfinished stir-fry.

I grabbed the bowl. "Maybe later, largeness," I said.

I thanked Doc Lee for his help, and he left.

SIXTEEN

My cellphone rang as I went out to walk with Spot. "Hello?" I said as I walked out my drive on a day that was as clear and bright as crystal.

"It's Anna. Do you have a moment?"

"Sure." Spot ran a circle around the Jeep, then trotted off past my cabin, down the slope toward the edge of the escarpment. Maybe he wanted to look at the view.

"Mr. McKenna, do you believe in free will?" Anna said.

Not what I expected. "What do you mean?"

"Just the idea that we are free to make our own decisions. That we can decide what to do next. That we aren't controlled by outside forces or events. Do you think we are controlled by physics? Or our biology? Or by our religions? If there is an all-knowing God, does he or she determine our actions?"

The topic seemed completely out-of-the-blue, but Anna's tone was so careful and sincere that she'd obviously thought about it a great deal. I realized that this was one of those times when I should think before I spoke. That I shouldn't be glib. Which, of course, made me nearly incapable of speaking.

"Well, I suppose that we want to think we are free to make decisions, right?" I said. I didn't know where she was going with this, and I found it a little bizarre that someone I hardly knew would call with such a question.

"Yes," Anna said. "But are we really free? Do we make decisions because we want to? Or do we make them because we have to?"

"We're kind of over my head on this, Anna. I'd guess that we make some decisions freely and others out of necessity. I need money, so I have to go to work. Like that. So maybe that isn't free will, huh?"

"Exactly," she said,

"But I'm fully aware that I don't really have to go to work. Maybe I'd lose my job if I didn't, but if I wanted, I could say, 'to hell with it.' I could kiss my job goodbye. So I still have a little free will."

She was silent a moment. I worried that I'd said the wrong thing.

"Why do you ask, Anna?" I finally said.

"I have a friend who says that we don't have free will." It sounded like she was talking about herself. "She says that I'm a classic example."

"Because you have made decisions out of necessity rather than desire?" I said.

"Exactly. My friend has been reading this philosopher named Schopenhauer. He was from Germany way back around the beginning of our country. And he said that we all believe that we're free and that at any moment we think we can change the course of our life, but that in reality we always have to do what we must rather than what we want. That we are controlled by necessity."

"Anna, what is this about? Why do you ask this?"

"Because if the decisions I've made weren't about finding some freedom from the man who attacked me and were instead determined by necessity, by my need for safety, then that means that I've lost three years of my life."

"You've been productive in those three years, right?" I said.

"That's what I wanted to think. But maybe none of it matters. Maybe I've simply gone down a road by necessity. That's worse than being attacked in your bedroom." Her voice was on a rising arc. "That's worse than losing your freedom. That's like dying!"

"Anna, I don't think that's true. Yes, you did some things out of necessity. But you still are in control of your life."

"No, I'm not! My attacker's in control! He's taken over my life. It's just like Schopenhauer said. I might as well have let him kill me three years ago!"

"Schopenhauer didn't say that, did he?"

"He may as well have. I've lost my life. I have no free will.

From the moment the stalker left the message on my answering machine, I've been under his control. I've lost everything!"

Her words had descended into darkness, into despair. Like she'd given up on life in the space of a minute.

"Anna, don't think like that." My voice came off stronger than I expected. "Your attacker is probably dead. So there is likely no necessity of living in fear of him. But we can't be sure of it. Caution suggests that you stay where you are and keep a low profile. But that doesn't mean that you've lost your life. You're just being sensible."

"The only way I can get my life back is to tell the attacker to go to hell. To live my life the way I want to."

"What do you mean?"

"To come back to the world. To come in from the cold."

"Not yet, Anna. Soon. But not yet. It is critical to remain cautious."

"You just said that you think my stalker is dead."

"Yes," I said, hesitating. "But thinking it is a world away from knowing it. Until we have solid evidence, it isn't worth taking the risk. The potential gain in freedom of movement is nothing against the potential loss if your stalker is out there."

"You're saying I have no free will. What Schopenhauer said. I can only act by necessity."

"No, Anna. What I'm saying is…"

She hung up.

SEVENTEEN

I was thinking about what Doc Lee said about the journal mentioning an important person with a recording box.

I didn't know any photography experts, so I called the Nevada Art Museum in Reno.

"This is Detective Owen McKenna calling on a research project that may help us solve a murder case."

"Oh, my," the soft-voiced, professional-sounding receptionist said. "I'm afraid you've reached a wrong number. This is the Nevada Art Museum."

"My inquiry is about art. Photography, specifically. Can you please refer me to an expert in early twentieth century photography?"

"Oh, I see. Well, I'm not sure exactly who would be best for that. I could transfer you to Sondra Moliere's voicemail. She teaches Photographic Portraiture at our E.L. Cord Museum School. Would that be okay?"

"Yes, thank you."

I left my number.

My phone rang 20 minutes later.

"Sondra Moliere returning your call." Another soft voice. Equally professional. Maybe it was a requirement to work in the museum world.

"Thanks, Sondra. I'm working on a case and an interesting question came up that may relate to your field. We have an old journal in which a Chinese/American laborer refers to an important person with a recording box at the construction site of something called the Sky Palace. I called you because I suspect that this refers to a photographer. The time would be during the early part of the twentieth century."

"That's an interesting notion, but I'm not sure I understand how I can help."

"Me neither," I said. "Does anything ring a bell? Was there an important photographer who would call his camera a recording box? Or did any of the early twentieth century photographers specialize in construction sites? Did any focus on something called the Sky Palace?"

"I'm sorry, but I would have to answer no to all of those questions. No photographer comes to mind."

"How would you suggest I research this? Is there some kind of comprehensive database of photographers where I could search by subject?"

"You mean, search for something like construction sites?" she said.

"Right. Or construction workers. Or the Sky Palace."

"No," she said. "Certainly, it is easy to find the common subject areas. Landscapes and portraits and such. But I can't think of a straightforward way to find construction photos."

"Any idea of whom I should call? Other museums? Galleries that sell photography?"

"Good question," she said. "Tell you what, you've piqued my curiosity. Let me check with some of my colleagues and see if they have any ideas. If I connect with someone useful, can I have them contact you directly?"

"Please. Let me give you my phone and email address, too, in case I'm not able to answer my phone." I read it off to her.

"I'm hoping to finish up a project today," she said. "If I hurry, I'll have some time before I go home. I'll try to get back to you later this afternoon. Would that be okay?"

"That would be wonderful. Thanks."

Sondra Moliere called back as I was preparing dinner.

"I haven't had much luck," she said. "What I did was call several people I know in the business. Dealers, curators, professors. Robert Calibre at the Crocker Museum was particularly helpful. He has quite an email list, and he said he would send out a bulk note with your contact info. I hope that was okay."

"Yes, of course. Thanks very much for your efforts."

"Good luck with your investigation," she said.
We hung up.

EIGHTEEN

L ate that night, Anna called me again.
      Street had long since called and told me goodnight-
I-love-you in that bed-ready voice that makes me pine for a life
where we crawled into the sack together every night. I had put
a split log on a bed of embers that may or may not have had
enough energy to begin life anew, poured a finger or two of
Chateau Routon port wine, and sat in the rocker in front of the
woodstove.

Spot got up from his comfy bed to consider what stores of
affection I might have in reserve. He perched his chin up on my
shoulder. I gave him a thorough head massage, starting with the
big neck muscles and ending with the fingertip routine up the
bridge of his nose and around the perimeter of his eyes and over
to his ears.

He'd shifted into that half-sleep state where his breathing gets
heavy and his eyes are shut, all while he's still standing, albeit
with his front legs folding. Just as his rear legs were losing their
steadiness and he was in danger of falling over, the phone chirped
and Spot woke up.

As I reached the portable off the little table, Spot lay down
on the braided rug.

The phone readout said the calling number was private.

"Hello?"

"Mr. McKenna? Is this too late to call?"

"No, Anna. Feel free to call anytime. And please call me
Owen."

"Owen. If you learn anything more about my attacker will
you call me instead of emailing?"

"Yes, if you give me your number."

"Oh, that's right. I guess there's no harm. Even if someone were to somehow get my cell number out of your phone, it's unlisted. So they couldn't find out where I live. And the cellphone company only has my P.O. box anyway."

She read the number off to me, and I wrote it down on a scrap of paper, putting a dash between every two numerals. If anyone found the scrap, it would be meaningless.

"I'm sorry if I'm bothering you by calling now. You're probably relaxing."

"No problem," I said.

"First, I wanted to thank you. You are trying to help me, and I've been incredibly ungrateful. I apologize for that."

"It's okay," I said.

"It's just that having something finally happen where I might get my life back, I can't stop thinking about it. I'm worried and scared and excited all at once."

"That's a normal reaction."

"Do you think it will happen? Will I be able to go back to normal?"

"Yes. Just be patient. We're not there, yet."

"Okay." Anna's voice was quiet. Resignation mixed with weariness.

"Earlier today you mentioned your dreams about your future," I said. "Plans you put on hold. What are they?"

"I think I mentioned that in my past life, I was a teacher. I taught science to fifth and sixth graders. Kids at that perfect age when they are so engaged, but they haven't yet become jaded. I loved being a teacher. But I chafed under the administration and their never-ending rules. And I always wanted to run my own show, so I began building my web design business, working on it weekends and every evening. I use some standard web design software but I also studied programming. And I've written some apps, one of which is selling a hundred downloads a day.

"Not far from the neighborhood where Tara and I lived were two girls who were students of mine. Maya and Lola. They lived in a run-down apartment building. The mother of one girl worked part time as a house cleaner. The mother of the other had a drinking problem and couldn't hold down a job. They subsisted on a little bit of help from some state and federal programs. Of course, there was no dad in either household.

"So Tara and I periodically invited Maya and Lola to our house to try to give them different inputs from what they were used to. The girls saw my computer work and expressed interest. They weren't interested in the computer, but they loved my colorful website designs. So I asked them if they would each like their own website. Not just a Facebook page, but the whole works with a professional email address."

"You mean like if my email was Owen at OwenMcKenna. com?"

"Yeah. You'd probably like it, too, huh?"

"I don't know if I'm that fancy," I said.

"Well these girls loved the idea. So I used that enticement as a way to teach them how it all works. We got them each a domain name, and we began to build each of them a website with photos and a page where they could post their blogs and so on. They gradually learned how to use web design software. They ended up creating great sites.

"Of course, as the girls grew older and started focusing on those things that teenagers occupy themselves with, they weren't quite so interested in the computer. But I stayed in contact. I convinced them that any girl with their technology skills had a huge advantage in pursuing college and careers. They were reluctant to stop texting their friends for even a moment. But I kept hounding them to stay up on the changes in software. We even had a schedule. Two hours after school every Tuesday and Thursday.

"When it came time to think about college, I helped them utilize their tech knowledge in their applications. Maya got a full scholarship to Sac State studying software engineering, and three and a half years later she graduated and got hired by Intel. You don't even want to know how much she makes. Lola got almost a full ride at a small technical school in San Jose. She quit school early when she got hired at a new tech startup. Small salary, but huge stock options. If the company goes big, that girl who grew up in a tenement will be worth millions."

"And all these years later, they still have their own websites?"

"Yeah! It's great. They're both happy with their careers. None of their other high school classmates who shared a similar limited background even went to college. And not that making lots of money is the end all, but these girls don't know of anyone else from their high school, regardless of background, who is doing as well as they are."

"And it was all possible because of the technology you taught them," I said.

"Yeah. I'm not bragging when I say it. I'm just recognizing what is. If you teach girls high-tech skills, it gives them a giant advantage in this high-tech world."

"Is that your dream? To teach high-tech to girls?"

"Exactly! I want to start a school, Owen! I want to focus on girls who have been marginalized by their circumstances, whether they grew up in the inner-city projects, or whether they just struggled with difficult family circumstances. I've done quite a bit of research. It can be like a charter school where they still get the basic subjects. But there would be an intense additional focus on technology.

"It would take a lot of money, but there are grants available. And I've talked to a couple of corporate people who said their companies might be willing to help."

"Because they would be the beneficiaries," I said.

"Right. The problem is that I can't move forward on this until I can rejoin the world. I'd have to be a public figure of sorts, running a school, seeking funding, promoting the concept. So it will have to wait until we know for sure that the dead hijacker was my stalker. And if he wasn't, then we have to find the stalker and put him in prison."

"A school sounds like a good plan, Anna."

"It would be great. I would so love it!"

"Changing the lives of girls who might otherwise have few opportunities," I said.

"Yes! Girls who might get pregnant and drop out. Girls who might turn to drugs. Girls who think that their future is going to be nothing more than that of the struggling people around them. I could offer them a dream. I could offer them hope. I could show them a clear path to great jobs. I could even show them how to start their own tech businesses." The excitement in her voice was effervescent.

"A lot of software engineers are women," I said. "I did something at Intel once and half of the employees were women."

"Sure. Women have lots of jobs in software. But I'm talking about the next level. It's like moving girls from the nursing side of medicine to the doctor side, to the cutting-edge research side. To do that, you have to get to girls when they're young, not when they're starting college or even high school. Of course, the business of software is complicated and women excel at it. But I'm talking about turning women into the creators of the next technology world. Dreaming up new paradigms. Building new companies. The boys who excel and ultimately create the new technology started learning it in middle school. Grade school. When we do that for girls, the world will change." She took a breath.

I waited.

"Do you want to know the name of the school?" she said. She made a little puff of air like she was about to giggle, but then she cut it off. I wondered if she'd ever laughed since she went into hiding. Did she smile? Her enthusiasm was a giant improvement over the fear and worry of our previous conversations, but I still doubted that mirth ever made an appearance in her day.

"Yeah," I said. "Tell me the name of the school."

"It's going to be called Reach For The Sky. And the subtitle is The Kick-Butt Tech School For Girls."

"Good name."

"I even have a place picked out. There's a smallish rundown office building for sale in Oakland. It's in a perfect area, with depressed neighborhoods on both sides. Of course, no way could I afford it. But if I could raise some money, get some grants, find an angel patron or two, I could maybe swing a mortgage. The building alone would cost a million dollars, but it would be so worth it. The layout is perfect for what we'd need. There are spaces for classrooms and dorms, too. Of course, it's just a dream, but I checked about getting some serious broadband put in and found out it's totally doable. Plus, I've looked into public transportation from there to San Jose, Santa Clara, even Palo Alto. My girls would be able to take field trips from our tech school to the greatest tech centers in the world."

"Where they can see just how to kick butt," I said.

"More than that," she said. "I'm going to teach them to take charge. Look at how many of the biggest tech companies in the world are right here in Northern California. Google. Apple. Facebook. Hewlett-Packard. YouTube. Intel. Adobe. Twitter. Oracle. Cisco. Yahoo. eBay. PayPal. Netflix. Almost all were started by young men or even boys who knew technology and had the confidence to believe they could do something better. The systems and mechanisms for greatness are already in place. Now we need only show girls how to gain access." Anna's voice was so intense I could feel it over the phone. Like audible sunshine.

"I can do that!" she continued. "Just think of it! Half of our population has been overlooked in the high-tech gold rush. It's like when society finally opened the doors for girls to become doctors and lawyers and professors and architects and astronauts. Technology is the last frontier. When we really start teaching technology to girls, when our society lets the second half of our population into the world of technology, the coming boom will be like nothing we've ever seen before!"

"It sounds great, Anna."

"Really?" Her voice was mixture of hope and wonder and disbelief... and a little bit of desperation.

"Really," I said.

NINETEEN

The next morning I was up before dawn. I took Spot out for a walk in the predawn twilight. Although I was still in the shady darkness from the mountain to the east behind my cabin, to the west across the lake, the Sierra crest was catching a bit of pink from the approaching sunrise, and it bounced alpenglow back to the Carson Range on the east side of Tahoe, giving a faint illumination to the forest. We followed the trail that winds north from my cabin, through the forest on the mountain slope. The fall air was crispy cold, and the birds and squirrels and chipmunks were already awake and industrious and noisy in their pre-winter preparations. Spot turned off the trail and charged through the forest, demonstrating that, whether it is their nose, their eyes, or their ears that lead them, dogs can navigate in the dark.

Ten minutes out, where the trail curves to follow a wrinkle in the mountain's skin, Spot ran to a large Jeffrey pine that we both had visited in the past. He sniffed it and the surrounding area with unusual interest. I stood and watched in the growing dawn light as he inspected the tree bark, the tree base, the area around the tree. Then he bounced on his front legs and stood up on his rear legs to his full six-foot-four height, his front claws gripping at the tree bark. He put his nose into the bark furrows, six feet off the ground, taking deep breaths.

"What is it, boy?" I asked, moving forward. He ignored me, and kept up his inspection.

Studies have indicated the breadth of the world that is available to a dog's nose. Your dog can tell everything that you've eaten in the previous day or two. If you've been somewhere your dog has been, your dog will know it when you get home. Your dog will know if you've come in contact with someone he knows.

Your dog can tell if you've been near another animal. And if it is a dog or cat or horse or some other animal that your dog has had previous contact with, he will know it even if you didn't touch that animal. A dog can tell if a person is angry or sad or worried or happy based on that person's smell. A dog knows if a person has merely been near another person who has smoked a cigarette or a cigar. If you buy a new brand of shampoo, your dog can tell the difference. If you switch from margarine to butter, your dog will notice. Upon meeting any woman, a dog can tell if that woman is pregnant, even before she or her doctor knows. A dog can be trained to smell a specific cancer with greater accuracy than any medical diagnostic technique. If you decide to take the stairs instead of the elevator at work, as soon as you get home your dog will be aware that something was different about your day. Dogs can even be trained to smell blood sugar on a person's breath and warn a diabetic of an impending problem long before the person realizes it themselves. So I fervently wished that Spot could speak English and tell me what he had discovered.

Spot dropped back down to all fours and walked S-curves here and there around the tree, sniffing the dirt.

"What is it, boy?" I said. I squatted down, leaned back against the tree and looked through the forest toward the view I'd seen many times. Framed by the trees was my cabin a half-mile away, sitting small and dark across the distant mountainside.

I stayed squatting for a minute as I considered the implications. Unfortunately, it was still too dark for me to fully inspect the site.

By sunrise, Spot and I were driving down the mountain. The unusually cold nights of late September had turned the aspen stands a brilliant golden-orange hue. They caught the first of the sun's rays and contrasted so strongly with the green pine forest that I thought they must look like marigolds from outer space.

Three hours later, we were on Interstate 80 approaching the coastal ranges. I turned south on 680, the shortcut route to the South Bay and, I hoped, a quicker drive than taking the Bay Bridge into San Francisco and heading down the peninsula.

The grassy rounded East Bay mountains shimmered their last golden glow before the rains of winter would turn them back to light green velvet. Rush hour was over as we made a fast cruise through Walnut Creek and Danville and the other communities east of the Oakland Tunnel. As the highway angled southwest, we went through the notch in the mountains and came into the giant basin of the Bay Area, a huge inland sea that was connected to the ocean by a strait so narrow that it was missed by early Spanish explorers as they sailed up the California coast.

The air was unusually clear. I could see across the bay to the San Francisco peninsula with the redwood-capped Santa Cruz Mountains that formed its backbone. The ocean fog that sustained the great trees was just visible, pushing up from the Pacific on the far side, feathering through the giant trees where Skyline Blvd followed the ridgeline, and flowing like slow gray rivers down the valleys to the Bay.

I cut across the north side of San Jose and turned north on 280, a candidate, as it approached Stanford, for World's Most Beautiful Urban Freeway.

Spot stood up in the back seat trying an ineffective stretch in the confined space. I pushed the button to crack his window, and he stuck his nose three inches out into the 70 mph wind, sniffing out the mysteries of the beautiful and undeveloped rolling landscape, the giant radio telescopes on the hilltops that listened to the whirring hum of the galaxies, the miles-long particle accelerator buried under the freeway where multiple Nobel laureates have learned about the largest aspects of the universe by smashing together the smallest bits of matter, the ancient redwoods that were already aged giants when the first Spaniards sailed north in their galleons, the fog that was older than life itself.

Eventually, Spot suffered wind-in-the-nose fatigue, and he lay back down.

I found the Woodside exit and drove west toward the peninsula's mountainous ridge. Large estates were scattered in the hills, separated from each other by horse pastures, paddocks, barns and other horsy structures. I found a turnoff and then another and then a third and came to several townhouses in a row. They were each neat and tidy and a contrast to the single-family mansions nearby.

I found the unit where Melody Sun had lived until she refinanced and got upside down on equity versus debt. The realtor's sign was small and discreet.

I knocked and, as I expected, no one answered. I went to the left and knocked on the neighbor's door. No one answered. I moved to the right and knocked.

The door opened, and an old man looked up at me. He squinted against the light.

"Hi, I'm looking for my old friend Melody Sun who used to live next door to you. Do you know how I can find her?"

The man squeezed his lips together, pushed them up into his nose, and shut the door in my face.

I moved another door to the right and knocked. No answer.

I moved yet again. Pretty soon I'd be knocking on doors in Palo Alto. I knocked on another door. A young woman answered. I repeated my speech.

"You don't know what happened?" The woman frowned. "Melody…" She paused, leaned out from the door and looked both directions. She looked at me, wondering, maybe, if I was safe. "Melody moved," she finally said.

"I know that the bank foreclosed her townhouse. But I don't know where she moved. Can you give me a forwarding address?"

The woman studied me for a bit. "How well did you know her?"

"Not well. We met after her cousin Grace died. But I haven't been in contact with her for some time. I was hoping to touch base with her again."

"Well, I don't want to upset you, but Melody lost everything. Not just her house, but everything. When she left here, she had her little truck, a sleeping bag and a few clothes in the back, and that was it."

"Do you have any idea where she moved?" I asked.

"That's just it. She didn't move anywhere. She was homeless. She said she'd be living out of her truck. See, after her cousin died, Melody met a man, got married and moved here with him. But then she lost her job, her husband took all their money before he ran off, and she had nothing for rent. I offered to let her stay with me, but she wouldn't hear of it."

"Did she have a cellphone?"

"She cancelled it," the woman said.

"So you have no way of contacting her?"

"No."

"When did this happen?"

"Three weeks ago. I came home from work one night to see her in the driveway putting her stuff in her truck. She'd been really depressed in the months leading up to that point. Especially after she realized that her husband had emptied the bank account before he left. It was the stress of that that caused her to lose her job."

"I never met him. How long was he around?"

"I don't know. He was with her when she bought the house, and he didn't leave until a year later. That was six months ago. Everything went downhill for her from that point. Lost the husband, her job, her money, the house. She drove off that same night that I saw her packing, and I haven't seen her since."

"Do you know where she worked?"

The woman shook her head. "Some software company."

"Did Melody use Sun for her last name? Or did she take her husband's name?"

"You ask a lot of questions."

"I care about her. Wouldn't you ask questions?"

The woman thought about it. "Melody Sun was the only way I ever knew her. I thought Sun was his name, too."

"Did Melody say anything to you before she left?"

"Not much. I asked if she wanted to stay with me. I asked if I could help. I even asked if I could give her some money. But she said no to everything. And when I asked where she was going, she said that she'd heard about a women's shelter up in Marin, someplace that's run by a bunch of Unitarian ladies. She was thinking of going there for a day or so to get her bearings. But she said she mostly wanted to be alone, that she might just hit the road and drive to the end of the earth. I remember that it sounded kind of ominous to me."

I thanked the woman and went back to my Jeep. I called Street. When she answered, I explained what I learned.

"Would you like me to look up the shelter online?"

"Yes, please."

"If you had a better phone, you'd be able to do it from there."

"Yes, but it would take me two years of computer classes at the college to learn how to use the phone. If I wait two years, any chance of finding Melody will be long gone."

"You're a funny guy," Street said, no humor in her voice. She paused. "Here it is. It's called The Connection, The Place Where Women Find Their Future. It's a non-profit sponsored by the Unitarian Universalist Ladies Auxiliary. The shelter's address is not posted. Probably because some of the women there are pursued by bad men. But there's a phone number. You could try that." Street gave it to me, and I hung up and dialed.

"Unitarian Universalist Church of Corte Madera." A woman's voice.

"I'm looking for The Connection, please," I said.

"In what regard is your inquiry?" Guarded. Not friendly, but not unfriendly, either.

I explained who I was and that I was trying to locate Melody Sun.

"I'm sorry that we cannot give out any information on the phone. But perhaps you can come to our church. I'm sure you'll understand why we need to be extremely careful. The safety of our residents comes before all else."

"Yes, of course."

The woman told me the address.

I got back on 280 and headed up to The City, followed Highway 1 through the Presidio and headed onto the Golden Gate. The fog enshrouded the bridge, snaking in tendrils around the vehicles. Periodically, a cloud tunnel opened up a view of a ship on the water below or of Alcatraz in the distance.

On the north side of the bridge I climbed the slope through thick fog, went through the tunnel and popped out into clear air, the fog held back by the mountain ridge that rose to the north and continued to Mt. Tam.

The Unitarian Universalist Church was on a side street in a stand-alone commercial building that looked like it had once been a small grocery market. I parked and walked in.

The entry opened onto a large room with two parallel semi-circles of chairs. At the focal point was a round barstool. The back wall of the room was a whiteboard on which was written 'The 6 Keys to Community' in dry marker. Below it said, 'In every demographic, a Socratic Dialogue is one of the best ways to produce engagement and inclusion.'

Religion meets the Intelligentsia.

One side of the room had a large counter with an espresso machine and stacks of porcelain espresso cups on paper doilies.

To one side of the entry was an office. I pulled open the door and let myself in.

A woman was at a desk. There was an open doorway in the back wall of the office. Through the opening I saw another woman at another desk. They both looked vaguely like Jodie Foster, good-looking but without playing it up. Both were dressed well in business casual, grays and browns. From a distance, neither woman appeared to wear any makeup or jewelry other than small earrings. Both had hair that could only be described as sensible. I smelled no perfume. Both spoke on the phone, articulate voices, lower-pitched than is common, intelligent word choices. No small talk. NPR's All Things Considered came from a small radio on the top of a bookshelf.

The women's desktops were neat, clean, organized. There were no donuts and coffee. No plaques with engraved aphorisms. No heart-shaped stickers saying 'have a great day.' No cute little frog sculptures sitting with crossed legs on the edges of the lamp bases or file cabinets. No pictures of children in little plexi frames. No coffee mugs with sports logos being used as pencil holders.

On the front table were a stack of New Yorkers and another stack of Atlantic Monthlys. In a bookshelf was the complete collection of Will and Ariel Durant's The Story of Civilization, the first such collection I'd ever seen that had enough wear to look like the books actually may have been read. The other titles were largely about Humanism and Secularism and Free Will.

There were no pamphlets or wall-mounted icons or paintings or sculptures or altars or anything else of a religious nature.

By the voice of the woman in front of me, I could tell that she was the person I spoke to on the phone from Woodside.

She hung up, made a careful note in her day-planner, and looked up at me. "Yes? How can I help you?"

"I'm Owen McKenna. I spoke to you on the phone about Melody Sun."

"Yes, of course. May I see an ID, please?"

I pulled out my PI license.

She studied it. "Please give me a moment." She stood and walked into the back office. I heard their soft voices but not the words. She came back.

"Please step back here, Mr. McKenna." She led me into the other office. "I'd like you to meet Samantha Abrams. She is our director. She will be glad to help you."

The other woman stood up, shook my hand. "Good to meet you, Mr. McKenna." I saw that she was now holding my ID. She handed it back to me.

The first woman left and shut the door behind her.

"Mary said that you were inquiring about Melody Sun?"

"Yes." I explained my background on the SFPD and how I'd met Melody after her cousin Grace's death. "I'm trying to locate Melody to give her the news that we have likely found her cousin's killer. I understand Melody has been having a hard time. It may help her to know that the murderer may finally be punished."

Samantha held my eyes for a long moment, then she looked down and fiddled with a button on her blouse. "I'm afraid I have bad news for you, Mr. McKenna. Melody arrived here in a very bad state. Serious depression, despondent over her circumstances. In the space of a few months she'd gone from being a woman with a relatively happy life to a woman who was homeless and penniless. She lived with us for six days, and each day she seemed to get worse. Our on-call psychologist worked with her. He said that Melody was suffering from serious depression and needed to see a psychiatrist and get on an appropriate drug regimen as soon as possible. He also said what we could all see, that Melody was fiercely intelligent. But of course, intelligent people sometimes have the worst time with depression. So we made an appointment for Melody the next day. But Melody left that afternoon and didn't come back.

"Early the next day, we got a call from the Golden Gate Bridge Patrol. Melody's pickup had been found at four in the morning parked in the middle of the bridge. The truck was sitting at an angle as if she'd jerked it to the side and stopped. The front door was open, and the engine was running. Melody was nowhere to be seen. There was a sticky note on the steering wheel that said, 'Sorry, I can't take this life anymore.'"

"She committed suicide," I said.

"They never found the body. But they told us that they often don't. Even when jumps are witnessed and the witness continues watching, the body often sinks and is never recovered."

The news stunned. Maybe Melody's death wasn't connected to Grace's death, but the coincidence seemed too strong. When Grace was killed, I'd seen the devastating effect on Melody. It was impossible not to think that Grace's murder had started a cascade of events that culminated in Melody taking her own life three years later.

"I'm sorry," I said.

"Yes, it is hard. Several of the other residents at The Connection have been very upset. They felt for Melody. They understood her pain. We are being extra vigilant with them."

"Were you able to contact her next-of-kin?"

"Melody told us that, other than the husband who disappeared months ago, she has no family."

I stood. "Thank you for your time."

"You're welcome."

TWENTY

Agent Ramos called as Spot and I were just starting up the first big slope in El Dorado Hills that marks the beginning of the foothills.

"Sergeant Santiago told me about Watson saying that Nick O'Connell was the hijacker," he said. "We got O'Connell's booking photo. It's better than the artist's sketch, but not much. I showed it to Street. She can't make a positive ID, but she says it's a good possibility. I'd like to bring you a copy. I can be at your place in fifteen minutes."

"Great. I'm coming up Fifty, but I'm only at Cameron Park, so I'm still about an hour and twenty minutes out."

"Okay, I'll come in an hour and twenty minutes," he said.

Ramos was in his Suburban in my driveway when I pulled up. He was talking on his cell. I waved at him and took Spot on into my cabin.

He rapped on the door five minutes later.

When I opened the door, he took a step back and frowned at Spot, who was pushing out between me and the doorjamb.

"I have on black pants," he said. "Your hound has white hair." There was no expression on his face, but his voice was tight.

I pointed at Spot. "All of those spots are black hair," I said. "So some will blend in."

Ramos gave me a dead look.

I pushed sideways with my hip so that Spot was squeezed against the door opening and couldn't easily get to Ramos.

"Spot, you wouldn't shed on Agent Ramos, would you?"

Spot looked up at me. His tail thumped against the closet just inside the front door.

"That Beatles song Love Me Do is on the radio," Ramos said. "His tail is beating the same tempo as the song."

"I guess you passed his love test."

"Probably just wants me for lunch."

"I doubt it. He hasn't chewed on anyone with a law degree in a week or more."

"Maybe we don't taste good," Ramos said. It was the first time I'd ever heard him attempt humor.

I took Spot's collar and held him back as Ramos carefully stepped through the door.

Ramos walked past the rocker and hitched a hip on one of my two barstools that sit on the front side of my kitchen-nook counter. He hooked a heel on the bottom cross support. His black shoes were as polished and shiny as his black hair and moustache. The creased fronts of his pants made sharp edges.

I had Spot lie down on his cedar-chip bed.

Ramos reached out the photo, expecting me to walk over to get it. Could be condescension. Could also be he was afraid to walk near Spot.

I took it from his hand.

The shot of Nick O'Connell was a study in what a photo can't reveal.

"The big hair and beard and eyebrows go with my memory of the hijacker," I said. "But I can't recognize anything else about him. His eyes and nose seem average. If you Photoshopped in different eyes and nose, nothing would change. This guy was probably the hijacker. But that means it could be anyone. The hair and beard are suggestions, nothing more." I handed the photo back.

Ramos held up his hand, palm out. "That's an extra copy I made for you."

"Thanks."

I filled Ramos in on the remaining details of the events since I spoke to Watson.

"Anna must wish she'd never contacted her birth mother," Ramos said when I was done. "Grace got murdered, and Anna acquired a murderous stalker who wants a journal that she knows nothing about. Now Melody has jumped off the Golden Gate."

Ramos stood up and, moving in an arc to keep his distance from Spot, walked to the sliding door and looked through the glass out toward the perimeter of mountains encircling the lake.

"How did Anna escape the bedroom attacker?" he asked, still facing the lake. "She some kind of commando?"

"I don't think so. She's just thorough. She made a point about how Grace taught her to be a careful planner. Apparently, Grace emphasized that you can confront any scary possibility by simply preparing for it very well. If Anna had had military experience, she almost certainly would have focused on arming herself with weapons. But from her description, it doesn't sound like she even considered weapons. All she wanted was an escape path."

"Good point," Ramos said, turning from the sliding glass door. "Maybe Grace suspected that harm might come to Anna, and the preparation lesson was because of that. What do you make of it?"

"I don't know. I've been uncomfortable with this case since the beginning. We have supposedly caught Grace's killer. But it doesn't feel right. Catching a murderer doesn't answer the question about why Watson – or someone – murdered a woman who seemed no threat to anybody. Until we understand what the connection was between Watson and the hijacker, I won't feel better."

Ramos frowned. His face was a study in extreme focus. I wondered if he ever relaxed. Probably he applied the same intensity to that, too.

Ramos said, "Anna told you that her attacker twirled a knife. Sounds like what Street said about the hijacker."

I nodded.

"Watson opened up to you," Ramos said, "and you're the guy who caught him. He wouldn't even talk to us."

"Maybe you wore him down, and I got a lucky break," I said.

"Don't bullshit me with false modesty, McKenna. You obviously knew how to open him up."

I waited a beat. "Watson referred to O'Connell as a knife man. I asked what he meant, and he described this man as being something of an artist with how he used a knife to do his violent deeds. He also mentioned that O'Connell did a twirling stunt with his knife."

Ramos said, "The way that Anna's stalker made a demand that she follow his instructions, it's just like what the hostage taker did when he called you. Acts like O'Connell. Sounds like O'Connell. Works a blade like O'Connell."

"Right. Here's another puzzle that makes no sense. Anna said that Grace took her to the San Francisco Library and showed her a book on the Gold Rush. In it was a mention of something called the Mulligan War."

"Meaning?" Ramos said.

"Some land dispute back during the Gold Rush that involved a person named Mulligan and a person named Gan Sun."

"What does that have to do with Anna and Grace?" Ramos asked.

"Just that Grace's great, great grandfather had violent struggles. The Mulligan person tried to lynch him. It's like trouble runs in the family."

"Quite the coincidence. But it's a real stretch to imagine that all of this has any connection to a dispute that took place a hundred fifty years ago."

"I would agree," I said, "except Anna said that Grace mentioned that someone named O'Connell was involved with Mulligan and Gan Sun."

"It sounds like the journal is at the center of this." Ramos reached over to the toothpick holder on the kitchen counter, pulled one out. He looked at it up close, turned it around, and worked it into a place in his teeth. Upper right side. Three o'clock. He levered it back and forth, then pulled the toothpick out of his mouth. He removed a handkerchief from his pocket and carefully wiped the tip of his tongue. Next, he wiped the toothpick off, set the pick on the counter, folded the handkerchief three times just so, and slipped it back into his pocket.

I had no idea if Ramos had ever studied the Grace Sun case. If he had, he would know about the journal being found on Grace's body, and he would know that I knew about it. Not mentioning it would be obvious.

So I said, "When Grace's body was found, she had a journal

tucked under her shirt."

"The journal Anna's attacker was looking for," Ramos said, nodding.

"Right. It was written in Chinese and it was mostly blurred by water. A Berkeley prof couldn't get anything useful out of it. The fact that the attacker told Anna he wanted the journal," I said, "suggests that it contained something valuable. Maybe Watson and O'Connell were both after the journal and they developed a plan. Watson chatted Grace up and got invited over for tea. He brought O'Connell in the door with him. Tensions rose. Grace and Watson fought, and she scratched him, to which O'Connell responded by caving her head in with the frying pan. That would explain how both of them were involved, and it would explain why Watson sounded sincere when he said he didn't kill her. If O'Connell killed her, then O'Connell would save himself by getting Watson sent up for the murder. Yet Watson wouldn't want to accuse O'Connell because, without DNA evidence, he'd have to admit that he was part of the crime. He'd be convicted as an accessory."

"An awkward reconstruction," Ramos said. "But possible. And the hijacking? How do you explain that?"

"More awkwardness. Whatever goodies the journal describes, Nick the Knife wanted them for himself. With Watson out of the way, he could have gone after them. So he concocted a way to get me to bring in Watson."

"The question remains," Ramos said. "Why didn't O'Connell just kill Watson instead of getting you involved?"

I shook my head. "Got me."

"Any idea where the journal is?" Ramos asked.

I reached over next to the toaster, picked it up and handed it to him.

"I thought the Grace Sun murder is still an open case," he said as he flipped through the journal.

"It is."

"Wouldn't this be evidence in the case?"

"Yes," I said.

"Does your possession of this raise a concern that you might be breaking the chain of custody?"

"It does."

Ramos looked at me.

"But at each step we documented and signed and crossed our hearts and swore fidelity to the law."

Ramos tossed the journal onto my counter. "Can't even read it, it's so blurry."

"You read Mandarin?"

"Never tried, so I can't say definitively that I don't."

More humor. I was impressed.

TWENTY-ONE

After Ramos left, I dialed the Dreamscape.

"Tahoe Dreamscape, where you ride your Tahoe Dream," a young woman answered. She put a little edge of huskiness into her voice. It probably increased sales to men a little and decreased sales to women a lot more.

"My name is Owen McKenna. May I please speak to the owner?"

"I'm sorry, the owner is not available. But I can forward you to the voicemail of our managing cruise consultant Darren Fritz."

"If the owner isn't in, I'll speak to Captain Richards."

"I'm sorry, but Captain Richards' voicemail box is full. The last few days have been…" she stopped talking, suddenly realizing that the reasons for Richards' sudden hectic schedule were not something she should talk about.

"May I speak to whoever's currently in charge?"

"Like I said, I can put you through to Darren Fritz's voicemail. Otherwise, all I can help you with is ticket sales."

I realized that it was her job to keep callers like me from getting past the gates. I didn't enjoy being rude, but I needed to save time.

"And your name is?" I asked.

"I'm Traylynn, sir, and I have incoming sales calls to answer, so I'll have to put you on hold while you decide if you'd like to leave a…"

"Traylynn," I interrupted, "if you put me on hold you'll be getting a personal visit at home from local law enforcement." I can lie as well as anyone else. "I'm the detective your hostage taker put on his little show for. Two men died, which is not an insignificant event on your boat. Now you can either connect me to the owner of the boat, or to Captain Richards, or you can give me the owner's personal cellphone number."

"But…"

"I understand that you're under orders to do none of those things. So you're going to have to make an executive decision, Traylynn."

"I'll get in so much trouble. If I ring his phone, I'll lose my job." The huskiness was gone. Her voice was now a high-pitched squeak. If I pushed her, she'd start crying.

"Then tell me his cell number. I won't say where I got it."

I waited. Her breathing had a little whimper in it. I heard pages turning.

"Okay. The area code is three one six." She read the number to me. "And you won't tell anyone where you heard it? Please?" She was pleading.

"I won't. Thanks." I hung up.

I looked up the area code. Wichita, Kansas. I dialed the number.

"Ford Georges speaking." Just three words and the soft voice sounded intelligent and arty and a bit pretentious. Like a museum curator or classical composer with a touch of drawl. He pronounced Georges as if it were the word gorgeous only beginning with a soft G.

"Ford, my name is Owen McKenna."

"Oh my. Owen McKenna. I'd never heard of you before a couple of days ago," he said. "But of course you are now a large figure in the Tahoe Dreamscape world. I've been meaning to call. I do hope you're okay. That was a terribly stressful drama you got dropped into. And you handled it well."

"I'm okay."

"Special Agent Ramos said you would be. He said you're tough, that you'd seen worse. By the way, how did you get this number?"

"My job. I'm a detective."

"Oh. Of course. You know how to compromise the database. Or one of my people."

"I'd like to talk to you. When will you be in Tahoe, and when can we get together?"

"I'm actually in Tahoe now, but my schedule's awfully full. This week is tough because..."

"Ford," I interrupted, still frustrated after talking to his ticket saleswoman. "I'm not going to play a schedule game with you. Pick a time today or tomorrow. Cancel an appointment. Or skip dinner."

"Well, I normally check with Teri. Let me grab the calendar." I heard some movement and shuffling noises. "How about an hour from now? We just got our liquor delivery here on the boat. I could open a bottle of Moet. Not that that would pay you back for your efforts on our behalf. But I owe you. Would that be good?"

"Fine. You want me to come to the Dreamscape?"

"Please. You know where it's docked? Crystal Bay?"

"I'll be there."

I was on the road, heading north toward Incline Village when my phone rang.

"Hello," I said.

It was Anna. "I keep thinking about my attacker," she said.

"Me, too."

"It's been three years. I've been living with such fear," she said.

"Yeah."

"And from all indications, he is almost certainly the guy who drowned," she said.

"Probably. But we don't know for sure."

She was silent a moment. "I'm thinking that I don't need to hide anymore," She said.

"I'd wait. I don't yet understand what this is all about. Until I do, I think you should keep your head down."

"You don't really understand my situation, do you? You don't have a clue how hard this is, living in hiding. To not be able to go home, walk the streets, eat at a restaurant, go out with old friends."

"Anna, I know..."

She interrupted, "I email them, of course. And I've explained the situation to some of them. And some of them understand.

Others think I'm crazy. But the ones I haven't told? The ones I care very much about but who don't have the kind of history with me where I could tell them what happened? They're nice, but they think I've just blown them off. Like I don't really like them at all, but I'm just communicating out of guilt or something. Do you know what that feels like? Do you have any idea what kind of pit you get in your stomach when you're trapped by circumstances that you can't explain? And if you broke your silence and did tell them what happened, they would think you're a paranoid schizophrenic."

"What I meant was…"

"It's so easy for you to tell me to keep my head down," she interrupted. "But I'm the one who has no life. I'm the one who has to look both ways before I even walk out my door. Well, I'm not going to do it anymore! I'm not going to live in fear, to let someone else control my life! I have things I want to do. I can create some good in this lousy world. I can start my Reach For The Sky tech school for girls. I can make a difference!"

"Of course, you can, Anna. Just wait a little longer. You are still doing good with your work."

"No! You don't get it, Owen! As long as I'm living in a straightjacket, I can't do anything seriously good. If I come back to the real world, I can get those grants. I can go to the board meetings of those educational foundations. If I can make my presentations in person, I know I can get the funding for RFTS. But if I stay in hiding, whatever I have that's special to offer the world is a moot point. I'm a nobody. I'm like a cat who won't come out from under the bed. A life lived afraid isn't a life, Owen!"

I tried to comment, she protested, and we said a terse goodbye.

TWENTY-TWO

The Dreamscape's home was a pier near Stateline Point at the west boundary of Crystal Bay. I drove up the East Shore and went through Incline Village. It was a spectacular fall-postcard afternoon. The aspen were in full color, and the golden yellows shimmered against the sparkling blue water backdrop.

The road curved counter-clockwise around Crystal Bay. Where the road dipped down near the water, I got a glimpse of the Dreamscape floating at its pier out on the point. It was a pretty sight, and the yacht radiated an essence of luxury. In a mile, the road gradually rose up toward the little town of Crystal Bay where the line dividing California and Nevada came down through the middle of the Cal Neva Resort and was painted on the hotel floor. Once owned by Sinatra, the glitzy hotel was a meeting spot for people like Marilyn Monroe and the Kennedy brothers.

A couple of blocks before the main intersection in the one-stoplight town, I turned left to follow a twisty road that I thought would take me down to the Tahoe Dreamscape's home pier.

I came instead to a small parking lot near a beach vendor with a tiny business shack sporting a sign that said Jackie's Jet Boats. Nearby was a row of personal watercraft. The Dreamscape was not in view. I was in the wrong spot.

I got out and trotted over to the shack. A chubby man whose excessive tan was far down the path toward melanoma stood up from his tall stool and leaned out the shack door. His sun-bleached sandy hair was pulled into Rasta-man dreadlocks that looked like they'd been moistened now and then but not washed for a year or more. I didn't want to get too close lest creatures like the ones Street studies leaped at the chance for a new host planet in a galaxy far away from their current home.

"Hey, bro," dreadlocks said. "It's still light out for another couple of hours. Beautiful afternoon for a thrill ride. The weather's warm, and the tourists have gone home. You'll have the lake to yourself."

"No doubt. Are you Jackie?"

The man made a big grin. "One and only. You want a boat? I've got a late-season special on the rental."

"Thanks, Jackie. I may take a ride. But not today. I have an appointment on the Tahoe Dreamscape. I thought it was down this road."

Jackie looked very disappointed. He slowly backed up two steps, back into the mini-shack and sat down on the tall barstool. The impact made a little stand on the counter behind him shake. What looked like a selection of jet boat keys swung in unison like a display rack of dangly earrings.

"Dreamscape's the next road down," he said, stabbing his thumb over his shoulder.

"Thanks," I said, and left.

I went back up to the highway, drove to the next turn, and headed back down to the lake.

The Dreamscape floated peacefully next to its pier. The buildings and houses of Incline Village dotted the woods across Crystal Bay. Above them were the ski runs of Diamond Peak, lonely and green, awaiting the snow and skiers that would arrive in hoards by Thanksgiving.

The Tahoe Dreamscape parking lot was tucked into the trees above the Dreamscape pier. Spot had gone a long time without movement, so I decided to bring him along.

He's tall enough that I don't need a leash. I held his collar as we walked down the asphalt path to the timber steps, down and out to the pier where the Dreamscape floated, looking, in the warm glow of the setting sun, younger and more romantic than the boat on whose rust-streaked deck I had attempted to negotiate with the hijacker five days before.

Spot heeled like he was class valedictorian, as dogs often do when you have a good grip on their collar. We walked out the pier to the boarding ramp, a 36-inch wide gangplank with a roller apparatus under the end that rested on the pier. As the big boat rocked with the gentle lake swells, the ramp oscillated back and forth on the pier decking, its little wheels polishing well-worn grooves in the pier planks. Spot turned with me and walked up the ramp like he'd been walking gangplanks all his life.

I unlatched the little gate at the gangway opening and we stepped onto the foredeck.

It felt like a different boat to me post-hostage trauma. Without the terrified crowd and the heavy weight of life-and-death drama, the layout felt more comfortable, the aisles and companionways less cramped, the open decks perfect for showing the lake and mountain views. Yet the railing where Street had been tied, a thin metal tube that wouldn't have been notable in the past, now looked frail and insufficient to the job of keeping people safe from the depths of the ice water. And the boat design, which I once would have admired for its interesting lines, appeared chunky and gawkish.

I tapped three times on the salon door, turned the latch, and led Spot inside.

"Hello?" I called out. "Anyone home?"

There was no response.

I walked past the corner booth where I had held Street close to me a few days before.

At the rear of the salon were two sets of double doors. I headed toward the portside doors and pushed through into the dining cabin. It was a small plush restaurant. Ten maple tables of Scandinavian design were each encircled with six matching chairs. I called out again, but got no response.

Spot and I weaved our way through the tables. At the rear of the dining area, also on the portside, were the swing-doors to the galley. I looked in, but the lights were off. On the starboard side was the exit to the lower aft deck and beyond it the tender deck where an inflatable boat was stowed. Spot and I went back outside. I glanced up both outer aisles that connected fore and aft decks. Nobody was present.

The aft deck had a large staircase that went both down and up. We went up, Spot's nails clicking on the metal steps. The large upper aft deck projected rearward as far as the stern below. Around the perimeter of the deck were decorative torch lanterns on tall tapered rods. The lanterns and rods were painted with bold zebra-stripe patterns. With the lanterns lit, an evening cruise on the Dreamscape would be a very memorable affair.

At the front edge of the upper deck were two steps up to the bridge. We went up. A man was visible through the rear glass of the bridge. He stood between the captain's chairs, facing forward toward a broad instrument panel with multiple rows of gauges, two small computer screens, a large old-fashioned analog compass, a stack of electronic stuff that was reminiscent of an old-fashioned stereo system, and other devices I didn't recognize. The man held a phone to his ear, and as he spoke, he gestured with his free hand like a conductor directing the philharmonic.

I walked up and tapped on the glass of the rear door. He turned and waved me in as he kept talking. If he was surprised at Spot's presence, he didn't show it.

I pulled open the door and walked in.

The man closed his phone, slipped it into his pocket.

He walked up to Spot, his hand out, casual, not looking directly at Spot. "Somebody mentioned this guy in conjunction with you," he said, as Spot gave him a sniff. "I see why they call this breed the Apollo of dogs. Wow. A watchdog this size doesn't even need teeth."

"But you don't hesitate to approach," I said. "You obviously know dogs."

"Growing up on a ranch outside of Wichita, you learn animals. They're mostly all the same when it comes to judging other beings. If you want to avoid aggression, you act indifferent. Of course, you have to feel indifferent, be indifferent, inhabit the whole concept of indifference, otherwise they will sense the charade. But if you succeed, potentially hostile animals will correctly perceive no threat and leave you alone. Bulls, roosters, mama coyotes. Even grizzly bears and music professors." Ford crinkled his mouth into a half smile. "That is, if the music professors aren't hungry, ha, ha." He scratched Spot under his chin. "This guy must have been fed recently." His hand moved up to finger Spot's ear stud. He bent down so that his face was a few inches from Spot's. "Love the rock, hon! You're so cute!"

The man reached to shake my hand. "So you are Owen McKenna. Ford Georges. Good to meet you." He gave my hand a gentle squeeze. As we shook, he touched my shoulder with his left hand. Then he looked me in the eye. "Thank you so much for saving our boat. We owe you more than we can say."

"You're welcome."

Ford was a solid, rangy guy in his middle forties, maybe four inches and twenty pounds shy of me. He wore a purple silk shirt over black silk slacks. His sock-less feet sported woven leather shoes with very thin soles like what I imagined on an Italian movie director. Ford had one of those hip haircuts where the top hair was gelled, combed and parted down the middle. The back and sides of his head were cut so short that you could see his childhood scars, his adult pores, and a tiny vein that squiggled its way through the territory above his left ear like a creek meandering through the Kansas prairie. That same ear sported two small sparkling studs similar to Spot's, although probably made of real diamonds.

"No doubt you've got many questions about what happened," he said. "But I can't be of much help. My wife Teri and I weren't on the boat. We have stay-aboard quarters below decks, but we mostly office at home, and it turns out the business of running a boat is ninety percent business and only ten percent boat. We've never actually taken one of our cruises together as passengers. We keep saying that we should pretend we're customers, eat the Emerald Bay dinner that we're famous for, the whole works."

"You haven't always been in the cruise business?"

He shook his head. "Insurance business. I retired and bought this boat. Best way I could think of to get out of Wichita."

"You did well in insurance."

"When my dad finally accepted that a masters degree in music was a good indication that I wasn't going to take over the ranch, he told me that if music didn't work, I should pick a service career instead, preferably something with no lights, no excitement, no razzle dazzle to distract me, because that's how a guy can make steady bank. Of course, I wanted the lights and the excitement and the razzle dazzle. I dreamed of taking my clarinet to a big city, eventually moving on to one of the premier orchestras and a recording career as a soloist. But in the end, I didn't have the chops. So I took my dad's advice and started a small insurance agency in Wichita. It turned out he was right. And in Kansas there isn't much to waste your money on, so I built up a sizable kitty. Now I'm working twice as hard and barely making expenses, but I'm not bored. And the views here are at least as good as endless miles of wheat fields." He made a big grin.

"Who else besides Captain Richards works as crew on the boat?"

"Chief Mate Allen Paul, and our three deckhands, Joshua Tolman, and the twins Andy and Warren. If you want Andy and Warren's last name, I'd have to look it up. They are both new to our boat in the last month."

"Were any of them onboard during the hijacking?"

"Yes, of course. Paul is always onboard when we sail. And that day, Joshua and Warren were our deckhands."

"When is a good time for me to show them a photo?"

"The police already showed them mugshots, if that's what you mean. Unfortunately, they couldn't identify anyone."

"We've got a new person we're looking at," I said. "I'd like you to take a look at him as well."

"Happy to. Of course, you remember that I wasn't there. But you're thinking that this guy may have been around at other times."

"Right. Or involved with you in some other capacity."

I pulled out the shot of Nick O'Connell that Agent Ramos had given me and handed it to Georges. He took it, held it close, scowled at it.

"It's a blurry photo, hard to tell much. Guy's got a lotta hair, that's for sure. Makes it hard to see his face. I don't think I've ever seen him."

He started to hand the photo back, then snatched it back and stared at it, his scowl deepening.

"Wait. I think I have seen this guy. I don't know where. Maybe at the gas station. Or maybe he was on the boat on one of the few days when I'm pulling water duty. Something about the intense eyes seems familiar. It reminds me of when I was in

Norway. Those people with piercing blue eyes."

He handed me the photo.

"Not much blue color in the picture," I said.

"Right," Georges said. "But that's the feeling I'm getting. Like I'm seeing that Norwegian intensity in his eyes."

"And you have no idea where you saw him."

Georges frowned, stared out toward the mountains on the far side of the lake, shook his head. "No. I can't pull that out of my head. It could've been anywhere. Grocery store. Bank. Maybe it'll come to me at three in the morning. I'll let you know if it does."

"I'd like to show it to your wife," I said.

"Certainly." He punched an intercom button. "Teri? You onboard?"

The answer was too scratchy for me to understand.

"Follow me," Georges said. "She's below decks in the forward stateroom. I can give you the tour."

We retraced my steps down the staircase to the lower aft deck.

"The former owner of the Dreamscape was a Turkish businessman. Made his money exporting Turkish goods to the EU mostly and around-the-world partly. Rugs and other home furnishings. He found this boat rusting away in a Greek boatyard. So he bought it and rebuilt it sufficient to suit Cleopatra. A decade later he sold it to the comedian Sammy Tuley. They sailed it from the Mediterranean to SoCal, and Sammy kept it at Marina del Rey. But that all happened just before the big lawsuit where Sammy lost everything. You probably remember it.

"Anyway, Sammy's loss was serendipity for me. I got the boat in the bankruptcy sale. The original shipyard had designed the bulkheads such that the boat could be cut into multiple sections. One of the divisions was right here." Georges waved his arm from right to left over his head, pointing at the steel structure. "So we sliced and diced it and put the pieces on trucks to deliver to Tahoe where we had it reassembled at that boatyard over on the West Shore."

Georges gestured toward the front of the boat.

"Of course, you've seen the main salon, the dining room, and the various decks. But the best part of the boat is below decks. Come."

Georges led us down the grand staircase to the lower level. At the bottom, he opened a recessed panel at the base of the staircase and flipped several light switches.

"This is the lounge," Georges said, waving his hand in a sweeping arc.

The room was decorated like a nineteenth century bordello. The walls were covered with red velour fabric. Each porthole was wrapped with a wide, circular, gold frame done in an elaborate Italian Renaissance style. There were multiple groupings of chairs, all upholstered in red fabric and each with its own small table. On the tables were old-fashioned lamps with red cloth shades. From the perimeter of each of the shades hung a ring of glass beads that shimmered. In each corner of the room was a fainting couch with several chairs arranged around it. I envisioned Manet's Olympia and three of her sisters as corner focal points for the room, lying back, propped up with red velvet pillows, entertaining the clientele when the weather was too inclement to sit out on the decks, asking the men to buy them another glass of triple-priced sherry.

"I'll take you forward in a minute. But first let me show you the engine room."

Ford Georges walked to the rear of the lounge and opened a door on the starboard side. The door looked heavy and was thick with foam insulation. "Check it out," he said. "This was the biggest part of the remodel the Turkish man did." He flipped on a light.

Georges walked into a room that was as neat and clean as any engine room on a Navy ship. Spot and I stepped over the bulkhead threshold behind him. Two giant engines, each five feet tall, took up most of the space with the rest filled with pipes and tubing and wiring conduit and gauges and meters and auxiliary generators and motors. Spot raised his snout and sniffed the air, his nostrils flexing hard. Except for a single oil stain on the floor under a hydraulic fitting, the engine room looked clean enough for surgery.

"Twin Cummins diesels," Georges bragged. "Built for torque.

Eleven hundred horsepower each. The Dreamscape may be big, but she can sprint at nineteen knots if Captain Richards buries the throttles. The former owner also installed bow thrusters, and then Sammy Tuley gave her all new marine electronics. Radar, GPS, auto-pilot, night vision cameras. The Dreamscape is simply the most advanced craft on the lake."

I nodded my admiration, realizing that if it were my boat, I'd probably show off the powerplant and techie-stuff, too.

Georges turned to go. I noticed a ladder and hatch that led up through the ceiling, although I couldn't place where it would come up into the main level. Perhaps near someplace on the lower aft deck.

"Lots of passages on this ship," I said, pointing to the ladder.

George grinned like a proud parent. "To be expected with three levels on a hundred-foot boat. Four levels, if you count the tender deck. I once counted how many ladders and hatches and stairways there are to get up and down from the various levels. I got to over a dozen, and I'm still not certain I found them all."

He led us back through the lounge and into a hallway with multiple doors.

"These are the staterooms, six in all. We haven't yet figured out how to put these to proper use. But we're thinking of doing a circumnavigation cruise. Two or three days. Give it a food focus. We could make ports-of-call at the different lakeside restaurants. Bring on a big-name chef for onboard cooking classes."

Ford led Spot and me forward to a small sitting area. A steep, narrow ladder stairway with handrails climbed up toward the salon above. The sitting area had four doors, two on each side, no doubt leading to staterooms. The forward door was open, and Georges walked into the main stateroom. He still hadn't expressed any reservation about Spot, so I continued in with Spot without asking permission.

The forward stateroom was under the foredeck where I'd engaged with the hijacker. Although it narrowed to a point at the front, it was very large and closer in size and style to a luxury hotel suite than any boat cabin I'd ever been in. Paneled in shiny dark wood, it had a king-sized four-poster bed to port, two chairs and a loveseat to starboard, a charming woodstove and near it a circular rack that held split wood. There were three more doorways, all closed. One, no doubt, was the private head, the other perhaps a walk-in closet, and the third was probably another ladder stair passage to the foredeck.

In one corner, a woman sat at a large desk looking at a columnar pad and punching numbers into a calculator. She telegraphed smart, high-school cheerleader in her mid-forties. Short, bouncy blonde hair, a round face that was more cute than pretty, and a shapely, trim figure that could still handle tight sweaters without embarrassment. She wore a pink sweatshirt that said 'Go Giants.' On the front corner of the desk lay a large tabby cat. He had a front leg up and turned in, and he was licking between his toes. When he saw Spot, he stopped mid-lick and stared, his paw still turned to his mouth.

"Teri, this is Owen McKenna," Ford said.

"So glad to meet…" She looked up, saw Spot, gasped with pleasure. "Oh, my God, what an amazing dog!" She came around from behind the desk. "What's his name?" She squatted down in front of him.

"Spot," I said.

At the sound of his name, he lifted his head and looked at me.

"That's perfect!" she said. "Spot!" Still squatting, she ran her hands all over Spot's face, and down his chest. He endured her attentions with his standard reaction, a steady wag, medium-slow speed. The woman rocked forward from her ankles onto her knees and hugged him, her face against the side of his neck, her arms reaching up and over the back of his neck. Spot's head went down her back. His panting tongue flipped little drops of saliva onto the back of her pink sweatshirt.

The cat on the desk hadn't moved. His paw was still lifted, frozen, toes to his nose. I saw the face of another cat peering out from behind a file cabinet. Above the cabinet was a little curved indentation in the wall of the boat with a porthole window at its focal point. In the curve sat another cat, staring intently at Spot.

Ford reached over to a sideboard that had a small fridge below and various bottles above. "What would you like? I have several ales, Jameson, and as I mentioned, Moet Chandon champagne."

"Whatever you're having."

He reached for the Moet. As he began untwisting the wire, he gestured toward his wife who was hugging Spot.

"Do all women respond to your dog like this?" Ford Georges asked.

No," I said. "I can think of at least three women who haven't thrown themselves on him."

"Be nice if we had some of his magic, huh? Women throwing themselves at us." He popped the cork and poured a healthy splash into three tall champagne flutes that he'd set out. He set one on Teri's desk, handed one to me, and raised his to mine. We clicked glasses. The stream of bubbles rising from the bottom of the stem sparkled in the light from the overhead cans. In the quiet of the insulated stateroom I could hear the hiss of the bubbles popping.

We sipped as the woman continued to grope my dog. She eventually stood up and began cooing to Spot.

"Look at this! He's so tall, all he has to do is lift his head up and he can sniff my chin!" She leaned toward him and touched her chin. "And he has an ear stud! I didn't even see it before. Oh, you big handsome brute! Gimme a kiss."

Spot licked her chin. The woman giggled.

"Never tried licking a woman's chin," Georges said. "Maybe that's the secret."

Finally, the woman turned toward me. Her sweatshirt was speckled with short dog hairs, black and white. She shook my hand and said, "Hi, I'm Teri Georges, chief assistant to every crew member. You've already met Ford, assistant to the chief assistant. It's good to meet you, although I wish it were because of different circumstances."

I nodded. One of the cats, large, orange and tiger-striped, walked bravely across the floor toward Spot. Although Spot would never hurt a cat, I gripped his collar to prevent any moves that might scare a feline.

"Not to worry about Edgar," Ford said. "Any thoughts I might have had about being the alpha male around here were dashed when he got to be about one year old and slashed my chin into strips of flesh all because I attempted to move him off my lap one evening. He is afraid of no animal except the vacuum cleaner."

Edgar walked toward Spot and then cruised on past, just two feet away and below Spot's head, as if Spot didn't exist. Impressive.

"Now, Rosalind and Celia, they are a bit more typical," Ford said, pointing at the two cats over by Teri's desk. "They'll hang back for awhile, take a measure of the situation and then decide if they want to engage or not. If they think Spot is acceptable as a heat source, they'll eventually curl up next to him."

"Three cats, none of whom are afraid of dogs. Impressive."

"Oh, they're the outgoing ones. The others won't even show their faces."

"You have more cats?" I said.

"This is just the beginning," Teri said. "There's Portia, Jessica, Nerissa, Hortensio, Kent and Viola." She turned to Ford. "Have I forgotten anyone?"

"Only Lucentio, but he's forgettable."

"Imaginative names," I said.

"That's Teri's doing," Ford said.

Teri looked up from the cats and Spot, a little embarrassed grin on her face. "You're here to ask about the hijacking."

"Yeah," I said. "Standard stuff, really. Can you tell me anything about it or the two men involved?"

She shook her head. "We've talked about it, but nothing seemed out of the ordinary. Of course, we weren't on the boat that day. We almost never are. But nothing unusual presented itself, if that makes sense."

"Was there anything unusual that happened regarding your business or your personal lives before or after the hijacking?"

They both shook their heads, Ford Georges slow and thoughtful, Teri faster. "I even looked at our books," she said. "Like, did our sales figures change or did our payables jump one way or another? Of course, what would that have to do with a hijacking, but I just thought, look for something different."

"But you didn't find anything different," I said.

"No. I went through our purchase orders, wondering if we'd taken on any new vendors. I checked with the crew to see if we changed any routines, bought fuel someplace new, changed caterers. But everything was the same as always."

"Business as usual until the hijacking," I said.

"Business as usual."

I pulled out the photo of Nick O'Connell. "I wonder if you recognize this man."

She took the picture and frowned just like Ford had. She stared at it for fifteen or twenty seconds.

"Yes, I kind of think I've seen him before. See how his eyes are – what would you call it – intense, I guess. This picture is washed out, but you can tell he's got really light eyes. That's what I recognize. Do you think he was the hostage taker?"

"We have some reason to think so, yes."

"God, that's really creepy, isn't it? To look at his face and realize that he perpetrated such a crime. Maybe it sounds brutal, but I'm glad he fell overboard."

"Anything come to mind about him?"

She shook her head. "No. But the longer I look at this, the more I think I've seen his face before, especially those eyes. But I can't remember where. You know that feeling when you've met someone before and then you see them out of context? Like you're standing in line at the DMV or something, and you recognize the guy in front of you, but you can't place him because you usually see him behind the meat counter at the supermarket?"

I nodded.

"Well, that's this guy," she said. "I've seen him. I wouldn't swear to it in court. But I'm pretty sure." She handed me the photo.

"Call me if you think of when and where?" I said.

"Yes, of course. And if I do, will that earn me more face time with Spot?"

Spot looked at her.

"Absolutely." I turned to Ford. "Has either of you noticed anything else out of place, before or after the hostage taker? Strange customers, unusual phone calls, any sign of tampering on the boat, anything missing or moved?"

"Not that comes to mind," Ford said. "But Teri did." He looked at her. "What was that you said, hon, about the gate?"

"Oh, just that a few days ago – I think it was the day before the hostage situation – I had to run to the hardware store for some WD-Forty spray. Our galley door had developed a terrific screech when it shut. It was early in the morning, and I was the only one on the boat, so when I left, I locked up. But I didn't lock the gangway gate because it is unnecessary when everything else is locked. Kind of like leaving the picket fence gate unlocked after you lock the house. It's not like someone is going to steal an old two hundred pound anchor off the deck, right? Anyway, even though I didn't lock the gate, I know I latched it. But when I got back from the hardware store, it was unlatched, and the gate was open. It's not the kind of latch that can accidentally come unlocked. So I know someone opened it when I was gone. Nothing was missing or damaged. Nothing was wrong. But I noticed because, even though people have occasionally come onboard outside of cruise hours, it is rare. Even more rare to leave the gate open. People just naturally shut it behind them, especially when they find it latched when they arrived. I looked around for a business card stuck into a door or something, but I didn't find anything. It wasn't a big deal. I wasn't scared or worried. But I noticed, that's all. Do you think it could have anything to do with what happened?"

"Hard to tell. Maybe the hostage taker came onboard to check the layout of the Dreamscape. Or maybe it was just a neighbor kid. In addition to the doors, did you lock the windows?"

Teri looked alarmed, then went pink in her cheeks.

"Well, no, I didn't think of checking them. But they shut with latches. So if they're shut, they're latched. If not, you can usually see some space at the edge. An inch of light coming in the side. I don't remember seeing anything like that. But no, I didn't go up and down the boat and check every window. My God, I don't even know how many of them there are."

"What about the hatches?"

The pink deepened toward red. "Well, I… I guess it's like the windows. They are latched most of the time. But I didn't verify that every hatch was latched. I'd never be able to leave the boat if I had to check every opening."

"If a window is unlatched, can you climb through it?"

"Anybody but a real big guy," Ford said.

Teri's frown deepened as her eyes widened.

"Let's say one of the salon windows was unlatched," I said. "If someone crawled through, would they be able to obtain access to any other interior part of the boat?"

Teri nodded. She looked sick.

"What part?"

"The swing doors to the galley and the dining room don't lock. At the corner of the dining room, there is a hatch and ladder that leads down to the lounge. From there you could get to most of the lower level."

"Including this stateroom where you have some office files and such," I said.

"But I do keep this stateroom door locked. The only other access is the ladder stairs and hatch to the foredeck. But we never use it, so that hatch stays locked. He couldn't have gotten into this room."

"But an intruder could have gotten to most of the rest of the boat. That is, if a salon window were unlatched."

"Even worse," Ford said, looking pale. "Captain Richards never locks the hatch up to the bridge."

"Where does that come down?"

"The salon. The ladder stairs on the wall, midway down, port side." Ford swallowed. "Christ, the guy could have stolen the boat. Not like he could hide it for very long on Tahoe. But still. Think of the liability."

"Where do you keep the ignition key?"

"In the bridge. It hangs in a hidden place just in case a tourist has drunk too much during one of our pier parties."

"Pier party?" I asked.

"It's actually the best business idea we've had yet," Ford said, a bit of a grin coming back onto his face. "We only need one deckhand and the catering service. No captain or chief mate or dock boy. No fuel or operating costs beyond a little electricity. Turns out that landlubbers love to hang out and party on a boat. Some like it even better than the cruises because there's less wind and no fixed amount of time you have to stay on the boat."

"With fewer crewmembers, a wayward guest could poke

around the boat quite a bit without getting attention," I said.

Ford Georges looked at me hard. "What you mean is, the hijacker could have come on board during a pier party and scoped out the boat's layout and whatever else he needed to plan his hijacking."

"Yeah. Did you have a pier party before the hijacking?"

"Goddammit!" Georges shouted. He made a jerk as he said it. Champagne slopped out of his glass and hit the carpet. One of the nearby cats snapped his head around at the sound and stared at the carpet as if looking for a mouse. "Three days before. A big party. Any number of people could have wandered the Dreamscape without calling much attention to themselves." Georges turned a quarter turn, staring at the door to the stateroom, clenching his jaw.

After a minute, Georges spoke. "This picture," he said, gesturing at the photograph in my hand. "Do you know who it is?"

"A man named Nick O'Connell."

"Do you know anything about him? Did he have a record of violent crime?"

"Not on the books," I said. "But he had a reputation as a violent guy."

Ford nodded. "That certainly would fit what I heard about his actions on this boat. I hate to admit it, but I'm kind of glad I wasn't on the boat during the situation. I'm not the typical go-to guy when it comes to situations that require physical courage. But if I'd been here, I might have charged him. It's strange to be offstage when the most significant thing that's ever happened on the boat goes down. It makes me enraged." Ford Georges had a sudden look of discovery on his face. "Maybe the hijacker did a little research and figured out that we wouldn't be here on the day he hijacked the boat. Maybe that figured into his plans."

"Maybe," I said. I pulled out two of my cards and handed one to Teri and one to Ford. "Let me know if you think of anything? Or if you remember where you may have seen this man. Even if you're not sure. Call right away."

"Not to be too dense," Ford said, "but if this guy was the hostage taker, then why such interest? When the bad guy dies, I'd think that law enforcement would be more relaxed about nailing down the details of what happened."

"We probably are more relaxed," I said. "But there are extenuating circumstances that make it critical we understand exactly what happened and why."

Ford nodded. "I see. And you can't tell me just what those circumstances are."

"Someday," I said. "Tell me, please, where do I find Captain Richards and the Chief Mate Allen Paul and the deckhands?"

"Let me get you their contact info." Ford walked over to a file cabinet, opened it, found a file and made notes on a piece of paper. He handed it to me.

I thanked them both and said goodbye. Teri gave Spot one more aggressive hug, and we left.

TWENTY-THREE

"It's our connections to each other that make life worth living," Street said, a statement that seemed unusual coming from a bug scientist.

It had been a very long day. Finally, I was alone with my sweetheart, out on my deck post-barbecued shish kebobs, looking down at the lake and up at the moonless sky. The air was crispy cold with hints of the coming winter. Spot was sitting next to us, leaning against my leg.

"Certainly true regarding my connection to you," I said. "What makes you think it?"

"I was out on my walk," Street said. "There was a family coming toward me on the trail. The parents seemed distant from each other. But their two young girls ran ahead of them. The girls were very engaged with each other. They had these little animal drawings on their faces. 'You're a donkey,' one girl shouted, pointing at the drawing on the other girl's forehead. 'You're a pig,' said the other girl. Then the girl with the pig reached up to the drawing. It turns out they were stick-on drawings. She peeled it off and put it on the other girl and shouted, 'now, you're the pig!'

"It was such a simple thing that gave them enormous pleasure. They ran through the woods, shrieking with delight."

"A connection at its most basic," I said. "It reminds me of talking to Anna. She told me about a school she wants to start. She calls it Reach For The Sky, a Kick-Butt Tech School For Girls."

"Good idea," Street said.

"The thing is, here's this woman who has been through all this trauma. You'd expect her to have the dreariest of attitudes.

But when she starts talking about what she could do for under-privileged girls, she lights up."

"Making a basic connection," Street said.

The stars above were astonishing in their brilliance and their number.

I stood behind Street, holding her to me. "Probably a lot of connections out there. I forget what you said about how many stars there are."

"Astronomers don't really know," Street said. She leaned her head back against my chest. "But they know it's such a large number that it's beyond comprehension. In our galaxy, the Milky Way, there are billions of stars. And the Milky Way is just one of billions of galaxies."

"And each of those uncountable stars is like our sun."

"Sort of. They come in a wide range of types. And because they are different sizes and each has a different combination of gases, they emit different wavelengths of energy. Some are yellower like our sun. Some are bluer. Some shine brightest in the range that is outside of our vision. There are also a lot of unusual stars, neutron stars, white dwarfs, supernova, pulsars, and other strange characters."

"Like a regular community of mostly regular people but with the standard assortment of oddballs and weirdos."

"Yeah. All stars share the same basic characteristics in the sense that each star is a huge collection of gases – mostly hydrogen – that are squeezed so strongly by the star's enormous gravity that the hydrogen atoms fuse together to make helium. And if there is enough size and resulting gravity, the helium atoms fuse together to make other, heavier, atoms. And in the process a little mass is lost in each fusion. The mass is converted into energy, enormous amounts of energy."

"The thing Einstein figured out," I said.

"Important parts of it, yes. His famous equation e equals mc squared describes how much energy you get from that conversion of mass into energy."

"And that is what heats the universe."

"That's what heats the area around the star," Street said.

"I'm missing something?"

"Just that while the stars are very hot, and they keep their local neighborhood nice and toasty, the universe in general is very cold and getting colder."

"Why?"

"Entropy. It's a basic principle of physics. Energy dissipates. It always flows away from areas of concentration. Plus, the universe is expanding really fast. Maybe faster than the speed of light. And another law of physics is that as matter expands it cools off."

"If there's only so much energy, and if it has to occupy a bigger space, the temperature will be cooler?" I said.

"Exactly."

"So entropy basically means that hot things always tend to cool off," I said.

"Well, pretty much, yeah."

We were silent for a bit, staring up at the enormous sky, looking at millions of pinpricks of light that had been twinkling through the universe since the beginning of time.

Street broke the silence. "I think at some root level that people, like all life, tend to draw together as a kind of reaction against entropy. It's as if our connections with each other, our communities, are temporary hotspots in the cooling universe."

"There are," I said, "some things that don't cool off with time." I traced a line from her temple, down her cheek to her neck.

"What would that be?"

"The heat you generate in me." I ran my hands down the sides of her body. Despite her thick clothes, her curves were manifest.

Street turned in my arms and looked up at me. "Well," she giggled, "you could be the exception to the second law of thermodynamics."

"I'm not just a momentary hotspot? Entropy doesn't apply to me?"

"Maybe we better check," Street said. She took hold of the front of my shirt and pulled me into my cabin.

TWENTY-FOUR

In the morning, I headed south into town and turned up Kingsbury Grade. I cruised past the building where Street has her bug lab and turned into my office lot.

Spot and I got out of my Jeep and went inside.

The mail delivery service had stuffed some bills and junk through the slot, but the answering machine light was steady.

I tossed my jacket over the back of the desk chair, loaded the coffeemaker and turned it on. The details of the case were many, but they led to no conclusions. Maybe if I just did some serious detective thinking.

When the machine stopped gurgling, I poured coffee, sat down in my chair and leaned back to a cacophony of squeaking chair mechanics.

If there isn't a rectangle of sunlight coming in the window, Spot normally lies down near the door. But today he walked over and sat next to me, turning his head so he was looking directly at my face from about 18 inches to my left. It's his equivalent of a toy poodle standing on its hind legs in front of you, begging for attention or a treat or both.

"What?" I said.

Spot stared at me. His tail swished the floor. Then he flicked his ears and swung his head to the door. His ears were making their little adjustments. 12 noon, then 1:30, then the left one swiveled to 10 a.m. while the right one hovered at 2 o'clock.

He puffed air through his jowls.

Someone knocked twice.

"Door's open, come in," I said.

A woman walked in. She looked mid-thirties, tallish, and biggish.

Spot had already jumped to his feet and gone around to sniff her.

She pet him, moving with a pronounced lightness as if she were a sprite half her size. She wore a long navy wool coat and under it black boots with heels that gave her a certain elegance and made her biggishness seem comfortable. With her movement came a waft of air that smelled a bit like fresh-cut celery. She had large hands, and on her right little finger a gold ring. Her face was solid, with heavy features. Stage looks. She'd be handsome at a distance.

"Owen McKenna, I'm Anna Quinn." She walked over, leaned over my desk, and reached out her hand and smiled.

I stood up and shook. "Quite a surprise," I said.

Her smile glowed. Her teeth weren't especially straight, and her gums were more substantial than she probably wanted. But she beamed. I'd never before had the sensation that I could feel the warmth in a person's smile. But Anna's smile was like sunshine.

"When I looked you up after you first contacted me," she said, "I learned that you had a big dog." She rubbed the sides of his head.

He wagged.

"Meet Spot," I said.

"Oh, look, he has an ear stud," she said. "Well, well, Spot," she said as she touched the sparkling rhinestone, "don't you have the bling to go with your size."

He wagged harder.

"And what caused the hole in his ear?"

"A run-in with some avalanche-control dynamite."

Anna looked at me, eyes wide. "He was in an explosion?!" She turned to Spot. "Poor baby! You should come home with me. I will be more protective of you!"

Spot pushed forward in her grip and turned so that he was sideways next to her. Then he leaned against her, still wagging. Anna had to put one foot out to brace herself.

"You probably think I'm out of line coming back to the real world," Anna said, "but I can tell you that I haven't felt this free in three years. It is really great!" She held her arms out at an angle and rotated 360 degrees like Audrey Hepburn in Roman

Holiday.

I pointed to my single visitor's chair. "Please."

"Will this hound want to climb into my lap if I sit down?"

"Yes. But he knows it's an unreasonable thought. He'll probably be content just to put his head on you."

"And get more white hair all over this coat," she said as she looked down at the coat which was not so navy now as it had been a few moments before.

"Sorry. I have one of those roller things. We can roll it over you before you go."

She sat, looked at Spot, patted her lap.

Spot immediately stepped forward and leaned against her some more. Anna hugged his head, rubbed around his ears.

"What motivated your appearance?" I asked.

"I finally got level-headed about all of this. It just seems so obvious that the man who tried to kill me was the hijacker. You, of course, are playing it super cautious, not wanting me to take any chances. But all of life is taking chances. And the more I thought about my doubts, the more they were like dandelion seeds in the wind. Every time I held them up to the slightest examination, they were too flimsy to stay put. I also decided that I was tired of being afraid. What's the point of trying to be cautious and protect your life if it's not a life you want to live?"

I nodded.

"You think I'm being careless," she said.

"A bit. But I understand your reasoning. I'd probably do the same thing."

"You'd come out of the woods?"

"Yeah."

"But you think I shouldn't have. Why?"

"I want to know what's going on. When I can't settle a case, when I don't understand what's happening, I go into a protective pattern. My instincts tell me to gather up the critical people and things and bring it all in out of the risky weather. Board up the entrance to the cave, stoke the fire and hold tight until I can figure out exactly what's going on out there."

Anna gave me a blank look. The pleasure that was on her face when she'd walked into my office was gone.

"Do you agree that the man who came after me was almost for certain the hijacker?" she asked.

"Yes."

"So you think that, almost for certain, I'm safe?"

"No."

"Why?" Anna let go of Spot's head and folded her arms across her chest. Indignant. Spot lifted his head to look at her. He sat his rear on the floor and hung his head, eyes droopy. Then he slowly slid his front paws out until his elbows touched the floor and he was lying down. Now Anna's lap was high where it had been low. He lifted his chin up and set it across her thighs. As if she were unaware of what she was doing, Anna rested her hands on him, one on the back of his neck, one on his head. The hand on his head folded one of his ears down flat. It looked painful, but Spot was already taking the deep breaths of sleep.

"The reason I don't think you're safe is that the hijacker may have told others about you and the journal. Either the journal was valuable enough, or the information in it was valuable enough to kill you for it."

"But I knew nothing about the journal."

"Right, but he didn't know that. And we know he didn't work alone. He had an accomplice on the hijacking, a man he may have told about you and the journal."

"The man he threw overboard."

"Right. And he may have had other accomplices that are still alive."

Anna looked frustrated. "So where are you going with this? Outline for me what kind of big risk you see out there in the dark," she said.

"Just that if other people learned about you and the journal, they might be after you."

"Look," she said. "The hijacker killed his helper and took a hostage. Obviously, he was totally wacko. So even if he spun some story about me and the journal to others, what's the chance that they would be that wacko, too?"

"I've learned that the hijacker had a relationship with a militia group," I said. "These guys are not model citizens. You said yourself that he could belong to a gang where their gang identity is spinning knives."

"That was my paranoia talking. The little voice in my head trying to justify why I've been hiding these last three years."

"Where have you been living?"

She hesitated. "I guess there's no reason to keep it a secret anymore, now that I've come out. Fresno. It's a great, sleepy little city in the farming country near the south end of the Central Valley. No one goes there except truckers hauling produce. No one pays it any attention. It's probably the most overlooked big city in California. Perfect for hiding."

"Who knows you're here in Tahoe?"

"Just my friends Lacy Hampton and Ben Merrill. It's Lacy's family vacation home where I'm staying. She's a nurse in Fresno and comes up for two weeks every fall. She drove up a week ago. I just got here last night. And Ben teaches website design at the community college in Fresno. He occasionally consults me on the business side of web design. He's a good guy. There's nothing romantic between us. We just have coffee together. They are the only two people that I've totally confided in about my predicament."

I nodded. I handed her a pen and paper. "Can you give me the address where you're staying?"

Anna scribbled it out and handed it back.

I knew the area. "Up on what we call middle Kingsbury," I said. "Not too far from here. What kind of car are you driving?"

"A Camry. White. Two thousand seven." She gave Spot a pet. "You really think I might still be at risk." She looked a little worried and a lot exasperated. I'd obviously destroyed her mood, her hope.

"Yeah. More now than before."

"Why?"

"Because you came here. Anyone involved in this case would have reason to watch me, my cabin, my office. They could perceive me, rightly or wrongly, to be the biggest threat to their purposes. If they have been watching, then they may already have seen you."

"But you're in the business. Surely you would notice if someone was staking you out."

I shook my head. "That only happens on TV. In the real world, it is very easy to take a bag lunch up into the forest." I pointed out the window. "A person could spend an entire day up above that outcropping of boulders and I'd never know it. Or they could sit in a vehicle across the street in that lot. If they had tinted windows, I would never see them. Or they could be in any number of different businesses, watching out a window. There are a lot of windows with views of this office building."

"Okay, I get it. What do you think I should do? Go back to Fresno?"

"That would be smart. Someone may already have seen you here. But if not, the less time you are in Tahoe, the better. I can follow you until we are far south, and I believe that no one is following. Grace taught you to be prepared," I said. "I think leaving Tahoe would be the best way to be prepared."

"And if I stay? I can only be prepared for certain, narrow situations. When the man came in my room, I had an escape plan. But out in the world, there's not much I can do."

"Yes, there is. Not in the same sense as escaping from a bedroom. But you can be ready for something unexpected."

"How?"

"Notice your surroundings. Look around before you go to your car or get out of your car. Look out the windows before you leave any building. Keep your doors locked. Stay in at night. Never go anyplace alone."

"Well, that last one is impossible. I came up here alone. And Lacy is in Reno shopping today and then meeting a friend for dinner. She said she wouldn't be back until ten or eleven. So I'll be alone until then."

"You could stay with me," I said.

"What, like a babysitter? You must be kidding."

"No, I'm not."

"I'm sure staying with you would be an overreaction," she said.

"Then be ready at all times."

Anna was shaking her head. "Look, I'll be careful. I'm naturally cautious. But if someone runs up and grabs me, there's not much I can do. Besides, I'm a runner. I run away from any little thing. Like when the man came into my bedroom. A regular timid mouse. If someone grabbed me, I'd die of a heart attack."

"There're lots of things you can do. Scream for one. You'd be amazed at how many women don't scream when they're attacked. One of the things they teach you in self-defense class is how to yell and shout at a potential attacker and, if he touches you, to scream. They have you practice it. Most women can't even do it in class at first. The natural tendency is to not call attention to yourself. It requires practice."

"It's not like I can go around practicing screaming."

"You can role-play it in your mind. Like an actor mentally reciting her lines without actually speaking. You envision someone acting threatening, and you envision shouting at him, STOP! DON'T COME CLOSER. I'LL SCREAM! Then you envision screaming if he grabs you."

Anna looked doubtful. "And what then? What if someone grabs me and I scream and he tries to stuff me in the trunk of his car or something?"

"Then you physically attack him."

"That's ridiculous. You don't understand. I'm not a fighter. I'd die of fear. I go limp in the knees at the thought. And even though I'm not a small woman, any man is going to be a lot stronger than me."

"Even a small woman has a good chance of stopping an attacker if she is focused and practiced."

"Mental practice," Anna said. She didn't roll her eyes, but her tone of voice suggested as much.

"Yes. Of course, physical practice is always best. But mental practice is better than nothing."

Anna leaned back in her chair, radiating skepticism. "Okay. What do I do?"

"First thing to remember is this: if a man grabs you, assume that he plans to kill you. He may not, but you have to assume it. It doesn't matter if he has a gun or a knife. Always fight back. It may save your life."

"But I've heard of women getting raped at gunpoint and then being let go. If they'd fought, they might have gotten killed."

"Hypothetically, that's true. But you can't know who is

planning to pull the trigger and who is just using an unloaded gun for show. Fighting might prevent the rape in the first place."

"So how could someone like me fight? Even if the man didn't pull the trigger, he would still overpower me."

"Not if you don't give him the chance. Men might be stronger, but a woman can kill with her hands and feet if she has the presence of mind. Remember the most vulnerable areas on a man. If he's at a bit of a distance, your best weapon is a kick. Women have strong legs. Here, stand up and let me show you how to do a front snap kick."

"Give me a break." Her tone was dismissive. "You want to make me try karate in this office?" She sounded repulsed by my suggestion.

I walked over. "Come on. Stand up."

She remained sitting, Spot's head still on her thigh. "I'm a grown woman. Thirty-five years old. I've never done anything athletic in my life. I'm hardly going to start now, here in this little room."

I reached for her hand, lifted it off Spot's head, pulled. "Up."

"Owen, this is embarrassing me. I'm the bookish type. I could no more kick a person than I could do a handspring."

"If your life is ever in danger, you'll be glad I showed you."

She looked at the ceiling and sighed.

I pulled Spot off her and lifted her up.

"I don't believe I'm doing this," she said as she stood. "I can barely ride a bicycle. I will never be a karate person."

"Don't think of it like karate. Think of it like saving your life."

She breathed heavily.

I moved next to her, standing at her side a foot away, facing the same direction.

"Are you right-handed?"

She nodded.

"Okay. A front snap is exactly as it sounds," I said. "There's no wind up, no telegraphing intent. You just raise your right knee up waist-high and snap your foot up and out in one smooth motion. Aim for his groin." I bent, grabbed her right knee, and lifted. "Up to waist level. That's right. Now snap your foot out."

"You must be kidding."

I was still holding her knee. "Snap your foot out," I repeated.

She made a limp snap, lost her balance, and fell to the left, away from me. I caught her, but just barely.

"That was good," I said. "Now let's do it again."

She made another weak effort, lost her balance again and had to hop backward a couple of steps to keep from falling.

I kept working with her, and she practiced kicking the air in front of us. She stopped.

"Okay, I get it," she said.

"No, you don't. Keep kicking."

With a big breath of frustration, she kicked again.

"It is important to keep your balance, and it is very important to lift your toes up so you make contact with the underside, the ball of your foot. If not, you can break your toes."

She kept stopping, and I kept making her go on.

Ten times. Fifteen times. Twenty times.

"You can practice this any time," I said. "The more familiar it becomes, the more effective it will be."

"Like Grace said," Anna said. "Be prepared."

"Exactly. Now if your kick doesn't stop him and he grabs you, you can still stomp down on the top of his foot, up high where the bones rise up toward his ankle."

I took off my shoe, and we practiced the foot-stomping move with my shoe as a stand-in for my foot. Twenty times.

I continued. "Most men expect that you will cave when they grab you. They tend not to control your hands the way they should. In most situations, you will have a good chance of reaching their face."

Anna scoffed, "Like scratching them is going to stop an attack."

"No, you don't scratch. You take your thumbs to their eyes."

She scrunched up her face. "That's disgusting."

"Not as disgusting as what they are planning to do to you."

"I just push my thumbs into their eyes?"

"No. Don't think of it like pushing. Think more explosive.

You jab your thumbs and rip and gouge. You're not trying to apply pressure. You're trying to take their eyeballs out. Most women have the thumb strength to remove a man's eyeball, and no man will continue an attack if you do that."

Anna shuddered.

"If you can't get to their eyes, you may be able to punch their throat. Let me show you how to do an elbow punch."

I lifted her arm, bent it, then had her swing her elbow in an upward arch, forward and backward. We practiced until she could make it an explosive move.

"An elbow to the Adam's apple will traumatize your attacker. If the blow is hard enough, it can crush the larynx and be life-threatening. You can also strike the throat with the edge of your hand. Or you can make a fist with your knuckles extended and punch him in the throat. And if your attacker ever gives you the opportunity, never pass up the chance to kick him in the throat or face or temple. A woman's kick is a formidable weapon."

"And you don't think any of these moves will cause an attacker to shoot me."

"They will absolutely cause some attackers to shoot you, the same attackers who will shoot you anyway after they rape you."

Anna spent some time thinking.

"Let me see if I have this straight," she said. "Even if an attacker has a weapon, I ignore it. If he gets too close but hasn't grabbed me yet, I yell STOP! DON'T COME ANY CLOSER! If he does come closer, I kick him in the groin or the knee. If he grabs me, I scream as I try to gouge out his eyes. Then I chop him in the throat or stomp the top of his foot."

"You are a good student," I grinned.

"I have some thinking to do," she said. "I think I'll go now. And yes, I'll be careful and watchful." She walked to the door, then stopped and came back.

"Owen?"

"Yeah?"

"I know I'm a difficult student. But you are doing an amazing job of hanging in there with me. Thanks." She raised up on her toes, kissed my cheek, then left.

TWENTY-FIVE

I found the condo where Captain Frank Richards lived on the North Shore near Carnelian Bay. It was part of two six-unit buildings on a hill set back from the expensive waterfront houses. The developer had designed it with the entrance road and guest parking area on the lake side of the condos so that no trees would ever grow up and obscure the view.

The address that Ford Georges had written down said that Richards's unit number was B-2.

I pulled into an entrance road that made a few nice but unnecessary curves around a couple of artificial mounds covered in thick sod. I parked in a spaced labeled B-2 Guest. I walked up a path made of terra cotta pavers. It wound around some boulders that had been stacked up in an unlikely pile. Then it wound around some raised flower beds built of stacking landscape stones. As I got close to the buildings, the path curved this way and that between some small trees that had been put in where, probably, some big trees had been taken out.

I paused to appreciate the spectacular view of the blue lake with Freel Peak, Tahoe's highest mountain, looming 4600 feet over the South Shore, 28 miles distant.

The condo Richards lived in was the second from the left on the right building. The man who answered my knock was gaunt and grizzled, tall and skinny, with large, brown, scratchy-looking sideburns. He looked vaguely like a large bottle brush.

"Captain Richards?" I asked.

He nodded. "Frank," he said.

"Owen McKenna." We shook. "I was the man who…"

"Not like I'm ever gonna forget your name," he interrupted. "Worst day of my life. The WORST. And it was all about getting you out to my boat. You figure out what really happened, yet?"

"Working on it," I said. I handed him my card.

Frank motioned me in, and we sat in two chairs that faced the view.

Frank pointed to his beer. "Get you something to drink?"

"No thanks."

"My day off," he said, taking a sip. "This helps me." He set the beer down. "Two guys down. One of them murdered. Your girlfriend almost murdered. I still get shaky when I think about it. Can't sleep." He took another sip. "All on my watch."

"Not your fault," I said.

"The guy told me to cut my engines. I was so shocked, I froze. Couldn't think. Next thing I know, he's yelling at me on the phone. I finally came to my senses and pulled back the throttles. But it was too late. The hijacker threw that guy overboard just to teach me a lesson. A man died all because I was too slow to think."

I shook my head. "You weren't the reason he tossed his helper into the lake. He planned to do it."

Frank looked at me. "You really think so?" His eyes were the kind of red and swollen you get from hours of misery. His lower lip twitched.

"I know so. The hijacker brought two chains. He planned for two victims. You can let yourself off the hook."

Frank turned and looked out the window. "What do I do now? How do I get past this?"

"Give it time."

He didn't move. In time he said, "I'll try."

"Do you recall seeing this man before?" I handed him the photo of Nick O'Connell.

Frank studied the photo, then shook his head. "I've thought about it in the time since. Like, what if he'd once been a passenger on a previous cruise. The thing is, you start wondering that, pretty soon you're thinking that the guy was wearing a wig and a fake beard and if you take them off in your mind, he could be practically anybody." He looked at it some more, then handed the photo back.

"Did you notice anything unusual in the days before the

hijacking?"

"How do you mean?"

"Anything. Maybe you found some passenger poking around where he shouldn't be. It could be someone else, nothing like the hijacker. A woman. A boy."

"An accomplice," he said.

"Yeah."

He thought about it. "No. Every day was the same. But Teri Georges – she and her husband Ford are the owners – she did ask me if I'd come on the boat one morning when we didn't have a cruise scheduled. I guess she'd left the boat to run some errands, and when she came back, the gangway gate was unlatched."

"Had you?"

"No. I had run down to Reno to get some stuff you can't get up at the lake."

"What about your deckhands? What kind of guys are they?"

Frank made a little shrug. "Regular, I guess. Andy and Warren Wellesley are twin brothers who graduated high school last spring and are taking a year off before college. After we close up shop for the winter, they plan to work at one of the ski resorts."

"Where are they from?"

"Bay Area. Somewhere on the peninsula." Frank held my card by the edges, flipped it over, flipped it over again.

"Good guys?" I said.

"Straight as arrows. I heard them talking to Joshua once. He's our other deckhand. Joshua Tolman. He's more of a normal kid. Been in a little trouble, I guess, but nothing more than I was when I was a kid. Anyway, Andy and Warren were telling him that they'd never drunk alcohol and never smoked pot. It fits with their personalities. They're the kind of guys that future mothers-in-law dream of."

"Could you imagine them giving information about the boat to anyone?"

"You mean, if someone approached them and started asking questions?"

"Yeah," I said.

Frank shook his head. "If someone tried to compromise Andy and Warren, they're the kind of kids who would come right to me about it. If I wasn't around, they'd tell Ford and Teri. Of that, I'm sure."

"What about the third deckhand, Joshua?"

"Well, he's not the straight-up kid that the other two are. But still, he lives with his parents, and all he cares about is girls and skiing and skateboarding."

"What if someone offered him money for information about the boat? Which doors are kept locked. How many people are on the bridge when you sail. Stuff like that?"

Frank shook his head. "I can't see Joshua for it. He even drinks milk at lunch. You ever seen a bad person drink milk at lunch? Honest to God, I've noticed that over the years. Joshua may have gotten some driving tickets and been cited for smoking weed, but people of questionable morality always drink something other than milk."

"One last question. Your Chief Mate Allen Paul. Do you know him well?"

Frank thought about it. "Absolutely. We never met before we started working together, but our working time has been close. Not to put too fine a point on it, but a captain and his chief mate are like a surgeon and his chief operating room nurse. You have to totally rely on your second in command. Total trust. Total understanding. You know what the other person wants and you give it to them before they even ask the question."

"Then you would probably know if Allen saw or noticed anything unusual in the last week or two as well?"

"Probably," Frank said. "I would say that until the hijacker, it was life-as-normal for all of us. Look, Owen. Let me tell you something. Of our entire crew, I'm probably the one who's less rock-solid than the others. I'm not saying I'm a bad guy. I'm a good guy. I'm just saying that it's human nature to try different things. More than the others, my life has been kind of messy. Broken relationships with women. A string of different jobs, not much common ground to them. I've always been a bit of a drifter. This job working for Ford and Teri is the best job I've ever had. I'm really lucky that I got it. I'd had some time on a tugboat on the Bay, and I happened to meet Ford and Teri after they'd bought this boat but before they shipped it up from SoCal. The timing was perfect and, frankly, they didn't know anyone else who knew something about running a large boat. Pure serendipity.

"Anyway," Frank continued. "While I've had a bit of a checkered past, I'm reliable and trustworthy. What I'm saying is that our other crew members are probably even more reliable and trustworthy than I am."

I thanked Frank and left.

Over the course of the next two hours I found and met Chief Mate Allen Paul at his house. I also caught Joshua Tolman and Warren Wellesley together just as they were leaving the Tolman house on their way to pick up Andy Wellesley at the Sierra Nevada College Library where Andy was looking up employment information for the various ski resorts.

After talking to all of them except Andy, I discovered that they were exactly as Captain Frank had described them, seemingly solid and trustworthy. All were forthcoming, and not one of them was able to add anything to my investigation.

I was back to my starting point.

TWENTY-SIX

That night, after Spot and I had gone home and eaten dinner, the phone rang.

"Hello?"

"It's Anna. Okay, I'm being hyper-vigilant like you said."

"Good."

"Earlier, when I came back to Lacy's house, there was a vehicle down the road. A guy was standing behind it, leaning in the back, like he was looking in his toolbox or something. He had long white hair and a big white moustache. But he wasn't real old. Maybe middle fifties. Thin and fit."

"Have you ever seen him before?"

"No. Anyway, I went out a few minutes ago to get my book that I'd left in my car. The vehicle was still there, just down the street. The neighbor's outdoor light was on. It was hard to see because there was reflection on the windshield. But his white hair and moustache were obvious. He's just sitting in his car in the dark."

"Are the neighbors home?"

"I don't think so. The house is dark. Only the outside light is on."

"You think the man is waiting for them to come home?" I asked.

"I would guess not. Earlier when it was light out, I saw some flyers stuffed into their front door. And on their sidewalk was a phone book in one of those plastic sleeves. It looks like they've been gone awhile."

"The woman you're staying with, is she home, yet?"

"No," Anna said. "Lacy called ten minutes ago to check in and say that she was leaving Reno. But I don't know how long that means she'll be."

"You're on middle Kingsbury. Another hour and ten minutes."

"Any chance you saw the license plate on the vehicle?"

"No. It's dark and it's down the street a ways. I should mention that it's the only other house on the street. So I'm pretty much all alone up here except for that stranger."

"What kind of vehicle is he in?"

"I don't know. One of those old, open-air things like what they use on a safari. Only, we're talking fifty years ago. Sixty years ago. It's rusted and ungainly-looking. It has a cloth top that doesn't fit properly. Probably homemade. Knobby tires. Gas can hanging off the back."

"Like an old Land Cruiser?"

"I have no idea what that is."

"Are your doors and windows locked?"

"Yes. Well, I think so. I just have the one key, and I locked the door behind me when I came in."

"How many bathrooms are there?"

"That's a weird question. Two, why?"

"I want you to double check the locks on the doors, then close the curtains and turn on several lights, inside and out, including the lights in just one bathroom. Turn on the water in the bathroom and let it run. Then lock the bathroom door knob and shut it from the outside."

"Oh, Christ, Owen. You're scaring me."

"Turn your cellphone on vibrate only, then quietly slip out the back door. Go back into the forest and wait for me to pull up. Don't come out until you actually see me and Spot. Hurry."

"Owen, aren't you being alarmist?"

"Anna, go now. Hurry!" I hung up.

Spot was already looking at me, his brow furrowed and ears perked up at my tone of voice.

"Let's go, largeness."

He jumped to his feet, and we ran out of the cabin.

I drove down the East Shore, running the Jeep up to 75 where the highway was empty and slowing to 55 where there was traffic. When I came to the South Shore, I turned on Kingsbury Grade and raced up the curves. Halfway up the mountain I found the turnoff, followed a twisty narrow road and made another turn onto the dead-end street that Anna's friend lived on. The mini-neighborhood's two houses were down by the end, one on the left that was dark except for a single light under the peak of the garage roof. Down about 60 yards on the right was Anna's friend's house. Light glowed in several of the windows.

I pulled into the drive next to Anna's Camry and came to a quick stop in front of the open garage, my headlights shining inside. One side of the garage was cleared for a single car. The floor on the other side was crowded with a snowblower, gas can, recycle bins, two mountain bikes, a kayak, and yard tools. In the corner leaned multiple skis and snowboards. Next to the corner was the doorway into the house. The door was kicked in.

Where the knob and deadbolt had been was splintered wood and hanging screws. One large shard of wood leaned out across the doorway.

I jumped out of the Jeep, jerked open the back door to let Spot out and sprinted in through the garage. Light spilled out past the broken door.

"Anna!" I shouted as I pulled the splintered wood aside. "Anna!" There was no answer.

Spot pushed his head in next to me.

"Spot! Find the suspect!" I gave him a smack on his rear. He ran past me into the house, his head high, air scenting. But he stopped, swiveled his head left and right, turned and looked at me. Which meant that no one was currently in the house.

The doorway brought me into the open area between the kitchen and the entry. Lights were on in the kitchen, but the entry was dark. Spot looked toward the kitchen. A quick glance revealed that it was empty. To the left, a hallway went down toward the bedrooms. Light shone from a doorway at the end of the hall. The sound of running water permeated the house. I ran down the hall and pushed open the door. The knob and latch were unbroken. The shower was running, and the rug was pushed up against the bathtub as if someone had sprinted out of the bathroom. I turned off the water to kill the noise.

I glanced in the dark bedrooms, but they appeared empty.

I ran back to the kitchen. It was neat and clean. The only thing out of place was the woodblock knife holder on the counter near the chopping block. It lay on its side, all the knives spilled out. Several of them sprawled across the counter. Two were on the floor. I counted the slots. Four narrow, three wide. Then I counted the knives. Four narrow, two wide. If the holder had been full, then one of the big knives was missing.

Maybe Anna grabbed it to protect herself as soon as she heard the intruder. Maybe the intruder took the knife from her.

Just to be sure, I ran out the back door. Spot followed me. I called out Anna's name as I dialed 911. She didn't respond.

When the dispatcher answered, I gave a fast report. The dispatcher said a patrol unit would arrive soon.

I hung up, ran back inside and looked in the bedrooms. Two were dark. One was lit. One of the dark ones was messy and strewn with lots of personal effects. The mess from a search is nothing like the mess from someone who doesn't put everything away. This mess indicated owner rather than guest. This bedroom was Lacy's.

The lit bedroom was neatly made up. There was a small roller suitcase on the floor. I unzipped it and opened the flap. I didn't want freshly laundered clothes. I needed something Anna had worn. To one side was a cloth bag that didn't seem fresh like the other clothes. Inside was a T-shirt and a pair of jeans. I pulled out the shirt, returned to the back door of the house, and called Spot.

When he came, I put the shirt on his nose. "Smell the shirt!" I said to him. I put excitement in my voice.

Spot looked at me, realizing what I wanted.

I pushed the shirt against his nose again.

"Smell the shirt and find the victim!" I pointed him out the back door and gave him a pat.

He trotted out behind the house while I held the back door open to watch. He looped around a pine, went past a Manzanita bush, took a big turn to the left, then came back to the house. He pushed past me, went inside and down to Anna's bedroom. I told him how smart he was.

I called Street and explained what was happening. "A woman

from Fresno named Lacy Hampton is driving back from Reno to her vacation house on Kingsbury. She's going to find that her houseguest Anna Quinn has disappeared, probably kidnapped, her house is damaged, and when she gets here it will be full of cops." As I said it, a siren rose in the distance.

"You need help," Street said.

"Yeah. Please. I don't know if Lacy has friends in Tahoe. If so, they may be fellow vacation home owners and are probably out of town."

"It'll take me a bit to get out of here."

"Thanks so much," I said. I gave her the address, then went outside to the driveway to wait for the cops.

Something sparkled in the faint light near the curve. I walked over and picked up a cell phone. It was severely scratched and one end was crushed as if someone had stepped on it. I opened it up. The screen stayed dark. I pressed the button to turn it on. Nothing happened. The battery seemed secure. My guess was that it was Anna's phone. Her attacker found it and stomped it hard enough to kill it.

An hour later, Diamond and a deputy and two crime scene technicians were at the house while Street sat with Lacy in the kitchen drinking coffee. Lacy put on a good face, but you could see her shake. I knew that when Street left, Lacy would fall apart. But Street had made a house full of cops tolerable for the moment.

I called Agent Ramos and filled him in on the details of what happened.

"No sign of the white-haired man?" he said.

"No."

"Is the vehicle she described around?"

"No."

"Do you have an idea of who may have taken her?"

"Other than the white-haired man, no," I said.

"Have Sergeant Martinez call me when he's done," he said.

We hung up.

I found Diamond and told him that Ramos wanted a call.

Diamond nodded and kept working.

An hour later, Diamond gave his okay for Lacy to leave and she went with Street to Street's condo. Diamond and the Douglas County deputies stayed behind to finish their business.

I was driving away as my phone rang.

TWENTY-SEVEN

"Hey, honey bunch," a woman said when I answered. The voice was warm and smooth and had the polished, rounded tones of a professional actor. Which meant Glenda Gorman, the non-actor, ace reporter for the Herald. Her casual tone told me that she hadn't been listening to her scanner, didn't yet know about Anna and Lacy and the man with white hair and moustache.

"Glennie," I said. I was having trouble shifting from Anna's kidnapping. But if I didn't want Glennie to pick up on the stress, I had to speak with normal voice and normal words. "Since when am I honey bunch?"

"Standard nomenclature for men in the back of my black book."

"I rate inclusion in the black one?" I turned off of Lacy's neighborhood street and onto Kingsbury Grade.

"The back of it's for the men who are taken but should have met me first. I'm calling with something you might find interesting."

"Okay," I said, knowing that with Glennie every favor was expected to be returned in kind with information. "All ears."

"Our advertising director at the Herald showed me an unusual classified ad that ran this morning. Made me think of you. I'll read it, and you'll know what I mean. It says, 'I have information about Grace Sun's daughter. Meet me on the beach-side lawn at Valhalla. Six a.m. tomorrow.'"

"Why do you think I'd be interested?"

"C'mon, Owen. You think I don't have sources? I know that the hijacking was about the murderer of Grace Sun."

I realized that there was no point in protesting. "Valhalla is the grand hall on the Tallac Historic Site, right?" I said, still trying to sound casual, chatty. "Where people get married. I remember the stone fireplace that is so big you can walk inside the opening. But I'm trying to remember where the turnoff is."

"If you come around the South Shore and head out toward Emerald Bay, the turnoff is just past Camp Richardson."

"Got it," I said. "Any idea about who placed the ad?" I asked.

"No. I asked our receptionist and she said there was an envelope under the door when she came to work yesterday. It had the ad typed out and more than enough cash to pay for it. Like right out of a spy movie. Because it was unusual to get an anonymous ad, they ran it by the publisher who said there was no policy requiring an ID on the person placing the ad. They didn't see any legal reason why the ad couldn't be run. On one hand, they thought they should contact law enforcement. On the other hand, they didn't want to infringe on anyone's civil liberties."

"The paper takes its responsibilities as a member of the press seriously," I said. I cruised past my dark office building, came to the bottom of the grade and turned north toward home.

"Yeah. Anyway, now you can investigate and tell me what you learn."

"You are a bold woman, Glennie. The Tallac Historic Site is out of the South Lake Tahoe City limits. I'll contact Sergeant Bains at El Dorado County."

"Oh." She paused. "Hey, say hi to him, will you?" Glennie's voice sounded wistful. I remembered their short, intense relationship from the previous spring.

"Will do."

"You think you'll go to Valhalla tomorrow morning?" Glennie asked. "See who turns up?"

"Might be a good idea. But I have to ask that you don't come."

"If I do, I'll stay back. Don't worry. I won't mess anything up." She said it in a jaunty way.

"Glennie, I hear that tone and I worry that you don't really mean it. I should tell you that I think the guy who placed the ad might be dangerous. Any person who would want to come to meet him might be dangerous as well. And it's still dark at that hour this time of year. You could regret it."

"Okay, I promise that I won't come close. Is that good enough?"

"Yeah. Thanks."

"And you'll reward my reserve by telling me everything you learn," she said.

"Yes, if I don't think there will be dangerous repercussions. No, if I think it could put you at risk."

"But you'll tell me eventually," she said. "After any risk has died down."

"Yes, but only because I understand that that is a condition you'll put on keeping your distance tomorrow morning."

"You are so onto me. I like perceptive men."

"Thanks for the tip, Glennie."

"Sure. What's with the daughter, anyway? Probably most women who get murdered have kids, and half of those kids are daughters. Is this one special?"

"Yeah," I said.

"And that's all you're going to say."

"Yeah."

We said goodbye and hung up.

TWENTY-EIGHT

I couldn't sleep. I'd told Anna to stay undercover. Even so, I knew that she'd come to Tahoe because of a chain of events that I set in motion.

I beat myself up for hours, wrestling the sheets, gritting my teeth. I got out of bed and paced. When I tried sleeping again, it felt like pressure was building in my head. I finally got up for good at 4:30 a.m. I gave Spot some dog food to nibble while I drank a two fast cups of coffee. Spot looked at his food with suspicion, then looked at me with melancholy.

"I know. Wretched, miserable pretend food. But if you actually had to chase down an elk or something for your breakfast, you would appreciate it a little more."

He turned back and looked down at his food, then lay down and sighed.

We left in the dark.

While Spot is usually an asset when I need to make an impression on somebody, he is a detriment to any undercover operation. I knew I would be engaging in the latter, but depending on how things worked out, I might need the former as well. So I brought him along.

We drove south down 50 and into South Lake Tahoe. The rest of the Tahoe world may have been asleep, but the Stateline hotels were brightly lit. Although it was still a couple of months away, two of them had signs advertising coming concerts for Thanksgiving weekend, the traditional beginning of ski and snowboard season.

I headed across the line to the California side, drove through South Lake Tahoe, turned right at the Y and headed out toward Emerald Bay.

The Valhalla turnoff was just past Camp Richardson as Glennie had said, but I thought it would be best to approach from a less predictable direction. I continued on another quarter mile or so and parked near the Taylor Creek Visitor Center. I let Spot out, and we headed down the dark path, away from the highway, into the black forest. I held onto Spot's collar as we went past the stream profile chamber where you can view the creek from underground and watch the Kokanee salmon and rainbow trout swim by at eye level.

Spot didn't hesitate as we walked through the darkness, his night-vision nose and ears filling in where his eyes left off. I took his lead, blindly thinking that he wouldn't get me into trouble. But I put my free arm out in an effort to detect trees and branches before they knocked me down or ripped out my eyes.

The forest near the Tallac Historic Site has multiple trails, fun for beach-goers and mansion-tour-takers to explore during the day, but confusing at night. At one point we came to a vague opening in the woods, which I took to be a split in the path. I was lost.

"Okay, largeness," I whispered. "You decide."

Spot pulled to the left, so I followed.

We curved left and right and left again. Soon, the world opened up.

Through an opening in the woods was the big black lake under a star-filled sky. We stepped through some brush and went down several feet to sand. The beach on this part of the shore is a narrow strip when the water is high in the spring. But in the fall, just before the onslaught of snow begins, the lake is at its ebb, and there is plenty of sand next to the frigid water.

I guessed the time to be about 5:30 a.m., a half hour before the predicted action. The lake was a huge black swatch with a 75-mile-long ring of faint, twinkling lights, sparser to the west and northeast sides where much of the shore was park and wilderness. The neighborhoods to the southeast climbed up the Kingsbury Grade and Zephyr Heights hillsides like a modern American version of the French Riviera. Large vacation homes with broad decks stacked up three, four and five levels high were anchored into the steep slopes. Across the far north reaches of the water was a continuous curve of lights twinkling from homes and businesses 22 miles distant, from Incline Village on the right to Tahoe City on the left.

The early morning air was chilly. The lake's humidity had washed over the woods and left a layer of hoarfrost on the bushes and the beach that was now visible in the thin light of the stars. Spot pulled his head down to sniff the ground. I stared, trying to see if I could perceive footprints. Nothing was visible except some faint marks in the frost that may have been raccoon footprints tracing an ambling pattern down the beach.

We walked east toward town, toward Valhalla. I didn't want to get too close and scare anyone off. But it was so dark, and we were still far enough away that I thought it was okay to stay out of the forest for a bit.

I kept watch on the woods to the right. When a dark opening appeared, I stared, willing my eyes to sense something. There were some short steps up from the beach. We walked up. In the darkness was another opening of sorts in the forest. I could just make out the outlines of a large building. The Baldwin Estate, a massive log home and the first of three early twentieth century houses that made up the Tallac Historic Site.

Spot and I stood motionless, waiting, watching, listening. And for Spot, sniffing. I tried sniffing, too, but all I could detect was cold humid lake air mixed with the scents of pine and fir.

Nothing appeared. We continued along a path.

After a few minutes, we came to another mansion, this one bigger and more modern in design but still from the same period. The Pope Estate.

We continued on through the darkness.

There was another opening in the forest. The Heller Estate, with its grand rustic hall named Valhalla. Around Valhalla are old-growth Ponderosa pine, giant trees that, thanks to the foresight of Santa Anita Racetrack founder Lucky Baldwin, were spared in the clear-cut that took nearly all of Tahoe's forests and reconfigured the wood as reinforcements for hundreds of miles of mining tunnels under Virginia City.

I pulled Spot behind one of those Ponderosas, and we waited. Periodically, I peeked around the tree, looking for movement on the grand lawn between Valhalla and the lake.

Other than the vast darkness, there was nothing to see but a few distant lights flickering through the trees over at the cabins of Camp Richardson.

Nothing moved, and there was no sound other than the waves that made a gentle lapping in the darkness, a soft murmur like the song the mermaid Lorelei sang as she lured sailors to their death on the Rhine.

If Valhalla had any beautiful feminine spirits wandering the grounds since the roaring '20s, I would have to rely on Spot to detect them.

The ad had given no specifics of location other than the lawn in front of me. I imagined that any people meeting would walk out in the middle of the lawn, the better to be seen in the darkness.

I'd worn a dark jacket and hat. By staying close to the tree, I thought I would remain incognito to all except another dog. And if someone brought a dog to the meeting, Spot would give me advance notice.

If anyone coming stayed off in the trees like me, I'd never see them. But then, neither would the person who placed the ad. It made sense that a person responding to the ad would wander around looking for their contact, perhaps calling out a 'Hello, anybody there?'

The air was still and quiet enough that I would likely hear their words over the lapping waves.

I paid close attention as 6:00 a.m. approached. Except for the sound of a few vehicles out on the distant highway, there was no indication of any person.

It seemed that the person placing the ad would likely wait in an obvious location. How else to let a potential purchaser of information know where to go? But I saw no one.

Nor did I see Glennie, though I assumed that she was out there, probably sitting and shivering in her car.

By twenty after, I started to wonder if I should walk out and pose as someone responding to the ad. The downsides were obvious. It could be dangerous if someone was lurking, waiting to leap out and harm the person who showed up. Another possibility would be that I'd find the person who placed the ad and, while talking to him or her, scare off the person the ad was intended to attract. And I wanted to know who would be attracted as much as the identity of the person who placed the ad.

I waited longer. Maybe the person who placed the ad was waiting in a warm vehicle on the drive at the back side of Valhalla, watching with binoculars, disappointed that no one responded to the ad. Although I noticed as I had driven down the highway earlier, the Forest Service gate at the entrance to Valhalla was shut and, presumably, locked.

In most ways, it made sense that no one would show. Even though the Herald was the biggest paper in Tahoe, there were locals who didn't read it, and many tourists probably never even saw it. The chance that the ad was seen by the intended person were small at best. I kept waiting. No one ever came.

At 6:30 Spot and I walked out from behind my tree. In case the ad writer was still waiting, I strolled down the lawn for all to see me. I paid attention to Spot, wondering if he would suddenly swing his head toward a scent. But he just maintained the standard countenance he exhibits in the dark, ears forward, nose sniffing aggressively, his head swinging left and right.

After crossing the lawn, I turned to go down to the beach. The sky was pinking to the east, and it threw oscillating magenta reflections onto the lapping waves. I strolled down the frosty sand toward the Beacon Restaurant, then about-faced and headed back west, toward Kiva Beach.

I didn't see the body until Spot made a sudden look toward the water and pulled me off balance.

The man was face up in the water, eyes open, arms straight out from his sides, legs spread wide. Even in the faint dawn, I could see the ugly hole in the center of his chest, black with blood.

The body bobbed head-first against the shore just below the grassy picnic area. His long hair, undulating in the waves, was ghostly white. His out-sized, walrus moustache was white, too. It was likely that he was the man watching Anna from the street the previous evening.

I put in a call to 911, and because Spot doesn't like dead

bodies, took him over to the lawn and waited.

When I was done explaining to the 911 dispatcher, I called Agent Ramos. He sounded awake and alert despite the early hour.

"Got something that may be connected to the hijacking," I said. I explained about the ad in the paper and how I came to find a body on the beach. He said he'd be over in about an hour.

Two El Dorado Sheriff's deputies showed up first. I showed them the body and told them what I knew.

Sergeant Bains showed up a bit later, a model of what a sergeant should be. With a sharp combination of smarts, knowledge, and people skills, he took charge of the scene without any firm words, and the other cops seemed pleased to do exactly what he asked as if they wanted nothing more than to earn his respect and praise.

I explained about the ad and showed him where the body was.

He put his men to work, and I gave them space. Ten minutes later he came over to where I sat with Spot on the bank where the Valhalla lawn broke and went down to the beach.

"An ad seems an unreliable way to find someone," he said. "Did you just happen to come upon it?"

"No. Glennie Gorman called and told me about it."

"Oh. How is that girl?"

"Same old Glennie," I said.

Bains and she had met each other during the avalanche case, dated intensely for a time, but then pulled back from each other. My sense was that Bains would have liked to stay connected. But Glennie was high-strung and high-energy, and it would take an unusual man to keep her happy for very long.

"Kind of miss her," Bains said.

"Anybody would," I said.

We heard someone approach and turned to see Agent Ramos walking across the grass, squinting against the morning sun, carefully lifting his polished shoes up and down to minimize the effects of moisture from the melted frost.

We all shook. Then Bains explained what they'd found.

"The victim is an unidentified male, approximately fifty-five to sixty, his pockets empty. He suffered severe trauma to his chest.

It appears that something large penetrated his chest from front to back, entering through the sternum and exiting just to the left of the spine."

"Shot with a shotgun slug?" Ramos said.

"Probably not," Bains said. "The entrance hole looks to be an inch or more. Larger than even an eight-gauge shotgun slug, not that anyone uses eight-gauge anymore. And if the victim had been shot with a shotgun slug, the exit wound would have been extensive. As it is, the exit is not much messier than the entrance wound. Never seen anything like it. The body was also in the water, so the cause of death could technically be drowning. But I doubt it. It looks like whatever penetrated his chest may have gone directly through his heart."

"Let's have a look," Ramos said. He bent over, wiped the dew off his shoes, then headed down the beach.

The deputies stood near the body, which they'd pulled out of the water and up onto the sand. The body was face up.

Ramos pulled up on the creases of his trousers and squatted down to take a look.

"Could be the white-haired man that Anna Quinn described before she was snatched," Ramos said as he studied the entrance wound. "Roll him so I can see his back?" he said, obviously reluctant to get his nice clothes wet and dirty.

The deputies each took hold of the body, one at the shoulder and one at the hip. They lifted it up onto its side.

Ramos looked at the exit wound and frowned. "I've never seen anything like it, either, Bains."

"Notice how the flesh projects both rearward and forward," Bains said. "If a projectile went all the way through, it would just project rearward."

"Looks like somebody killed him with a stake," I said. "Then he wanted to retrieve the murder weapon. Maybe it didn't protrude far enough out the back side to grab. So he pulled it back out from the front."

"That would take some strength and some guts," Ramos said. He used his finger to draw a diagram in the sand. I saw what he was getting at.

"A stake through the sternum would be caught by the

fragments of shattered bone," he said, "all angling back, making it nearly impossible to pull the stake out the way it came."

Bains looked at me. "Be like getting a barbed fish hook in you. It can't go in reverse. You have to push it on through the flesh to get it out."

I nodded.

"But," Ramos continued, "if there was nothing to grab on the back side, the killer would have no choice but to pull from the front, maybe placing his foot on the victim's chest as he yanked it out. That would explain the flesh going both ways."

Bains looked a little sick.

Ramos stood up, brushed his pants off. "At least, we have a clue where to start looking," Ramos said.

"What's that?" I said.

"The victim is Davy Halstead, leader of the Red Blood Patriots."

I reached down and pulled up on the right sleeve of the body's shirt. The blue squiggly lines were similar to what I remembered from Nick O'Connell's tattoo. Like two infinity symbols, one over the other.

"Militia tattoo," Ramos said. "Probably all the Red Bloods have it." He turned to Bains. "Sergeant, the Red Blood Patriots are in your county. Let's you and I compare notes on this."

Bains nodded.

I said, "Makes it look like the Red Bloods were involved in Anna Quinn's kidnapping."

Ramos nodded.

"Do you have enough information about the Red Blood Patriot's world to know where to look for her?" I asked.

"If we find probable cause, yes." He glanced down at the body of Davy Halstead. "We'll see if this body provides any evidence. I'm not optimistic." Ramos looked back at me. "And your next move?"

"Breakfast."

The van arrived to take the body away.

"Let's keep the victim's identity private for the next day or so," Ramos said. "We don't technically know the ID for sure, anyway."

Bains looked at the deputies, then at me. We all nodded.

"Where are you parked?" Ramos asked me.

"Over by the Taylor Creek Visitor Center."

He looked at my dog.

"I don't need a ride," I said. "I'm happy to walk. But thanks for the thought."

He nodded.

Glennie Gorman appeared over by the Valhalla grand hall. She walked across the lawn, nodded and exchanged a few words with Agent Ramos as they passed each other. I walked up to meet her. She pet Spot, then gestured at the men sliding the gurney with the body on it into the van. "Looks like I missed some excitement."

"A dead body. No one else showed."

"Murdered?"

"Looks like it. Has a good-sized hole in his chest."

"Gunshot?" she said.

I shook my head. "Looks more like he had a stake driven through his chest."

Glennie's eyes grew very large. "Do you think he was killed by the person who placed the want-ad?"

"Maybe. Maybe not. Maybe he placed the ad. I've told you everything I know about the situation."

Bains walked up at that moment.

"Hi Glennie. Long time."

Glennie smiled. "Has it been that long? I guess so. I have such clear memories." Slight pause. "We had a good time together."

"Yeah." Bains gave her one of those lugubrious smiles where his mouth was cheery at the same time his eyes looked a little misty. "If you ever…" He stopped, swallowed, smiled some more. "Good to see you, Glennie."

She nodded at him.

"I gotta go," I said. I took Spot's collar, made a little wave and headed back down the beach.

I turned at Ski Run on my way home and went into the new Red Hut for an Owen's Omelet, hashbrowns, and coffee.

I saved a third of the omelet and brought it out to Spot. He was standing on the back seat as I came out. Because he's too tall to easily get his head out the window without having to hang his head, he does this thing where he puts his right legs on the floor. That puts his head at the proper height to fit out the window while his left legs are bent on the seat. His tail was on high-speed, going back and forth between the front seat and the back seat, slapping them hard enough that I could hear it from outside.

"Got a treat, your largeness. But you're gonna have to fight for it." I stood close and held the box behind my back. He used his snout against my waist and elbows to push me left and then right, trying to get at the box behind my back. Great Danes were developed in the medieval ages for hunting wild boar. They were bred to be tall so they could grab the boar from above. And they were bred to have incredibly strong necks so they could hold the boar until the hunters came. My game was for Spot to use his neck strength to muscle me off balance. I spread my legs to brace myself, and still he pushed back and forth hard enough that I had to take a step sideways.

"Score," I said.

I pulled the omelet from behind my back, opened the box and Spot used his professional omelet-vacuum technique to make the egg levitate and shoot into his mouth like in a cartoon. I couldn't even see him swallow. Spot licked his chops and then licked the cardboard box.

I pulled it away before he could eat the cardboard.

The landscape didn't register as I drove home. All I could think about was Anna. I wondered who had her now that the man who had watched her the night before, the man I assumed was her kidnapper, was dead.

TWENTY-NINE

When I got home, I called Diamond.
I got voicemail at all of his numbers. I left messages.

I sat down to think and try to make a picture in my head of how the pieces fit. But they wouldn't go together.

Nick O'Connell put on an elaborate, tragic show in an attempt to get Thomas Watson arrested for Grace's murder. Watson had sold weapons to both Nick and Davy Halstead, leader of the Red Blood Patriots. All three apparently had reason in the form of a valuable journal to go after Anna. Davy, the only one who had been both alive and free, was watching Anna last night. Then Anna was kidnapped and Davy was killed, probably, but not necessarily, by the same person. Of the three men involved, only Watson was still alive, and he was in jail.

I had no other suspects.

What I kept thinking was that the militia called the Red Blood Patriots was at the center. Davy started it. Nick was involved at least to the extent of helping acquire weapons. And Thomas Watson was connected as the weapons supplier.

I needed to find out more about them.

I looked online and found a few references in old newspaper articles, but nothing else. No names, no addresses, no emails, no websites. In an era when everything was now online, it was a remarkable level of privacy.

Diamond called back.

"About to have lunch," I said. "Come up the mountain to join me? I can update you on what happened this morning."

"Would love to, amigo, but work calls. I'll stop by later."

I called Street and asked her the same thing. She was sorry that she had to meet a bug census deadline for the Forest Service.

"Any news about Anna?" she asked.

"Unfortunately, no." I told her about finding Davy Halstead's body.

"So Anna's disappearance could be connected to the Red Blood Patriots," Street said.

"It looks like that, yes."

We said goodbye, and I spent the next two hours trying to figure out who had Anna and where they had taken her. My frustration was extreme. When my brain was sore from stressing and worrying about her, I attempted to distract myself with some aimless paper work, then did some aimless housework. I tried to ignore the building pressure, tried to focus on something less dark than men who prey on others.

Spot and I ate in, barbecued cheeseburger and fries for both of us, although in different proportions. As always, I marveled at Spot's focus and concentration as the burgers cooked. If researchers studying the science of desire put their electrodes on Spot's head when I fired up the charcoal, they'd shelve Pavlov's most famous work as trivial. Spot's enthusiasm for cheeseburger was an order of magnitude beyond any previously-known life force.

Because of Spot's proclivity for turning all meals into instant meals, I cut his food into pieces to force him to enjoy it longer. He knew what was happening and stared at me the way a starving lion would stare if you took a fresh side of beef and started carving it into little hors d'oeuvres. To exacerbate the situation, I reached for his dog food to provide some dilution and extension.

Spot's brow furrowed further.

"What'sa matter? All I do is grab the bag o' beige chunks and you look unhappy."

Despite my flavor alterations, when I gave the okay, Spot's performance was appropriate to someone who held a Ph.D. in Instantaneous Eating.

Diamond knocked on my door at 9 p.m. I knew before I answered that it had to be Diamond or Street because Spot made only the smallest of woofs at the knock and began wagging hard as he stared at the solid door.

I let Diamond in. He gave Spot a rough pet, then sat in my rocker.

"Relax your fists," he said to me.

I looked down and saw that my hands were knotted at my sides. I straightened my fingers. They didn't uncurl easily.

"Worry and stress ain't gonna make you find her sooner," he said.

I told Diamond about the ad, the body, Ramos's ID of the victim as Davy Halstead, leader of the Red Blood Patriots.

"Ramos would like us to keep the identity quiet for the time being," I said.

Diamond nodded.

"Got a question about gang tattoos," I said as I fetched him a beer.

"You remember where I work? Douglas County is ranching country with a resort corner up here at the lake. Not many gangs."

"Right." I handed him a beer. "But you're a smart guy, and you read the trades. So I figured you'd know more about tattoos than I do. The hostage taker had a tattoo on his wrist that looked like two infinity symbols, one stacked above the other."

"Don't know much, but I'm guessing it's not infinity symbols. Probably, you look at it the other way, it's stylized eights. If so, number tats aren't what most city gangs use these days. More like country rednecks. Number tats are big in the militia movement."

"The Red Blood Patriots never got to Douglas County?" I said.

"I hope not." Diamond reached over to where Spot was lying next to him and gently knocked his knuckles on Spot's head. Spot lifted his head and opened his mouth to pant. He thumped his tail once on the floor.

"The numbers usually represent letters or the number of words in a saying," Diamond said. "Eighty-eight is code for Heil Hitler, because H is the eighth letter in the alphabet."

"How do you know this stuff?"

"It sticks in your mind when you've got brown skin because most of these militia groups are about guns and white supremacy. People of color and Jews are the enemy. White power groups want to wipe us out because we are of course inferior, and we are gradually polluting their race."

"It's getting better, don't you think?"

"Some white people would say that. And I'm inclined to agree. But not all others with brown skin think so."

I raised my eyebrows.

"Some militias are just about boys with their guns. But more are about hate. The type who are drawn to those groups liked it when blacks were just property and picked the boss man's cotton. But when Lincoln did the Emancipation thing and said that blacks weren't property anymore, that was upsetting. Then, when the Fourteenth Amendment said that blacks could be citizens, too, that was too much. They've been trying to kill them off ever since."

"You were born in Mexico City and became a naturalized citizen. How do you fit in?"

"Brown skin. Practically a brother in the eyes of the Nazis."

"Maybe the militia boys are just insecure," I said.

Diamond nodded. "Ever since Jesse Owens kicked those blond German butts in the thirty-six Olympics." He upended his beer, swallowed hard. "'Course, there are Hispanic gangs and black gangs that also use number tats, but they are few and hugely less powerful than the militia movement."

"You're pretty facile with this amendment stuff."

"Had to know it to pass the citizenship exam," Diamond said.

"Most native-born Americans don't know it."

Diamond grunted. "A true patriot would know and defend the principles that this country was built on. Easy to wave a flag and put stickers on your truck. Harder to know and support the bill of rights and the central components of the constitution and the amendments."

"I looked up the Red Blood Patriots and struck out," I said. "They must have an oath of secrecy for their members. You got an idea of where I could go for more specifics on militia groups in general?"

"There's a guy at UNR. Frank Stein. I read about him in the New York Times. Caught my eye, a prof from Reno in the Gray Lady. Anyway, he consults for the ADL. He probably knows more about militias than anyone."

"What's the ADL?"

"Anti-Defamation League," Diamond said.

"Rings a bell. Remind me what they do?"

"Their main focus is fighting discrimination against Jews."

"No small thing, there," I said.

"Yeah. Most people of color can track hundreds of years of discrimination among their ancestors. But Jews have been hounded for thousands of years."

"I'll look him up. Thanks."

It was late, and Spot and I walked Diamond out to the Green Flame, his beautiful old Karmann Ghia.

"Not on duty," I said.

"You think I would drink beer on duty?"

"How come you're up on this mountain if you're not on duty?"

"A friend calls and leaves a message. I knock on his door when I'm off duty. Something wrong with that?"

"No, Diamond. Something's very right with that. Thanks."

"Welcome." Diamond got in the car. Rolled down the window, his arm making fast little circles with the hand crank.

Spot took a step forward, his head even with the top of the car's window.

"Anyway, I just came to visit your hound," Diamond said, reaching up to pet Spot.

"I knew that," I said.

THIRTY

The next morning I looked up Frank Stein at the University of Nevada Reno. He taught Political Science. I called and found out that he had just left his office to head across campus to give a lecture and would be out of class at 10:50. Just enough time to meet him.

I took Spot and drove up and over Spooner Summit, cruised with a tailwind down the winding 3000-foot descent to the valley and caught the new freeway bypass around Carson City. Reno was only 30 minutes north on 395. Some kind of weather system was pushing through and making strong wind gusts. The Nevada Highway Department had turned on the No-Trailors-Or-Campers sign in Washoe Valley. I cruised on past the exit where the larger vehicles had to turn off to follow the wind-sheltered two-lane road that hugged the mountains to the west. I took the freeway slowly as the wind rocked the Jeep.

As I came over the rise below Slide Mountain and the Mt. Rose Ski Resort, Reno sparkled clear in the bright fall sun, all traces of smog blown east toward the desert. I went west on 80, took the North Virginia exit and crawled around the UNR campus looking for a parking place. Everything was taken. I finally found a lot with a single open space, and I parked beneath a blue sign that warned that if I didn't have the appropriate windshield sticker, my car would be towed.

I got out and turned to Spot, who had his head out the rear window on the driver's side. "If the tow truck comes, be nice, and maybe the driver will give you to a good home." I put his head in an arm lock and gave him a knuckle rub. He wagged.

I asked three different students for the hall where Stein taught. All three of them had to dial down the music in their ears and ask me to repeat the question. They each gave me a different answer. I eventually found a sign with a campus map. A man I guessed to be Stein was walking out of the lecture hall as I approached.

Stein was a stooped man in his seventies. He wore a snappy-looking watchman's cap made of plaid wool that went with his tweed sport jacket and wool pants. Beneath the cap was salt-and-pepper hair that seemed to grow in tufts and patches and appeared to not enjoy the attention of a barber. His eyebrows were huge gray caterpillars that looked about to crawl off his face. Smaller, fuzzy creatures lurked inside his ears and nose.

I introduced myself and told him I was working on a case involving a suspect with a distinctive tattoo. "I was given your name, Professor Stein, by a law enforcement officer who said you were an expert on gang and militia tattoos."

He snorted and kept walking. "Expert, no. Outraged elder, yes."

I recognized that he fit a certain type, so I played into it. "You think this country is going to the dogs?"

"This country has decided that kids are not the critical trustees of the future but merely an inconvenience to be parked in front of the TV, or a video game, or Facebook, and fed fast food."

Stein gestured toward a group of kids on Virginia Street who seemed unlikely candidates for high school graduation, much less a university education. The boys wore their jeans falling off their butts, cuffs dragging in the dirt. The girls wore skin-tight, low-cut tops that showed lots of cleavage and belly rolls, and low-cut pants that revealed their thongs.

Stein huffed. "Now we're enjoying the benefits of an entire generation whose idea of nutrition is high-fructose corn syrup, whose idea of education is survival reality shows, whose idea of entertainment is gross-out YouTube videos that show people in eating and farting and vomiting contests." Stein knocked his elbow onto my arm just in case I wasn't paying attention. "What happened to eating your vegetables and reading books?" he said. He was speeding up, his energy output in direct relationship to his emotional temperature.

"What happened to ambition and yearning and intelligent pursuits?" he said. "For thousands of years, people have tried to create an intelligent society, to make us a better species. We celebrated a liberal arts education and studied the classics in literature and art and music and philosophy. Now it's only taken twenty or thirty years to devolve into a society of militant ignorance. I've got kids in my class who can't write a single literate sentence. They use this new texting language where letters and numerals substitute for entire words. Either they never use capital letters or they only use capital letters. Used to be, Freshman English was just a bit remedial. Now, Freshman English is fourth grade stuff. I had a kid turn in an essay the other day. Every line was like a list. All nouns. I told the kid that a complete sentence had to have a verb in it. He said, 'What's a verb?'"

Stein was now at a near-trot, his breathing a series of short pants. He turned up some stairs and went into another building. I held the door for him.

"These kids in that last class of mine… Will any of them ever go to a library? An art museum? The symphony orchestra? If I mention Archimedes or Pythagoras or Newton or Shakespeare or Mozart or Michelangelo, they have no idea who I'm talking about. Same for Roosevelt and Churchill and Stalin. I should be glad they know that Lincoln was a president. But they don't know what he did or when he did it. They can't tell me the three branches of our government. They don't know why any of our past wars were fought. They can't find Germany or Japan or Korea or Vietnam or Iraq on a map."

Stein opened a door that said Frank Stein, Ph.D., Political Science. He walked into an office that was crowded with piles of books, on shelves, on his desk, on the floor. He balanced his briefcase on top of one of the piles, sat down on an old desk chair. Stein took several deep breaths, exhaling hard.

"By now you're wondering if I'm just a frustrated geezer suffering dementia. But I rant because of your question about militia tattoos. These guys are the essence of mindlessness. A charismatic leader who read the Cliff Notes on Mein Kampf tells his followers to engrave their bodies with some asinine racist phrase or an arbitrary set of numerals that are supposed to be code for the phrase. And his minions do it. They don't know what it means. They don't understand the history. They don't have a clue about its implications. But they think it is cool, and it gives them a sense of power and significance. They now have a mark. They're part of a group. They love feeling that they're one of the herd. They are cattle, eager to follow somebody, anybody. They are proud not to think for themselves because thinking is geeky-nerdy and very uncool. They don't see brotherhood in thinking. Brotherhood comes from the tribe. Us against them. Special handshakes and secret symbols. It's the new hip. And they show it on TV, which anoints it, gives it value."

He slid a pad of lined paper toward me, tossed a pen onto the pad. "Can you draw the tattoo?"

I attempted the symbol and made a mess of it, scratched it out, tried again. "I don't remember the specifics well, but the tattoo was like two infinity symbols, one over the other. A friend thought it was eighty-eight turned sideways, a Heil Hitler code."

Stein turned the pad toward him and looked at it.

"Yes, I think your friend is right. The same old thing keeps going round," Stein said, his voice suddenly weary. "It started out as a Celtic symbol and then got co-opted by anti-Semitic hate groups. We've studied this for so long, and it makes less sense than ever." Stein opened his file drawer, pulled out a bottle of water and drank from it as if he'd been dying of thirst.

"Do you know that we did a survey of anti-Semitic militia group members, and a majority of them can't tell you the reason they hate Jews? Can you believe it?" Stein stared at me. "They hate us, but they can't articulate why. They don't offer up religious reasons. They don't cite any historical precedents. They don't even know what Hitler said about us. You'd think that they would try to find something to legitimize their hate."

"But that would be impossible, wouldn't it?" I said.

"I don't mean that they could find justification in the common sense use of the word. I mean that they could find august people and institutions that promoted anti-Semitism. Then the militias could at least cite them in their motivation for hating Jews."

"What august person or institution, as you say, would promote hating Jews?"

Stein shook his head at me.

"How many years should I go back? Of course there are the multitude of obvious events, bookended by the First Crusade on one side and the Holocaust on the other, events sanctioned by both church and government. But I'm thinking more about people like Martin Luther who wrote in the sixteenth century that Jews who didn't convert to Christianity should be murdered. I'm thinking about the Catholic Church, which, as recently as the early twentieth century, allowed that while hating Jews as people was a bad kind of anti-Semitism, hating Jews as successful businessmen was fine. They called that a good kind of anti-Semitism, and they promoted it, wrote about it in church publications." Stein finished his water, then held the plastic bottle up at eye level and crushed it in his fist.

"But the militia members could care less about historical precedent. They just hate without reasons because they're hard-wired to find someone to be the fall-guy for whatever is wrong in the world. Their leader says that Jews should be annihilated, and the rank and file say, 'Where do we sign up?' It fills their need for an us-against-them world view. So they dehumanize and persecute some other tribe, which helps define their own tribe.

"The person who has done this most effectively in our local area is a man named David Halstead. He started a group called the Red Blood Patriots. Right over the Sierra Crest down in the foothills between Placerville and Auburn. Their mission, like that of so many militias, is to overthrow our government and, in the process, round up all people of color and, especially, all Jews. What Davy Halstead has told his followers is that Jews are the people behind the government conspiracy to take away all guns and seize all private property. Halstead is a truly hateful guy. He should be…" Stein trailed off and looked out the window. There was a group of young women on the lawn, all holding actual textbooks, an animated study group. But I don't think Stein noticed.

"Davy Halstead was found dead yesterday morning," I said.

Stein jerked his head back toward me. "How'd he die?"

"He was murdered."

I watched Stein carefully. It wasn't much of a reach to imagine him deciding to enact a little frontier justice of his own. But I couldn't see it even if he had the strength to put a stake through Halstead's chest.

"Probably mutiny within the ranks," Stein said. "These boys live in an atmosphere of violence. If they have a dispute, their rule is violence before discussion."

"Did you know of a man named Nick O'Connell?" I asked.

"Just heard of him recently from a guy I know in law enforcement. O'Connell was a recent recruit to Halstead's group who drowned during the hijacking up at the lake. Apparently, he was the hijacker. I did a little research on him to get a sense of his influence in the militia world and see if he warranted further study."

"You sound very thorough," I said.

"That's my self-appointed job. The Anti-Defamation League is a good organization that has lots of scruples about doing things the right way. I make contributions to their work, but I do it from the side. My way. The Frank Stein research institute. I don't want anyone – and I think the ADL agrees – to think that I'm an ADL mouthpiece or spokesperson.

"So I study guys like Nick O'Connell. I read their writings, watch their YouTube videos, peer into their brains, learn about their hate. I have lots of resources, and I've developed a few informants. You'd be surprised what you can learn with a hundred bucks. I've become quite a proficient researcher online. I know the websites where these guys post their diatribes."

Stein took a deep breath, his nose whistling. "I think the best defense is to understand the breadth and depth of those who would like to put us back into the ovens. A man like you would probably think that I should have a private investigator's license. But I know the requirements. I stay just this side of that line. And I report all that I learn to Special Agent Ramos up at the lake. You probably know who he is."

I nodded. "Have you seen any videos of O'Connell?"

Stein shook his head. "But I saw videos that mentioned him. He had a reputation in the drug and militia underground. He sounded like the devil. He was some kind of a knife expert. One comment I read was that he liked to cut flesh. But he wasn't a leader. More of a second-in-command."

I tried to remember who else had said that about Nick O'Connell, but it didn't come to me.

"No loss to the world with O'Connell gone," Stein said. "The men who follow these leaders and who engrave their bodies with the hateful tattoos, they are to be reviled," Stein said. "But the leaders, the would-be Hitlers who build these groups and shape their hate, they are pure evil. David Halstead. Nick O'Connell. I believe in and support our system of jurisprudence, but these are the people we can do without."

Stein said it with such venom that I again wondered if he had a little vigilante blood in him.

"Do you know how I can contact the Red Blood Patriots?" I asked.

Stein narrowed his eyes. "A phone number or email? No. They are much too secretive. But Halstead has a tract of land in the foothills where the Red Blood Patriots do their military exercises. There are some buildings there under the trees. They're well-hidden, but you can just make them out on the Google satellite photos. We believe some of the Patriots live there. Others live in the surrounding countryside. But if you go there and your disguise isn't very good, you might get yourself killed. Then I would have that on my conscience."

"Dr. Stein, I'm an ex-cop. Twenty years SFPD. I'm experienced, cautious, sensible. You can tell me the location."

He shook his head at me as if to say that I was a fool. "We believe that the Red Blood Patriots have killed three people who poked into their business. One was an ATF agent who disappeared a few months ago. He'd been working undercover on the gun show circuit in Nevada. He was last heard from as he was following some men in a pickup. They had left a show in Reno and were headed west into California.

"Another likely victim was a member of a rival militia group in Oregon. We think he went in under cover as if to join the Red Bloods but in reality had a darker purpose. We don't know what. Steal weapons? Try to join up, influence other members, and stage a coup? All we know is that he was seen going into the compound and he never came out. The boys in Eastern Oregon where he was from have been talking about attacking. Like some damn horde of infidels coming out of the north. Unbelievable."

"Who was the third person you think they killed?"

Stein gave me a hard look. "A reporter from Sacramento. A free-lance writer who has done features for The Reno Gazette Journal, The Sacramento Bee, The Chronicle and others. She contacted me for information. I didn't tell her about the Red Blood Patriots, thank God. She got that information somewhere else. Anyway, one of the editors – I won't say at which paper – had given her an assignment to write about the militias. Militias In Our Midst was her working title. She was seen in the area asking about the Patriots. Then she was never seen again. Later, a tourist passing through the foothills said he overheard some guys in a foothill bar. They talked about the reporter bitch and how she really put up a good fight." Stein looked down, his face dark.

"If you won't tell me where the Red Blood Patriots hang out, I'll get the information from someone else."

Stein reached into his briefcase and pulled out a notebook. He flipped through the pages.

"There is an auto shop called the Good Fix Garage that is owned by Halstead and his brother Harmon. Harmon runs the garage. He's a bit of a dimwit and isn't an important figure in the Red Blood Patriots. One way or another, you can get in touch with some of the Patriots through Harmon. I'll write down the address of the garage." He wrote on a Post-it and handed it to me. "The Patriot land is a quarter section – one hundred sixty acres – roughly north of the garage and west of the highway, but it is not on the highway. In the public records it is described as having no legal access. Which means you'd have to explore the local logging roads to find a way to drive in there."

"Thanks." I stood and shook his hand.

Stein looked at me. "It is a mark of how dangerous these guys are that they attracted a shark of the magnitude of Nick O'Connell. You go into their lair against my advice. It's best to let groups like us watch from the outside. We keep the sheriff informed, and he responds as he sees fit."

"I appreciate the warning," I said and left, with dark foreboding in my mind as I walked back across campus.

Thankfully, my car hadn't been towed. Spot was still inside.

THIRTY-ONE

The address Professor Stein had written down was in a foothill town near Highway 49 between Placerville and Auburn. Gold Country. Home for tens of thousands of good people who willingly pay their taxes and respect their government and its laws even if they disagree with some of them. And, apparently, also the chosen home ground for the Red Blood Patriots.

I got back on 80 and drove west out of Reno, up the canyon to Truckee, over Donner Summit and down the long glide to Auburn. I pulled off the highway and found a walk-up taco restaurant. I ordered four beef jumbo tacos.

"Have you eaten here before?" the pretty young brown-skinned girl said in native-born American English. "Because if not, I should warn you that our jumbo tacos are really big."

"No problem. I'll have really big help eating them. I'd also like two milks and a large bowl of water."

"I'm sorry, you want, like, water in a bowl?"

"Please," I said. "A large bowl. It's for my dog." I gestured over my shoulder toward Spot, who had his head out the window, nose and pointy ears perked up and aimed toward the taco smells.

The girl gasped when she saw Spot, then broke into a huge grin. Her teeth were crooked, but very white.

"But we don't sell water. And we don't have bowls. I don't know what to say. They trained me to take special orders, but they never said anything about dogs."

"How 'bout a hose? Do you have one of those?"

"No. We took it in for the coming winter."

"A faucet?"

"Of course! You have to have a faucet to put a hose on!"

I was so obtuse.

"May my dog use your faucet?"

The grin came back. "Yeah, sure!"

So Spot and I fortified ourselves, then headed south on the Gold Country highway.

The rundown town was two-horse in size and one-horse in pretensions and probably no horses lived there. The fanciest building was the Good Fix Garage, an old gas station with peeling paint that no longer sold gas. I parked and walked in through one of the two open garage doors.

The garage was dusty and musty and hot and smelled of oil and cigars and beer and something else that I recognized but couldn't place. I turned around, looking for any staff. There was a late '70s Bronco up on the lift, its two rear wheels off and leaning against a large red tool chest. On the other side of the chest was a door that led to the office. I stepped over an air wrench and hose and compressor and stuck my head in the office doorway.

It was a small room with an ancient counter on which sat what was probably the original cash drawer and Skoal rack from the 1950s glory days of gas stations.

The walls had been papered with gun posters, glued edge-to-edge wherever there weren't windows. Assault rifles, big-bore sniper rifles, and hunting rifles. Gatling guns, Tommy guns, MAC 10s, Uzis. Revolvers, pistols, semi-automatics. Zip guns, air guns. Next to the door was a poster that showed pictures and listed the features of bullets from tiny .22s on up to .50-caliber rounds that were closer to artillery shells than bullets. Exploding bullets, armor-piercing bullets, tracer bullets, incendiary bullets.

I realized what the smell was that seemed familiar.

Gunpowder.

No doubt the Red Blood Patriots liked to load their own ammo.

Behind the counter was a more ominous poster. It detailed the features of shoulder-launched assault rockets, small, finned missiles that could be carried in your pack yet had the power to blow a house into splinters.

At the back of the office was an old green metal desk. Sitting behind the desk, talking on the phone, was a rugged, handsome man in his fifties. He had thick gray hair that looked like a movie star's.

The man raised a finger in acknowledgment. I nodded. He kept talking about the shocks on the Bronco.

Behind the man was the only non-violent poster in the office, a map of the surrounding area. It was part topo map with the lines that show elevation, and part history map that showed old gold sites. The map had been marked with black Xs and arrows and small notations that I couldn't read from where I stood. I looked for a square labeled Red Blood Patriot Country, but they'd forgotten to put it on the map. In the corner of the map were two numerals.

88.

The man got off the phone.

"Help you?"

"Yeah. Looking for a guy named Harmon."

"I'm pret' near the only Harm these parts," he said. "Ain't saying fer sure, but far as I know, a guy want someone named Harm, a guy want me."

I looked around. "This your garage? Cool. I always wondered if I coulda done this, fixing cars and stuff. Keeping people on the move."

"It's my brother Davy's business. Only he's not here much. He did real good with Harley Davidson stock. Timed every one of the five stock splits to the day. Now he's semi-retired, and I mostly run the garage."

Harmon didn't yet know that his brother had been killed the previous morning. I took a moment to figure how to play my next move.

"Awesome," I said. "See, I's havin' lunch at this taco joint up the road in Auburn? And I got talkin' to this guy who's parked next to me. He knows you... big guy in a red Dodge Ram half-ton. Ring a bell? Sweet paint job. You pro'bly know it. Got the blue pinstripe. Name's Bob, I think he said. Innaways, we're both deer hunters, and he say he nailed a twelve-point down these parts last fall. So I tol' him that I'd never ask where he dropped such a trophy, but maybe he could just gimme a tip about good huntin' in the area. You know, general locations where a guy might see some buckskin."

Harmon frowned at me, a flicker of concern darkening his face. I was treading on sacred ground.

"So Bob," I continued, "he say pretty much anywhere in Gold Country is fruitful. That kinda stuck in my ear. Fruitful. Ain't heard no hunter talk like that. But there it was. Maybe Bob read books or somethin'. Innaways, Bob say to me that if me 'n my hound was headin' south on forty-nine, I should stop at the Good Fix Garage 'cause ol' Harm knows these woods better 'n anyone else."

"Well, that's true, and I can truthfully say there ain't no good hunting around here," Harmon said.

"You're kiddin'."

Harmon shook his head. Real serious. "Nope. Our hunters are good. They already got all the deer."

"Well, hear me out if you got a sec." I stepped to the side of his desk and pointed at the map behind his head. Harmon rotated his desk chair to see what I was pointing at.

"See how this area here got this big ravine goin' through it, 'n this whole side is a west-facin' slope? Well, I been studyin' deer for better part of twenty year, and I made up a theory 'bout it. You know how a cougar will sit up in a tree and drop down on a deer, all stealth-like? The deer go into the trees for cover, but it turn out the worst thing to do. Bam!" I clapped my hands. "Jaws 'round the back your neck!"

Harmon made the tiniest of flinches.

"Innaways, any buck with a big rack has lived a long time and learnt how to stay outta the cougar's jaws. So I think – this is what I call my theory of bucks – I think the big buck stay outta the trees. 'N where's that? On the west-facin' slope where the trees don't grow 'cause the sun is too hot and the ground is too dry. A big buck'll just stay in the tall grass. And if a cougar comes their way, that ol' buck'll pro'bly lower that rack 'n charge! If I were a cougar, no way I'd wanna be shish kebab on a buck rack. Whadya think?"

Harmon did a slow headshake and looked at me like I was nuts.

I kept talking. "So I'm lookin' at this west slope." I traced the topo lines with my finger, covering a wide area of country not far from the garage where we stood.

Harmon didn't react.

I moved my finger to a new area. "Or this slope," I said. "Or this one."

"No, not that one," Harmon said. "Don't go there."

"Oh, you hunted that area? Come back with all your ammo, did ya?"

I pointed to another area. "What about this place? You ever hunted there?"

Harmon thought about it. He stood up and pointed at the map. "I'd say this slope or the first two slopes you pointed at would be yer best bet. But this one? I know that country. I can state that I never seen a deer anywhere around there."

"Hey, that's a good tip," I said. "Save me from wastin' my time. I thank you. Now I can test my theory." I shook his hand, moved to leave, then turned back. "Hey, you wanna take a break? I'd like to buy you a beer. You're my kinda guy."

Harmon shook his head the way he'd shake it if someone offered to let him hold their snake.

"Okay, Harm. But I owe ya. You 'n me ever end up in the same bar, I'm buyin' a round for all your buds. Mark my word 'cause my word is better 'n King Tut."

I walked out to the Jeep. Spot had his head out the window. I rubbed Spot's head and said, "Bingo."

THIRTY-TWO

I drove out of town in the direction of the area that Harmon categorically stated contained no deer. As I got close to the big west-facing slope I'd seen on the map, I pulled off the highway and drove forward into a short, up-hill dead-end that was thick with brush and overhung with Black oak trees. A young buck burst out of the cover and bolted up the slope above me. I gunned the Jeep under the brush, the branches making new scratches over the old scratches in my paint job. I stopped and set the brake.

I had to push hard to open my door against the pressure of the brush. I deflected brambles away from my face, went around to the right side of the Jeep where there was a bit more space, and let Spot out. He immediately ran toward the brush where the deer had disappeared.

"Spot!" I shouted in a low voice.

He powered up the steep slope a bit, then stopped, not because of my voice, but because the slope was closer to vertical than horizontal. Like many predators, he instinctively realized that deer have anti-gravity that makes them run faster the steeper the slope. And it was hot, the Mediterranean foothill climate unabated by the fall season. More nap-in-the-shade weather than run-up-the-hill weather.

I walked out of the dead-end and onto the highway. Spot followed, staying in the tall, dried grass at the side of the road, trotting with his nose down. Probably sniffing out militia members. I heard the sound of a vehicle from behind a curve. On instinct, I called Spot's name and ran off the road toward a group of oaks. Spot bounded after me, always excited when I run.

We were under cover when the vehicle came into view. It

was an old Chevy Blazer, painted camo, four guys in it, wearing camo. The windows were down. They were talking loud enough to be heard over the roar of the bad exhaust system. Based on the raucous laughter, somebody was very funny.

After they passed, we went back to the highway. A quarter mile down, I saw a foot trail that climbed up the steep slope at a gradual angle. Spot went first, exhibiting the standard dog enthusiasm for trails. If he could talk, he'd say, "A path! Let's see where it goes!"

I followed. In just a few minutes we were a hundred feet or more above the highway. Two cars and a pickup approached from the north. Just in case any of the vehicles' occupants were leaning forward so they could look straight up through their windshields, I held Spot and we squatted down in the high grass. In another minute or two, we had hiked high enough that I didn't think anyone would see us from the highway.

We came to a fold in the landscape, which provided a good view of the slope above. It rose up to a ridge. Along the crest of the ridge, just barely visible when I squinted my eyes, was a fence. I couldn't make out the details, except that it seemed tall. I wanted a closer look.

I left the gradual trail and hiked straight up the steep slope toward the fancy fence. After half a minute, I turned. Spot stood on the trail below, looking up at me, wondering when I would come to my senses. I continued upslope. In places it was steep enough that I had to put my hands on the ground in front of me to help keep from sliding back on the slippery dry grass. A glance back revealed that Spot had decided to join me. He labored up the slope, his body language telegraphing his distaste at exercise for exercise's sake.

The air was biting hot and full of nature sounds. Grasshoppers snapped their wings as they lurched through the air. In the distance came the buzzsaw racket of cicadas advertising some big event, maybe a sex orgy or their impending takeover of the world from humans. The crispy golden grass made crinkly noises under the pressure of a breeze so hot that the more it blew, the hotter you got. My panting was so loud that mountain lions from miles away would be perking up their ears and calculating the meal count a large dying animal like me would provide. The only sound I hadn't heard was an agitated rattlesnake, which I knew were numerous in the foothills, but which no doubt had the good sense to stay indoors on such a hot afternoon.

When I got to the fence, I sat on a nearby boulder and rested, ruing my oversight of not bringing a half dozen bottles of water.

The view behind me was grand. The valley was spectacular with its golden hills and stands of Black oak and winding road and the American River in the distance, still full of rushing ice water that originated from Lake Aloha up at 8400 feet on the east side of Tahoe's Crystal Range.

The view in front of me was ominous. The fence was made of wire so heavy it would be difficult to cut with a bolt cutter. The wire had been spray-painted camo. I guessed the fence at ten feet tall. The top had curving loops of razor wire like what you see around prisons and military installations. On the inside of the fence was a dirt road that paralleled the fence. It didn't take much creativity to imagine guys wearing camo, patrolling in camo Blazers, with the camo assault rifles they'd purchased from Thomas Watson strapped across their chests.

Stein had said that Halstead's land was a quarter section, which means a square, one half mile on a side.

There was a large ring of high hills that were warped and bent like a bicycle rim that had been run over by a truck. The hilly rim was topped by the fence, which looked like a great wobbly camo necklace a half-mile in diameter, much of which was visible from my vantage point on its east edge. At the center of the necklace were two depressions in the landscape, one maybe three hundred feet below me, the other only a hundred. The depressions were connected by a valley that flowed out of sight toward the south. In each depression were groupings of oak trees, a natural result of water drainage.

After a bit of study, I realized that there were several buildings in each depression, carefully tucked under the shady cover of the trees. Although the fence and dirt road would be easily visible from aircraft and even from satellites, the buildings and associated vehicles would be largely out of sight. The dreaded big-brother government would not easily detect the activities of this particular group of disgruntled citizens.

Spot made a sudden puff through his jowls. He stared through the fence toward one of the groups of buildings. He wagged his tail.

I didn't know what he saw, but I grabbed him and pushed down on the back of his neck.

"Down, Spot!" I whispered. "Lie down."

He eased down, still wagging, staring intently.

I tried to follow his look. At first, there was nothing. Then I saw movement a bit to the side. A man was walking as if on patrol. He held something long, no doubt a rifle. More intimidating was the dog to his side. Even from a long distance it looked like a Bouvier des Flandres, a French/Flemish dog in the 80 – 110-pound range. The Bouvier was bred for herding, but it has become prized for its superior guarding characteristics. Although Bouviers don't look as serious as German Shepherds and Doberman Pinschers, they are formidable animals. If it was trained as a guard dog, it would be at least as dangerous as any militia man with his mere guns. Even if the dog wasn't trained, its natural protective instincts would still make it very difficult to get past.

I wondered how David Halstead's boys came and went from the compound. Although I couldn't see the road from where I sat, it appeared that the logical access would be the valley to the south. It would make sense to put the drive down in that valley, under the trees. There would be a guarded gate where the drive came to the perimeter fence. I probably couldn't talk my way past an armed guard, and I certainly couldn't get over a razor-wire-topped fence. Or could I?

The more germane question was whether there was any point in trying something that might get me killed.

There was no doubt in my mind that the Red Blood Patriots were the center of much of what had happened. And I was beginning to think that the compound in front of me was as likely a candidate for Anna's prison as anywhere.

Nick the Knife had been involved with the Red Blood Patriots and Davy Halstead was watching Anna before he died. I didn't know the identity of the man who Nick had dropped off the

Dreamscape, but because no one had reported anybody missing, he was probably a loner without family. And his association with Nick suggested that he too might be a member of the Patriots.

The person who took Anna could be anyone, but the evidence – all circumstantial – suggested that her kidnapper may well be a Patriot, someone who learned of Anna's potential inheritance from Davy or Nick or Thomas Watson or even Nick's helper in the hijacking. When he realized that all but Davy were no longer a threat, he may have staged a coup, killed Davy and taken Anna.

I had no indication of where Anna was being held or even if she were alive. It was likely that her kidnapper forced her to talk and reveal whatever she knew. It was equally likely that once he realized that she possessed nothing valuable, he would kill her.

Nothing felt right. It was like a big, deadly real-world version of the Sunday crossword puzzle on the subject of murder, where I still had nothing but inscrutable clues and hadn't yet figured out a single word.

THIRTY-THREE

The heat of the lowering, searing, afternoon sun drove me up from my boulder. The guard and his dog had disappeared, so I walked along the outside of the fence toward a distant oak which would have shade. Spot followed, slowed by the heat. When we reached the tree, Spot immediately walked over to its shadow and lay down. He rolled onto his side, and his big tongue flopped onto the grassy dirt.

I sat on the ground next to him and wiped my forearm across my forehead where sweat ran into my eyes. We were both dehydrated and needed water, but even more, we needed a break in the shade. While we rested, I pondered what I might learn from Davy Halstead's crew. It was immediately obvious that, should I approach his followers directly, the answer was nothing. There were lots of militias, and each had a different focus, but they all shared a strong disaffection with government. This hostility universally drove them to acquire weapons, and whether those acquisitions were legal or not, they would not abide anyone from outside of their group making inquiries about their activities.

The only thing that made sense was to walk away. I could try to convince the county sheriff or Agent Ramos that Anna's kidnapping warranted a search of the Patriot's compound. But it would be futile. Without evidence, there was no probable cause, which meant no judge would issue a warrant.

If Anna were alive, she could be held anywhere. But the most likely place that I knew of where she could be held out of sight and hearing of others would be somewhere within the fenced tract of land before me.

No matter how I presented myself to them, I would still be an outsider trying to get info about their members and their activities. No way would they have any reaction other than a strong and possibly violent mistrust of me. Which left only one other approach.

I had to go in unobserved. Back-country trespass.

I momentarily entertained the notion of a secret tunnel into the compound that I could breach from underground. Not likely. Nor could I safely hire a helicopter to drop me in from the air. Exciting in the movies, but not realistic for the real world. I'd already ruled out going in past the guards at the front gate. Even if they had a regular delivery vehicle where I could stow away under the cargo, it would probably take weeks of surveillance to figure out how to plan it. That left going over or under or through the fence.

It didn't look electrified, although maybe it was monitored by hidden surveillance cameras. I could climb it, but getting over the razor wire would be difficult. The jagged wire looked sharp enough to slice through any tarp or blanket that I might try to drape over the top. And the wire was designed to be non-rigid. It would sag and snare in a nasty way. I could bring up a bolt cutter, but I would probably find that the wire was hardened. I'd seen bolt cutters that had managed only a few cuts before hardened wire had dulled them into uselessness. I could bring up a shovel and dig a tunnel, although the fence was set into the ground. Perhaps there was even a concrete curtain under the fence. I kicked at the dirt, pulled out my pocketknife and stuck the blade into the dry hard dirt. The blade went in less than two inches before it would go no farther. The sun-baked ground appeared harder than asphalt.

I looked up at the oak above me, wondering if there might be a tree somewhere that overhung the fence, allowing me to drop in. The answer was found in one of the oak's branches that had grown toward the fence and had been sawed off. I assumed that they had trimmed all of the trees near the fence.

The sun lowered close to the distant hills, although its heater setting was still set on broil. I realized that I needed to start down the mountain.

"C'mon, Spot, let's go," I said. Spot didn't move.

I started to walk away. I looked back after I'd gone ten yards.

Spot had lifted his head. "C'mon, boy. I'm leaving. It's all downhill from here."

He pushed himself to his feet. Yawned. Lowered his head as if it were too heavy to hold up. Started walking. Watching him come out from the shade under the oak, I had an idea.

The oak had been trimmed so it didn't overhang the fence. But it was still fairly close to it. If I could drop the oak and control its direction, it might land on the fence, crushing it and making it easy for someone to do a balance-beam walk up its inclined trunk, scramble through its branches, and jump down on the other side of the fence. The trick would be cutting the oak by hand because the noise of a chain saw would bring attention. Another trick would be controlling its fall. Unlike straight pine and fir, which can be directed by the shape and size of the hinging wedge one cuts into the tree before the final cut, oaks often grow with their center of gravity substantially out to one side of the trunk. No amount of careful hinging can change the way such an oak will fall. Off-center trees can only be directed with a hydraulic claw arm on a truck, or by cables tied to other trees. I had no such luxury.

I went back to the tree and walked a circle around it, judging its center of gravity. The branches were uneven in size and length. The trunk had a slight S-curve. And there was some old scarring on the trunk that would weaken one side. Even so, I thought it might be possible to direct its fall onto the fence. Of course, first I had to cut it. By hand. The tree was two feet in diameter. Cutting oak is closer to cutting rock than cutting soft pine or fir.

As Spot and I hiked back down the mountain, I put the concept out of my mind as unreasonable at best and unworkable at worst.

I backed the Jeep out of its hiding place, drove to Placerville, parked on the main street of what locals call Old Hangtown and pulled out my phone.

THIRTY-FOUR

Sometimes when you aren't concentrating on a subject, it comes to you unbidden.

My unbidden subject was Thomas Watson's comment when I talked to him in jail.

"I didn't do it," he'd said in reference to Grace's murder.

Those of us in law enforcement hear it all the time. The line is a cliché, the first thing out of the mouths of every crook from shoplifters all the way up to burglars, robbers, and murderers. Even idiot white-collar criminals say it when they lose the discipline to obey their lawyers and keep their mouths shut. I'd heard it so often that, like all cops, I had an encyclopedic sense of the line's every nuance.

And since Watson had said it in the jail cell, it kept coming back to me when I was working on something else.

The reason for Watson's words making such frequent visits to my subconscious when I didn't expect it was obvious. Unlike all the other times I'd heard the line, this time I believed it.

I couldn't say exactly why. Something about his tone, his inflection. Some kind of pain in his voice. Some sense that he telegraphed veracity in the other things he'd said, and so maybe there was some truth to this statement as well.

So I thought about it. A woman is killed. She has your skin under her fingernails. They make a positive identification of your DNA. If you know you didn't do it, then consider the possible explanations.

I called Joe Breeze at the SFPD expecting his voicemail at 7:30 p.m.

He answered.

"Working late, Inspector?" I said.

"Just getting warmed up. You already forget about the dedication of SFPD professionals? But then you, private sector poster boy, probably have a glass of cabernet in your hand as we speak."

"Right. Hey, I'm tracking a militia group, and I have a question for you."

"Something about the journal I filched for you?" he said.

"Kind of. I need the name of the lab and technician who worked with the DNA under Grace Sun's fingernails."

"I should quit my job and be your secretary," Breeze said. He didn't sound happy.

"I could take you on as an unpaid intern."

"My pay being proximity to the famous investigator and the opportunity to observe greatness up close," Breeze said. "Couldn't put a price on that." Breeze didn't say it like it was a joke.

"Yeah. Anyway, all it takes is you pull open a file drawer. If I remember correctly, it's left of your desk. The gray file cabinet, not the brown one. Second drawer from the bottom."

I heard heavy breathing.

"Send you your favorite Havana smokes if it makes you feel better," I said.

"I quit that cigar shit last year. Now I'm the picture of health. Smoke-free, two hundred five pounds on a five-eight frame, and growing."

I couldn't tell how much of Joe's anger was about me pushing the limits of favors or about the struggle of weight gain and a job that mostly involved sitting at a desk and doing paperwork. I heard the noise of a file drawer slamming shut. Papers flipping.

I said, "Then all I can offer for reward is that the information you give me may help prevent an innocent man from getting the big sleep."

"Yeah those wrongful executions are expensive. Lucky for the state that you and your white horse are saving them money. Here it is. For some reason, we farmed it out. Must be our own lab was too busy. The lab that did the work was called Evidence Inquiries, Inc. There's a signature on one of these report forms, but I can't read it. You got a pen?"

"Yeah."

Breeze read off a phone number, gave me the date and ID number off of the report.

"Thanks, I really appreciate it."

"Right," he said and hung up.

I looked over to the back seat where Spot lay prostrate, his tongue out panting, still trying to blow off excess heat. "Okay, largeness, time we found some supper."

He didn't respond.

I went west on the freeway to the Bel Air supermarket in Cameron Park where I got a deli sandwich, a quart of milk and a ten-pound bag of dog food for Spot. It wouldn't last more than 24 hours, but I expected to be back home before then. We ate out back where I found another faucet. Then we drove down to the valley floor, found one of the lower rent chain motels where they let you bring in a dog for an extra fee.

"We allow small dogs only," the woman at the check-in counter said, a stern look on her face.

I nodded solemnly. "Right. He's got a big personality, though," I said.

"Isn't that the way it always is!" she exclaimed. "The littlest guys, they always think they're the star attraction of the circus."

"You know it," I said.

Once I figured out where my room was, I drove around and brought Spot in the end door of the building.

"Be quiet and act small," I said as I let him in. He took off running down the long hallway.

"Spot! Come!"

He ignored me. A door opened about 30 yards down. A woman backed out, pulling a stroller behind her. She swiveled the stroller our way and shut her door. The toddler saw Spot racing toward them, raised both arms, waved and shrieked with excitement. The mother screamed.

Spot did an about-face and raced back toward me. I had my key card in the door slot. The light turned green, and I pushed in the door.

"Sorry," I called out to the woman as we disappeared into the room, hoping we were far enough down that she couldn't tell which room we were in.

A minute later I heard the squeak of wheels go past my door. A little kid was shouting.

"Mommy, I wanna big doggy. Mommy, I wanna a BIG doggy. Mommy!"

"Quiet!" she shouted back.

The next morning I dialed the number Breeze had given me.

"Evidence Inquiries." A young voice, male, pitched up high like a choir boy.

"Detective Owen McKenna calling in regard to a report you did for the SFPD three years ago. The ID number on the report is eight, seven, B, R, I, M as in Boy, Robert, Ida, Mary. I need to speak to the technician who worked on it."

"And the name on the report?"

"There is an illegible signature, nothing more."

"Okay. Hold on and I'll transfer you to the Eight-Seven group."

I waited until a woman answered, "Sharon Wilsonette." Older voice. Not-so-high-pitched.

I repeated myself.

"Let me look that up." She made little humming sounds while I waited. Sounded like a Sondheim tune. "Here it is. Jonathon James was the lead technician on that."

"May I speak to him?"

"I'm sorry, he's since left the company."

"Do you have forwarding contact information?"

"Now, Mr. McKenna, as a law enforcement person, you know that companies are not allowed to give out personal information on their employees."

"Right. But you are allowed to have a friendly chat with an old friend of Jonathon's."

"Old friend?"

"You work a murder case together, you forge a special bond," I said. "Grace Sun was the victim's name. It was one tiny good thing that came from that investigation, getting to know Jonathon well."

"If you knew him well, you'd know he hated the name Jonathon and that he went by JJ."

"Of course. JJ and I talked about that very thing over beers one night."

"If you knew him well, you'd know he never drank alcohol."

"That's right. He was drinking O'Douls, non-alcoholic beer. So did JJ start his own lab like he talked about?"

There was a long pause. "As everyone and anyone who had anything to do with JJ knew, he had no intention of starting a lab. This job was just a side gig to help pay for medical school. He graduated two years ago and is now a resident at a hospital in Oakland."

"Sure, now I remember. Except, I forget which hospital."

"Of course you would forget because it's only one of the biggest names. I'm afraid I have to go now."

She hung up, and I called various Oakland hospitals. The automated phone system allowed me to go directly to the person of my choice by entering their initials. At the first hospital, the robot voice said it was an invalid entry. At the second hospital, the robot voice asked me to choose between two different JJs.

I made my selection, waited, and was given another menu. I made another selection. Repeated the process a third time. Then I was put on hold where I listened to a recorded voice tell me that my call was very important to them and that due to unusually high call volume the wait times were long and that I could always find the answer to my question by visiting the hospital's website, which the recorded voice spelled out slowly and laboriously twice. Then the message repeated over and over.

I wondered about the writers who wrote phone scripts that contained such multiple, blatant lies. If my call were really important to them, they'd have a real person answer the phone. If the high call volume were actually unusual, they wouldn't have a permanent recording saying it. And the chance that the answer to my question could be found on their website was about the same as the chance of getting treated promptly in their ER.

Like lots of businesses, the hospital obviously thought that their customers were of little importance, and they simply wanted us to go away and stop bothering them.

Eventually, a real woman answered.

"Nurse Frances, third floor," she said.

"Detective Owen McKenna calling for Dr. Jonathon James with a side bonus offer for you. If you actually speak to me and don't put me on torture-hold, I promise I won't come to your nurse's station during your shift and have a messy psychiatric breakdown."

"Oh, hon, I'm so with you on that! Besides, you have a nice voice, and your bonus offer is quite enticing. Now let me see his schedule. You're in luck because Dr. James is working another thirty-two hour shift, so no matter when you call, he's always here. Not only that, because our residents sleep like Equus, he'll be glad for the interruption."

"What does that mean, sleep like Equus?"

"They learn to sleep standing up. But unlike horses, they sometimes lose their balance and fall over. Very embarrassing. Especially when they're assisting in the OR. Oops, I probably shouldn't say that. So if you're listening, Big Brother, it was just a figure of speech. Do you think I should spell that, Detective? The robo operator doesn't have very good voice recognition. They might think figure-of-speech is bigger-a-leech."

"I'd pass on the spelling. They wouldn't recognize that, either."

"Anyway, the interruption of a phone call is quite welcome. Except, we have a little problem, you and I. Our PA system is down, and I can't keep talking to you while I go look for Dr. James. Tell you what, I'll set the phone down without putting you on hold. Maybe I'll put a little Post-it note on it saying that if this phone is hung up, the patient on the other end is going to undergo spontaneous combustion. Would that be suitable?"

"Frances, next time I'm in Oakland, can I bring you a box of chocolates and a rose?"

"That would be suitable, too."

A minute later, I was talking to Dr. James.

"Sure, I remember that case," James said, no sleepiness in his voice at all. "The skin sample your people sent us was quite substantial. It included several hair follicles, too. Made the DNA sampling much easier than it might have been."

"Was that a surprise, getting hair follicles?"

"How do you mean?" he asked.

"Just that the skin came from under a woman's fingernails. In my experience, it was a lot of skin. Most middle-aged women would not be that successful at gouging their attacker. In your experience, would you agree that it was an unusual amount of skin?"

"I agree. Although I've known some older women who might do Grace Sun one better. Younger women might be stronger, but older women sometimes burn with a hotter fire."

"Could the skin have come from someplace else?" I asked. "Would your analysis see that the same way?"

"You think your department faked up the evidence? Like the victim didn't really have skin under her nails?"

"No. Grace actually had skin under her nails. That I know. What I mean is, what if someone planted the skin there?"

"You don't have a very high opinion of your fellow cops," James said.

"No, that's not what I mean. I'm wondering if her murderer planted the skin there."

"You mean to frame someone else?"

"Yeah. The killer could have pulled out someone else's skin and packed it under her nails. In your opinion, if that had happened, would it have affected your test results?"

James was silent on the phone. "I'm just running our procedures through my mind. As long as the skin wasn't contaminated by a third party's DNA, I can't see how your scenario would change anything. So no, I don't think it would change the results of our tests."

"What if the skin under her nails came from a part of a person's body that a victim normally wouldn't scratch during the course of an attack?"

"Like where?"

"Someone's leg, for example. Would that affect your tests compared to, say, skin from someone's face?"

Another pause. "This is unfamiliar territory for me, Detective. As a scientist, I'm reluctant to speak on a subject on which I'm no authority."

"Then just give me your gut sense. Off the cuff."

"Off the cuff, I'd say that skin from a person's shin would of course have the same DNA but would look different from skin from a person's face. However, the difference would probably not be easy or even possible to scientifically identify. Usually, we just get some skin cells. If we had a big enough chunk of skin, it might look different. Coarser. And lighter if their face and arms had more sun coloration than their legs did. Although that might not apply if the person was African American."

"What about the hair follicles?" I asked.

"Hair and hair follicles from a leg would probably be heavier and courser than from an arm. But not as heavy as a beard. I don't recall the sample enough to remember that."

"One more question. If someone were framed by skin evidence that was planted, is there anything about DNA testing that would reveal it?"

"Not that I can think of. Unless the victim actually did scrape the skin of the attacker before the attacker planted more skin under their nails. Then we might have noticed tissue from two different sources. I don't recall anything like that. But it would say that on the report. Does that answer your question? Because I'm late for an appointment."

"Yes. Thank you very much for your time. And doctor?"

"What?"

"When Nurse Frances comes up for review, put in a word for a raise, if you can. You'll want to keep her around as long as possible."

"You noticed, too," he said. "Or, as she would say, 'Oh, hon, I'm so with you on that.'"

When I hung up, my sense that Thomas Watson didn't kill Grace was even stronger. I couldn't prove it. But I could see how it could have happened.

Watson had winced when he stood up from the jail cell bench. He rubbed his leg. Pulled up his pants to reveal an ugly old wound. Without any apparent guile he simply explained that he had tripped and hit his shin on a curb while he was in San Francisco. It happened around the time of Grace's murder.

A murderous opportunist – whom I now believed to be Nick

O'Connell – could easily have been following Watson. Maybe that was how O'Connell had learned of Grace in the first place, by overhearing Watson talk to Grace at the library. O'Connell could have watched Watson stumble, then collected some of the skin that got scraped off on the curb.

How O'Connell came to kill Grace was a mystery. Perhaps he broke into Grace's apartment, surprising her when she came home. But that wouldn't explain the presence of the tea. It was possible that Grace, calculating how better to survive, had struck up a conversation with the intruder and even made him tea. But it seemed unlikely.

O'Connell was a knife man. So why did he hit Grace with the frying pan instead of using his knife? Did she use the frying pan to knock his knife out of his hand? Did he take the pan from her and hit her over the head? He may not have assumed that he was going to kill her. But he came prepared just in case such an event happened. He brought along the bits of Watson's skin and rubbed them under Grace's fingernails, framing Watson for the murder.

Three years later, frustrated that the authorities never brought Watson in, Nick O'Connell hijacked the boat to get me to catch Watson. Now, with Watson in custody, O'Connell would have been free to act on whatever information he'd gotten from Grace without worrying about Watson getting involved. That is, if he hadn't fallen off the Tahoe Dreamscape.

I made a call to the District Attorney of San Francisco County. It took some convincing to get them to transfer me through.

"Madam District Attorney, former SFPD Inspector Owen McKenna calling," I said when she answered. We'd previously met, but I didn't expect her to remember me.

"Roberta to you, Owen."

"The power of your office hasn't gone to your head."

"It's just a job, and a pain-in-the-ass job at that. What's up?"

I told her why I was calling. She was polite and generous with her time, and, in an unusual break from my expectations, she didn't interrupt.

When I was done, she said, "Of this scenario that you

present, how much of it is your wish versus belief predicated on evidence?"

"Actually, I have no evidence for this notion. I originally wished for – and believed – that Watson was guilty. And the only evidence we have in this crime points to his guilt. But I've changed my belief because of everything I've learned in the meantime."

"So this is all about a hunch that directly refutes the DNA evidence?"

"Yes," I said. "But before you dismiss my idea, consider how many times in your career that your belief about someone's guilt or innocence was in conflict with the current evidence." I wanted to elaborate, to sell her on the idea, but I decided to leave it alone and just let her think about my question.

"Okay," she said. "A second question. What do you think is the likelihood that you will eventually obtain evidence to support your idea?"

"A strong likelihood. If I had to put a number to it? Seventy percent."

"Then you may say that I will take a hard second look at the situation if the suspect cooperates and the information he provides leads to credible evidence indicating that he is not the murderer."

"Thank you, Roberta," I said.

THIRTY-FIVE

Two hours later, Spot and I were stuck in the permanent slow-and-go that is I-80 near Berkeley. Eventually, we got through the toll booth and onto the Bay Bridge. I always felt sorry for Oakland the way it had to play second string in the city lineup just like San Jose, yet without San Jose's claim to being the high-tech epicenter of the world. But when you see San Francisco's hills and skyscrapers framed through the Bay Bridge's towers, you have to concede that The City gets to play Varsity Ball just on looks alone. Fair or not, people don't go to California from around the world and then send home postcards of Oakland.

I took the Ninth Street exit, made the three lefts for 8th, Bryant and 7th, and found a parking place near the San Francisco County Jail. I told Spot to be good, went inside and did a lot of talking before they let me talk with Thomas Watson in an interview room.

Watson was carrying a book. He set it on the table next to him. The cover said Langston Hughes.

"Poet, right?" I said.

"Actually, this is a biography." Watson sounded aloof, as if intellectual gunrunners read biographies, and cops just read comic books. Or didn't read at all.

"Did you know that Langston Hughes wrote fifty books?" Watson said. "And a play that was performed on Broadway over three hundred times? He was also a newspaper columnist and a war correspondent and a novelist and children's book author. And he wrote amazing poetry."

"Got a favorite?"

Watson thought about it. "I keep going back to the one about holding fast to dreams," he said, no doubt knowing that I'd have no clue what the poem was.

"The sentiment is appropriate to the reason I'm here," I said.

Watson gave me a long look. "You talking about your dreams or mine?"

"We have strong evidence against you in the murder of Grace Sun. If you have entertained any thoughts of acquittal, they would not seem like reasonable hopes but more like dreams. I'm here with an offer of a quid pro quo, something much more concrete than that dream."

"I'm listening."

I decided to stretch the truth a bit. "The San Francisco County DA has intimated that if you come clean with me, if you tell me all you know about Grace Sun and Nick O'Connell, she will consider dropping the murder charges against you."

Watson opened his eyes a bit wider.

"This means you think I'm innocent, in spite of the DNA evidence?" The way he said it, it sounded like he knew he was guilty.

"Innocent of murdering Grace? Probably. But if the information you give me suggests that you've committed other crimes, then that is a separate issue."

"And you're doing this why?" The aloofness had shifted toward suspicion. Maybe contempt.

"Same old cliché. I'm a law guy. I want justice done. You may be an evil person. But if someone else killed Grace, I want him or her caught."

"And whether or not the DA drops the charges will be based on what you tell her? Your judgment?" He scoffed.

"I can't make any promises, but I can give her my recommendation. It's all you've got."

"How do I know you'll follow through on this?"

"You don't. It's a risk you'll have to take. But unless your information reveals that you are guilty of other crimes as serious as murdering Grace, it's a no-lose situation for you. If you don't cooperate, you will face life in prison with no chance of parole at best and death row at worst."

"Okay. What do you want to know?" He sounded cagey.

His attitude instantly infuriated me. "I'm offering you a huge possibility and you respond by playing games? I just told you what I want to know! Everything about the case! How you know Nick. How you know the Red Blood Patriots. Why Grace was killed. Tell me every detail, damnit!"

"Okay, okay!" Watson took a moment to calm himself.

I waited.

Finally, Watson spoke. "The story is basically about Nick. Nick the Knife O'Connell, the most dangerous man I ever met."

THIRTY-SIX

Thomas Watson was sweating.

"Several years ago," he said, "I met Nick O'Connell at a gun show in Vegas. O'Connell said he wanted to buy a bunch of gear for a paramilitary group. Full auto AK forty-sevens. Ammo. Flash suppressors. Ranger Armor Vests. Helmets. Some night vision equipment.

"I was able to acquire most of it. I met with Nick several times over the course of our transactions. He was quite the talker. I'm a good listener. We both like Margaritas. I learned about the Red Blood Patriots and their dues-paying members. These men are basically a bunch of disaffected white guys who hate people with brown skin, and really, really hate people with brown skin who have good jobs. And they also think women are lower class citizens than their dogs.

"They love belonging to the Red Blood Patriots because the group makes them feel powerful, and it gives them purpose. It elevates their hate to a sense of mission. And best of all, the group encourages them to play soldier and fire their weapons. Most of these men probably couldn't get into the Army, although if they had they would have chafed at the discipline and probably would have gone AWOL. So they're happy to pay monthly dues to Davy Halstead in return for some kind of meaning, no matter how vile it is."

"Davy is the leader," I said, keeping things in present tense so that he wouldn't guess that Davy had been murdered. I didn't want him to think about anything other than telling this story.

"Right. Davy is their general, their minister, their father figure, maybe even their direct line to God. Davy created the Red Blood Patriots in the manner of a church. He is like many charismatic cult leaders, using a calculated mix of commandments and cajoling to get what he wants. And the fealty of his flock is unquestioned."

"And Nick was part of this group," I said.

"Only in name. He was too smart to be a member in spirit. But he was happy to take their money and serve as a weapons procurement agent."

"If he didn't believe in the mission, didn't they see through him?"

"I think Davy did. But Davy is smart. He could see that Nick, with his weapons skills and his mercenary background, could teach them a lot. So he basically hired Nick to bring the Patriots into the big leagues in regard to weapons. Maybe Nick taught them some tactics, too. Nick told me he had extensive military background, but he wouldn't give details."

"If Nick had Special Ops experience, wouldn't dealing with the Red Blood Patriots be a big step down in street cred?"

"Ten years ago, sure. But we all age. When he was twenty-eight or thirty, he probably could write his own ticket to wherever he wanted to go. But you get a little older, you no longer have the physical authority to go with your knowledge. So you segue into running a private contracting business and sell your services to the military or big business. Or you get a regular job and forget about your past until it comes time to write your memoir. In Nick's case, he was too much of an outsider to do either. So he picked up whatever jobs he could. Less pay and less respect, maybe. But it fit his personality."

"Which was what?" I asked.

"Over-the-top, wired, intense psychopath."

"How did Davy get the money to hire Nick and buy expensive weapons and other gear from you? Even with steep monthly dues, it still wouldn't add up to much."

"The Red Blood Patriots is just a side gig. He's passionate about it, runs it like a cult church, but it's still only a hobby. Davy's main business…" Watson paused.

"I'm waiting."

"Davy makes his money running a meth lab. He's real smart about it. Instead of selling to individual addicts, each of whom are a security risk, he developed a single big customer, a biker gang in Arizona. He's a pro and they're pros. None of the principals do drugs. It's all about the money. They send a courier to pick up the product every month. Payment is by electronic transfer."

"And the lab is at the Red Blood Patriots compound?"

"Yes. It would seem counter-intuitive because if anybody were to look into Davy's activities, they would obviously focus on the compound. Maybe they'd find some illegal guns, but they won't find drugs."

"Why not?"

"The lab is well-hidden. None of the Patriots' members even know it exists."

"You learned this from Nick?"

"Yeah. Davy took him into his confidence. Probably was dying to brag to someone after all these years. Davy disguised some of the details, but Nick was smart enough to put together the real story. And it's a beaut.

"Years ago," Watson continued, "Davy bought one of those heavy metal storage containers like they use to ship freight on ships. He had the delivery people put it behind a cabin he had there on his big parcel of land. He rigged it with lights and such, and it made a nice shop. This was all before he started the Patriots. Eventually, Davy wanted to trade up to a bigger shop. So he bought a kit for a large pole building and put it up himself.

"Davy did all his own excavation work. Rented a front end loader with the backhoe on the rear, the cement mixer, the works. He'd done some construction work in years past, and he was so good with that tractor and the concrete block foundation that he was able to build a retaining wall into the big hill that rises up on the back side of his property. The retaining wall became the back wall of the pole building. The result left enough space on the front side of the pole building that he could put in a nice little patio between the pole building and the cabin. It was complete with a fire pit and some raised-bed gardens, and a loggia above.

"From what Nick understood, Davy did all the work himself, and the area can't be seen from any nearby property. So the only people who could have ever seen what was going on were the few Mexican laborers he brought in to help with some of the grunt work.

"Anyway, probably no one noticed that the metal storage container that had been there for years was suddenly gone one morning.

"Turns out that during a long night of excavation work, Davy embedded that storage container deep into the hill behind the cabin, backfilled around it, and then built the retaining wall in front of it. He even prettied up the area with some landscaping. Apparently, you go into the pole building and there's an honest-to-God secret door in the back wall."

"And behind that is the meth lab," I said.

"Right. Hidden like a cave. With lighting and a serious ventilation system."

"Does Davy do the lab work himself?"

"Yeah."

"Does he have a cover story? What do people think he does for a living?"

"More genius. Davy owns a rundown garage where he has an auto repair business. He also has a dimwit brother who helps run it and does some legitimate work like changing oil filters and such. But what Davy's brother is really good at is telling the story that Davy planted in his brain. And the story is that Davy was a guru of sorts for Harley Davidson stock investing."

It fit exactly with what Harmon had told me the day before. "Everyone who wants to know about Davy would eventually speak to the brother and be told the story that Davy basically retired on his investments," I said. "Providing perfect cover for running drugs."

Watson nodded.

"And Nick told you all of this."

"Like I said, Nick was a talker. He was also very good at learning things about people. And I'm a good listener. Being a good listener means knowing how to keep a person talking."

"Nick pass on anything else about Davy Halstead?"

"Nothing important. Just stuff like Davy Halstead's wife is a lonely woman who is so reticent she may as well be mute. And Davy's mistress talks about his impotence problem and how they fight. Everything else I heard is even less significant."

"Tell me about Grace."

"I learned of Grace from Nick. Davy learned about Grace from Nick. All three of us, Nick, Davy, and I, have attempted to make something out of what we learned. All of us have failed."

Watson took a deep breath, held it like it was a yoga exercise, then let it out.

"Nick had amazing perceptual abilities. He could meet a person, talk to them for less than a minute and know their background, their financial situation, their hopes and dreams and fears and worries."

"And he met Grace?"

"Not in the introduction sense. But he saw her at an author signing. He'd gotten season tickets to a lecture series at Berkeley. He said he was simply interested in hearing the authors speak. But I assume that he really went as a hunter/predator, looking to study the well-to-do crowd that attends such events. The truth was probably both. One of the authors had written a book on the role of the Chinese immigrant laborers in the Gold Rush. After the talk, Nick got in line to buy his book. There was a woman in front of him. When she got up to the author's table, she asked the man several questions about whether he'd ever heard of Chinese laborers striking it rich in the gold country."

"Which piqued Nick's curiosity," I said.

"Yes. So he watched and listened as she asked the author to sign the book to Grace Sun."

"Do you know the name of the author?"

"No idea. After that, Nick went home and began researching Grace Sun. He discovered a website about Gold Rush history where Grace had posted several times on a discussion thread about Chinese miners. In one of her postings, Grace said that she had a distant grandfather who had come from China. In another, she wrote about a journal that her ancestor had written in Mandarin and how much of it was damaged and too blurred to read. But the tone of her post was to suggest that the journal possibly hinted of finding gold.

"From that, Nick put together a scenario that basically said, what if Grace Sun had reason to suspect that her ancestor got rich in the Gold Rush and, if so, what if there was money or gold that was lost or deliberately hidden. Could the gold be found? Could the journal be examined by experts? Were there clues that Grace would never figure out but that might make sense to Nick?"

"Or to you," I said. "You kept quiet all along about Grace's potential treasure because you hoped that you could one day figure out what and where it was. And then you could retrieve it for yourself."

"Yes, I admit it. I wondered about it. too. So when Nick told me about it, I engineered my own little plan. I found out where Grace lived and followed her now and then. She often went to the San Francisco Library. Sometimes I was able to watch from a distance as she found books in the stacks and took them to a table to read. I made walk-bys and spied the titles and authors. I watched as she re-shelved the books. Once I saw her put a pink Post-it in a book to mark a page, and when I later pulled the book off the shelf, the Post-it was still there, and I could see what she'd been reading. After several visits, it was obvious from the books she investigated that she believed her ancestor had stashed away something very valuable. One of the books she'd looked at was even called *Hidden Treasure: How To Find And Retrieve Fortunes That Have Been Lost To Time*."

Watson rubbed his face as if he'd just awakened and was checking his beard to see how badly it needed shaving.

"It was after that that I talked to the librarian about Chinese history, and she told me about the woman who had been in researching the same thing. Of course, it was Grace Sun, the person I'd been spying on for a long time. I was so confidant that she'd never seen me that I met her and shook her hand, just like I told you before."

"Just because she believed that there was money," I said, "didn't mean it exists."

"Of course not. Not only might it not exist, it probably doesn't exist. And even if it does exist, it will most likely never be found."

"Yet you still pursued the idea, hoping to take for yourself something that rightfully would have belonged to Grace."

Watson looked down at the floor. "I'm as wicked as the next guy. But I didn't kill her. I have never personally, physically hurt anyone."

"You think Nick O'Connell killed her?" I asked.

"Good a guess as any. From what I read in the paper, nothing valuable was taken from her apartment even though the place was turned upside down. It sounded like someone was looking for something and didn't find it. My guess is that Grace's killer was Nick, and that she surprised him while he was looking for the journal she mentioned on the website posting."

"When we found the body," I said, "there was a journal tucked inside of Grace's shirt."

Thomas Watson made a single, intense jerk of his head as if someone had put electrodes under each ear and given him a high-voltage shock. It took him a moment to recover.

"Was the journal in Chinese?" he finally asked, his eyes wide even as he frowned.

"Mandarin, yes."

"What was in it? Although I suppose you won't tell me."

"Most of the characters were blurred as though the journal had been dropped in a mud puddle. We can make out almost nothing from it."

Watson's eyelids tensed and lowered as if he was scheming. "After all this time," he mumbled in a low voice, "it turns out to be true. I never really believed it."

"Does Davy Halstead know about the possible treasure," I asked, still using his name in the present tense.

Watson nodded. "He talked to us about it one night when I delivered the last of his order, some helmets, if I remember correctly. We celebrated our business with a late-night cognac. I was surprised because both Nick and Davy seemed like beer guys. Of course, I knew something of cognac from my international travels. So when Davy brought out three large snifters and a bottle of Courvoisier, I experienced one of those little seismic shifts. I realized that I had underestimated Davy."

"Courvoisier being superior to beer," I said.

"Of course," Watson said, completely missing my sarcasm. "So we hung out at the bunkhouse on Davy's compound and had a little party, and Nick showed us knife tricks, and we discussed Grace's mythic fortune, waiting out there somewhere for us to discover and claim as long-lost treasure that would belong to the finder."

"Was anybody else around who might have overheard you three talking?"

"No. The entire compound was empty. Davy is careful that way. Nick was sort of his confidant. And I was his supplier. He didn't want the rest of the boys to mix it up with us. He was like a corporate manager. You don't have drinks after work with the mail-room crew."

"When I first came and talked to you, you were willing to say that the hijacker was Nick, but you weren't willing to mention Grace's possible treasure. Why?"

"Because I didn't fully believe that I was in jail for the long term. It's like having a valuable secret in addition to some contraband when your parents catch you doing something bad. You only volunteer to show them what's in your pockets, what they can find out by themselves. You keep the secret to yourself."

"You told me about Grace's daughter. Did you also tell Nick and Davy?"

"Yeah. My tongue can be loosened by drink as well as the next person's. I shouldn't have. It didn't occur to me that she might be valuable. Although maybe she knows nothing. Not that it would make a difference. Later, Nick said that he almost got her once. But he and Davy have both tried to find her since then, and couldn't."

"What about Grace's cousin Melody?"

"Was she Grace's roommate?"

I nodded.

"For some reason, I never paid her much attention. After following Grace for a few weeks, it seemed clear that the other woman was just a roommate. If she had been important, I would have expected to see Grace and her going to the local coffee shop, or shopping together, or simply staying in together at night. But Grace was often alone in the evening while her roommate went out." Watson stared off at a vague distant place as if visualizing a memory.

"You're remembering something."

"Just that the roommate – or Grace's cousin as you say – unlike

Grace, she was quite an attractive woman, and she went out with several different men during the short time that I observed them. I got the feeling that the roommate was not so interested in finding a long-term partner as she was interested in simply having a man on her arm. Where Grace seemed thoughtful and discriminating and, maybe, a bit melancholy, the roommate seemed happy and smiley and shallow. I was more drawn to Grace. She reminded me of the line in that song about wanting the sadder but wiser girl."

"You never saw or met the daughter?"

Watson shook his head. "Never would have known she existed but for the casual comment that Grace made."

I pulled out the photo of Nick and handed it to Watson.

"Is that Nick O'Connell?"

"I couldn't say for certain what with all the hair and beard, but yes, it certainly looks like him."

"Are you saying that the hair and beard are a disguise?"

Watson looked up at me with another look of tolerance for the mentally deficient. "Of course."

"Were Nick's eyes intensely blue?" I asked.

"They were blue. But I don't know about intensely blue."

"One witness who saw him up close used that term."

"I suppose it would depend on the surrounding light. But I wouldn't describe them as anything other than blue. Ordinary blue. Blue-gray. But I don't recall if I ever saw him in bright sunlight. Maybe that's the difference."

"Do you remember if Nick had the double-eight tattoo like the rest of the Red Blood Patriots?"

"Sure. On his wrist. When I saw it, I was surprised. He didn't seem the type to do that."

"When was the last time you saw Nick?"

"About a year ago. I'd flown into Reno and was coming out of the airport's baggage area. One of the Reno hotel shuttles was just driving away with a load of passengers. Nick yelled my name out the window and waved."

"So that places him near Tahoe, but not in the Tahoe Basin. When was the last time you spoke to Nick?"

"Probably that night we drank Courvoisier with Davy. That

would also be about a year ago."

"Do you know who Nick's helper on the hijacking was?"

"The man he dumped overboard? No. If I had to guess, I'd say it might have been a man named Kyle. He was a loner with a shifty quality. He watched Davy a little too closely. I didn't trust him. Nick and Davy probably had a deal that was mutually beneficial. Nick gets some help on the hijacking, help without strings attached because the help was going to die. And Davy got rid of someone who was a problem. Maybe the guy learned something he shouldn't have. Or maybe he'd made Davy look bad in front of the other guys. Or maybe he was disloyal."

"Davy would kill someone for those transgressions?"

Watson looked at me like I was naïve. "Davy is one of the most amoral men I've ever met. Just like Nick in that way. He does what's effective in getting what he wants. There is no right or wrong, only what's pragmatic. He doesn't even have a temper. He's just a businessman without a conscience."

"So he wouldn't kill you for insulting him. But he'd kill you if your insult made his other men less likely to obey."

"Exactly."

"It sounds like Nick and Davy were in this together, trying to find the treasure before you could find it."

"I don't think so. I think each played the other, tried to make the other think that they were allies in looking for the treasure all while each planned to double-cross the other and take the treasure for himself."

"As were you."

"Yeah, I guess so."

"Why?" I asked. "You obviously did well on your gun venture. You didn't need any more money. Why such an effort to find this treasure?"

"Just because it is treasure. Buried treasure. The allure has captivated people throughout history. It's not about money or wealth. It's about discovering the secret. Did Gan Sun find or create a treasure? Did his grandson Ming Sun stash it somewhere? The excitement of finding this possible bounty is much greater than its monetary value. Financial reward is of no account compared to the history-making excitement of prying open some treasure box to see what is inside."

"What is your take on why Nick hijacked the boat?" I said.

"The only explanation that makes sense is that he wanted me out of the way. He thought I was close to finding the treasure, the treasure that probably is just a dream."

"Why didn't he just kill you?"

"I'm hard to kill. I'm careful where I go and how I run my affairs. Except for this little jail detour, I always carry. I'm even legal in California. And I have two bodyguards. So the only way for Nick to kill me would be to make the hit in public. In a grocery store or something. And that carries a large risk of being caught." Watson paused. "So it makes sense that Nick planned all along for this."

Watson stopped, gazed into space. "But I still can't figure out how he got my DNA to put under Grace's fingernails."

I pointed at his leg.

"What?"

"Your leg. The wound on your shin."

Watson looked truly shocked.

"My God! When I tripped and hit the curb!" His hand went unconsciously down his leg, his fingertips feeling the shin divot through his pants. "I remember that I was wearing shorts that day. Nick must have been following! He saw me fall, and after I shook myself off and hobbled away, he collected whatever flesh I left on the curb! Christ, that was brilliant."

"Can you think of anyone else who might be a danger to Grace's daughter?" I didn't want to tell him that she'd been kidnapped.

"You mean, someone who would pursue her because Grace might have given her valuable information?"

"Yeah."

"Well, other than Davy, no, I can't think of anyone else. Even if I got out of prison, I wouldn't be a physical danger to her. I'm not the type. And with Nick at the bottom of the lake, that leaves Davy alone. Unless he or Nick told someone else about the possible gold, but I can't see it. We all wanted it for ourselves."

I thought about it, decided there was nothing more to learn from Watson, and called to be let out.

"Hey, what about the DA?" Watson said as I was leaving. "Are you going to call her? Put in a good word?"

Watson had been very forthcoming. But his desire to steal Grace's treasure – if there was a treasure – disgusted me.

"I'll think about it," I said, and left.

THIRTY-SEVEN

It was still light when Spot and I got home.

I remembered the recent dark morning when we'd walked out on the trail that winds around the mountain north of my cabin. I took Spot back out on the trail to the overlook where he'd sniffed with such interest. When we got there, it was just like before. Spot was very interested in the Jeffrey pine and the surrounding area.

After looking around and seeing nothing, I decided to make a more thorough grid search of the area. I drew an imaginary rectangle that included the tree and the area ten feet to either side, as well as the area about six feet both upslope and downslope from the tree. Starting at one corner, I slowly walked one edge, studying the ground. At the far side of my rectangle, I about-faced and walked back, this time studying the ground a foot in from the imaginary edge. When I'd returned to the original side, I moved another foot in and went back across the rectangle. I had no idea of what, or if, I might find anything. But a grid search is the most effective way of forcing oneself to look at the entire area, even those patches that have nothing to attract the eye.

The tree grew at a transition point on the slope. To the sides of the tree where the trail went along, the ground was level. Above the tree was a gentle slope that was thick with duff and brush. Below the tree, the ground dropped off at a steep angle. A person watching my cabin from this distance would likely pace back and forth a bit to stretch his legs. But he would be reluctant to step below the tree because he would probably slip and slide on the steep dirt. If you weren't careful, you might not stop until you came to a stand of small Lodgepole pine 30 feet down.

I searched all of the area above the tree as well as to the sides of the tree, finding nothing. I didn't want to step below the tree, fall on my rear and slide down the mountain. So I moved down the trail to a point where the descent was less steep. I carefully stepped off the trail and, holding onto a small tree, eased myself down about ten feet to an area that was a little less steep and also had a few more handholds, a couple of young trees, some brush, and an exposed root of the large Jeffrey pine. Moving laterally, I studied the slope that was just below the trail and now roughly straight out from my head. On my second pass below the tree, I saw a bit of something that was light-colored. I picked it up.

It was a torn corner of thin paper like newsprint. It was shaped like a right triangle with the tear as its hypotenuse and clean-cut edges for the sides as if from the bottom corner of a catalog. One side was blank. The other side had some printing that began in the middle of a word that had been torn in half. The printing ended with a period. It said "tional foot soldier.'

I put it in my pocket.

When Spot and I got back to my cabin, I called Professor Stein and described it.

"I wonder if this suggests anything to you," I said.

"Of course," he said. "The phrase is 'Constitutional Foot Soldier.' This is the standard verbiage that militia groups use to justify their radical actions. It's especially helpful in recruiting. You're not joining a wacko group that stockpiles illegal explosives and automatic weapons and spews white-supremacist diatribes. You're going to become a constitutional foot soldier and defend our nation's Second Amendment rights against the Socialist government's efforts to eliminate them. You're becoming an essential ally of the founding fathers, and without you, the greatest democracy on earth is doomed to a dystopian nightmare of thought control and the cultural hegemony of abortionists, atheists, people with brown skin, Jewish intellectuals and financial barons."

"Can you think of any other non-militia group or company that would put together a publication using these words in a different format and different meaning?"

"Why are you being so tedious? You call with a question. I take time out of my evening to give you the answer. There is little room for equivocation on this. You found words that either came from a newspaper article describing a radical right-wing militia or its equivalent, or it came from something published by a radical right-wing militia or its equivalent. Nobody of any significance today talks about constitutional foot soldiers in any other context. Now I believe it's time for me to go back to my wine and my book."

"Thank you, sir, for your time."

He grunted at me and hung up.

It wasn't a rock-solid connection to the Patriots, but it was very suggestive. Everywhere I turned, I kept coming across more indications that they were involved. Nick O'Connell and Thomas Watson and Davy Halstead were the only people I'd found who had knowledge of Anna and could presume that she had learned something valuable from her biological mother. All three men were involved in the Red Blood Patriots. The constitutional foot soldier printing came from a place on the mountain where someone was likely watching my cabin. Spot alerted on a strong smell where I found the scrap of paper, and he'd recently trained a similar olfactory focus on my office and on the outside of my cabin door. And before Anna disappeared, she called to say that she saw Davy Halstead on her street.

Now all three men were either dead or in custody.

I made several phone calls. To Agent Ramos, Sergeants Bains, Santiago and Diamond.

I asked them all the same questions. Had they learned anything about Anna Quinn's kidnapping? Did they know anything more about Nick the Knife O'Connell or Thomas Watson or Davy Halstead?

They all suggested ideas and put forth hypotheses. But none of them had experienced any epiphanies. When we were done talking, nothing had changed.

My previous thoughts still suggested that another Red Blood Patriot had overheard Nick and Thomas and Davy talking. Once Nick and Thomas were out of the way, this man realized that if he removed Davy Halstead, he alone would know about the supposed treasure, which, even if it did exisit, probably didn't amount to much. But a man eavesdropping on other men who spoke of gold might well imagine something much grander than common sense would suggest.

I visualized this other, unknown Red Blood Patriot following Davy Halstead and getting the bonus knowledge that Halstead had found Anna. Or maybe Halstead recruited him, and together they kidnapped Anna. Then the new recruit found an opportunity to put a stake through Halstead's chest and take over by himself.

All of which produced the question: Where was Anna? Was she dead, her body dumped in the forest? Or did someone question her and decide that she was hiding valuable information? If so, they would want to keep her someplace where they could wear her down. Starve her, deprive her of sleep, maybe torture her in an effort to learn what she knew.

Assuming that someone was able to eavesdrop on the information about the journal and treasure, it made sense that the same person would be capable of learning other secrets.

Like the existence of the secret meth lab buried in the hill behind the pole building at the Patriots' compound.

It was time to visit the Red Blood Patriots, at night, unannounced, on my terms.

I called Diamond a second time.

"Do you have, or do you know somebody who has a bolt cutter?"

"No, but I've seen them at the Home Depot."

"I need one tonight."

"Let me call Ron. We call him Ronald McHardware. Guy's got more crap in his garage than a hardware distribution center. I could borrow one from him."

"The hardware stores are all closed up here. If Ron doesn't have one, could you buy one and run it up the mountain to me?"

"Hey, tell you what," Diamond said, irritation in his voice. "Why don't I drop everything including this Tecate and become your private courier service."

"Please. It might save a life. I'll owe you, as will the person who lives. If she lives."

"And you're not volunteering Anna's name because…"

"Because then you might feel a duty to let the appropriate

county's sheriff know about my activity so they could help save her life."

"You're playing hero, going in alone," he said, derision in his voice.

"No. I'm being practical. One guy can probably get in without calling attention to himself. It would be a lot more difficult with two or more guys."

"No point in disagreeing with you anyway," Diamond said. "I know how you are."

There was a pause.

"Be there as soon as I can," Diamond said.

As soon as I hung up, there was a tap at the door.

I envisioned militia fundamentalists with AKs on full auto. But Spot was staring at the door, wagging his tail. You can't find more trust in church.

I pulled the door open.

Street came in, hugged me, then pushed back a little and put her hands on my chest. She reached up and traced the edges of my shirt collar. Spot burrowed his nose between us.

"What's wrong?" she said.

"Why do you ask?" I said.

"I can tell. You're distracted. Worried."

"I have an idea of where Anna might be."

Street's face clouded. "No, don't. Please." She shook her head.

"You don't even know what I'm thinking."

"Yes, I do. You're going to go after her. And you're going alone. I've seen and felt this too many times before. I can read the danger on your face."

The worry on her brow was intense.

"You should have help," she said. "And backup. But you won't because you think it will compromise your mission. Owen, this terrifies me." She turned her head against my chest and hugged me, her fear telegraphing from her body to mine. Spot pushed forward so that he completely separated us at Street's waist and my hips. We had to bend forward to still hug.

"I'm sorry, sweetheart. Yes, reinforcements would absolutely compromise my mission. And I know it's frightening. But please think of how terrified Anna must be. If she's still alive."

Street turned and looked up at me, her eyes distorted with heavy tears. "Of course, I know how terrified she must be! This isn't a simple thing, Owen. It's not like an equation where I can balance her fear against mine and say, sure, hon, go for it."

She put her head back against me.

"I'm sorry," she said. "I shouldn't have said that."

I held her head, my fingertips touching her face. I lowered my chin until my nose touched her hair. I inhaled her scent.

"You won't tell me where you're going, will you?"

"It's best if you don't know," I said. "Less risk to you."

"And you won't tell Diamond, either."

"Diamond always looks after me. His instincts make it hard for him to hold back," I said.

"When will you be back? When will I hear from you?"

"Sometime between early tomorrow morning and tomorrow night."

"Why such a long time frame? Don't you know where you're going?"

"I know where I'm going. But I may have to wait for some people to leave."

"To make it safer for you to make your move," she said, sniffling.

"Yeah."

Street shut her eyes. I saw her jaw muscles bulge. "What if you don't come back by late morning? What do I do?"

"Chances are good that I will."

She opened her eyes, looked up at me, her eyes moving left and right, searching mine. "But what if something goes wrong?" Her voice was tight, high, worried.

"Okay. If you don't hear from me by six p.m. tomorrow, call Diamond. Tell him to contact Professor Frank Stein at UNR. Together, they will figure out where I went."

"Will you bring Spot?" she asked. He lifted his head and looked up at her.

"Yeah. But I won't put him in any danger that I know of."

"Not that you know of," she repeated. "He can still get killed. You can still get killed."

I didn't respond.

"Am I right? This is going to be very dangerous, isn't it? It's not like Anna's tied up in some lonely place without anyone around. Is that the case? Tell me the truth."

"It is, Street. She may be alone in a small place, but that place is likely to be watched by at least one man."

"And he'll be armed," she said.

"I'm not going to lie to you. Yes, it will be dangerous." We were both breathing hard. "I'll take every precaution."

Street was crying harder.

"And what good will that be when I get a phone call from Diamond or some other cop telling me what happened to you?"

"Maybe no good at all," I said. I squeezed her hard.

Street held me for a long minute. Then she pushed away, blinked tears out of her eyes, and dabbed them away with her fingers. She looked up at me, her eyes red. She took several deep breaths, stabilizing herself.

"Okay," she said in a voice so soft I could barely hear her. "I love you." She kissed her fingertip, pressed it against my lips, and turned to walk out.

"I love you, too," I called after her.

THIRTY-EIGHT

I dug through my clothes and put on my black jeans, a black turtleneck, dark brown running shoes, a black knit cap. In the back of the closet hung an old dark navy windbreaker that I rarely wore but keep for such night operations. In my sundries drawer I found my black belt pack. On top of the fridge was a little box of sandwich bags. I opened the woodstove, found a crumbling chunk of burnt wood that had turned to black charcoal and put it in the bag. The charcoal went into the belt pack along with my medium flashlight and my Leatherman folding multi-tool. My smaller jackknife and penlight went into my pocket.

Last was fuel. We might be out in the elements for a long time, so I made a large meal for both Spot and myself.

Just as we were done, Diamond showed up and handed me one of the largest bolt cutters I'd ever seen.

"Thanks much," I said.

"Got you some line, too," he said, pointing to a coil of high-test nylon cord that he'd rubber-banded to the bolt cutter handle.

"For?"

"You cut your way through a pad-locked door, you might need to tie it open so it doesn't bang." He looked at me with narrow eyes, like he still thought I was being stupid. "Or a fence. Especially good for tying back barbed wire."

He handed me a plastic bag. "Some other stuff in there that might come in handy."

I took the bag and hefted it. "Like what?"

"Duct tape. A nested screwdriver set. Folding hacksaw. Energy bars. The LED headlamp is particularly useful."

I clamped my hands on his shoulders. "What can I say?"

"Nothing," Diamond said. "Just keep your head down. Like to have you back in one piece." He gave Spot a pet and left.

Five minutes later, Spot and I were heading down my twisty drive to Highway 50. I went around the south end of the lake, up and over Echo Summit and headed down the American River canyon.

My cellphone rang as the highway climbs from the cellphone shadow at the bottom of the American River canyon back up to the town of Pollock Pines on the ridge at 4000 feet.

"Hello?" I was in a hurry and didn't want to pull over, so I hoped the illegal conversation would be short.

"Mr. McKenna?"

"Owen, yes."

"My name is Tania Kadlec. I'm an assistant curator of photography at the Oakland Museum. I got an email from Robert Calibre at the Crocker Museum. He said you were wondering about whether any early twentieth century photographers took pictures of Chinese laborers. And in particular, there was a reference to something called the Sky Palace?"

Tania sounded Czech, and her beautiful voice was imbued with insecurity.

"Thank you so much for calling," I said. "I appreciate it."

"Well, I don't know if I can be helpful. Robert mentioned something about a murder case, and, well, I'm just calling about an obscure photo."

"I'd love to hear about an obscure photo. Tell me about it," I said.

"Okay. We have a patron who's quite wealthy and has donated many pieces to our museum over the years. Now he's getting on in years, and he's having us do an inventory of his art in preparation for possibly donating his entire collection to us. It's an incredible opportunity for us, and I've been appointed to oversee the photography and…" she stopped. "That sounds really, how do you say, crass, doesn't it?" she continued. "Like we're just cashing in on some rich patron…"

"Tania, it's okay. I understand. Museums need wealthy people to provide the art, and it's standard routine for those people to wait until they are old or dead before they give their art to the museum. In return, they know that the museum will provide a great viewing environment for that art. What you do for the wealthy is just as valuable as what they do for you."

"Oh, thank you. I'm… It's just that most people don't have quite such a sensible way of looking at these things."

"Tell me about your photograph."

"Yes, of course," she said. "Our patron has many great works, but this one is a standout. Tell me, are you by any chance familiar with the photographers called Group F-Sixty-four?"

"No, I'm sorry, it doesn't ring a bell."

"It was a group of well-known photographers who got together in the late nineteen twenties. Ansel Adams, Imogen Cunningham, Willard Van Dyke, and a few others. Their purpose was to show the world that Stieglitz and his New York friends were not the center of the photography universe. The Group F-Sixty-four look was one of crisp focus, exquisitely-framed images, mostly of Western landscapes, but also including portraits and nudes and close-ups of natural objects. They often felt that f-stop-sixty-four was the best aperture for creating their works."

I'd come out on the top of the Pollock Pines ridge. The winding highway had turned to high-speed freeway and I was up to 70, rocketing down toward Placerville.

"Anyway," Tania continued, "our patron has a beautiful black and white, silver gelatin print, eight by ten. Very sharp focus. A spectacular use of lighting and shadows. The range of values alone is worth noting. On the verso it's dated nineteen twenty-eight, and it says, 'printed for the de Young show, nineteen thirty-one.' It's signed by Edward Weston. He had a one-man show at the de Young Museum in nineteen thirty-one. Have you heard of him?"

"Of course. One of the three or four most famous American photographers of the twentieth century. What is the subject?"

"The photo shows several men working with large pieces of rock, laying them into a wall. Three of the men are Caucasian and two appear to be Chinese. It hasn't been authenticated, but it looks very much like Weston's other work and clearly fits with his oeuvre. I believe it to be a genuine Weston, which would make it very valuable."

"Tania, that is a big help. I very much appreciate it."

"Really. Oh, I'm glad. I worried that I would be bothering you by calling."

"No, absolutely not. Tell me, is there anything about the photo that might provide a clue as to where it was taken?"

"No. I've looked at it up close with my loupe. There are no specific identifying characteristics that I can find."

"What about things not specific?"

"How do you mean?"

"What is your gut sense? When you look at this building they're working on, does it look like something you recognize? A tall building going up in San Francisco? A dam or breakwater? A villa in Los Angeles? Could they be repairing a wall at one of the California Missions?"

"Oh, I see what you mean. No, none of those. But whatever I would think could not be backed up with any scientific evidence. It would be, what's the word, whimsy."

"That's exactly what I want, Tania. I want your whimsy. What do you think of when you look at the photo?"

"Well, this would really be whimsy."

"Perfect," I said.

"Last summer," she said, "two of my friends and I went up to Lake Tahoe for a vacation. We went all around the lake and looked at the amazing sights. One day we hiked down the long path to Emerald Bay and we took the tour of the Vikingsholm Castle."

"And that's what the photo looks like to you?"

"Yes. It looks kind of like these laborers are building one of the walls at the Vikingsholm." She paused. "And that would fit with the name you gave Robert Calibre."

My brain was blank for a moment.

"Which name was that?"

"You said it was called the Sky Palace. That would fit, wouldn't it?"

"Yes, Tania. Better than you realize."

I thanked her and hung up.

THIRTY-NINE

It was very dark by the time I came to my turnoff on Highway 49 in Placerville, the Gold Country Highway. I went north, up past where gold was discovered, past the turnoff to the Three Bar Ranch, home of Ellie Ibsen, the world's greatest dog-training expert whose search dogs had helped me on several cases. I continued several miles north to the same place where Spot and I had been a couple of days ago. I hid my Jeep under the brush I used before.

I pulled the baggie of charcoal out of my belt pack and rubbed it over my face and hands. Spot was very interested in this new makeup and stuck his cold wet nose on me in several places.

"Okay, largeness. Time for your nap."

I turned around to face Spot who sat on the back seat, his head jammed up against the headliner of the Jeep.

"Don't want to put you in front of men with guns just yet. And I may need your help later, so sleep well."

I tucked my wallet under the edge of the floor carpet where it curved up toward the brake pedal, and put on my belt pack. I stuffed in the goodies Diamond had gotten me except for the big roll of duct tape. I grabbed my windbreaker and bolt cutter, pet Spot and got out, locking him in the dark Jeep.

I needed my key to get back into the Jeep, but I didn't want to make things any easier for the Patriots just in case everything went wrong.

Thirty feet away was a Black oak. Using my flashlight, I walked around it looking for a little crevice or hole in the bark and found one at the split where one limb branched off another. I wedged my Jeep key into the notch, pushing the metal into the bark with some force so that it would be impossible for a squirrel to run off with it.

With no ID or key on me, I started up the dark trail, carrying the bolt cutter and using my flashlight in short bursts.

It seemed a long hike in the dark before I reached the fence. I was in full view of the dark world, but I didn't have much choice. I put on the headlamp that Diamond had brought and, kneeling in the dirt, I used the bolt cutter to cut a small hole. The fence wire must have been hardened, because it was very difficult to cut. The hardened wire immediately began to dull my cutter. Each subsequent cut became more and more difficult. I worried that the cutter would get too dull before I could make an opening. I downsized my intended circle. After I'd gone about half way around the clock, I had to work the cutter back and forth, over and over, twisting and rotating to cut the linked wires. Finally, the cutter became so dull it was unusable.

I bent the cut half-circle of wires as much as I could with my hands, then stood and kicked at it with my feet, trying to flex it up a bit farther. I cut a piece of the cord Diamond had given me and looped it through the half-cut circle of fencing. I ran it up and through the fencing links a foot above. By jerking and cinching, I folded the heavy wire circle back against the fence and tied the line off to hold it in place.

The opening in the fence still looked much smaller than anything I could crawl through. But I had no choice.

I got down on the ground, raised my right arm, put it through the hole, then stuck my head through the fence. I began to wriggle through. Cut fence wires hooked on my ears and hair and drew bloody scratches down the left side of my neck. I tilted my shoulders at as much of an angle as possible. Wires ripped at my shirt. I got my right shoulder through the hole, but one wire dug in near my left carotid artery, and I wondered for a moment if I would puncture it and die in a minute, pulsing blood coloring my corpse while I was stuck in a fence.

I shifted my position so the opposite wires skewered my right armpit in order to take the pressure off the left side of my neck.

Getting my left shoulder through was the worst. Wires that were effectively sharpened by the process of cutting, raked parallel grooves in my left deltoid and down the outside of my left arm as the opposing wires ripped the flesh of my right armpit. My left elbow seemed to stick on a sharp wire, and as I wrestled it free, I envisioned the bones separating like cooked chicken bones.

Eventually, I was through to my waist and from there it was mere scratches all around my body as I got my butt through and snaked my thighs and legs the rest of the way.

I stood up, blood coming from countless small wounds, and thought about the Bouvier that Spot and I had seen from a distance the previous time we'd climbed to the fence. With luck the dog was kept inside. But unless he was upwind of me, he would smell my blood along with my scent, and it would inflame his response. He would bark until let out.

If it came to a confrontation, I'd have to rely on my experience play-fighting with Spot.

I couldn't hurt a dog that was just doing his job. No club or cobble or other weapon was acceptable. A reckless decision by many measures, but such was the handicap of knowing dogs as well as I know people.

I'd thought of wearing heavy gloves for protection. But I knew from hours of wrestling with Spot that no kind of glove, not even a knight's chain mail could provide much protection against an animal with a bite that can break bones. I also knew from experience with Spot that there is a way – though not very reliable – to gain control over an attacking dog, and it requires that one is bare-handed for maximum control. I hoped that I would have the presence of mind to employ it, should it be necessary. So I went in without gloves.

Of the two depressions and their groups of buildings, only the northernmost one had lights on. I turned off my headlamp and went toward the south group of dark buildings, again using my flashlight as little as possible.

Perhaps the south buildings were vacant, with all of the soldiers in the north group, eating dinner and drinking whiskey. Or perhaps the occupants of the south buildings were on the early-to-bed program. Either way, I had a chance of breaking in without arousing attention.

It was very dark, with only faint starlight to see by. I went slowly, careful not to trip, aware that I could step in an unseen hole and break my ankle.

I walked a spiral curve from the fence ring in toward the south buildings, studying them for possible lights or movement. Despite the moonless darkness, I gradually got a sense of access points, likely paths for their vehicles, probable locations of doors, and possible locations for sentries should the Patriots be very paranoid.

As I got close, I was south of the south buildings. I kept looking for a cabin with a pole building behind it, and a hill behind that. If I found it, I would know that buried deep in the earth was the secret container with its meth lab and, hopefully, one very scared woman tied up and gagged, awaiting probable death.

But I saw nothing like what I was looking for.

There were two plain buildings with several windows at regular intervals. They looked to be of standard frame construction with composition shingle roofs, two-foot eaves and wood siding. There was also a large metal pole barn with no windows, no eaves, but multiple skylights. No light came from inside. The lack of windows suggested a purpose that they didn't want seen by anyone from outside.

I approached the metal pole barn first. In its end was a large oversized garage door big enough to drive a bus-sized RV through. It was locked from the outside by a sliding bar and a large padlock. I would need a cutting torch to get in. I moved to the first of the stick-built buildings.

It had a regular wooden door with a window pane. Peering in, I saw nothing but a distant red glow. I tried the doorknob. It was unlocked. I stood to the side of the wall, pushed the door in, and waited. There was no response.

I walked into the dark interior, moving slowly, keeping my hand along one wall. The red glow turned into a clock. 10:47 p.m. Farther away was another clock. 10:51 p.m. I moved sideways, put my hands out, found a platform, sat down.

It was a bed. I was in a bunkhouse.

I thought of digging through personal effects. But I'd have to use my one of my lights. I'd risk discovery by anyone passing by outside.

I left and went to the second building. It too was unlocked. I slid around the door jamb, moved slowly through the dark, and discovered I was in a kitchen/dining hall. It had a strong odor of garlic mixed with bleach. Again, I could perhaps learn something of the militia men if I wanted to risk a light, but I wanted to explore more before I took that risk.

I left and found the dirt road up the small ravine toward the other, higher depression on the fenced land, and the second, northern group of buildings.

Afraid to use a light, I moved slowly, ready to sprint into the brush on the nearby slope if I sensed a vehicle or men walking through the dark.

The northern group of buildings was well lit by the glow of a sodium vapor light. It flooded a large circle of yellow over the space between four buildings, one of which was a Quonset-style building with a large, arched corrugated roof. At the end of the building was a door with a pair of windows on each side. Lights were on inside the building, and I heard voices from within. Two of the four windows were open, and fitted into each was an exhaust fan that ran at high speed.

The long building to the left was a traditional stick-built design with a gabled roof and five double garage doors, all of which were closed. Nearby were parked two '70s Blazers, the old camo-painted Bronco I'd seen earlier on the highway down in the valley below, and three pickup trucks, one an old Dodge, and two late-model Fords. Not counting any vehicles in the ten-car garage, the vehicles in front of me could represent 18 or 20 men. From the raucous hollering that rose above the whirring nose of the exhaust fans in the Quonset building, they might be 18 or 20 inebriated men who carried automatic weapons.

I walked over to the dark, curved roof and inched my way toward the far end. I peeked around the corner. Light also spilled from this end of the building, but it came from just two windows, the only openings at that end. Both windows were open, serving as air intakes to cool the sweaty men inside.

There was a garbage dumpster twenty feet away from the windows, close enough that I might be able to hide in its dark, protective shadow and hear the voices inside the building.

I circled out through the dark and came up into the dumpster's shadow. I crouched down and peered around the edge of the dumpster, trying not to gag on the miasma of rotting garbage.

A couple of the voices were clear against the larger din of grunts and laughter.

"… up at the range. Those targets were perforated like from a shotgun!"

"That's what an automatic weapon will do. But instead of little buckshot, each hole is from a round that will take down a bear! Imagine putting that puppy over your shoulder and riding into town!"

"Guys!" A third voice trying to get attention.

"That was the AKs we popped those targets with. The Mac tens are accurate as a pea-shooter. All the power in the world don't do no good if you can't hit your target."

"Guys!"

"Accuracy don't mean shit if you're close enough that you can't miss. Gimme a Mac any day. I'll show them civil servants what we think of their rules and regs."

"GUYS!!! SHUT UP!" The voice was deep and thundering.

The building went silent.

"We commence at dawn. Mitch is gonna run tomorrow's drill. He'll take us through a full dress rehearsal. The bank will be represented by the south bunkhouse. This will be a full assault, the real thing. Live ammo. Do you understand what that means?

"And if we pull this dry run off, we're going to set the date. If, and I stress IF… If we make our objective, then we may be wholly funded from within for an indefinite period of time. But NO WAY will there be a stipend! This is a holy war! This is about saving our country from the New World Government! This is not a job with a paycheck! This is about fighting for your constitutional rights, your purpose! OUR MISSION! Now get your asses home to bed!"

There was the general noise of sliding chairs and people mumbling. I ran away from the small cover of the stinking dumpster, then trotted up the slope into the darkness. I turned to watch from behind an oak. I heard doors open at the far side of the building. Followed by voices.

Several men appeared in the wash of yellow light.

I saw a large, furry, black dog romping through the light, into the shadows, back into the light. The Bouvier des Flanders. Herd dog and guard dog extraordinaire.

The group of men ambled away from me, down the path toward the southern depression and the bunkhouse. The interior lights of the building went off, and two more men came into view. They turned the other way and walked toward the end of the building where the dumpster was.

Toward me.

"Christ, that dumpster stinks!" one of them said.

"Greg put those deer guts in it."

"He didn't bury them?! The hell was he thinking?! Davy said we always gut our prey down in the gully so the stink runs down into the gov'ment's property."

"Greg didn't know."

The dog ran toward them and trotted with them.

As they were about to leave the last wash of yellow from the outdoor light, the dog stopped, lifted his head to the night, spun a half-circle, made a deep growling woof, then sprinted in my direction.

FORTY

As the dog shot toward me, growling like a deadly predator, my instinct was to turn and run away. But I knew that I needed to confront him. And for that I needed to see.

I ran toward the light, toward the dog.

An intense, whispered voice came from below. "Big Bear sees something! Go get 'em, Big Bear!"

The dog didn't slow as he raced up the dark slope. If he saw my rush toward him, he was unfazed.

He stopped growling.

I watched his leaping stride, concentrated on his rhythm, tried to ignore his sudden, frightful silence. I remembered all the times that I'd engaged in full-body combat with Spot. Spot didn't use a crushing bite when we played, but he lunged and dodged and parried, and I developed a familiarity with canine attack techniques. I remembered the movements, the tricks. But this dog was a stranger. I didn't know his personal moves. I also had no idea if a dog that was engaged in play fighting acted the same as a dog in a serious attack.

But I had a belief that I understood the movements of dogs. And compared to Spot, the Bouvier was relatively small.

When the Bouvier got close, he burst forward as if doubling his speed, then leapt into the air. He rose from the ground on a rising arc. I dropped to my knees to be below him.

Like a large cat, he twisted in the air, lowering his head toward his moving target.

I waited an excruciating moment. A feint only works if it comes at the last beat.

When the dog was a mere three feet from locking onto my face, I raised my left hand to the side.

Dogs always go for the movement. He jerked his head to the side, his mouth open, ready to crush my hand bones. At the last instant, I snatched my left hand from in front of his jaws as I shot my right hand to the side of his neck in a fast swipe.

I hit him hard, grabbing a thick handful of neck fur in my right hand as I rotated my body and followed through with the weight of my body.

I drove him down onto the ground. He was as shocked as I was. I held the back of his neck fur as I landed on top of him. He struggled and writhed beneath me.

A one hundred-plus-pound dog is very strong. And a dog's jaws and teeth are sufficient to kill an animal four times his size if he can get a good grip on his prey. But a hundred pound dog is no match for a man who has his neck from behind.

I gripped his collar with my left hand, grabbed a better handful of fur with my right, and picked him up, front paws off the ground. I didn't want to choke him, just control him, so I kept his rear paws on the ground.

He stopped struggling, the reaction to domination. His life was in my hands and he knew it.

I walked over to an oak, lowered him down to all fours, and leaned against the tree with his body between me and the tree bark.

I released his collar with my left hand, but kept a firm grip on his fur with my right. I took Diamond's cord from my belt pack, stuck it through his collar and ran it tight around the oak so that his neck was immobilized against the bark. I tied the rope tight, stepped back, hands out, ready in case he got loose. But he was held firm. He didn't even growl or bark.

I turned toward the buildings below.

A man was thirty feet down the slope. He shined his flashlight in my face.

I was about to speak when I sensed the barest hint of a lightning-bolt striking the back of my head before the world went dead.

FORTY-ONE

I awoke slowly. Felt slime over my face. Thick goo. Stink like rotting meat. Odor worse than the gagging smell outside of the dumpster. A hundred times worse.

I realized that I was in the dumpster. My hands were tied behind my back.

My breath burbled through a gelatinous goo that filled my left ear, mashed around my left eye, over my nose, under my chin and into my mouth. The goo was warm and seemed to bubble. A garbage pudding made of rotting flesh. Shivering movement, as if the gelatin were alive.

Maggots!

Street had once shown me a great, writhing maggot mass in the rotting insides of a bear carcass.

I was face down in a maggot mass.

I exploded into a full-body convulsion, knees pulling down into the deer-guts garbage, shoulders twisting, head thrusting back. Spitting, yelling, choking on maggots. I blew the goo out from inside my cheeks, then vomited. Dry heaves. Spit and gag. Spit and cough. More spitting.

Threw myself sideways, banging into the side of the dumpster. Wiped my face on the rusted metal inside of the dumpster. Spit again and again, great, wracking, hacking, throat-gouging spit.

My head pounded as if it had been hit into the left field bleachers with a Louisville Slugger. My shoulders ached from having my arms pulled back. But nothing compared to the inside of my mouth. My tongue found a soggy bit of goo stuck on the inside of my cheek. A maggot. Spit. Another mashed onto the insides of my front teeth. Another pureed between my upper left molars.

I vomited again.

I raised my knees and wiped my gooed-over face on soaked jeans.

I leaned back against the inside of the dumpster, unable to breath, unable to think.

The torture of physical or psychic pain can be incapacitating. Yet the torture of revulsion can be as strong as either. In the space of a couple of minutes, I'd been broken. I would have signed any paper, confessed to any trumped-up charge, run through any fire if I could suddenly be clean and dry and wearing fresh clothes and in a place that was far from any maggots.

The best way to find calm in a seriously stressful situation is to take a deep breath, hold it, then breathe out slowly. But I couldn't take a deep breath. The gas in the dumpster was so thick with putrescence that I could barely tolerate the tiniest sip of air.

After five minutes of mind-over-matter struggle, I managed to replace horrific disgust with anger.

There was a line of light to the side above my head. I got my feet pulled in beneath me. I raised up just a bit, pushing my feet down into unknown gunk until they hit something firm. My upturned face rose to hit the metal at the inside corner of the dumpster. A tiny stream of fresh air came in past the edge of the lid and hit my face. I sucked it in, desperate for air that wouldn't poison me. But my thighs were holding me just above a deep squat so that I could keep my mouth and nose near the crack at the edge of the lid. My thighs began burning and quivering from the deep flex. I had to relax and sink back down into the garbage.

I leaned forward onto my knees, took a knee-walk step forward through the gunk. I looked up at the dumpster lid. There was another line of light, another infinitesimal bit of air coming in. I realized that the dumpster had two lids, side-by-side. I straightened up until my head hit one of the lids. I pushed against the lid with the crown of my skull, my temples throbbing with the pain of being knocked out. The lid moved a half-inch or so, but no more.

I knee-walked sideways, under the other lid. Pushed up with

my head a second time. That lid also moved just a bit, but no more. I sat back on my haunches and cranked my head back to try to see through the crack between the two lids. I had to rock sideways, back and forth, to get a sense of that line of light, to see that the line was interrupted by a dark object about six inches across.

Maybe the two lids were padlocked shut. I tried to recall what I'd seen when I'd come into the compound and hidden in the shadow of the dumpster. No image came to mind. I remembered seeing the dumpster. I'd hidden behind it. It had so reeked of dead, rotting flesh that nothing about its lids had registered.

Now, as I looked at the dark interruption in the thin line of light between the two lids, I envisioned handles or brackets welded to the lids. It looked like a 2 X 6 board had been slid in under the handles or brackets. If, in some way, I could slide that 2 X 6 out from the handles, maybe I could open the dumpster and escape.

I needed something to poke up through the crack between the lids and use to move the board. For that I needed my hands.

My hands were tied tight enough that my wrists burned. I pushed and pulled my hands from one another, seeing if there was any give in the cord that bound them. There was no flex. I needed some kind of tool, something sharp. The only possibilities were in the garbage beneath me.

So I sat down on my butt, leaned back, and thrust my hands down into the garbage. I felt and grabbed and squeezed. The garbage was mostly in plastic garbage bags. But many of the bags were old and the plastic disintegrated as I reached with my hands. The more recent bags had tough plastic, but were still easy to rip apart. Everything was covered with the slippery slime of rotting deer guts.

Each time I came across something of substance, I put it between my hands, explored it by feel. I stayed on the perimeter of the dumpster, avoiding the maggot mass that I thought was toward the center. I stabbed my hands down into the gunk, pulled up whatever I found. Then I scooted sideways and repeated the process, attempting to identify each item by shape and heft and texture and determine if it could be of aid to me.

I found a large boot, a drip coffee maker with no pot, a glass bottle, a large-caliber empty shell casing, a thick, bendy book like a big-city Yellow Pages, a bolt stacked with washers held in place by a nut, a dull chainsaw chain, an aluminum can, an old candle that was burned down in the center until the wick was gone, a disposable razor, a DVD disk, a plastic bag with unused tortillas... Wait. A disposable razor.

I felt around behind my back, trying to find the razor again.

It wasn't there. I went left, then right. I found a 9-volt battery, a crumpled pile of foil, a plastic bottle, broken eyeglasses, a piece of window screen, and, finally, the disposable razor.

I tried to figure how to work it. My hands were tied so that the inside of my left wrist was against the outside of my right wrist. As a right-handed person, that position made it difficult to get the razor into contact with the cord. I hoped that they'd used the cord that Diamond had given me as it seemed like something a razor could cut. Twisting my arm hard, I was able to rotate my right wrist so that both wrists were inside-to-inside. That position stressed my right shoulder and elbow and substantially limited my ability to manipulate my right fingers. I couldn't do anything with the razor. So I rotated my wrist back to its original position and, careful not to drop the razor, shifted it so that I was holding it by its very tip, then waggled it until I could catch it with the fingers on my left hand.

To make a shaving razor work, you have to hold it almost perpendicular to your face. And I couldn't get the end of the handle far enough out from my wrists to get the cutting edge to contact the cord.

I shifted it around so that I was using my thumb and index finger to hold the razor by its head, while the handle poked out the opposite direction. It was a terrific strain on my hand muscles, but I was able to scrape the razor head against the cord.

I heard a sound like a door opening, swinging out hard and banging against a wall. I went motionless.

Voices. Two men. Five times louder than needed for communication. Slurred words.

"I tol' you, Manny, dint I? I tol' you good."

"What? That you'd nail that sucker? So what, Gaver? If it

hadn't been for Big Bear, that guy wouldn't'a been distracted. You think that tall guy woulda let you play tee-ball with his head if he wasn't dealin' with Big Bear? You ever seen a man who could take Big Bear on a charge? Have you? Answer me."

"I dunno."

"'Course you haven't. Jackson trained that doggie. No dog Jackson ever trained has been taken by a bare-handed man. It's like he had some kinda James Bond training, grabbing that dog out of the air like he was a butterfly or something, and then tying him to a tree. Gentle with the dog, too. Like he's one of those martial arts dudes, all calm and into the Buddha thing. Then you whack him with your stick. Big deal. If he wasn't tying up Big Bear, he woulda been hog-tying you."

"Not with this S 'n W on my belt, he wouldn't."

"So you say, Gaver. But saying ain't the same as doing. If I's you, I'd be careful. There probably isn't a chance he's still alive, considering the way he flopped face-first into those deer guts."

"Hell, no, he din't even move, din't even jerk for air. Hard to think he was breathin'."

"Even so, until you know for sure, I'd watch your back."

"Even if he's still sucking intestines, by eleven tomorrow morning, when the sun gets high, that dumpster'll be hot enough to bake bread. By noon or one, he'll be baked dead as that deer. Teach him for hitting Big Bear. Davy'll be okay with me using the backhoe. Come one o'clock, I'll put his body where we put that ATF guy. Jus' like before, you'n me'n Davy will be the only ones who know. I got plenty of time to get rid of the body."

"Better not put it off, because the weather's supposed to turn. You won't even get that backhoe up the hill when it starts raining and the path turns sloppy."

"Who you think he is, anyway?"

"Gotta figure it's that guy Davy warned us about. The private cop from Tahoe. Davy said he might come 'round askin' about our group. Davy will be glad when he finds out what we did with him."

"Hey, check the time, we gotta spell the Mauer brothers on their watch."

The voices got softer as they moved away.

In time, I heard nothing more, and I went back to work with the razor.

I could feel the little blade bite into the cord. By using a short, repetitive shaving motion, I worked it over and over. Because a shaving razor is designed to take a tiny bite, it took many minutes. I had to transfer the razor from my left hand to my right so that I could straighten and flex my left fingers and prevent them from cramping. Then I shifted it back to my left hand to keep working.

Ten minutes later, I had cut the cord.

My shoulders ached as I brought my hands around in front of me. Now I had to get out of the dumpster.

I reached up and tested both dumpster lids to verify what I'd discovered with my head. Both lids moved just a little before stopping, possibly held in place by the six-inch object that I could make out in the crack between the lids.

If the lids were locked with something much more substantial, my only hope would be to find in the garbage some kind of a lever strong enough to use as a crow bar between the crack where the lid came down on the dumpster, and then bend the metal enough to get out. Which was about as likely as a SWAT team descending on the camp before the morning's sun baked me to death.

I began searching the garbage for a tool.

Twenty minutes later, I found an old, rusted, 14-penny nail in the gunk at the bottom corner of the dumpster.

I poked the nail through the crack between the lids and pushed it into the six-inch obstruction I'd seen earlier. The nail was barely long enough to reach the object. The material felt like wood, giving just a bit as I pushed the nail point up through the crack.

I levered the nail sideways. The wood didn't budge. I pushed the opposite direction. Maybe it shifted a tiny bit. Maybe not. I changed the angle of the nail, pushed it up and to the side, levering it again. The wood – if it was wood – possibly shifted a little more. I worked the nail over and over. I couldn't tell if I was merely gouging a groove in the material or moving the material. The possibility of escape seemed very remote. But I kept up the nail movement.

Ten minutes later, the wood made a thunking noise as its weight shifted. I envisioned the wood as a teeter-totter of sorts, first leaning a tiny amount one direction, then leaning the other direction. It gave me hope because it indicated that I was succeeding at moving the wood.

After another ten minutes, the wood came free from whatever brackets or handles held it, and it fell to the ground, banging the side of the dumpster with a loud thunk.

I didn't wait to see who would come to investigate. I pushed up one of the dumpster lids, standing up into cool, fresh night air. I held the lid so it wouldn't flop over and bang onto the back of the dumpster. Keeping a strong grip on the lid, I swung my leg up and over the dumpster edge, followed with my other leg, folded my body over the ledge, my feet contacting the ground, and closed the lid gently so that it wouldn't bang. I slid the board back under the handles.

The grounds were quiet, the men and the dog gone. The sodium vapor light was still bright, but the light that had earlier spilled out from the Quonset-style building was off.

I moved around the far end of the building, staying well into the darkness, watching for the silent rushing attack of the dog named Big Bear.

No dog moved, and I saw no man.

What I did see now that I hadn't seen before was a small dark cabin in the distance and behind it a pole building that backed up to a steep hill.

In the side of the pole building were windows, and in one of them shined a weak light.

FORTY-TWO

My impulse was to rush in, but I kept my distance. I moved sideways through the darkness, moving in an arc around the cabin. I felt for my belt pack and its flashlight, but it was gone, as was my headlamp, my jackknife, and everything else that had been in my pockets.

I went by a Jeep, a CJ-6 model from the '70s with the open top. I felt in the dark for the ignition. There was no key. I reached and felt above the visor. Nothing.

I came by a mound where someone had been piling compost. Near it was one of those large mobile utility carts mounted on two bicycle wheels. I stepped around it and continued moving in the dark.

The front of the pole building came into view as I came even with the back of the cabin.

The pole building had a tall garage door that was wide enough to fit four cars side-by-side and next to it a human door.

In front of the human door was a small, dull, orange glow. I moved closer. Slow. Silent. Creeping up at about the speed a vine grows on a hot summer day.

When I got closer, I saw that the glow came from the embers of a small fire. Two men sat in folding chairs in front of the fire. Their mission may have been guard duty, but it looked like they were asleep. Or drowsy drunk, their bodies slid down in the chairs, feet stretched way out, heads tipped back on the top edges of the chairs.

One of them moved and mumbled something. The other groaned.

Manny and Gaver, the night guards.

I worried that my stink would be obvious if they were

downwind from me. But the air seemed motionless. I stopped and sat down in the dark and watched them. In time, one of them made a startled jerk and sat up straight. He stared into the dark for a bit, then put another log on the fire. He pushed himself off his chair, kneeled in the dirt and blew on the embers. Over and over. Eventually, a flame grew under the new log. He sat back in his chair, reached a bottle off the ground and took a drink. Then he bumped the bottle against the other man's arm. That man sat up, took the bottle, and swigged a longer drink.

I got an idea.

I went back through the darkness to the utility cart. It had such a good balance that I barely touched its handle, and it rolled easily. I pushed it through the dark, over toward the pole building, where I left it behind some trees.

After forty-five minutes, one man told the other that he had to pee. I moved behind a tree. He stumbled across the dark toward me. I studied his form, looking for the shape of a weapon. It looked like there was a holster on his right hip. The man named Gaver had spoken of the gun on his belt. Gaver stepped behind a tree and urinated into a bush.

I had thought about what approach would work best. While he was still zipping up, I tackled him from the right rear side, my shoulder to the middle of his ribs. He made a sudden exhalation and folded as I propelled him into the trunk of a large fir. His head bounced off the wood, and he went down.

I unsnapped his holster and tossed his gun into some distant bushes. The gun clattered through branches, making even more noise than the man had hitting the tree.

Gaver was a good-sized guy with a large inner tube of heavy flab around his middle. I squatted, grabbed his jacket collar with one hand, his belt with the other, and picked him up.

With Gaver in a bent position, arms flopping and feet making pretend steps, I ran him forward, straight into the utility cart. His head hit the front, fiberglass wall of the cart, and he collapsed in a heap. Another loud noise.

"What're you doing, Gaver?" The other watchman Manny called out.

I picked up the cart handle and trotted Gaver along the way

that I'd come, toward the far side of the cabin. Manny's plaintive refrain receding in the distance, "Gaver? You okay? Hey, Gaver, where'd you go? You trip or something?"

I rolled Gaver back to the compost pile and let go of the cart handle.

He moaned and gasped. I grabbed his hair, lifted his head, knotted my knuckles and put a short right jab onto his jaw. He went still. I patted Gaver down. His overly-large Jim Bowie knife was in a sheath on his right thigh. His wallet was attached to his belt with a heavy chain. I took off his belt and threw it, the wallet and his knife into the bushes.

I trotted back toward the pole building.

"Gaver," Manny said, standing ten yards away from the fire, staring into the night. "Don't be a dumbshit. This isn't funny. We have a job to do. This isn't the time for jokes."

I stayed in the dark.

In another minute, Manny came walking farther out into the darkness, the campfire winking behind him. He had his gun and flashlight out, holding them together like a SWAT team member. He swung them back and forth, the light beam oscillating through the night. I stayed behind a tree, watching his rhythm. When he got closer and his beam went away from me, I made a silent run over to the dark side of the pole building. I waited in the dark while Manny called Gaver.

I planned to wait for him to give up and come back toward the campfire. But I saw him point his flashlight down to his side and lift something off his belt. I felt a jolt of adrenaline as I realized he had raised a walkie-talkie to his mouth.

I sprinted toward him.

"Sunrise, this is sunset. Come in, sunrise. We have a situation that..."

His words were cut off as I hit him from behind.

He exhaled a big whoomfing sound as he went down. The walkie-talkie flew through the air. I landed on top of Manny, and he made a grunt of pain. He reached out, gun in his hand.

I grabbed his wrist and pounded it onto the ground. Again. Harder. He let go and the gun spun away. Manny writhed under me. He was tough the way a wild animal is tough. He rolled and squirmed, punched and gouged, got my forearm in his teeth and bit down.

The pain was like fire just below my elbow.

I jerked my arm, slamming the side of his head onto the ground hard enough to break his skull. He made an amazing jerk and got out from under me. I jumped up, expecting him to flee. Instead, he turned and lunged toward me.

I bent so that he went by my side. I grabbed his jacket and added to his momentum as I stuck out my foot. He went down again. I landed on top of his back. We both slid on the ground right up to the embers. Manny kicked and jerked like a madman. I got my knee into his back but it didn't slow him down. He pulled a knife out of his pocket.

I reached into the fire, grabbed the unburned end of the log, lifted it high and smashed it down onto the back of his head. Coals sprinkled into his hair, but he lay still.

I brushed the coals out of his hair and rolled him away from the fire. He didn't move.

Nearby was the whiskey bottle that Manny and Gaver had been drinking from. I still had the taste of mashed maggots in my mouth. I took off the cap, took a mouthful, swished, gargled and spit. It tasted like cheap bourbon, and I'd never been more grateful for mouthwash in my life. I tipped my head back, poured the whiskey over my face and rubbed my sleeve over my cheeks, scraping away a layer of dried, rotted deer guts.

I removed Manny's knife from his hand, folded it shut and put it in my pocket.

Several yards away in the dirt came a voice over the walkie-talkie. "Sunset, do you read? Sunset, report. Sunset, we're on our way."

I ran to the pole building.

The door was unlocked. I swung it open and stepped inside.

FORTY-THREE

The inside of the building was like a large farm equipment shed. On the left was a front-end loader with the backhoe hanging off the rear. In the middle of the building was a bass boat on a trailer. To the right sat an old International Harvester Scout, without a top and so rusted that the fenders looked like they would fall off if the vehicle hit a large bump.

At the rear of the building was a long workbench that stretched all the way across the back wall. On one side of the bench was a fluorescent shop light throwing its cold greenish glow over that corner of the cavernous room. Near it was the window from which I'd seen the light outside.

The back wall was concrete block just as Thomas Watson had described, a retaining wall holding back the hill behind the building. At one-third intervals there were abutments made of the same block. They were perpendicular to the back wall, and their top edges rose up at a steep angle to meet the back wall about 8 feet above the ground. Davy Halstead was a smart engineer.

The surface of the back wall was covered with stolen highway signs, turned on end and attached to the block wall. Up close, you realize just how big they are, 5 by 10 feet, with rounded corners, and made of some type of pressed chip board with a smooth finish and painted with high-gloss paint. One was green and said Exit 296 in white reflective paint. Another was yellow and said Thru-Traffic Merge Left in black letters. A third said Colusa 4 Miles and Sacramento 72 Miles.

The workbench backed up to the signs. Screwed into the signs were tool racks and angle braces to which clip lights were attached.

I felt along the bench looking for divisions. The bench had

a 2 X 4 framework underneath that had been constructed into 2-foot by 8-foot sections to hold standard plywood ripped down the center on the long dimension. I felt along each section. One had a heavy-duty metal drawer slide attached to the bottom left side of the 2 X 4 structure. The next section had none. The following section had the same drawer slide attached to its right side. It looked like the brackets were designed to hold up the section of bench between them.

I felt some more and found the connecting rod that penetrated the rear wall, locking the suspended bench section in place. Pulling on it unlatched the bench section, and it slid toward me, then pivoted down on swing arms until it touched the floor, perfectly counter balanced by tension springs similar to those on a garage door.

A sign that read Exit Only was now fully exposed. There were two hidden catches on the right side, one 2 feet above the floor and one 6 feet. I unhooked them and the sign swung open. It was a good disguise and well designed, easy to operate from the outside or inside, but nearly impossible to detect unless you knew it was there.

Behind the Exit Only sign was a recessed sheet-rocked wall with a door framed into it. It had a regular knob and a heavy keyed deadbolt. The deadbolt had been forced with a crowbar. Maybe Davy Halstead had lost the key. More likely, the man who killed Davy couldn't find the key and had to jimmy the lock to use the secret room.

I turned the knob and walked into Davy's meth lab.

FORTY-FOUR

The meth lab in the metal storage box was like a windowless cave. It was damp and cool and dark. Despite the whoosh of what sounded like an exhaust fan, the air was thick with a burning odor that reminded me of ammonia or cat urine. Meth lab chemicals.

The only light came from a small desk lamp in the front corner to my left. It shined down on a counter that showed the white laminate surface at the edges, but was covered with brown stains elsewhere. Above the counter was a narrow shelf with supplies. Stacks of cold medicines, still unopened in their bright-colored packages. Multiple boxes of coffee filters. A row of shiny new glass beakers. Six small cans of kerosene. A big plastic jug of anti-freeze.

I walked over and turned the desk lamp so that it shined back toward the rear of the storage unit.

At the back wall of the metal box shined two little points of light about five and a half feet above the floor. I left the light in its angled position and walked back.

The two points of light grew into Anna's eyes. Terrified eyes. Eyes that looked almost alien in their fear and dread. Eyes on a body that was stretched up like Jesus on the cross. Eyes that had been hanging on the wall for days.

I realized that she couldn't see who I was.

"Anna, it's me, Owen. I've come to get you out of here."

Her head vibrated, but she didn't speak. Her mouth was stuffed with a beige rag like a sleeve torn off of a shirt. It ran around her head and through her mouth. Around her neck was a rope that stretched up to a tie loop at the upper edge of the storage container. She was currently standing, but she would choke to death if she fell asleep and sagged down. Her arms were out and up, a nylon line going from zip ties on her wrists to distant tie loops at the upper corners of the metal storage container. Her bare feet were lashed together. Assuming the goal of her captor was to make her confess to secrets real or fictional, I couldn't imagine a more effective way of breaking a person's spirit. She couldn't move or talk or sleep. That she was still alive suggested that she still hadn't given in to her captor's desires.

"I'm going to cut off your gag, Anna. Hold still."

I took Manny's folding knife from my pocket and raised it to the side of Anna's head, keeping it out of her sight. I slipped the point under the cloth behind her ear. My hands shook with tension. I knew that men would be on us shortly. Manny's knife was as sharp as a razor blade, and the fabric fell away.

"Thank God you're here," she said in a hoarse, ravaged whisper.

Next, I cut the rope that was tied around her neck. I worried that she'd collapse once her arms were freed, so I cut the rope around her ankles first. Then I positioned myself to catch and support her as I cut the rope around her left wrist.

As her armed dropped, she gasped in pain.

With that arm freed, she swung in and sagged. I got my arm around her waist and held her up as I cut the final rope on her right wrist. As that arm fell, she stifled a scream of agony, and I understood that her shoulder tendons and ligaments must be on fire.

I pocketed the knife, then shifted her so that I could pick her up. But first, knowing she'd be unable to put her arms around my neck, I tucked her arms in front of her so they wouldn't swing and cause her more torturous pain. Then I put my arm behind her knees, picked her up, and trotted with her out of the secret room, through the door, and into the pole building.

In the distance through the outside door, I saw approaching headlights. I knew that if I stayed in the pole building, we would be trapped and possibly die in a flurry of bullets. So I ran out the door into the wash of headlights, two sets racing up from the side of the cabin.

Still carrying Anna, I turned and ran with her into the dark bush, up the slope toward a stand of oak trees. It was a futile move, but I was panting, and I couldn't think of a better thing to do.

"Don't be foolish, McKenna," came a shout, ragged with anger. Someone had recognized me in the glow of their headlights. The voice sounded vaguely familiar, but I couldn't place it. "Come out of the woods or I send the dog," he said.

I kept running.

"Go Big Bear! Go get 'em!"

I stopped, set Anna down so she could sit on the ground and lean against the trunk of a big oak.

"Don't leave me, Owen," she pleaded.

"I'll be back as soon as I can." I trotted down toward the light, frustrated and angry at having to replay my moves from several hours before.

The Bouvier came running like a cat, fast and silent. I dropped down to my knees. He slowed.

"Big Bear, STAY!" I shouted as I dropped my arm in a dramatic motion toward the ground.

He slowed further, hesitating, no doubt remembering our previous engagement.

"GET 'EM, BIG BEAR!" the man below screamed.

"SIT-STAY!" I hissed.

The dog slowed to a trot.

I worried that the men below had me in their rifle sights. I needed that dog.

I got up and walked at a fast pace toward the dog and the light. In a moment, I'd be well-lit and an easy target for a man with a rifle. Big Bear stopped. I didn't want him to run.

"Good boy! Good dog!" I praised.

As I got close, he cowered.

I reached down, grabbed his collar with one hand and picked him up with the other.

I walked toward the four headlights, holding the Bouvier against my chest. The men were invisible in the dark behind the blinding glare. I didn't know how many men there were or where they were standing. As before, Big Bear didn't struggle. He completely submitted to my dominance.

I shifted Big Bear onto my hip and managed to get the knife out of my pocket. I flipped it open and held it by Big Bear's side.

"I've got Manny's knife," I said. "You want to get your dog back alive, you'll all get into one vehicle and leave the other. The woman and I will drive out of the compound. When we get to the highway, we'll leave your vehicle with Big Bear inside." It was a desperate attempt at a way out, but I had no other choices.

I tried to squint against the headlights, tried to sense any figures or any movement. It was hopeless. They could have moved off to the side to pick me off without harming the dog. I turned a circle. Unpredictable movement would make them hesitate. The dog was getting very heavy. After carrying Anna, my arms were fatigued.

"It's a good trade," I continued. "The woman obviously has no valuable information for you. I'll take her off your hands, no more questions asked. You have a good dog. You don't want to lose him." I kept turning. I held the knife so that it would reflect in the headlights. If the men had any brains, they would realize that my previous engagement with Big Bear showed that I knew dogs well. And anyone who knows dogs well is incapable of hurting them. But I counted on these guys being too stupid to put it together.

"Last chance," I said. "A vehicle in exchange for the dog."

From up the slope where I'd left Anna came a scuffling sound, movement in the dirt, a whimper.

I ran toward the sound. As soon as I was out of the main headlight beams, I set Big Bear down and ran bent over, holding onto his collar. When I got near the tree where I'd left Anna, I stopped, willing my eyes to adjust to the darkness.

She was gone. I turned and headed across the slope, scanning for movement.

A car door slammed. Then another. Then a third. I let go of Big Bear and sprinted down the slope toward the vehicles.

One of them shot backward, engine racing. It made a tight turn and stopped, shifted into forward. The second vehicle did the same. The two of them shot out past the cabin, went alongside the Quonset building, and disappeared. It was dark once again.

I ran to where I'd left Manny by the campfire.

I turned him, lifted him, shook him.

"Wake up!"

He was still out.

I ran to the dark bushes near the side of the cabin and kicked around looking for Gaver. Nothing. He must have gotten into one of the vehicles.

I turned and walked into his body.

He was heavy, but I dragged him over to the side of the old CJ-6 Jeep, reached in and turned on its headlights and flicked them to high beams. I dragged Gaver to the front of the Jeep, lifted his torso and positioned him so that his back was against my thigh and his face was ten inches in front of the left headlight. He was lit with such intense light that it looked like his sideburns would catch fire. I slapped his cheeks.

"Wake up, Gaver!" I hit him hard.

He moaned.

"Wake up. Hurry!"

Nothing.

Left, right. Hard enough to knock out his teeth.

"Wa're'y'doin?"

"Wake up!"

I took a deep backswing. Hit him hard enough to loosen his eyeballs.

"Stop!" His eyes fluttered, started to open. "Cntrnofflight!"

"Wake up!" I said again. "I'll turn off the light when you tell me where the key is."

"I'nknow'rkey!"

"That's it, Gaver. I'm done."

"Wait! I'll tell you!"

I pulled him to the side. He lifted his hand, rubbed his eyes. Then shot his hand up and grabbed at my face, gouging my nose.

My patience was gone. I spun him down onto his belly and kneeled on his back. I heard a crack. He screamed. I took the back of his hair and carefully positioned his head so that his face was directly into the dirt. Then I leaned on his head.

He screamed again, this time muffled by the ground.

"I'm going to give you one more chance to tell me where the key to the Jeep is. You will answer clearly. If you don't, I'm going to put all my weight onto your head, which will mash your nose back into your brain. I can't remember what they say. Either it kills you outright or you end up drooling on yourself for the rest of your life."

"In my pocket."

I picked him up. Walked him the six short steps to the side of the Jeep. I took his hair in my right hand and his left ear in my left.

"Reach into your pocket and pull it out."

He did so.

"Now step into the Jeep and start the engine. And remember that if you decide to drive away suddenly, your ear and scalp will stay with me."

Gaver swung his leg over the door sill of the open Jeep, and sat on the seat, his head bent sideways under my grip. He started the Jeep.

"Now get out."

He climbed out.

"Where do you keep your weapons?"

"Armory."

"Where is that?"

"Building next to the bunkhouses."

"Is that the south group of buildings? Down the ravine from the Quonset building?"

"Yeah."

"The other men who were here earlier, are they in the bunkhouses?"

"No. They went home."

"How do you get into the armory?"

"I dunno. It's always locked. Only Davy has the key. He's been gone a couple days. We ain't heard from him."

I turned Gaver away from the Jeep and faced the cabin.

"Time to run," I said.

"Really? You're letting me go?"

"I'm helping you to go. All you have to do is run. Ready. Set. Go."

Gaver ran. I held onto him just long enough to direct him to the cabin wall, then trip him at the last moment. He hit head first and dropped.

I got in the CJ-6, turned the headlights down to the parking light position and drove away by the yellow glow, past the Quonset building and down the ravine. I'd walked this part of the trail in the dark several hours before. In the headlights, it looked different than I imagined. When a light appeared down below in the distance, I turned off the parking lights.

I came to the bunkhouse. The light I'd seen was a dim yellow insect bulb above the bunkhouse door. There were two vehicles parked out front, an old Blazer and a new Ford pickup. Big Bear the Bouvier was in the Blazer. The pickup appeared empty. Lights were on inside the bunkhouse. A figure went by inside. Then another. Fast movements.

I could go in and get my head blown off. Or I could go get reinforcements.

I cruised on past at coasting idle, not hitting the gas, which would make engine noise, and not touching the brakes, which would flash bright red across the area. I came to an open gate in the razor-wire fence and followed the trail as it curved down to the left. When I could no longer see, I turned on the parking lights and again drove by the yellow glow. After a quarter mile of twisting and turning, I decided it was safe to turn on the headlights.

I went faster than I should, came to the highway, turned left, and was at my own Jeep twenty seconds later.

I parked the CJ-6 off to the side, ran to the oak tree, and found my key by feel.

I got in my Jeep. Spot jumped around. I started the engine and shot back up the highway. Spot's nose was all over me as he puzzled out the mysteries of rotting deer guts and maggots and vomit and bourbon and Big Bear the Bouvier and unwashed men and an unfamiliar woman wracked with terror.

I spun into the narrow opening and retraced my route, heading back up the trail toward the compound. At the appropriate times, I switched to parking lights only and then drove with no lights. I coasted to a stop off the trail a good distance before the bunkhouse, and turned off the Jeep.

Spot and I got out and moved into the darkness behind the oak that was closest to the bunkhouse. Both the Blazer and the Ford pickup were still there.

The bunkhouse door opened. A man stuck his head out and looked around. He radiated tension. He turned back inside. I heard a muffled shout.

"Are you ready? Okay, I've got the girl! You two are my cover. One on my left, one on my right. Ready? Go!"

The door opened. Two men ran out, each holding assault rifles. They stopped ten feet apart, watching the darkness, rifles up and ready. Into the gap between them came the other man holding Anna in front of him. He had one arm around her waist. She flopped, barely able to make her feet move. His other hand held a pistol. They were all in the wash of the yellow bug light above the door behind them. I couldn't see any of their features.

"Spot!" I hissed into his ear. I shook him to communicate the sense of urgency. I made a pointed gesture at the man on our right, then raised my arm back up. "See the suspect?!" I whispered louder. "Find the suspect!" I dropped my arm in the hard gesture that I'd used to train him. "Find the suspect and take him down!"

Spot shot off through the dark. I picked up a rock, took careful aim, threw it hard, then sprinted forward. The rock hit the end of the bunkhouse building just behind the men. They all jerked around, looking behind them.

Spot was now in the light, up to full speed, closing like a torpedo on the gunman to the right. I ran an arc to the left.

The first man to turn back around was the man who held Anna. "Look out!" he shouted.

The other men turned around. Now that I was up close, I could see that the rifles were AK 47s. They raised them toward Spot, but it was too late.

Spot had already made his attacking leap, leaving the ground at a low angle. Spot's man tried to raise his rifle against Spot's chest. But Spot's jaws closed on the man's upper arm, and they went down.

I focused on the other man. He had his rifle up, aimed at

Spot and the other man, reluctant to fire and hit his comrade. I charged on. He heard me and turned. But I was on him. He tried to swing his rifle. I grabbed it, pushed it up against his neck and ran him back into the bunkhouse.

A shot exploded as if to blow open the night. Louder than most rifles. A big-bore handgun behind me.

I hugged the man, his rifle stuck between us, and turned him around so that he was between me and the man with Anna.

The shooter turned before I could see his face, pushed Anna into the truck, jumped in after her, and started the engine. The truck's wheels spun and shot gravel as it took off down the trail.

I looked past the man I was hugging and saw Spot on top of the other man, his mouth on the man's shoulder, his growl sufficient to shake your chest. The man lay on his back. He'd stopped struggling in order to keep Spot from biting harder. But he was inching his rifle into position so he could get the muzzle up into Spot's chest. I ran my man backward toward a boulder, then let go of him at the last moment while hanging onto his rifle. The man hit the boulder and went over backward.

I turned, took two fast strides, and swung the rifle like a baseball bat. The barrel hit Spot's man on the abdomen. He grunted and let go of his rifle. I picked it up and turned around.

The man behind the boulder was reaching for his knife. I pointed the AK at him. He moved his hands out to his side.

Spot sensed that the game was over and let go of his man.

"Spot! Hold the suspect!" I shouted and pointed.

Spot's man rolled away.

"Hold the suspect!" I shouted again.

Spot grabbed the man's calf muscle and bit down. The man screamed. Spot growled.

I held two rifles. I took the magazine out of one, pulled the bolt handle back to eject the cartridge in the chamber, threw the pieces out into the brush. I gestured at the man on the ground behind the boulder.

"Get up."

He slowly stood. He was in his mid-thirties. Unkempt. Dirty.

"Over to the wall of the bunkhouse. Spread wide."

He moved slowly, got into position. I patted him down. Found his knife and threw it far.

"Over to my Jeep." I pointed.

He walked over.

"Stand by the front passenger door."

He did as told.

I kept the rifle on him while I opened the door. The duct tape that Diamond had given me was still there. I pulled it out. I directed the man back to the bunkhouse. "Back against the wall."

"I just did that," he said, sullen, like he hadn't just tried to kill me and my dog.

I jammed the rifle butt into his jaw. He collapsed in the dirt.

"Get up!"

He stood, rubbing his jaw, and got back into position against the wall.

"Spot, let go."

He wagged his tail.

"Let go."

He reluctantly let go, turned toward me, and wagged harder.

"Good boy! Good job!" I pointed the gun at Spot's man. "Up against the wall."

He limped with great drama and spread his arms and legs.

I found no other weapons on him.

I had them walk into the bunkhouse. Made one tape the other to a bunk bed. Very thorough. Had him truss his own feet to another bed. I finished his arms and quickly checked the first man, then put tape over their mouths.

"Let's go, Spot."

FORTY-FIVE

Spot and I ran to my Jeep, jumped in and raced down the trail and out to the highway.

I had no clue that specifically indicated which direction the man with Anna might have gone.

But I had a hunch that he'd want to get to the freedom of a highway. Interstate 80 was a good distance to the north. Highway 50 was closer to the south.

I turned south. The dashboard clock said it was 3 a.m. The Gold Country Highway was deserted. I ran the Jeep as fast as the tight curves would allow, Spot struggling to hold his footing in the back seat.

My breaths were short, my heartbeat fast. The tension of the past few hours had knotted my stomach and back muscles into coiled springs. The stress of nearly saving Anna and then losing her again was burning a hole in my gut.

I tried to take a deep breath. Then another. Clear the head. Calm the emotions. Get the brain back to a space where there was room to think.

The man with Anna had a long lead. I wasn't going to catch him soon if ever. I wasn't going to catch him by simply driving fast. I could only guess where he might go. Other than the compound, the only other obvious location was Harmon Halstead's Good Fix Garage. But it was too obvious. The man with Anna would never go there.

I tried to revisit everything I knew about the case in an effort to guess which way he'd turn when he got to Placerville.

To the west was Sacramento and not far beyond it, the Bay Area. Nine or ten million people would make it easy to disappear.

To the east was the Sierra, a vast landscape of mostly-deserted mountains.

As I reconsidered everything I'd experienced in the previous days, I noticed that one thing about the case kept being a central feature. I didn't know why. But everything kept coming back to Tahoe.

Grace was murdered in San Francisco. But Thomas Watson, her supposed murderer was found in Tahoe. Grace's daughter Anna was chased and escaped to Fresno, but she was ultimately kidnapped in Tahoe. The Red Blood Patriots were based in the Gold Country foothills, but their leader was found dead in Tahoe. The man who brought me into the situation did it by hijacking a boat in Tahoe. The journal that supposedly held secrets mentioned an important man who recorded the Chinese laborers. And when a curator at the Oakland Museum found an Edward Weston photograph that fit the description, she thought it looked like it was taken during the building of the Vikingsholm Castle in Tahoe.

When I came into Placerville, I turned left on Highway 50. East.

Toward Tahoe.

FORTY-SIX

I dialed nine-one-one.

The dispatch woman who answered was another unfamiliar voice. New hires.

"Owen McKenna calling. I need a conference call set up between Sergeant Bains at El Dorado County, Sergeant Martinez at Douglas, and Commander Mallory at SLTPD."

"I'm sorry, sir, please repeat your name and department and tell me why you are calling."

I tried not to yell, but I had trouble staying calm.

"A woman's life is at stake and I need to talk to those men now. Any one of them will vouch for me. HURRY!"

"Hold on, please, while I try to connect."

I was racing up the ridge above Placerville toward Pollock Pines. If it took too long, I'd drop down into the river canyon to the east and be back in cellphone shadow. I went past the Apple Hill Café at 80 miles per hour, high beams on, trying to watch for the eye-glimmer of the ubiquitous deer.

What seemed like several miles later, the dispatcher said, "Sorry for the wait, sir, I'm still trying to connect." Then, "Sir, I have Sergeant Martinez on the line."

"Diamond," I said. "I'm coming up Fifty from Placerville…"

"Sir, I'm sorry to interrupt, but Sergeant Bains is on the line."

"Hey, Bains," I said.

"McKenna," he said.

Then another voice. "Yeah?" Rough. Older. Groggy. It was Mallory.

"I'm reporting on Anna Quinn, the woman who was abducted

from Lacy Hampton's house. She's currently being held captive in a new Ford six-pack pickup, plate unknown, color very dark, possibly black, no topper. Vehicle is freshly washed. I believe the suspect is driving east from Placerville on Fifty. Suspect is armed and dangerous. I don't know his destination. I'm hoping you can put officers at the choke points on the South Shore. In Meyers at the base of Echo Summit. On Emerald Bay road out by Camp Rich. On Fifty in Stateline near Edgewood."

The highway peaked, then pitched down into the curves that led to the bottom of the American River Canyon, where the road began the long, final climb to Echo Summit.

"You got an ID on this suspect?" Mallory said.

"No."

Mallory made a loud, frustrated sigh.

"You got a guess?" he said.

"Only that he belongs to the Red Blood Patriots and is likely the murderer of the Patriots' leader Davy Halstead."

Bains said, "The man whose body you found out at…"

His voice evaporated as I followed the highway down around a piece of the mountain. I looked at my cell. The signal was gone.

Thirty minutes of high-speed driving later, I crested Echo Summit and saw the light bars of three sheriff's vehicles on the turnout. Their spots were turned onto a shiny black pickup. An older couple stood talking to two deputies. I pulled in and got out, announcing my name across the dark.

"McKenna," a familiar voice said. "Over here."

I found Bains standing by his Explorer, talking on his radio. He clicked off and pointed toward the older couple, then stopped and scrunched up his face. "Jesus, what's that smell?"

"Run-in with a deer carcass," I said.

I could see Bains frown in the dark. He took a step back.

"Anyway," he said, "Mr. Blake Weschler and his wife Nan were getting drowsy so they stopped for fresh air."

I realized what he was about to say. "What kind of car were they driving?"

"Expedition. White." He handed me a Post-it. "I wrote down the license plate."

"How long ago did they call it in?"

"That's the thing. They didn't. The suspect took their cellphone, too. They flagged down another car." He pointed toward a small red Nissan in the dark where two young men stood leaning against the hood. "José and Jorgé Romero from Davis called it in," Bains said, using the correct hor-hay pronunciation. "When we got here, the Weschlers estimated that the suspect had taken their car about fifteen minutes prior. That was ten minutes ago."

"And the pickup?" I said.

"Reported stolen in Stockton two weeks ago."

"Were you able to contact Diamond and Mallory?" I asked.

"Right away. But that still wouldn't have been soon enough. If the suspect drove fast, he could have gotten all the way past the Stateline choke point before Diamond's boys knew that he wasn't in a black pickup."

"So he could be anywhere," I said.

Bains nodded.

FORTY-SEVEN

I headed down the grade from Echo Summit, through the lonely, dark curves of early morning, past the avalanche-control artillery tower on the left, and onto the floor of the Tahoe Basin where nearly everyone was asleep. There were so few cars out that it should be easy to spot a white Expedition with a crazed driver and his broken female prisoner. I wasn't that far behind.

But the Tahoe Basin is huge, and it would be easy for him to park and hide on a back street or lift another car. I didn't have a clue what to do next.

Out of habit, I turned on Pioneer Trail, the faster route to Stateline and the east side of the basin. As I drove through the dark forest, the pressure building within me was intense. My gut clenched. I gripped the wheel as if to crush it. I wanted to lash out, to race up the highway and find the killer, force him to the side of the road, jerk him out of his vehicle.

I tried to revisit the standard principles of investigation. Sort out the case into what you absolutely know, what you believe you know but can't prove, what is mere supposition, and what is possible but unlikely.

There were only a few things that I absolutely knew. Anna had been in serious danger ever since she met her birth mother. In the beginning, before I knew about Anna, everything that had happened to her suggested that Nick O'Connell was her tormentor. And after Nick tossed his helper over the edge of the Dreamscape and then accidentally followed him into the water, everything pointed to Davy Halstead. Then Davy was found dead. Then another person connected to the Red Blood Patriots imprisoned Anna at the Patriots' compound, and, after I attempted to rescue her, snatched her from my grasp and disappeared. That's all I knew for certain.

Everything else was a murky soup surrounding blurred entries in a journal from another century, markings in Chinese that suggested that Grace's ancestor might have accumulated a treasure. And ever since Nick the Knife had heard Grace talking to an author who wrote about the history of Chinese miners, Thomas and Nick and Davy had all been fixated on the possible treasure. And they all believed that Grace had told Anna about it.

I thought about another of the basics of investigation, which was to treat all of your assumptions with skepticism.

A doe lifted her head from the side of the road and stared at me, her large eyes catching my headlights and looking sad and innocent. I slowed as I went by. She never moved, unaware that she couldn't trust the human species to be safe any more than Anna could.

I reconsidered all of the victims. There wasn't even any common aspect to the way the victims died. Grace had been bludgeoned to death. The nameless man on the boat got dropped into the lake with a chain around his neck. Nick fell into the lake wearing a heavy pack that dragged him down as effectively as a chain. Davy Halstead had a stake or something similar pounded through his chest. And Grace's cousin Melody committed suicide by jumping off the Golden Gate.

For the hundredth time, I thought about what I knew of Nick, the likely hostage taker. He'd always been the main puzzle. Hijacking the Tahoe Dreamscape was such a dramatic way of getting me to bring in Thomas Watson for Grace Sun's murder that it still made little sense to me.

I'd talked to him on the phone when he first called me, and I'd met him briefly on the boat. I'd seen his clothes, and his manner. I'd seen his pack with the wire, and I'd glimpsed his explosive belt. Street had seen him, too, and she'd gotten a glimpse of the 88 tattoo on his arm along with the intense blue eyes under his sunglasses. He didn't wear a mask as he had when he attacked Anna, but his big hair and beard and sunglasses were just as effective a disguise.

In the category of things I thought I knew but wasn't certain about, I believed that Nick the Knife was the knife-twirling man who wore a mask when he attacked Anna three years before. I'd shown his photo to the Dreamscape owners, Ford and Teri Georges. They didn't know his name, but they recognized him. He probably came aboard the Dreamscape to check it out before the hijacking.

It seemed that Nick O'Connell was the key to everything that had happened since. Maybe I could learn something about him online. The explosives and the twirling of knives were the things about him that were the most unusual and hence probably the easiest to track. I could track down how people learned to twirl and throw knives. I could cross-reference that with the Red Blood Patriots. If I found out about sources for explosives, maybe I would discover that there was an intersection among all three.

To my knowledge, the U.S. doesn't have a big black market for explosives. There isn't that much demand. But the U.S. does have a large legitimate market. The mining and construction industries use large amounts of explosives. As do highway building and demolition of old buildings. Ski resorts across the country use explosives for avalanche control, as do highway departments in mountain areas. I assumed that Hollywood creates all their explosions on computers, but maybe there is still a demand for the real thing. A dedicated person who wanted explosives for illegitimate uses could probably find many ways to steal them.

Once again, I thought about questioning even my most basic assumptions. And there I found what may have been a major oversight.

I'd crossed the town of South Lake Tahoe and was driving through the bright lights by the Stateline hotels, but I didn't see them as I struggled to grasp the implications of my thought.

It seemed a ridiculous notion. But the more I explored the possibility, the more it seemed plausible.

I worked through my wild premise as I drove, paying no attention to my route, my Jeep speeding up as my tension caused me to accelerate. I talked to myself, building my case, establishing what was the easy-sell part of it, the basic foundation stones and the supporting walls. The hard-sell part was the end concept, something that at first seemed ludicrous, like it could never be supported by facts. If I were looking at architecture, my idea would be like one of those ultra-modern buildings where it appears that the top is floating precariously as if it were held up by some secret architectural levitation.

But as I drove north toward Cave Rock, speeding faster, I began to realize that all of the supporting components for my ridiculous idea did in fact exist. It was like an unlikely building that, despite appearances, was in fact held up by cantilevered beams and hidden cables and a solid if improbable geometry.

I took a curve too fast, and the Jeep swayed as I brought it back into my lane. Spot suddenly stuck his cold wet nose onto the back of my neck, startling me. I reached back and rubbed his snout. "It's okay, boy. Driving too fast. Sorry."

My thought was triggered by what Street had told me about the little girls with donkey and pig drawings on their faces. She'd thought they were painted on, only to watch the girls peel them off. It reminded me that the same could be done with tattoos. Stick-on tattoos. From there I realized that a person could also purchase colored contact lenses.

I realized that Nick's big hair and beard and tattoo might not have been the only aspect of his disguise. I visualized the hostage taker standing at the bow of the Tahoe Dreamscape, yelling at me, threatening to dump Street into the lake. He spoke with a ragged voice, another easy way to disguise an aspect of your identity.

Of course, that still only suggested that he didn't want to be recognized after the hijacking was over.

I remembered him yelling at me about the pressure at great depths and how it would crush someone's ribs after it first squeezed the air in their lungs to nothing.

It was his knowledge of water pressure that made me realize what it was that nagged me.

He'd worn a custom belt, a wide, black nylon strap with multiple rectangular pockets to hold C-4 plastique or something similar.

I remembered where I'd seen a similar belt, and I now believed that the pockets on the hostage taker's belt didn't hold any explosives. Neither were there explosives in his backpack.

The belt wasn't designed to hold explosives at all, but rectangular pieces of stainless steel. The number of steel pieces could be adjusted so that the belt weighed just the right amount to counteract the buoyancy of the person wearing it.

It was a scuba diver's weight belt. Divers' wetsuits are quite buoyant, and divers need extra weight to stay under water.

Nick the Knife wore a blue jacket and pack that would blend in with the water. He looked like a big man partly because he had a thick wetsuit or drysuit under his clothes. Because of the buoyancy of his insulating garments, he made certain that he had enough weight in his belt to sink him faster than any lifeguard could swim. Then he purposely tripped on his shoelaces, fell over the railing of the Dreamscape, took a big breath, and faked his tortured, gargled descent into the ice water. As Bukowski dove in and tried to save him, Nick the Knife put on his look of shock and terror and then followed it with his open-eyed death stare.

When he'd sunk past 100 feet or so, beyond the point where anyone could see him, he pulled the quick release on the belt and let it fall. In his pack was a scuba tank with the regulator already attached. It would be easy for him to pull out the regulator mouthpiece of his scuba gear and begin breathing.

Then Nick took a leisurely swim two or three hundred yards away before rising to the surface to climb into a boat or escape into the forest.

Why? Was it possible that Nick's charade was just about making me think he was dead? It made no sense. I didn't even know who he was before he took Street hostage.

When I realized why Nick had done it, the impact made me exhale.

Nick the Knife didn't take Street hostage to make me think he was dead. And he didn't do it just to get me to bring in Thomas Watson.

He did it to find Anna Quinn.

FORTY-EIGHT

Nick had been looking for Anna ever since she escaped when he broke into her bedroom. Three years of searching.

Thomas Watson and Davy Halstead had been looking as well. But neither was as focused and dedicated to the pursuit as Nick. Then something changed.

Perhaps Davy or Thomas said something that made Nick think that one of them was close to finding her. Or maybe he realized that they both had the money and connections to find Anna, while Nick had few resources other than his determination.

Nick's brilliance was in hatching a plan to get a professional investigator to find her.

It was nearly perfect. Just as Nick wanted, after he hijacked the Dreamscape and took Street hostage, I began to pursue Thomas Watson. In that process, I also began re-investigating Grace's murder. I found out about cousin Melody's suicide and, with Street's help, Grace's daughter Anna that she'd given up for adoption.

Because Anna decided to trust me, she came out of the woods. It was easy for Nick to watch my cabin and office. When she showed up, he and/or Davy followed her to Lacy Hampton's home and carried her off. Then Nick killed Davy. I played into his plan so perfectly that I may as well have brought her to him myself.

She was his captive because of my stupidity!

I floored the accelerator, chasing a killer who had constructed a huge charade just to find a girl whose mother had a secret, a secret he desired enough that it drove him to kill. My anger was nearly incapacitating.

As I approached the first car on the highway, I realized that I was helpless. I had no idea where to look.

Maybe Nick's instincts would have him trying to put distance between him and me, heading east to Carson City or north to Reno. Maybe he wouldn't want to find a place to stop and hide.

I overtook the car in front of me. A minute farther up the dark highway, I passed a pickup. Then two more cars, followed by another mile of dark deserted highway. A white vehicle appeared ahead. An SUV. Just before Cave Rock. I stomped on the gas as I raced up to it. It was a Suburban, not an Expedition.

I shot past the SUV, careened north through the Cave Rock tunnel, then accelerated harder.

I dialed Street as I drove.

"Hello?" Her voice was groggy.

"Sweetheart, I'm calling to say that I'm okay."

Her sigh of relief was audible over the noise of the Jeep. I gave her a quick explanation of Nick the Knife and how I believed that he was still alive.

"My God! The man who nearly killed me is alive?!" I heard her breathing over the phone. She knew that Nick's primary goal hadn't been to kill her. But that didn't mean he wouldn't come for her again if it suited him.

"Don't worry," I said. "He won't come after you again. He has what he wants. I have to get off now," I said. "But can you do me a favor? Call Diamond and tell him that Nick O'Connell didn't die when he went overboard. Diamond can call the others. Tell Diamond that I believe that Nick the Knife has kidnapped Anna Quinn."

"No, don't tell me..."

"Yeah." I was now shooting past the road up the mountain to my cabin as I spoke to her.

"I'll call Diamond." Street's words were shaky. "Where are you headed?"

"I'm heading north up the East Shore. It's a long shot, but he could be somewhere in front of me."

Street was silent for a moment. I went around the curve by Glenbrook then pushed the Jeep up to 80 as I climbed up toward Spooner Summit.

"Owen," she said, her voice so soft I could barely hear her over the roar of the Jeep,

"Yes?"

"I know I can't tell you not to do this. Maybe Anna is still alive. Maybe she's already dead. But you know that man is a cold killer. He's sick and desperate and feral. I saw it in his eyes. He'll put a knife through your heart without even hesitating."

"I know," I said. Up ahead were taillights that were not getting any closer. A vehicle going as fast as I was. The red lights flashed bright for a couple of seconds then jerked left at the turn from 50 onto 28 going north around the lake. I accelerated hard to close the gap, then braked for the turn and cranked the wheel. My tires skidded through the turn. In my peripheral vision, I sensed Spot sliding across the back seat. I hit the gas, brought the Jeep back up to 70.

Street said something else, but I couldn't make it out over the roar of the engine.

"What?" I said.

"Please be careful." She was pleading. "Please."

"I promise," I said. "I love you." I folded my phone and stuck it in my shirt pocket as I came to the first curves up by the Spooner Lake Campground.

I took most of Highway 28 at half again the speed limit, careening the Jeep through the S-turns. Gradually, I closed on the vehicle in front of me. It was a dark van.

There was no oncoming traffic, so I swung out and shot around him.

The highway was dark with few vehicles. I kept up my speed, hoping that Nick might be going along at normal speed, as confused about his next move as I was about mine.

I raced north, trying to guess his moves.

On the lake side came the viewpoint parking area just south of Incline Village. I shot by. A moment later, I realized that there'd been a white vehicle parked in the dark.

I stood on the brake pedal, not caring about the screech of my tires. Came to a smoking stop. Threw it into reverse. Ran my Jeep up to the tach's redline going backward. Came even with the north entrance to the little lot. Stepped on the brake again and shifted back into drive. Spun the wheel and squealed into the lot.

Nick must have heard me brake. The white Expedition was already moving. He shot out the south entrance and turned north. I followed.

I raced after and got close, then dropped back a bit, not wanting to make him so tense that he did something stupid that could end in a fatal crash. We flew past the first residences south of Incline Village.

His brake lights flashed bright and hard in the night. He took a sudden left turn off the highway and onto Lakeshore Blvd. I closed ranks again so I wouldn't lose him as he raced by the mansions, the fenced estates, the big gatehouses with the automatic wrought-iron entrances. As he approached the stop sign intersection where Country Club Drive came down from the highway, he sped up, ran the stop sign, and slid into a right turn.

I'd wondered for a few moments if I was wrong, if I'd merely come upon some kids doing drugs in daddy's Expedition. But his high-speed flight convinced me that Nick O'Connell was alive and driving the big Ford in front of me. And even though I had no direct evidence that Anna was with him, I knew it just the same.

I followed as the Expedition powered past the Hyatt Hotel. A few blocks up Country Club, he stomped on his brakes and took a left turn into the Sierra Nevada College campus, the small, beautiful and exclusive school where a few privileged kids got to exercise their neurons when they weren't skiing or snowboarding on the mountains above or plying Tahoe's vast water playground.

I thought that Nick the Knife had made a mistake turning into the narrow college streets with the esthetically pleasing but confusing arrangement of parking areas. My vague recollection of the campus was that most of the routes had no alternative outlets. As he turned toward the famous Tahoe Center For Environmental Sciences, I thought I had him trapped.

But he jerked the Expedition up onto the sidewalk and careened between the trees near the library. There was a natural-landscaped garden area with only a walking path between the plantings, but the SUV plowed through at high speed, bouncing hard. He shot out onto another parking area with access from the other direction.

I tried to follow, but made a wrong turn and got trapped between trees that were too close to let me pass. I backed up and felt my bumper scrape and bounce. My Jeep slammed to a stop. I shifted into drive, gave it gas. My wheels spun, but the Jeep was stuck.

I jumped out and looked at the dark rear wheels. I'd backed over a small boulder and caught it under my bumper. I'd need a jack to get off. But I didn't have time. I went around to the other side, squatted down and sighted under the bumper. The boulder was like an egg, half again as long as it was across. Driving forward would tip it the long way. If I could jockey the Jeep a quarter rotation, the boulder would tip the short way.

I got back in and went forward and backward, turning the wheel back and forth, gradually rotating the Jeep. Then I shifted into 4-wheel-drive and gave it gas. I felt the rear of the Jeep lift up and drop down with a thud. The wheels dug into the dirt and I shot forward. I bounced across the landscaping onto a parking lot. At the far end, I went up the college's north access road and headed up to the main highway through Incline.

But I was too late. The Expedition was gone.

On instinct, I turned left to continue counter-clockwise around the lake, thinking that Nick wouldn't take Anna back the way he'd come.

I came to a red light near the Raley's supermarket in Incline, slowed to a near stop, glanced at the deserted cross street, and raced through the intersection. Up the road was the intersection where the Mt. Rose Highway climbed up to the highest year-round pass in the Sierra. I wondered if Nick had turned up the mountain. A sudden thought made me think he didn't.

Crystal Bay was to my left. Home of the Tahoe Dreamscape. Nick the Knife had hijacked the boat once before. Would he do it again? It seemed a far-fetched notion, but it was nothing compared to his faked death. And the Dreamscape offered him a good escape possibility. Nick could also threaten Anna with death by drowning in a last effort to get her to tell him what she knew. He could find another length of anchor chain, tie it around her, and drop her overboard. Then he could pull the Dreamscape up to any dock on the lake, steal another car, and escape.

Ford and Teri Georges had mentioned a mystery visitor to the boat during a time when they were gone. Nick had probably been that person. He'd likely have taken the time to explore the vessel enough to figure out how to orchestrate the hijacking. Did that include visiting the bridge and checking out the controls? Was Nick knowledgeable enough about boats that he could run the Tahoe Dreamscape? Did he possibly find where they kept an ignition key?

The road made a curve, then dropped down close to the water. I strained to see through the darkness across the bay. The Dreamscape pier was near the far point, just down from the town of Crystal Bay. The trees opened up. The boat was still there. There was a light down low on the pier. It blinked on and off. A second time. I realized that the light wasn't turning on and off. People had moved in front of it.

I sped up the highway as it climbed up above the lake. The turnoff to the Dreamscape's parking lot was dark. I found the entrance by feel more than anything else. Took it with too much speed. Slid off the edge of the asphalt. My wheels sunk into soft shoulder. I thought I was stuck. But then rubber caught something firm, and I came back onto the road. I went past the parking lot, heading for the pier. But as I got close and the Dreamscape came back into view, I saw that it wouldn't work. Although no lights were lit on the boat, it was already moving slowly along the pier, heading out to sea.

Even if I sprinted, there was no chance I could catch it and jump on.

I hit the brakes and skidded to a stop. Threw the Jeep into reverse, cranked the wheel, and shot back up to the highway. I turned left again, heading toward the little town of Crystal Bay, trying to remember which road I'd accidentally turned down when I went to the Dreamscape to meet Ford and Teri.

There it was. I turned off the highway and sped down a narrow ribbon of pavement, got to the bottom of a hill, went right, then left, and pulled into the parking lot near the small beach. I parked and jumped out.

A quick glance through the trees out to the lake showed nothing but dark water. The Dreamscape couldn't have gotten that far away in such a short time. Which meant that Nick O'Connell had never turned on the running lights, and he was making an illegal dark run toward the depths. There was a good onshore breeze coming over the water from the southwest. I turned my head a bit so my ears didn't hear the sound of the wind. Instead I heard from out on the water the rumble of distant diesel engines running hard.

I let Spot out of the Jeep and dialed Diamond to give him an update. I got his voicemail. I told him to call, hung up and ran to the boat rental where I'd talked to the man who ran Jackie's Jet Boats. When he was in the beach shack, I'd seen the display board with all the keys hanging on it like earrings.

The throb of the Dreamscape running through the night came louder than before, the sound riding on the breeze as the big boat headed out of Crystal Bay.

The racy jet boats were lined up on the beach waiting for a final warm weekend or two when a few off-season tourists might want to have some cold-water fun. There were two sizes of boats, ones designed for two or three people and smaller ones that would only fit one rider.

I read the number off one of the larger ones and ran over to the little office shack. The door was so rickety that I was able to put a soft shoulder block next to the latch and pop the door open.

I found a small desk lamp inside and flipped it on. The display board was gone. I looked in the file cabinet. Under the counter. Nothing. He'd taken the keys home with him.

On the right rear corner of the desk was a note that said, 'trouble starting, runs rough, needs tune-up.' Taped to the note was one of the keys.

On the waterproof key fob was written the registration number. I memorized it in the light. Ran out and found the matching boat. It was one of the small ones. No way could Spot try to ride it with me. Maybe it wouldn't start, either. But I didn't have any other options.

Spot ran around me as I pulled the jet boat down the short stretch of sand and into the water. It bobbed in the waves, its tail end just touching the sand.

I wondered if the little boat had a bilge that could collect explosive gases. I didn't see a pump switch. One way to find out.

I hit the starter. The engine cranked a bit, caught once, then nothing. I cranked it again and again. It didn't fire. Maybe it was like some car engines, which, in starting mode only, can be cleared of excess gas by opening the throttle all the way.

I pulled the throttle trigger all the way and cranked the engine. After several revolutions, I let the throttle fall back to idle.

It coughed, fired, coughed again. I kept cranking and gave it a touch of throttle.

The engine fired and started, running very rough. It smoothed out a bit as the idle speed increased, then began coughing over and over.

Maybe if it warmed up a bit…

I called Spot and trotted back toward the Jeep. Halfway there I realized that he hadn't come. I turned to look back.

Spot stood on the beach by the jet boat, unmoving, looking at me. He realized that I was going to leave him in the Jeep.

I called him again.

He turned toward the dark lake.

I thought about it. Spot was nearly always worth the trouble of bringing him. But I couldn't figure out how to get him on the boat.

The jet boat coughed, then resumed its idle. I scanned the beach. Saw something that gave me an idea. Probably a ridiculous idea.

Over at the far end of the line of jet boats, up on the sand, was a small fiberglass dinghy, no doubt used to ferry people out to the boats that were tied to buoys. Coiled at the bottom of the dinghy was a short line that was tied to the bow cleat.

The little boat was surprisingly heavy. I lifted on the gunwale and dragged the dinghy over to the water next to the jet boat. The bowline was just long enough to tie to one of the recessed brackets at the rear of the jet boat and leave about fifteen feet between the two crafts, enough distance, I hoped, to tow the dinghy without creating instability.

"Spot. In the boat," I said, snapping my fingers. I pointed at the dinghy.

Spot looked at me. He'd experienced my crazy ideas before, several of which had involved boats.

"Go on. Get in the boat. You didn't want me to leave you. And there isn't enough room on the jet boat."

He stuck his head into the dinghy, sniffed, took two steps back, looked at me again.

I went over to the jet boat, pushed it out into the water. As jet boats are designed for day use only, there were no running lights, which suited me fine.

I repeated my little speech to Spot. He couldn't understand the specific words. But dogs pick up meaning from the tone of voice. I knew that he understood what I wanted. But I also knew that at some doggy cognition level, he was also wondering whether it was a stupid idea.

He'd been in a wide variety of small boats and had even ridden on a surfboard. But he'd also nearly succumbed to hypothermia in the icy water of Tahoe. Since then, he'd approached all water rides with skepticism.

I dragged the dinghy out into the water. It floated near the jet boat. Spot stood on the dry sand, looking at me. In the faint light of a distant parking lot light, I could see his head. He had his pointy ears up and forward. Curiosity. But his brow was wrinkled in deep furrows. Worry. That meant he was getting the message.

"One more time, boy," I said, floating the dinghy back to the sand beach. "Get in." I pointed again. "Hurry up."

Spot came over, stared in the boat for a bit, then lifted one front paw and set it in the dinghy. The little boat rocked precariously.

"Go on."

He put his other front paw in. I grabbed the little boat to keep it from capsizing. He jumped his rear legs into the boat, then stood with all four legs spread wide as the dinghy rocked beneath him.

In the past, I'd tried to teach Spot to hunker down for stability when in a moving vehicle. I could never get him to lie down when on a tippy platform, but he'd learned to sit his rear down and keep his front legs spread wide.

I got him into position between the two seats of the dinghy, then waded over to the jet boat. I climbed aboard, straddling the seat. The boat had a safety lanyard attached to the ignition kill switch. I slipped it over my wrist. If I fell off, the boat's engine would stop, and Spot wouldn't be pulled across the lake without me. I grabbed the handlebar, squeezed the trigger throttle and gave the engine enough gas to ease forward until the line between the two boats became taut. Then I accelerated slowly, watching in the dark to see if my boat would throw water onto Spot.

The jet boat coughed and wheezed and hiccupped, but still had enough power to pull the dinghy with no apparent stress. Spray shot out behind me to the sides. I saw Spot shake his head, so I knew that some water was hitting him, but from what little I could see in the dark it seemed more like a strong mist than a drenching soak.

Spot kept his head forward into the wind just like when he sticks it out the car window. Like all dogs, when it comes to air in the face, Spot lives by the principle that says if a little is good, more must be better.

Soon, I was going 25 mph, and the jet boat showed no signs that there was any limit to its speed.

I thought that the boat would easily go fast enough to catch up to the Tahoe Dreamscape even if the Dreamscape was at full throttle. But I didn't know if the dinghy would track well at that speed without porpoising and throwing Spot out.

I kept turning around to watch behind as much as I faced forward. The little boat skimmed the water, floating across my wake from left to right and back again in a gentle oscillation. Now and then its bow raised up under the pressure of the wind and Spot's head would momentarily disappear. But the towline kept the bow from going too high. I'd put Spot in a ridiculous situation. We must have looked like something in a Dr. Seuss book.

Catching the Dreamscape was complicated by not knowing

where it was. With the jet boat roaring, I couldn't hear the Dreamscape's big rumbling engines. I scanned the horizon as we raced out into the vast dark void that was Tahoe in the predawn hours. If the dark shape of the Dreamscape came between me and shore lights, I might see it. But large sections of the East Shore were wilderness park and had no lights at all.

I shifted my course left, toward that shore, thinking that if the Dreamscape was in that direction, I'd have to be close to find it in the night.

The Dreamscape was a big boat, 100 feet long, with the kind of hull that was designed to cut large ocean waves. It wasn't a boat meant for velocity. But Ford Georges had bragged about the big diesel power plant and how the Dreamscape could push 19 knots. So I squeezed the jet boat throttle trigger and gradually sped up to 30 mph. Water starts to feel hard beneath a boat hull when you get over 30. The dinghy bounced harder, but Spot stayed in.

After I'd gone about a mile into the water, I throttled back to idle. The jet boat and dinghy coasted to a near stop. The dinghy floated toward me.

"Hey, largeness," I said, pulling on the line and bringing the dinghy alongside the jet boat. I reached out to give Spot a rough head rub. He was soaked with cold spray.

He stood his rear legs up, reached a paw out to the gunwale. The dinghy rocked under his shift of weight.

"Sorry, dude. One rider per boat. You gotta sit back down."

I listened to the darkness. The diesel throb of the invisible boat was louder. It came from our port side at about 11:30 on the clock dial, which put it between us and the dark East Shore, just a bit north of the Thunderbird Mansion.

"Back down," I said to Spot. "Sit." He ignored me.

I pulled his boat forward alongside the jet boat and pushed him back to a sitting position. With a little push on its bow, the dinghy floated back until the towline was again taut.

As I reached for the handlebars, a tortured woman's scream ripped across the water from the direction of the unseen yacht. The piercing shriek rose in pitch and volume and became ragged with horror.

FORTY-NINE

As Anna's scream faded into what sounded like a choked death rattle, I ran us back up to our previous speed and then on past until we were flying across the dark water at 40 mph. I put us into a big, leaning curve to the left, aiming for the dark eastern part of the lake.

There was just a slight breeze, so the chop on the water was light. But even the small waves transmitted jarring shocks into the racing jet boat. Glancing behind, I saw Spot down in his low sit, front paws spread as wide as they can go. The little dinghy bounced alarmingly, occasionally appearing to leave the surface for short moments. I worried that the dinghy might flip over. But if Anna was still alive, if I wanted a chance at saving her…

My cellphone rang in my pocket. I fished it out, looked at the screen.

"Diamond," I shouted.

"Sí. You wanted something."

"Talk loud," I shouted. "I can barely hear you. I'm heading after the Dreamscape. Nick the Knife is alive. He's got Anna and he's taken the Dreamscape."

"Street called me about Nick," he shouted. "You're going to board the Dreamscape?" Diamond said, his words tiny against the whine of the jet boat.

"Going to try."

"You on a speedboat?" he shouted.

"One of those small jet boats."

"I'll call Bains. Maybe we can shake loose a chopper."

"Never mind that right now," I yelled. "I've got a question."

"What?" Diamond shouted back.

"I want to tell you some names. Portia, Jessica, Viola, Nerissa,

Lucentio. What do they mean to you?"

"Nothing, other than that they're all names from Shakespeare."

"What kind of names?" I yelled back.

"Just characters. Probably regular names back in sixteen hundred."

"What about Kent, Hortensio, Rosalind and Celia? Is there a common aspect to the characters?"

"I'm no Shakespeare expert."

"You are compared to me," I yelled. "Think."

"Nothing in common," Diamond shouted. "They come from all different plays. King Lear, Taming of the Shrew, Merchant of Venice. Tragedies, comedies, tragi-comedies."

"Keep thinking," I yelled.

"Sorry. Nothing comes to mind. You think Anna's still alive?"

"Maybe. But I need to know about the names."

"What can I say, Owen? They're just names!"

"Okay, thanks," I shouted.

"Wait!" Diamond said.

"What?"

"Maybe it's the disguises," Diamond yelled.

"What do you mean?"

"All those characters, what they have in common. They all used disguises so that people would think they are someone else."

"Just what I needed. Thanks." I hung up.

In another half mile I saw the Dreamscape, its hulking form barely visible against the dark shoreline. No light showed from any of its decks nor from any of its portholes. It looked like a phantom ship. Wherever Nick had Anna on the boat, there was nothing to give away the location.

The jet boat was going much faster than the yacht. I came around behind the big boat's stern, gliding up the main wave of its wake at a gradual angle so that we didn't catch too much air.

As the jet boat lifted a bit and landed, I swiveled around to watch the dinghy go into the air. For a moment in the darkness I couldn't see Spot. My gut clenched. The dinghy slammed back down onto the water, much harder than the jet boat. Then I saw Spot, pushed down by the impact, his chest down on the dinghy floor.

The dinghy didn't flip. I turned back to focus on the ghost ship roaring through the darkness.

The center of the Dreamscape's wake was a broad flat swath of water rough with bubbles from the prop turbulence. The jet boat and dinghy both seemed to skid sideways on the bubbly surface.

I slowed the jet boat down to 25 as I approached the port corner of the Dreamscape's stern. Because of the darkness and the roaring spray coming off the yacht, it was hard to tell precisely my closing velocity. I didn't want to risk crashing into it.

Hovering just a few yards from the big boat, I tried to figure the best way of boarding the Dreamscape. I could jump onto the big boat as I let go of the throttle. The safety lanyard would pull free, stopping the jet boat. But then Spot would be left adrift in the dinghy. I had to get Spot onto the Dreamscape first.

"You're a dead man, McKenna!" a male voice shouted over the roar of the yacht and jet boat. The same ragged, rough voice I'd heard when I first met the hostage taker at the bow of the Tahoe Dreamscape. Nick the Knife.

I looked up to see a vague black silhouette against the starlit night sky. He stood at the rear of the upper deck. As he moved, I sensed that his left arm wrapped around a smaller figure, holding the person in front of him.

Anna.

Nick raised his right arm up and back. While he held Anna in front of him with his left arm, his body snapped forward as his right arm came down in a fast arc like a pitcher throwing a fast ball.

I saw no projectile, but his arm motion was focused at me. I jerked the handlebars to the left. The jet boat lurched. I heard a loud crunch of fiberglass behind me.

I turned around. Just behind the seat was a large javelin sticking through the rear of the jet boat.

FIFTY

Adrenaline burned through my system. It was difficult to breathe.

The javelin stood six feet tall. It gradually leaned backward toward the water, its pointed tip prying up vinyl and padding and fiberglass. I steered back to the right. The motion made the spear flop to the left. It popped out of the seat and fell away into the lake.

I kept my hand on the throttle and began steering the jet boat back and forth, weaving behind the speeding yacht.

"You didn't hear me, McKenna? You're going to the bottom of the lake just like Kyle did. And when I'm done with the girl, she's joining you."

"Owen!" Anna screamed. "Get out of here while you have a chance. He'll kill you, Owen. He's… arrrgh…" her voice was choked off.

With my left hand, I reached back to the bracket where the dinghy's towline was tied. I pulled some slack into the line, gave my hand a quick twist to wrap the line around my hand, then undid the slipknot. My hand was now holding all of the drag of the dinghy with Spot in it. The line felt like it was cutting through my hand.

I forced myself not to look up and instead focus on my task.

While I steered the jet boat back and forth to make a difficult target, I visualized how I was going to board. The most important thing would be to move very quickly so that Nick couldn't easily take aim with another javelin. I went back and forth another two times, then made my move.

I swung back to the starboard, dropped back a bit, then gunned the jet boat. The dinghy pulled as if to rip my left arm out of its socket. I raced forward in the dark. As I cruised past the starboard side of the Dreamscape's transom, I leaped off the jet boat and onto the yacht's boarding platform, still holding the towline to the dinghy.

The drag from the dinghy was too great. It was about to pull me off the stern and into the water. I flailed my other arm, grasping at air. My fingertips brushed something. I bent, trying to gain an inch or two. I groped frantically in the night.

My fingers gripped the ladder rail at the front of the boarding platform.

With the lanyard pulled from the jet boat ignition, the engine went silent, and the boat immediately slowed to a standstill and disappeared into the dark, just missing the dinghy.

The yacht vibrated under my feet as it raced forward.

The boarding ladder was short and steep. It went up and over the edge of the transom and onto the tender deck. The handrail that I gripped was spaced out from the transom about a half a foot. I slid one of my knees in behind the railing for support, then reeled in the towline hand-over-hand. I tried to be fast to minimize the time that Spot and I were easy targets for Nick.

When the bow of the dingy touched the boarding platform, I jerked the towline around the handrail and made a fast slipknot. I reached out to the bow of the dinghy and jerked it halfway up onto the boarding platform.

"Spot! Come!"

He stood.

Another javelin crashed down into the boarding platform, just off the dinghy's bow, midway between Spot and me. Its tip went into one of the narrow gaps between the spaced boards. It traveled half of its length before friction brought it to a stop. There was no light other than starlight, but the spear was so close that I saw the wild patterns of black on white. I'd seen them before, but I couldn't remember where.

I grabbed Spot's collar. He made a little jump as I tugged him out of the dinghy. I pulled him over and down, close enough to the transom that I hoped we were out of sight from the killer up on the deck above.

In a holder on the transom was a bar with a curved end used

to aid swimmers climbing onto the boarding platform. I took off my windbreaker, draped it over the bar and held it out in view of the man above us. I moved it so that it could be mistaken as me coming up the ladder over the transom.

A third javelin crashed down directly through the jacket.

"Spot, hurry!" I jerked Spot up. Put his front paws up on the top of the ladder. Lifted his rear legs up onto the steps. With a push from me, Spot jumped over the transom. I leaped behind him, hoping that we weren't taking enough time to allow Nick to grab another javelin and get into position.

I nearly tackled Spot as I grabbed his collar and dove forward. We hit the forward wall of the tender deck, which was underneath the trailing edge of the upper deck.

I breathed deep, realizing what I'd missed all along.

I remembered the pattern on the javelins. They were the rods that held up the lanterns on the deck of the Tahoe Dreamscape. Lift them out of their holders, slide off the lanterns, and you have a deadly weapon waiting for you. A bunch of them, all lined up on the upper rear deck of Ford and Teri Georges' tour boat. Put there in advance for ready use as weapons. And it was on the boat where I saw the errant package that looked like a holder for contacts. Contacts that I now realized weren't ordered for vision correction, but to make Nick's eyes look intensely blue.

I shouted up toward Nick the Knife who was probably still on the deck above.

"It was an impressive strategy, Nick. Hijacking your own boat as Nick the Knife while your new identity as Ford Georges gave you a cover. The hijacking fooled me. It set in motion a plan that would get me to find Anna for you."

"Yeah," he shouted back. "Dying was the brilliant part, wasn't it?" His voice was just audible over the roar of the engine and the wind. "That and the false identity out of Wichita, Kansas."

"If I'd paid more attention, I would have figured you out a long time ago."

"But you didn't, McKenna. And you'll be dead soon, just like this girl. I'll have her ring, and your bodies will never be found. I've taken over the Patriots. I'm beginning to build my empire."

I had no clue how to get to him. As soon as I appeared up the stairs to the upper deck, he would put a javelin through my chest. If I kept him talking…

"What was the point?" I shouted. "Find the treasure from Anna and Grace's ancestor and sell it to pay off the boat mortgage?" I turned and ran my hands over the rear wall of the tender deck, feeling for something, anything, that I could use to try to disarm the man.

Nick didn't immediately respond to my question. I worried that he had moved. If I didn't know where he was, I'd be out of luck. When he spoke, his voice was wistful. I could barely hear him over the roar of the yacht.

"True, the tour business will never pay off a boat mortgage as big as this one. But that doesn't matter. The point is that I deserve the Chinaman's treasure. I'm the only heir to my maternal grandmother. She was Katherine Mulligan, granddaughter of Seamus Mulligan who lost his life because of the Chinaman. If the Chinaman had stayed in China where he belonged, my ancestors would have been rich. I would have been rich. The money is mine."

There was no point in pointing out that Mulligan had tried to lynch his Chinese neighbor Gan Sun.

Over the roar of the yacht came a grunt. A javelin thudded into the deck a foot from my leg. I jerked and scrambled away, pulling on Spot's collar. I realized that Nick had moved to the side of the upper deck and was leaning over the edge, throwing back in at me and Spot.

"Nice try, Nick," I yelled. I wanted to make him doubt himself. "But you don't even know your own boat if you think you can hit me from there. I'm out of your line of sight."

I leaned toward Spot and whispered. "C'mon, Spot." I pulled on his collar, and we scrambled up the few steps from the tender deck to the rear deck where the staircase that rose to the upper deck was broad and open and offered easy line-of-sight to us. I pulled Spot up the side passageway toward the bow of the boat.

The view across the lake showed that the shore lights in all directions were similarly far away, which suggested that we were approaching the middle of the lake. There was a distant cluster of lights that looked like Tahoe City. Those lights were at four o'clock on the Dreamscape dial. That put us traveling south, heading toward a point south of Emerald Bay. Baldwin Beach, maybe. Ten or twelve miles away. If no one got to the bridge in time to stop the Dreamscape, and if no other boat got in our way, we'd run aground in about 30 minutes.

I had to get Anna from Nick's grasp and stop the boat before that happened.

But Nick understood the basic principle that makes hostages so attractive to psychopaths, which is that taking a hostage renders intervention moot. Any course of action that compromises the hostage taker also risks the life of the hostage. In broad daylight, and under perfect conditions, a sniper can sometimes take down the hostage taker without harming the hostage. But that situation was nothing like being on an unlit, unfamiliar yacht in the night. Maybe I could find a way to turn on some lights, but that would just make Spot and me an easier target. I needed to create a surprise action that would create more risk to Nick than to Anna.

The main stairway to the upper deck was back at the rear of the dining cabin. Spot and I were already well past that. We continued forward on the starboard aisle.

In the middle of the yacht were ladder stairways, one on each side. They went from the main level up to the upper deck just aft of the bridge. When we came to the starboard ladder stair, I saw in the darkness a life ring hanging on the outer wall of the lounge. It had a line that had been gathered in a neat coil and hung on a bracket. In my pocket was the knife I'd gotten from Manny at the Red Blood Patriots compound. I used it to cut off the line where it attached to the life ring.

Extending below the handrails were sections of metal gridwork. I cut off a section of the line and used it to tie a taut trip-line from the left grid panel across to the right grid. I positioned the cord about eight inches above the lowest step. Spot stuck his head next to me, wondering what I was doing. "See this, Spot?" I whispered. "Don't trip on this." He didn't know the words, but maybe they'd help him remember the line was there. I put his nose on the line.

Next, I moved with Spot around the front of the lounge

cabin, back down the port aisle, and tied a matching line across the ladder stair on the port side of the yacht. I put his nose on that cord as well.

From there we went back to the lower rear deck and approached the main staircase from the side. I whispered in Spot's ear, "Stay." I didn't want him moving across the stair opening because his white-with-black-spots pattern was the opposite of camouflage in the dark.

I cut another, longer, section of line and tied it across the wide stairs, moving fast to minimize the chance that I would get a javelin through my chest. When I was done, I had put a hazardous cord across the three main stairways from the main level to the upper level. If Nick encountered my cords going down one of the stairs, he'd fall a good distance. My hope was that if he still held Anna, the distance wouldn't be so great that it would seriously wound her, but far enough that Nick would be stunned.

I pulled Spot up to the dark nook behind the main stairway. On a dark boat at night, the nook provided even more cover. We waited, Spot lying in the ready-to-jump position, elbows spread wide, rear legs knees-up. I squatted next to him.

I figured that Nick would tire of waiting for me, and he would soon take Anna into the bridge house and slow the boat before we raced too close toward shore. But the boat didn't slow. No lights came on above me. There was no sound of human movement, only the steady roar of the yacht's engine.

After a long minute of waiting while the yacht continued to charge across the lake, I began to think I'd made a mistake. It had taken me so long to put up my trip-lines that Nick could have easily taken Anna down the aft stairs while I was working on the mid-ships stairs. Or maybe there was another stair or ladder I didn't know about. When Nick had given me the boat tour, acting as ex-insurance agent Ford Georges, he had bragged that there were over a dozen stairs and ladders and hatches that allowed for vertical movement among the boat's four levels.

I watched the distant shore lights. The world had rotated a bit. Instead of going in a straight line toward the southwest corner of the lake, it appeared that the boat was tracing a gradual arc toward the west. It was too dark to see clearly, but it looked like we would eventually turn toward Emerald Bay. I hoped I was wrong. Otherwise, we'd crash ashore much sooner than I'd originally thought. And unlike running aground on a gentle sandy slope like Baldwin Beach, there was the possibility that we'd come ashore on a rock-strewn landscape. A collision with boulders would be much more abrupt than sand.

After another minute, I couldn't wait any longer.

Bending down with one leg forward and one leg back, I was able to position my thigh in front of the trip line. When I tugged on Spot, he stepped over both thigh and cord. I let go of his collar and he continued up the stairs with me directly behind. We were halfway up when a terrible, muffled scream rose from somewhere below my feet.

"Spot, come!" I said as I turned and leaped down four steps, clearing the cord. I hit the deck and spun in a circle, trying to sense where the scream had come from. Spot came down behind me, also leaping over the trip cord.

There was no more sound, just the steady dull roar of the racing yacht.

I yanked on the doors to the lower staircase, but they were locked. The doors were made of steel. Breaking through would not be simple.

Then I remembered the multiple hatches that Nick O'Connell/Ford Georges had mentioned. I had tried the one on the foredeck. The only other ones I knew about were inside the locked salon.

I tried to breathe, tried to think. When Teri Georges talked about the person who came on the boat during her absence – which I now knew was a bogus story to direct me away from her husband – she mentioned the hatch and companionway from the bridge down into the salon.

I sprinted forward, stepped over the trip line on one of the mid-ships stairs and went up two steps at a time to the upper deck.

Spot followed and stayed next to me as I ran across the big deck and up the short stairs to the bridge.

The door was locked.

I went down to the deck and lifted on one of the javelin rods that held up the lanterns. It slid out of its holder tube. Rotating the javelin like a long baton, it was easy to kick the lantern off of its top end. I'd never thrown a javelin before, but it had a natural balance. I took aim and hurled it at the dark window in the bridge house door.

The javelin exploded the tempered glass into tiny fragments. I reached through and unlatched the door.

It was worth it to take the time to slow the boat.

I found some toggle switches on the wall and flipped them, hoping they would turn on lights, but they did nothing. I felt in the dark for the throttle handles. There were two levers that felt correct, but they were in the idle position. They flopped forward and back when I pushed them. Nick must have disconnected them when he sped up the boat. Squatting down, I reached under the control panel. I waved my arm in the dark, hoping to find loose throttle linkages. There were two cables, a rod, and some wires. Nothing changed when I pushed and pulled on them. I took a strong grip on the wires and tore them loose.

The boat roared undiminished across the lake.

I stood and ran my hands across the top of the panel, feeling in the dark for the ignition key. I found no key. I turned knobs and flipped switches. Nothing changed.

At least, I could avert disaster by putting the boat into a turn so we'd just keep tracing circles. I grabbed the wheel and rotated it. It spun freely, disconnected from the steering mechanism.

Nick had obviously made a plan for this kind of possibility and arranged things so the controls could be disconnected. There was probably a second, small cockpit on the main level, perhaps behind a closed door at the front of the salon or up on the bridge deck above my head. It could be that there was a way to enable just one cockpit at a time. But Nick hadn't shown that to me when he put on the Ford Georges persona and gave me a tour of the boat.

On the port side of the bridge, just to the rear of the chief mate's chair, was a vertical hatch-type door. It was unlocked and opened to reveal a ladder. I stepped onto the ladder and was halfway down into the salon when I realized that Spot was above.

I needed him.

I climbed back up, bent over him, and wrapped my arms around his abdomen.

"Okay, boy. This is no big deal. Rear first, just the way humans go down a ladder." I reached out to the ladder, pulling him with me. I put his front paws on the rung. He couldn't grip it, but he could support some of his weight so that I didn't have to carry him.

I was in a panicked rush, but I needed to reassure him with a calm voice.

"Remember the ladder down into the mine during the forest fire?" I said. "Same thing. Only no smoke this time, no falling embers. Piece of cake."

I lifted his rear up, got his rear legs over the hatch collar and guided them down onto the first ladder step.

"Attaboy."

Spot resisted as I put a foot out and down onto a rung.

He was big and strong, and I couldn't have dragged him against his will if we'd been outside in the dirt. But I had a good grip around him, and we were going down, which made gravity my ally. I managed to pulled him with me over the opening in the floor. His rear paws flailed. But he worked his front paws down the ladder like a trained circus dog. We were down in the pitch-dark salon in a moment.

We ran back through the dining room to the staircase. I went down it fast, feeling the steps with my feet, the walls with my hands. Spot came after me with no hesitation.

At the bottom of the stairs was the bordello-wannabe lounge. I thought of going into the engine room to see if I could find a way to stop the engines. But I would likely just lose more time turning valves and flipping switches with no result.

I went to the lounge's forward doors, into the hallway with the staterooms and trotted forward to the sitting area.

Light showed at the bottom of the door to the forward cabin. I reached out and gently tried the latch.

Locked. Maybe that door was steel, too. I couldn't tell in the dark.

I had no choice.

My best sidekick is powerful. But I decided instead that the long hallway offered a better approach. I went back down the hall twenty-some feet and maneuvered Spot behind me so I wouldn't hit him when I ran. For direction in the dark, I took a careful look at the thin line of light under the stateroom door. Then I exploded forward like a sprinter out of the starting blocks.

I tucked my elbow in and hit the door with my upper arm and shoulder.

The door shattered, wooden pieces exploding inward. I tried to stay upright. But my feet couldn't keep up with my momentum, and I fell in a sliding skid as if to tag home plate with my fingertips.

FIFTY-ONE

I slid, face first, into the big forward stateroom. Cats with Shakespearean names scattered. Anna was on the bed, arms up above her head. She was trying to scream, but an outsized gag like a pillowcase was stuffed in her mouth and tied around the back of her head. Nick was at the side of the bed, his back to the woodstove. He had tape looped through the zip tie on her wrists and was running it to the left corner post of the bed. Teri had hold of Anna's hands. She held a wire cutters and was working it on Anna's ring finger. The gold ring sparkled through dark red blood. Behind Teri, in a huge ceramic pot to one side of the bed, was a grouping of the decorated rods that supported the lanterns on the upper deck.

Javelins.

As I hit the floor, Nick leaped up, his reaction deadly swift. He picked up a fireplace poker from a holder next to the woodstove and swung it at my head. It just missed and rang off the floor. I grabbed it on the bounce, jerked it from his hand, and tossed it away. Nick dove onto me.

I knew he was strong, but his frantic manic attack seemed to possess a kind of double strength. We grappled and rolled.

He let go of me with his right arm, giving me a big advantage. I got on top of him, one hand on his left wrist, my other hand on his throat. At the last moment, I realized the folly of it.

His right arm came up with a shiny knife. I leaned forward and put a forehead butt into his face, The blade missed me by inches.

We were too close for me to get his knife hand, so I jammed my elbow down onto the upper arm flesh just below the shoulder. He screamed. The knife clattered to the floor. I grabbed it and threw it into the corner. Then I lifted his head a half-foot off the floor and slammed it back down. Nick went limp.

"Spot, watch him!" Spot looked at me. I grabbed his head, pointed him toward Nick, gave him a little shake. "Watch him!"

I turned toward the bed.

Teri Georges was backing away from Anna, a feral intensity in her darting eyes. Her arms were out in front of her, and she held the fireplace poker in both hands like it was a baseball bat. Her arms still telegraphed cheerleader strength. She looked crazed.

"You must have known that getting involved with Nick O'Connell carried a huge risk," I said, trying to distract her. I moved sideways, my hands open, ready for her swing.

Her eyes narrowed.

"Hard to believe that he convinced you to go along with his plan to murder Grace," I said.

"You don't have a clue," she said.

I moved closer. She lifted the poker higher, like a batter ready for the pitch.

She clenched her jaw, and I flashed on a memory. Three years ago. Grace's cousin trying to come to grips with Grace's murder. The same clenched jaw. A look that gave me empathy, then. Contempt, now.

"As Melody Sun," I said, "you had a good life. You could have shared in Grace's possible fortune. Instead, you faked your own suicide and signed on to Nick's sick plan."

"She was a righteous bitch." Melody's voice sounded like the hiss of a rattlesnake. "So high and lofty with her ideals and her dreams. Everybody loved Grace so much. It made me sick. Grace, with her charming awkwardness, and her masculine body, and those giant hands. Instead of it making life a challenge, it made life easier for her. I did better in school, but she always had the better job. I was first runner up to prom queen. I was the better musician. I could draw and paint. I was coordinated and athletic. The boys liked me." Her voice had changed to a whine.

"But Grace always came first. People felt sorry for her size and her hands and her man-ish look. And when she got pregnant, she didn't even have the courage to keep the baby. So she gave it up. Then she had the audacity to complain about how life was so harsh, how people looked down on single mothers. She was a hopeless loser."

Melody was circling, poker up in the at-bat position, ready to swing.

"I couldn't have babies, and she could. But she thought a baby was a problem, not a gift. I detested her attitude. And just when I thought that maybe I was done putting up with her, along comes the daughter she gave up for adoption. So I had to endure a never-ending lovefest between them." Melody shot a poisonous look toward Anna on the bed.

Anna looked deadened, her body curled as if to implode. Yet, I saw the reflection of light in her eyes. She had narrowed them as if squinting. The squint wasn't about bright light. It looked like anger, and it gave me hope.

"The whole world consisted of Anna and Grace. Grace and Anna," Melody said. "Instead of that daughter being outraged that her own mother got rid of her like some kind of parasitic pest, she acted like Grace was some kind of goddess. It made me want to puke! It was suffocating, and I couldn't stand it!"

As she said it, I made another little mental leap. One that explained why Grace and cousin Melody looked nothing alike.

"It sounds like you hated that you were adopted, Melody. You focus on how you were given up by your own mother and raised by Grace's aunt and uncle, right? And now you want to punish Anna, your relative through adoption. So you hooked up with Nick, and you both changed your names and got a boat."

I saw Melody making little telling motions in her shoulders.

"Is your plan to kill Anna? That will really set things right, won't it?" I said, tensing.

Melody lifted her foot and stepped sideways as if at the plate and swung the poker so hard that it flew out of her hands. The sharpened steel missed my head and clanged against the wall of the stateroom.

As fast as I registered the movement, she spun and pulled a javelin from the ceramic pot. She raised it, aimed it toward me.

"Cut with your pop psychology, McKenna! That doesn't work with me."

"Think about it, Melody. Anna is a sister in kind. A fellow

adopted daughter. But you have such contempt for your own kind that you torture her. It shows how you feel about yourself."

Behind Melody, Anna squirmed on the bed.

"So you did whatever Nick wanted you to?" I glanced over at the prostrate figure on the floor. Spot was still watching the man, but his attention was drifting.

"If you think Nick orchestrated this, McKenna, then you're dumber than I thought. This was my plan and my revenge. He was my pawn, and he did what I said. When I caved in Grace's thick skull, he was so stupid that he said he would let me set him up for it in return for promises of riches. And when I put Thomas Watson's shinbone skin under her nails and told him that Watson would eventually be blamed, he was like a dog, panting, waiting until I gave him his reward. He knew he was nothing more than an enforcer, a second lieutenant, a knife man. I dangled the ultimate prize of money and a new life and endless days of physical reward. Like most men, he was just like a stupid stallion who cared about nothing other than the mare in heat. For that simple thing, he did whatever I said."

I turned and saw Nick on the floor, his eyes open, staring past Spot to Melody. I stepped away from him, toward the sideboard, picked up a bottle of Jameson whiskey, and held it like a club.

Behind Melody, Anna struggled on the bed, tugging at the line that tied her to the bedpost. Her eyes telegraphed fear and anger. Spot turned and looked at her. I wondered how to get Anna untied without getting my head run through with a javelin. I wondered how to use Spot without getting him skewered, too. I tried not to think of the yacht racing through the night on a collision course with the shore.

"But you never found Grace's journal," I said. "You never learned where the treasure is."

Nick used his legs to inch toward the vase with the javelins.

"I had a good idea," Melody said. "Grace had made hints about some kind of diary entry and how a gift she gave Anna completed it. I realized that it was about money and that the ring was part of it. I sent Davy Halstead to watch you. When you found Anna, and Davy followed her to where she was staying, I had Nick pick her up and shut up Davy for good. Nick likes being a tough guy. Just like when that militia man Kyle called me and told me he'd overheard something about me. I told him he could be in on my plan if he helped Nick hijack the boat. Kyle was so dense that he suspected nothing until Nick dropped him into the water. But the genius of my plan was getting you to bring Anna out of the woods."

She turned and sneered at Anna.

"That vile woman was so suspicious that she didn't respond to my reasonable emails. But you were the perfect dupe. I knew you'd find out about her and contact her. I knew she'd look you up. I knew she'd find out about your reputation and learn that everybody thinks that Owen McKenna and his big dumb dog are some kind of safe zone. Little do they know. It was obvious that Anna would come out of the woodwork and into your false comfort. Then I'd get the ring and force her to tell me what I want to know."

Nick's arm suddenly swung out and snatched a javelin out of the pot. I dove onto him, grabbing the javelin. We rolled, the javelin between us. I was about to call Spot, but Melody came into my peripheral vision, javelin held high.

She threw it.

I twisted.

The point of the javelin glanced off my leg, hitting the nerve bundle on the inside of my knee. Electric pain shot up my leg. I couldn't move.

Spot grabbed Melody's ankle, and she screamed.

Nick jumped up next to the bed. Raised his javelin back, its big sharp point aimed at my chest.

Anna did a sudden spasmodic stomach crunch on the bed, pulling her arms down against the tie line for support. She shot a front snap kick up into the air above her body and caught Nick's chin with the ball of her foot. He dropped the javelin. Staggered back. Reached for his face.

Anna twisted sideways, flashed out a second snap, lower. Her foot struck his solar plexus. Hard.

Nick grunted and doubled over.

I reached for the poker, but the nerve electricity in my leg was still acting like a stun gun, paralyzing me.

Nick stumbled forward, leaped over me, and ran out of the stateroom door. I struggled to my knees.

"Spot!" I yelled, hoping that Nick no longer had a weapon on him.

Spot let go of Melody's ankle. She bent, reaching her hands to clutch where he'd bitten her.

Spot looked at me, his face a mix of confusion and eagerness. He sniffed my face. I grabbed him around his chest. Shook him for emphasis. Raised my other arm.

"Find the suspect!" I did the pointing motion, dropping my hand toward the black hallway where Nick had disappeared. "Find the suspect and take him down!" I smacked him on his rear.

Spot shot out into the darkness.

There was movement behind me. I spun.

Melody had grabbed a javelin. She threw it toward me in a practiced throw.

I jerked to the side. The javelin crashed into the wall next to my head. It broke in half with a loud snap. Fiberglass splinters rained through the air.

Melody was reaching for the last javelin in the ceramic vase, but I was up. I picked up the javelin that Nick had dropped and hobbled toward her. A little feeling was coming back into my leg, but it collapsed as I tried to put weight on it. I hopped on my good leg.

Melody brought her javelin back to throw. Her eyes were demonic.

I shifted my grip on my javelin. Swung it as she released hers.

They connected, one breaking and folding. They clattered to the floor.

Enraged, Melody ran to the corner and picked up Nick's knife. She held it out and charged me, uttering a loud guttural roar. I dropped to the floor. Stuck my leg out.

Melody tried to jump over me, but her foot caught on my leg. She went down. Landed on her hands, knife skittering away. Her jaw hit the edge of the broken door. She collapsed.

I hobbled toward the knife. Brought it to Anna. Cut the rope and tape that bound her hands. Pulled out her gag. Helped her to a sitting position.

"Hurry!" I yelled, hoping the command would cut through her shock.

I pulled her to her feet.

We stepped over Melody, went out the door into the black hallway.

My leg was a mass of pinpricks as the nerve tried to recover from the javelin blow. I stumbled through the dark passage, feeling the walls with one hand, dragging Anna with the other.

We felt our way down to the lounge and the staircase. I could only step up with my good leg, so I did a leaping climb, two steps at a time with the good leg, lifting the numb leg behind me.

From below the stairs came the powerful vibration from the engines. The locked doors had swing bars on the inside that opened them.

We went out onto the rear deck. The glow of stars and distant shore lights were bright compared to the blackness below. To the east was the faintest hint of the coming dawn. I looked around for Spot or Nick, but I saw nothing.

The yacht continued its roaring trajectory across the lake.

I pulled Anna down the side aisle toward the bow, watching for Nick to appear.

If he'd gone up the stairs, maybe Spot would have caught him. But if he'd climbed up a ladder through one of the many hatches, Spot might still be searching. Nick could be waiting for us, another javelin raised and ready.

When we got close to the bow, I looked ahead and saw that the starry sky had been replaced by the dark mountain above us. Directly in front of us was blank darkness. I paused for a moment, trying to make sense of what I was seeing. Then I understood.

We were heading directly for the Rubicon cliffs. They looked less than a quarter mile away. The Tahoe Dreamscape was about 45 seconds from impact with a solid wall of granite.

And I didn't know where Spot was.

"Spot!" I called. "Spot!"

If he was close, maybe he'd hear me. If not, my words would be drowned out by the roar of the racing yacht.

We came around the front of the salon.

I tried the door.

Still locked.

Spot might be trapped inside.

I gritted my teeth against the nerve pain and put my best sidekick against the window in the salon door. Glass shattered.

I reached through, found the latch, turned the lock.

Anna came with me into the salon.

"Spot!" I ran through the blackness to the rear of the salon. Poked my head into the dining room. "Spot! Come!"

There was no response.

I ran back forward and glanced out the front of the salon. The cliffs of Rubicon were rising in the sky above us.

Something moved. An odd shape at the pointy front of the bow.

I pulled Anna with me across the foredeck.

It was Spot. He stood over Nick who was flat on his back. Spot's jaws encircled Nick's neck. I knew the posture. It wasn't a biting maneuver, but a holding maneuver.

Despite the faint starlight, I could see the fear in Nick's eyes. "Good boy, Spot!"

I held tight to Anna and pulled her with me over to the gangway gate at the side of the bow railing. I unlatched it and slid it to the side. Below was a rush of black water mixed with the foam from the bow wave.

"Can you swim?" I shouted over the roaring yacht.

"What? Yes. Why?"

I pointed at the wall of rock. The cliff loomed above us. We were less than twenty seconds from impact.

"The boat is going to crash. You need to jump off. Now."

"You're crazy," she said. Despite the darkness, I could see that she was terrified.

"No, I'm not. I mean it. Jump."

"I could never jump," she shouted, her voice a panicked cry.

I looked again at the fast-approaching wall of rock.

"It's going to be very cold," I said. "But we'll come for you. It will take a minute or two."

"What?" she shouted.

I picked her up and threw her, screaming, off the deck and into the black ice water below.

Her shriek stopped as she hit the water and the boat rushed on ahead.

I sprinted back to Spot.

He still had his jaws on Nick's throat.

I put my hand through Spot's collar and looked at the looming wall.

The roar of the Dreamscape grew exponentially as the sound echoed back from the vertical wall of rock. We had maybe three seconds at the outside.

"Spot, come!" I yelled. I took his collar and sprinted with him toward the open railing gate. As we got close, I tightened my grip on his collar in case he wanted to hesitate.

We leapt up and out in a broad arc, six legs bicycling through the night. The impact on ice water was hard. The temperature was a gasping shock.

A moment later, the Dreamscape hit the cliff.

The impact was an explosive boom, followed by metal popping, grinding, twisting, ripping as the boat crushed itself against the immovable wall of granite.

The bow collapsed and disintegrated and was followed by the yacht's midsection. The first wave from the impact hit us, lifting us up, pushing us back. I still had Spot's collar, and I frog-kicked my best, pulling us away from the impact.

A second wave, reflecting off the rock, hit us. This wave was bigger and choppier. We tossed and spun. I inhaled water. Spot struggled to swim up the wave. I kept pulling him.

The yacht's engines kept roaring for several seconds as the stern raised up, props exposed to the air. Freed of the resistance of water, the props spun faster and faster in a screaming rise of RPMs. Then came a muffled explosion followed by the squeal of tearing metal. The prop whine quickly dropped in pitch until it stopped. It was followed by a sudden, eerie silence.

I tread water. Spot swam in a tight circle around me.

What was left of the front half of the yacht had disappeared beneath the water, raising the stern farther in the air until the wreckage was near vertical, the dinghy still tied to the tender deck ladder and dangling like a dead gray beetle in the black night. Then the stern with the attached dinghy dropped back down the way a whale's tail flukes slap the water. As the bulk of the Dreamscape wreckage submerged, there was a whooshing sound of water rushing in from the sides to fill the sucking void.

The stern was about to disappear. I realized that the dinghy was still floating. I let go of Spot and swam toward it with my fastest crawl. Maybe I'd get sucked down into the vortex of the sinking boat. But Anna was out there at risk of hypothermia. As was Spot. As was I.

We needed the dinghy.

I grabbed the little boat and pulled on the end of the line where I'd tied the slipknot. The line came free. The dinghy bobbed in the waves caused by the crash. I held the line and swam away from the sinking yacht.

There was a last moaning, screeching shriek of metal being torn in two as the Dreamscape sunk beneath the surface. I felt the swirl of a powerful current pull at my legs, trying to suck me down into the icy blackness. The current lessened. Then, from many feet below came an eerie, scraping howl of submerged metal against the underwater cliffs of Rubicon. It was followed by a creepy silence and a small gurgle of eddy currents created by the huge yacht as it began its descent down one of the tallest underwater cliffs on the planet.

I found Spot about twenty yards out. Despite the ice water, he was still strong. I got his front paws up over the gunwale of the dinghy. Then I raised my thigh beneath his rear feet. He pushed off and jumped into the little boat.

Spot stood with his head hanging down over the bow as I swam with the dinghy out into the black lake.

"Anna!" I shouted. "Anna! Where are you?"

I swam another 20 yards.

"Anna! Anna!"

My muscles were beginning to seize from the cold.

I swung a leg up and over the dinghy. The gunwale of the little boat tipped down toward the water. Spot came close, making it much worse.

"Spot! Lie down! Lie down!"

He sat.

I pulled myself up, got an arm into the boat, kicked hard, and rolled over the gunwale, flopped into the dinghy.

Spot was all over me.

"Let me up, Spot!"

I stood. The little boat rocked. Threatened to capsize.

"Anna! Anna!" I peered out at the blackness. Shivers wracked my body. "Anna!"

I heard a small sound off to one side. I turned. Shouted. "Anna!"

There was a tiny light object out on the slate-black water's surface. It moved.

I jumped into the water, bowline in hand. "Anna!"

I drew close to her. She was sputtering. Arms moving. Thrashing. No focus. Face bobbing in the waves. Choked intake of water followed by gasps of air.

I grabbed her from behind. Lifeguard carry.

"I've got you, Anna. Take a deep breath. You're safe. We're going to get you into the dinghy. Here it is on your right. I'm putting your hand on the boat. Hold on. That's it. Now your other hand. Good."

This time, Spot stayed in his spread-eagle sit.

"Okay, Anna, grip hard while I get your foot over the edge. Left foot first. That's it. Now hang onto the boat with your hands while I boost you up and over. Ready? Up we go."

I got my right hand under her hip while my left hand gripped the boat. I worried that the boat would tip enough that water would surge over the gunwale and sink the boat. So I gave my strongest kick as I pushed Anna up into the air like I was punching up a world-record shotput.

Anna flopped into the boat. She coughed and choked and gagged. When she belted out a big crying wail, I knew she'd be okay.

The ice water was sapping my strength, but I thought I could last another couple of minutes.

I wrapped the bowline around my waist and knotted it, turned toward the north, and swam the woman and my dog toward the beach at the north end of the Rubicon cliffs.

EPILOGUE

Late that morning, Doc Lee came out of the ER to talk to Street and me in the waiting room.

"Anna's going to be okay. The wire cutter cut down to the bone on the sides of the finger, but the tendons on the top and bottom were spared."

Street shut her eyes and breathed hard.

"The ring was really tight. But I had to take it off to stitch her up. Had to do the cold hand, warm ring, glycerin trick."

He handed it to me. "She said you might like to see it."

I nodded.

"Interesting Chinese writing on it," he said.

"Could you make anything out?" I asked.

"Yeah. Hanzi engraved in gold beats blurry writing on paper any day. The characters were on both the inside and outside of the ring. As best I can determine, it says, 'As this ring came from rushing water, the source for its sisters is six paces from the Sky Palace toward calm water.'"

Three nights later, we took a shovel, mallet, chisel, trowel, broom, bag of mortar, and a mixing box. Jennifer Salazar was out of town, but she let us borrow her new little runabout. The rain was cold and steady, but the wind was calm, so we took it straight across the lake to Emerald Bay. We had the nylon top up, but the center windshield panel was flipped open, and Spot stood in the rainy passageway between the two halves of the windshield. His front paws were up on the bow seat, rain-soaked head thrust up and forward like the carved bust on the prow of a square-rigger. Diamond sat in the Captain's chair on the right side, piloting the boat with a stiffness appropriate to a guy who grew up in Mexico

City and never set foot on a boat until he got a job with the Douglas
County Sheriff's Department.

Anna sat in the left seat on the other side of Spot. Street and I
took up the rear bench seat. The chop was quiet. Diamond drove
at half-throttle, just barely high enough to keep the boat on plane,
which kept the engine roar low enough that we could talk in loud
voices but without shouting.

"This boat," Anna said, "and that monster house where we
borrowed it, who do they belong to?"

"Young woman of substantial means," Diamond said.

Street told Anna how we'd met Jennifer Salazar a couple
of years before, and how she came to have a huge fortune and
practice a personal philanthropy from which my bad-guy pursuits
occasionally benefited.

As we approached the entrance to Emerald Bay, Diamond
dropped the throttle to the slowest forward speed. We idled our
way through the narrow passage.

Although the main campgrounds were closed for the coming
winter season, there were several boats moored in the distance at
the boat campground. While rain dampens how sound carries
across water, it was critical that we didn't draw any attention from
people who might be on Emerald Bay, so we spoke in whispers.
After we were through the narrow opening to the bay and away
from the shallow rocks, Diamond turned off the running lights.
Diamond had nothing but very dark clouds silhouetting even
darker moutains to help him sense the shape of the bay.

I reached into my pack and pulled out some bottles of water
and passed them around.

"What's this for?" Street asked.

"Fuel. We may have a long night in front of us."

"Great fuel," Diamond said.

"Not the water. The bread."

"You made more bread?" Street was raising her voice. "After
your last debacle?"

"Shhh. And it wasn't a debacle. It was just a practice run."

"Street told me about it," Diamond said. "Sounded like you
developed a new kind of high-tech cement."

I pulled the bread out, passed it around and followed it with a camping tin that I'd loaded with sharp cheddar. Everyone broke off a piece of bread.

"Oh, my God," Street mumbled through a full mouth.

"You scored, dude," Diamond said.

Anna turned to Street in the dark. "A man who bakes bread this good," she said. "He must be a wizard in the kitchen."

Street started giggling. "Not quite the description I usually use," she said.

After twenty minutes of slow cruise, Fannette Island appeared out of the dark off our bow on the port side. I pointed at it, and Diamond nodded. Spot turned his head to stare. What looked like a tiny little bump from the highway up on the mountain above was a looming black butte seen from a little boat down on the lake.

Diamond made a correction and we went by the island just fifty feet from its shore. The waves lapping against its granite perimeter were loud enough to hear over the sound of our idling motor.

We beached on the wide swath of sand near where Eagle River entered the lake at the head of Emerald Bay. Diamond jumped over the bow, getting his feet wet in the shallow water. He tugged on the boat and pulled it far enough onto the beach that the rest of us were able to jump off onto rain-wet sand. While I ran a line up to a tree, Spot ran up and down the beach, eager to source all of the night smells that were enhanced by the rain.

Back in the forest sat the Vikingsholm castle, its windows dark and ominous, its turret looking like a place to imprison medieval princesses.

I put my arms around Street and Anna. With Diamond across from us we made a loose huddle.

I whispered. "At the back of the Vikingsholm, on the side away from the lake, are the original servant's quarters. After Lora Knight gave the estate to the California Park System, they decided it made sense to have two or three employees sleep in those quarters rather than drive in and out every day. They may be asleep now. Or not. But if we are quiet, they might not hear us on the lake side."

All four of us were silent as we walked up the beach toward the forest where the Vikingsholm castle stood hulking under the black canopy of the giant Ponderosa pines and the mountains towering

3000 feet above us.

I stood with my back to the castle door, took six paces toward the lake and stopped.

"Your feet tingle?" Diamond whispered.

Anna made a nervous giggle.

I got out the mallet and cold chisel and began to cut the mortar joints around one of the granite slabs that made up the large entry patio. The clinking sound of chisel on mortar was loud. But I hoped it couldn't be heard around the back side of the castle.

Street had a penlight. By cupping her hand around its end, she was able to shine it now and then without spilling much light to the side. But most of the time, she turned it off for security, and I worked in the dark. I swung the mallet at the chisel by feel, missing my target almost as often as hitting it. The rain slicked the mallet surfaces so that even when I succeeded in hitting the chisel, the mallet often slid off and struck my chisel hand.

After interminable pounding, I'd cut the mortar from the entire perimeter of the first big slab. Diamond and I got on one end, and Street and Anna each took a side. Anna could only work with one hand, but she was a strong woman, and her help was critical.

We got our fingertips under the rock and with great effort tipped it up on end. Diamond and I rolled it like a great wheel ten feet away and leaned it against the castle wall.

I picked up the shovel and began digging. The soil was sandy, and the shovel blade went in with relatively little effort. Three feet down, I stopped to breathe.

"How deep do you think he would have buried it?" Street asked.

"Don't know."

"Maybe we should move sideways."

So I got down on my knees and went to work on the next slab, chiseling out its mortar perimeter. It was a bit smaller than the first and we four got it lifted and rolled out of the way like we'd been rolling granite for years.

This time Diamond dug. He went down, then went sideways, so persistent and energetic that it was as if he thought that trying harder would make the concept of buried treasure materialize beneath our feet.

"This patio could have been re-laid several times over the years," Anna whispered in the dark. "Somebody with a backhoe might have found whatever was buried here. Or the total amount of money or gold might be no big deal. Like it could fit in a little pouch that we'd dig right past in the night without ever seeing it. We should have brought a metal detector. Why didn't we bring a metal detector?"

"I meant to," I said, "but I forgot."

"We even talked about it," Diamond said.

"I screwed up. Sorry."

Diamond's shovel made a clink in the hole. "Got something," he said.

We all kneeled around the hole as he reached down and felt with his fingers. He worked at it for a bit and finally came up with a cobble. "False alarm."

We chiseled out another patio slab, and I dug for awhile. We'd excavated enough that I was able to take the dirt I was digging and toss it sideways to the other side of the growing hole. When I found nothing, we stopped to reconsider.

"How much mortar can you make with that bag you brought?" Diamond asked.

"Maybe enough to re-seat the slabs we've excavated plus one or two more."

"Then we should be thoughtful about which slab we take out next."

We all stood back and looked at the mess. Street shined her light for a moment. Multiple pieces of granite leaned up against the outside of the Vikingsholm. There was a huge hole in the middle of the patio and next to it, a big pile of dark, wet, muddy dirt.

Street walked over to the grand front door.

"When a Chinese American says six paces," she said, "does he mean the same thing as a six-six Irish-Scottish American ex-cop who does everything on a large scale?"

"I watched Owen pace," Diamond said. "He was quite modest in his steps."

"Modest for Owen might be really large for Ming Sun," Street said.

Anna walked over. "I used to have a favorite Chinese restaurant. The owner was a second generation Chinese American and he walked about like this." She walked with small steps.

"Okay," I said. "Do that from the front door."

Anna backed up to the door and took six small steps. She was a long way short of the hole we'd dug.

"Let's try digging there," I said.

I chiseled up another slab, and Diamond dug with energy.

Five minutes later, we once again heard a sound that was different from digging sand. This time, it wasn't a clink, but a chunk, and Diamond once again said, "Got something."

Diamond kneeled down and dug with his fingers, working his fingertips around the edges of the object. He pulled out a bag that was about the size of a quarter loaf of bread. He set it down.

"It's like heavy leather," he said, "but hardened."

Anna felt it. "Like it was coated with pine pitch," she said.

"Something that bugs and bacteria can't attack," Street said.

Street pointed her penlight at the top of the bag while Diamond worked at the tie. It crumbled apart in his hands. He pulled open the top. Street shined the light in the opening. Anna looked inside and gasped. "Shiny yellow powder! And a nugget! Unbelievable! I wonder what it's worth."

Diamond hefted the bag. "Little bag, but it weighs about the same as a large bag of charcoal. Maybe twenty pounds."

"Last I heard, gold was selling for much more than a thousand dollars an ounce," I said. "Could be a lot of money."

Diamond looked at me.

"I'm just a private investigator," I said. "You do the math."

"Sixteen ounces to a pound," Diamond said. "At just a thousand per ounce it would mean sixteen thousand dollars a pound. Times twenty pounds is three hundred twenty thousand dollars."

"My God!" Anna shouted.

"Shhh!" I said. "This is rightfully yours, but if you shout it to the world, someone's gonna come, and the next thing you know the state of California will take it away from you. They will find some small print somewhere that suggests that because Lora Knight gave this land to the state, the gold belongs to the state."

Anna was waving her arms in the dark. "I can do so much

with this! I can help those kids. I can start the Reach For The Sky school!"

"I like the other name," Diamond said. "The Kick Butt Tech School For Girls."

"Me too," Street said.

"We gotta put all this dirt back," Diamond said. He started shoveling dirt back into the hole.

"Wait," Street said. "How do we know there isn't more down there?"

Diamond stopped. "That bag wasn't full. Wouldn't he have filled it if he had more gold?"

"Yes," Street said. "But only if he had just a little more. More than that, he might have started another bag so he didn't stress the seams."

So Diamond dug some more and made another chunk with the shovel. The hole was deeper than before, so he lay down on the nearby slab and reached in with both arms and pulled out another bag.

And another bag.

And two more after that. Five bags. 100 pounds or more.

We refilled the hole, jumped on the dirt to tamp it down, re-mortared the granite slabs into place, and used the broom to sweep away excess dirt. We succeeded mostly in making a muddy mess. When we were done, we brushed the loose dirt off the granite slabs and loaded the gold bags into Jennifer's boat.

I untied our line, and Diamond and I pushed the boat out into the water.

As Diamond, Street and I turned to get into the boat, we realized that Anna and Spot were gone.

We turned, peering through the dark night.

Down the beach, where Eagle River emptied into Emerald Bay, was movement. Spot was easy to see in the sky-lit dark, his areas of white fur tracing circles and arcs, around and around in the sand.

At the focal point of his loops was Anna. She ran through the rain with a galloping gate, cutting tight turns, doing a dance of leaps and sprints, then twirling like a little girl, her arms held high, reaching for the sky.

About the Author

Todd Borg and his wife live in Lake Tahoe, where they write and paint. To contact Todd or learn more about the Owen McKenna mysteries, please visit toddborg.com.